THE LOST AND
THE DAMNED

―THE HORUS HERESY®―
SIEGE OF TERRA

THE HORUS HERESY®

Other Novels and Novellas

Many of these titles are also available as abridged and unabridged audiobooks.
Order the full range of Horus Heresy novels and audiobooks from
blacklibrary.com

THE HORUS HERESY®
SIEGE OF TERRA

THE LOST AND THE DAMNED

Guy Haley

BLACK LIBRARY

A BLACK LIBRARY PUBLICATION

First published in 2019.
This edition published in 2022 by
Black Library, Games Workshop Ltd.,
Willow Road, Nottingham, NG7 2WS, UK.

Represented by: Games Workshop Limited – Irish branch,
Unit 3, Lower Liffey Street, Dublin 1,
D01 K199, Ireland.

10 9 8 7 6

Produced by Games Workshop in Nottingham.
Cover illustration by Neil Roberts.

A CIP record for this book is available from the British Library.

ISBN 13: 978-1-78999-934-1

See Black Library on the internet at

blacklibrary.com

Find out more about Games Workshop
and the worlds of Warhammer at

games-workshop.com

Printed and bound by CPI Group (UK) Ltd, Croydon, CR0 4YY

THE HORUS HERESY®
SIEGE OF TERRA

It is a time of legend.

The galaxy is in flames. The Emperor's glorious vision for humanity is in ruins. His favoured son, Horus, has turned from his father's light and embraced Chaos.

His armies, the mighty and redoubtable Space Marines, are locked in a brutal civil war. Once, these ultimate warriors fought side by side as brothers, protecting the galaxy and bringing mankind back into the Emperor's light. Now they are divided.

Some remain loyal to the Emperor, whilst others have sided with the Warmaster. Pre-eminent amongst them, the leaders of their thousands-strong Legions, are the primarchs. Magnificent, superhuman beings, they are the crowning achievement of the Emperor's genetic science. Thrust into battle against one another, victory is uncertain for either side.

Worlds are burning. At Isstvan V, Horus dealt a vicious blow and three loyal Legions were all but destroyed. War was begun, a conflict that will engulf all mankind in fire. Treachery and betrayal have usurped honour and nobility. Assassins lurk in every shadow. Armies are gathering. All must choose a side or die.

Horus musters his armada, Terra itself the object of his wrath. Seated upon the Golden Throne, the Emperor waits for his wayward son to return. But his true enemy is Chaos, a primordial force that seeks to enslave mankind to its capricious whims.

The screams of the innocent, the pleas of the righteous resound to the cruel laughter of Dark Gods. Suffering and damnation await all should the Emperor fail and the war be lost.

The end is here. The skies darken, colossal armies gather. For the fate of the Throneworld, for the fate of mankind itself... The Siege of Terra has begun.

DRAMATIS PERSONAE

THE EMPEROR	Master of Mankind, Last and First Lord of the Imperium

The Traitor Primarchs

HORUS	Warmaster, Primarch of the XVI Legion
FULGRIM	'The Phoenician', Primarch of the III Legion
PERTURABO	'The Lord of Iron', Primarch of the IV Legion
ANGRON	'The Red Angel', Primarch of the XII Legion
MORTARION	'The Lord of Death', Primarch of the XIV Legion
MAGNUS THE RED	Primarch of the XV Legion
ALPHARIUS	Primarch of the XX Legion

The Loyal Primarchs

JAGHATAI KHAN	'The Warhawk of Chogoris', Primarch of the V Legion
ROGAL DORN	'Praetorian of Terra', Primarch of the VII Legion
SANGUINIUS	'The Great Angel', Primarch of the IX Legion

The High Lords of Terra

MALCADOR THE SIGILLITE	Regent of the Imperium
KELSI DEMIDOV	Speaker for the Chartist Captains
HARR RANTAL	Grand Provost Marshal of the Adeptus Arbites

OSSIAN	Chancellor of the Imperial Estates
SIMEON PENTASIAN	Master of the Administratum
SIDAT YASEEN THARCHER	Chirurgeon-General of the Orders Hospitalis
NEMO ZHI-MENG	Choirmaster of the Adeptus Astra Telepathica
BOLAM HAARDIKER	Paternoval Envoy of the Navis Nobilite
JEMM MARISON	High Lady of the Imperial Chancellory
GENERAL ADREEN	Lord Commander Militant of the Imperial Armies
CONSTANTIN VALDOR	Captain-General of the Legio Custodes

The Kushtun Naganda, 'Old Hundred' Imperial Army Regiment

KATSUHIRO	Conscript
RUNNECAN	Conscript
ADINAHAV JAINAN	Acting Captain

198th Palace Aerial Defence Squadron 'Bright Hawks'

AISHA DAVEINPOR	Squadron Mistress
YANCY MODIN	Pilot, flight one
DANDAR BEY	Flight Master, flight two

The VII Legion 'Imperial Fists'

| MAXIMUS THANE | Captain, 22nd Company |

The IX Legion 'Blood Angels'

| RALDORON | First Captain, First Chapter |

AZKAELLON   Captain, Sanguinary Guard

The VIII Legion 'Night Lords'

GENDOR SKRAIVOK   'The Painted Count', Acting Legion
                            Commander
THANDAMELL   Terror Master
LUCORYPHUS   Raptor

The XII Legion 'World Eaters'

KHÂRN   Captain, Eighth Assault Company
LOTARA SARRIN   Shipmistress, Legion Flagship, the
                            Conqueror

The XVI Legion 'Sons of Horus'

EZEKYLE ABADDON   First Captain
HORUS AXIMAND   'Little Horus', Captain, Fifth
                            Company
TORMAGEDDON   Possessed Space Marine
FALKUS KIBRE   'Widowmaker', Captain, Justaerin
                            Cohort

The XVII Legion 'Word Bearers'

ZARDU LAYAK   'The Crimson Apostle', Master of
                            the Unspeaking

The XX Legion 'Alpha Legion'

LYDIA MYZMADRA   Operative
ASHUL   Operative

The Dark Mechanicum

KELBOR-HAL   True Fabricator General of Mars

| Sota-Nul | Martian emissary to the Warmaster, Mistress of the Disciples of Nul |
| Clain Pent | Fifth Disciple of Nul |

The Adeptus Mechanicus

| Zagreus Kane | Fabricator General of Mars-in-exile |
| Vethorel | Ambassadress |

The Adeptus Titanicus

Esha Ani Mohana VI 'Great Mother', Legio Solaria

Thernian 7th, Imperial Army regiment

| Hanis oFar | Trooper |
| Fendo | Trooper |

Others

| Thuria Amund | In-system traffic controller, Bhab Bastion |
| Azmedi | Beastman |

ONE

When strikes midnight
Bombardment
We will stand

Bhab Bastion, 13th of Secundus

On the thirteenth day of Secundus, the bombardment of Terra began.

The enemy aimed the first shell deliberately at the centre of the Inner Palace, the Sanctum Imperialis, the Emperor's own quarters. It screamed a song of fire as it tore apart the atmosphere over Himalazia, falling through the furious storm of anti-ship cannonades and defence laser beams coming up from the Imperial defences. The assault on the Warmaster's fleet was so intense that the shell went almost unnoticed. Its flight was short, being cut apart by a net of las-beams as soon as it was detected.

But it was seen.

The Emperor's Praetorian watched its brief descent, his stern features unmoved. Two others stood with him, mighty lords of the Imperium both. The Great Angel and the Warhawk saw the momentary flash also.

Three armoured giants forged in the fires of yesterday's knowledge. They were brothers, after a fashion, born of the same science and the same inhuman genius.

The Praetorian's name was Rogal Dorn. His armour was of gold. His hair was shocking white. His sculpted face was as severe as any patriarch from mankind's long history. There was no room for compromise in his expression.

Sanguinius, the Angel was named. He was garbed in gold as bright as Dorn's panoply. His armour covered all his body save his face and his snow-white wings. He was beautiful, a divine being incarnate pulled down from heaven and exiled in the soiled world of men. He observed the universe sadly.

The Warhawk wore gleaming white. His adopted people called him Jaghatai Khan, the first name given for his prowess, the latter because he was their king. He kept the name. Like his brothers he went without his helm. Below a tall topknot his face was proud, wild, always on the verge of a smile, but troubled, like the sky at summer's end edged with autumn's clouds. He sought out death simply for the joy of laughing at it.

'Midnight, as the old reckoning has it. The symbolic spearcast,' said the Khan. 'Our brother marks his enmity for us. It is a challenge. A promise of his victory. We did this on Chogoris, when armies met. This shot is meant for the three of us.'

'Such arrogance,' said Sanguinius softly.

'Horus was well gifted with confidence. It has grown wayward. He is too sure of himself.' The Khan shrugged as if Horus' fall had been an inevitability. His glorious armour hissed and sighed. 'Arrogance is close kin to hubris. He will fail because of it.'

Dorn turned his gaze to the Warmaster's armada. Not since the Principia Imperialis had mustered at the opening of the Great Crusade had such a fleet of void-ships gathered over Terra, and never before had so many come as enemies. Terra's iron children returned to their origin with murder in their hearts, to spit hatred onto the cradle of mankind. And yet, for the moment, they held back, weathering the storm of explosives and violent energies hurled at them from the ground.

Thousands upon thousands of ships crowded every orbit, so many that their lights outcompeted the stars and sun and turned night and day into a single, ceaseless murk of red war-glow, strobed with vicious flashes. Void shields deflected the Palace's attack, spilling unclean colours across the upper atmosphere in such amounts that they encased the planet in vile aurorae.

Bells rang from every Palace tower. Sirens wailed. Tocsins clamoured. Guns rippled out asynchronous drumbeats. The sky crackled and boomed with the discharge of mighty weaponry. The Palace defences had been firing since the moment the ships came within effective range. The fleet was so densely packed the defenders could not miss. As the brothers watched, a ship came apart, shedding debris meteors.

The enemy's response was that single shell.

'Why do you wait?' Dorn said quietly. The ramparts of the Bhab Bastion were empty except for the three brothers. The question he uttered for the sake of speaking, for recently he felt himself falling too often into silence. 'Come to us. Break yourself upon our walls.'

'He waits no more,' said Sanguinius. His voice, once melodious, was strained. 'It begins.' He lifted his hand and pointed.

The sky sparkled a billion times as every ship in the fleet spoke together. *The Emperor will fall*, the pattern of light seemed to say. *We have come to wreak ruin.*

'Every war I have ever seen has hidden beauty,' said the Khan. 'But I have seen few sights quite so entrancing as this.'

'A fleeting beauty,' said Dorn. 'And deadly.'

The shells hit the upper atmosphere where they drew flaming lines through the sky.

'All things are fleeting,' said the Khan. 'Life is short and full of woe. One must wring every moment dry, and drink in the experience it has to offer, good or bad.'

The space above the Palace was full of the downwards arcs of munitions, and the straight lines of las-bursts stabbing upwards. The air shook with matter hurtling from the void. Booming reverberations echoed from the peaks of the Himalazian massif, resounding around the whole world, girdling it in sound even before the first shot detonated.

'How can you see the good in this?' Sanguinius asked the Khan. As he turned to look to the Warhawk the first shells burst over the Skye orbital plate, the last of Terra's artificial satellites. It hung low to the horizon, near the Inner Palace, its wide arrays of grav engines labouring to keep it aloft. The munitions exploded harmlessly, their fury vented into the warp by void shields. The dome of the plate's protective aegis shone with baleful energies.

'Joy is an act of defiance,' said the Khan. 'With joy, we win, even if we lose. To have lived well is a victory all its own, for we all die. Death is unimportant to the laughing warrior. A poet makes tragedy glorious. That is why.'

The shells hit the main shields seconds after hitting Skye. The aegis was wrought with ancient knowledge jealously harboured by the priests of Mars. The voids comprising the aegis reacted, and roofed the Earth with fire. Storms of flame shot out complex tangles of discharge lightning. The Palace shuddered with the effort of buried machines as halls of generators fought to hold back the bombardment from the spires of the city. Beyond the aegis' protection the ground bucked. Towers of nuclear fire roared skywards from every horizon. Tremors shook the world. As the first round of shells hit, the fleet's energy cannons awoke, hurling shafts of burning light and streams of plasma down, so that the void shields danced, and the view of the ships was lost.

The Emperor's Praetorian looked into the inferno in the sky. His eyes focused somewhere past the fleet, deep into the hidden void, as if he could see beyond the bounds of the Solar System and the material universe and out into the warp, where the fleets of Roboute Guilliman made all haste to the Throneworld. His gauntlets gripped the lip of the parapet tightly.

'We will not fall,' he said with utmost certainty. 'We will stand.'

Altai Wastes, 13th of Secundus

Thousands of kilometres away, in a land where cold wind cut over bare peaks, other eyes watched the skies. From Altai, the Palace was a glow reflected from the heavens. The curve of Terra hid the Palace and the mountains it usurped, but the Emperor's home dominated the globe. One was always certain where it was, no matter how far distant, for in an empire of a million systems, Terra was but a small place.

Horus' fleet swam above the city shine, like sparks over distant forest fires. To the watchers on the mountainside the first shell fell obviously down the sky in a bright tear-track streak. In the long slit lens of high-powered magnoculars, it shone even brighter.

Myzmadra lowered the magnoculars from her mask lenses. The lenses and magnoculars worked together to snatch at the light and drag the image so close to her that she felt she could feel the shell's re-entry heat. Bringing the magnoculars down ended the illusion, and she shivered with the cold, though she wore a voluminous cloak over her body-glove. Puffs of air exhausted of oxygen blew away from her breathing ports in misty curls.

'Is that the signal?' Ashul didn't feel the cold like her. He tolerated the high altitude better too and so wore no mask. His left eye was shut gently, the other pressed to the scope of his sniper-las, watching the shell as it came apart under the anti-munitions beams.

'It is as good as any,' she said. 'We have to be quick. Altai is a long way from Southern Himalazia.'

The mountain over the valley had a perfectly squared chunk removed from it. At the bottom of this square the sun could never touch was a mining town built around a monorail halt, currently crammed to capacity with people rounded up for the final conscription.

'There will be no more trains after this,' said Ashul.

The glaring light cast by the town's tall lumen pylons picked out every individual in the crowd as clearly as rocks in the desert under noonday sun. He swept his sight over them, idly calculating beam diffraction and the difficulties of distance kills.

'You can get us in there?' he asked.

'Do you think I can't?' said Myzmadra.

Over the Palace, the bombardment began in earnest. The sky flashed, and the earth shook.

Ashul shrugged. 'Our luck has to run out sooner or later.' Privately, he felt their luck was exhausted when they'd been sent back to Terra. Not so long ago he made the mistake of telling Myzmadra this. 'Our orders keep coming, but the assets dwindle. Now the end.' He waved to the rising false dawn of the bombardment. 'This is the last run for us. We'll get caught, or we'll die in the crossfire.'

'Do you care?' Myzmadra said.

Another cynical shrug. 'I still believe in the Legion, if that's what you're asking.'

'It wasn't.' Myzmadra divested herself of her kit, all of it – cloak, pouches, weapons, everything she carried. She did so methodically. Only when she stripped off her bodyglove did she begin to hurry. In the glare leaking from the town her naked body was cast into a relief as pronounced as the Altai Mountains: peaks of muscle, deep valleys between. Goosebumps formed all over her. Everyone has weaknesses, thought Ashul, being cold was one of hers. She was his.

'Do you care about dying?' she said.

He wished she hadn't put it so baldly.

'I do care. I thought I wouldn't,' admitted Ashul. 'Death in the abstract is a friendlier fellow than death in the flesh, and he's breathing down my neck right now.'

She kept her mask on, because anyone who could get a mask like that in the Altai wore one. They were relatively common despite their expense. From a backpack, she pulled out padded utility clothes worn by the workers, and a heavy, waist-length jacket. She shuddered noticeably as she clothed herself again. The bodyglove was a far more efficient form of insulation than the worker's uniform.

'You've become afraid,' she said.

'I'm no coward,' said Ashul. 'We're all going to die, one way or another. I'm still with you. You asked, I said. I don't want to die, but I will if I have to. I'd prefer it if it made a difference.'

'We'll make a difference.'

'What are our orders, even?'

'Free rein,' she said. 'Havoc. We'll find something.'

'Will we?' he asked flatly.

Myzmadra gave him a look he had come to know only too well. Her face was invisible under the mask, of course, but the look was there, on her face, right now. He could tell from the tilt of her head. He could tell from the tone of her voice.

'You do your job, Ashul.'

He got up and dusted his knees off. His rad counter gave out five slow clicks; the mountains were rife with residual radiation from one of Terra's forgotten wars. He'd read somewhere that the region used to be quite beautiful, a land of rivers, forests and steppes. He couldn't believe this freezing desert could be any other way than what it was today. He couldn't even imagine it. That was always his problem, he thought, no imagination. That was why he never believed the Emperor.

'I will,' he said. He dumped his rifle with some regret. It was a good gun.

His other possessions – stub pistol, knife, rations and such – were common enough to pass as the authentic kit of a dirt miner.

They wrapped their belongings in plastek before placing them in a cleft in the stone and heaping rocks on top of them. They would not be coming back, and nobody would find the cache, but old habits died hard.

'Alpha to Omega,' he said.

'Alpha to Omega,' she responded.

They snuck down the mountain. The muster point was simmering with tension. The few officials present struggled to keep order. Everyone was scared. Nobody on Terra had slept well for months; hellish nightmares tormented all the world.

The crowd, heaving with irritation and fear, absorbed Ashul and Myzmadra without ever noticing they were there.

TWO

End of the line
Eternity Terminus
Through the Palace

Eternity Terminus, 13th of Secundus

Bolts rattled in the pitch-dark, startling Katsuhiro from the numb, aimless terror that had replaced sleep. The door to the cargo container swung down and out on creaking hinges, slamming hard onto rockcrete. Light that wasn't so very bright but seemed as glaring as a plasma flash flooded the compartment. When his eyes adjusted, lumens grouped in berry bunches on iron vines were the first thing Katsuhiro saw of the Imperial Palace. Beyond the lights was a ceiling of coloured glassaic, softly backlit. Everything else was obscured by the throng crammed into the freight container. Since the very beginning of the sixteen-hour trip, there had been standing room only. His legs shook with the effort of remaining still so long. If it weren't for the bodies rammed in beside him, Katsuhiro would have fallen.

Trying to crane his neck to see better invited a sharp spasm of cramp. His kitbag pulled at him, sending spiders of pain

over his scalp and making his shoulder ache. The bag had
been plucked from a pile of identical bags and slung around
his neck when he boarded. There had been insufficient room
for him to adjust it. He blinked and cracked his stiff spine.
As if summoned by the pop of his bones, the noise outside
started abruptly, and overwhelmingly.

Whistles blew. Voices bellowed.

'Move, move, move, move, move, move!'

The passengers were slow to obey. The groans and mut-
ters of men and women long confined turned to shouts as
burly men reached into the containers and hauled individuals out at random. After hours and hours of the rattling,
stifling quiet of the train, the noise was terrifying. Despite
the demands of the marshals outside, the conscripts shuffled
forwards in the dazed way common to large crowds. They
were hemmed in by the people around them. Progress was
tortuous. The light outside remained unreachable. Biting
gusts of thin air blasted into the container, churning up the
damp, sweaty fug. There had been nowhere to relieve themselves. Urine stink stung Katsuhiro's eyes.

The threat of a shock maul's buzz motivated the first
row onto the platform, and the occupants of the container
surged. They toppled out, some falling, trampled by those
behind. With no more agency than a molecule of water,
Katsuhiro drained towards the open ramp. The lights and
the beautiful ceiling drew nearer and nearer, then the man
in front of Katsuhiro was yanked forwards hard by the bag
around his neck, and Katsuhiro went after him, falling into
the Imperial Palace and the open gullet of war.

Thousands upon thousands of people were spilling from
containers clamped to flatbed trucks into a monorail terminus. Katsuhiro could not see far, but the pressure of
many people pushed at him from all directions. Voices

shouted, wailed, screamed and begged in cacophonous profusion.

A marshal half caught Katsuhiro, and a flash of a face behind an armoured visor joined all the other fragments of sensory information that fought their way into his mind. Badges of the Adeptus Arbites surmounted with unfamiliar heraldry flashed past and Katsuhiro was shoved into the reeking flow of humanity pouring towards destruction. Bells and sirens sang from every quarter, and from far away there came a steady thudding, as insistent and dull as a thousand hearts. He was turned around in the crowd, sucked into eddies in the human river before being shoved back out into swift currents. Men and women of all kinds jostled him: scribes, old warriors, algae farmers, technicians, rich, poor, young, old. Every hue of skin and eye and hair present upon Terra was there. Every uniform and badge of occupation Katsuhiro had ever seen, and thousands more besides. His head spun with the overload. More details stabbed into his awareness, painful as darts. Decorations on the walls, a noble face captured in a marble relief. A sign proclaiming his location to be Eternity Terminus, Sub-Platform 99-8-Epsilon. The expressions of his fellows, two in particular – one blue-eyed and leering, the other brimful of fear – struck him. Hands grabbed at him. He was funnelled between a stack of boxes and a gun slapped into his hands. The crush increased as the crowd slowed unbearably. Elbows played his ribs as if they were bars on a semandron. The smell was dreadful. The noise was worse. Then he was out the other side, pushed along with gathering speed. All the people on the platform had only two things in common: the mass-produced lasguns clasped in their uncertain hands, and the kitbags slung around each of their necks, dragging them into hunches. Some struggled, now they were moving, to switch the straps to their

shoulders, but there was as little space on the platform as
there had been on the trains. Katsuhiro saw a man drop his
gun. When the man bent to pick it up, the weight of the
crowd pushed him down. Katsuhiro did not see him rise.

Katsuhiro blundered into a pillar, raising more bruises to
add to those he already had. His feet snagged on something
soft. He glanced down to see a dead man, blood running
from his nose and ears, crushed by the herd. He recoiled,
rebounded off a giant stacked with vat-grown muscle, bald,
squinting and full of violence.

'Watch it,' the giant growled. Katsuhiro backed away apolo-
getically, and the crowd caught him again, whirling him away,
while from above the rapid, hurried heartbeats boomed on
and on.

The platforms opened out and the ceiling sprang away
from them, lofted upwards on giant piers of stone and plasteel, the crowd spreading across the vast concourse sheltered
beneath. The panes of coloured glass lost their individual
form, merging into a display that stopped the breath in
Katsuhiro's lungs. Captured in glassaic, men and women
stood victorious upon a field of battle. Suppliants bowed,
defeated, holding out their hands in fealty towards the figure dominating the centre of the piece.

'The Emperor!' Katsuhiro gasped. So lifelike was the display,
so radiant the figure, that for a second the addled Katsuhiro
thought the Master of Mankind was standing above them
in judgement. A triple thump of the ceaseless hearts broke
the spell, stuttering the lumens behind the image and cracking certain panes to shards. Colourful, razored rain fell that
brought blood and screams from the crowd.

The conscripts slowed again, spread out and dawdled, as
a swift river is arrested by a lake. Katsuhiro had a moment
to catch his breath. The sheer size of the muster was sinking

in, and it terrified him. Empty trains were pulling out, fresh ones rolling in. Hot engines and overtaxed rail levitators baked the scent of metal into his nostrils.

Grille-gates rattled somewhere off to the right. Whistles blew again. A line of marshals, or arbitrators, or whoever they were, formed across one side of the plaza. More gently this time, the crowds were directed towards a row of arches and through the opened gates. Katsuhiro passed through into the terminus' hidden spaces, utilitarian cargo halls of new rockcrete where cranes and conveyor belts sat idle. All were bereft of the usual goods, and full instead with the chiefest currency of war, that of human bodies. Armies and armies of people shuffled within.

Issuing from a line of officers at the far side, men pushed their way deep into the crowds, grabbing people and directing them to groups that grew swiftly.

'You, you, you, you.' There were no pauses between their words. Gloved hands grabbed shoulders, hung coloured chits around necks and impelled the dazed populace of Terra towards the officers behind them. 'You, you, you,' they barked from helm speakers and external voxmitters, the voices roughed to inhumanity as they rounded up the nations of the world, broke them apart and pressed them towards their deaths. People cried as friends, lovers and families were separated. The officials did not notice nor did they care. 'You, you, you.'

Katsuhiro's time came soon enough. A leather gauntlet grabbed him, a second dragged a green plastek chit on a chain over his head, catching his ear painfully in the process, and shoved him on his way. A small desk greeted him. Numbly, he presented his token to the army officer behind, which earned him another shove, and so, as aimless as driftwood, Katsuhiro came to a slow, grounded stop with a hundred others all clutching green plastek and blinking fearfully.

'What do we do?' said a lean woman, wasted by years of short rations. Thinness was a look common to them all.

'You be quiet,' shouted a uniformed man with a harried face. 'And you wait.'

The man moved on without paying them any more attention, pushing himself sideways like a blade through the recruits.

'You there!' he shouted. 'You there! Stop–' and he was gone, his commands vanishing into the chorus of voices echoing in the cargo hall.

Katsuhiro shook. Shock, lack of food, cold and the effort of standing upright for so many hours were each enough alone to upset his humours. Together, they brought him close to collapse.

A warm hand slipped around his side and pulled him close. Ordinarily Katsuhiro would have recoiled from such unexpected intimacy, but now he welcomed it.

A small, powerfully built man had him. Shorter by a few centimetres than Katsuhiro, he had to look up to address him. He was filthy, and stank of oil and stale clothes, but his smile was genuine.

'It is cold, isn't it?' he said. 'Enough to knock you down if you aren't used to it. Winter at the top of the world!'

Katsuhiro frowned at him, growing embarrassed by the embrace. Being so close to someone else bothered him. It was not the done thing in his subculture. Needing the support shamed him more.

'Yes,' he managed. 'Thank you. Please, let me go. I am fine now.'

'You sure?' The man released him anyway. The man's left hand grasped the straps of his kitbag and rifle, both slung neatly over his right shoulder. He held out his dirty right hand. 'The name's Doromek. From Baltica.'

Katsuhiro swallowed his distaste and limply shook Doromek's hand.

'Katsuhiro,' he said.

'Dragon nations, eh?' said Doromek. 'We've got a fine mix here and no mistake. Tell you what, let's get you sorted out. You want to get that bag strap off your neck.'

As Katsuhiro struggled the bag over his head – it had somehow gained weight since it had been hung there – the man continued talking.

'You'll find some tablets in there. Recaff tabs, salt and glucosium energy blends. Take one of each. Chew them up, don't just swallow them – it'll get the spit flowing in your mouth and make it easier for your body to process them. You hear me?'

'Is there water?'

'Not yet,' said the dirty little man. He looked behind him. Flustered officers were arguing with a man in the robes of an adepta alien to Katsuhiro. 'They're not coping very well,' said Doromek. 'Hurry up though, we'll be moving out soon.'

'Where to?' he said.

The man snorted. 'Where do you think? The fighting. You hear that noise?' He pointed upwards. 'The bombardment has begun. The traitors are here. This is the big...' He frowned at Katsuhiro's fumbling. 'What are you doing to your kit? Give me that.'

Doromek grabbed his bag. Katsuhiro surrendered it. Doromek set it on the ground. Once he had the drawstring open Katsuhiro saw the contents neatly arrayed, all sealed in plastek packets. Doromek moved aside.

'You need to learn your way around this. This one, this one and this one.' He pointed with a strong, broad finger.

Katsuhiro ripped open the packets his new companion indicated and placed the pills in his mouth. 'Thank you. I have no idea what–'

A hard-faced woman barged her way into their conversation.

'You two. Shut up,' said the woman. 'They don't like it if you talk. I don't want the attention.'

'But someone's got to tell us what's going on!' Katsuhiro protested.

Another responded to this, a man even thinner than everyone else, who was cleaning his nails with a worn knife. 'They don't have to tell you anything, my friend. Nobody does.'

'You're soldiers,' said the woman nastily. 'There are things expected of you. Shutting up is one of them.'

'I'm not a soldier, I'm a third-grade enumerator for the Eighty-Sixth Nihon nutrient complex,' said Katsuhiro.

The woman shot him a grim smile. 'You were. You're a soldier now.' She drew back, looking around at the swelling gaggle of people. 'Now just shut up.' She held a finger to her lips. Above the cut-off of the half-glove she wore, her nails were incongruously well manicured.

She scowled at him and turned her back.

'Charming lady,' said Katsuhiro.

'Glad to see you're recovering your sense of humour.' Doromek lowered his voice. 'But word to the wise, don't antagonise the likes of her.' He watched her carefully as he spoke. 'I recognise bad news when I see it. That one's a fighter.'

A whistle blew. The officials had apparently resolved their argument.

'Green chits!' The man was non-military, his voice unsuited to bellowing over a crowd's noise, and Katsuhiro struggled to hear what he was saying. 'Green chits follow me!'

Without waiting to see whether all in the group had heard

him or not, the official turned about, and shoved his way through the throng towards more gates in the back of the cargo hall.

They were taken in their groups through a massive service corridor, emerging some minutes later via a side tunnel onto another fantastically decorated public platform. Hundreds of maglev trains awaited them, their insides welcomingly lit. The far end of the platform was open to the outside. The icy wind blasted in unimpeded. The bombardment's racket roared over the trains. The firelight flicker of exploding bombs had taken the place of sunlight.

Men yelled themselves hoarse to no effect. Only those with voxmitters and vox-hailers had any hope of being heard, and then their commands battled one another into incomprehensibility. The moment of calm in the cargo hall seemed as if it had never happened. Katsuhiro was herded urgently onto the carriages. By the doors, menials with buckets collected chits, snatching them violently from people too dazed to understand what they were supposed to do. A single-sheet flimsy was thrust into Katsuhiro's hand, and he was shoved hard from behind into the carriage.

'Move down! Move down!' A voice crackled over the train's vox-speakers.

Katsuhiro stumbled his way along the aisle. The train was luxuriously appointed, each set of seats half screened from the rest by high backs and panels of frosted plastek imprinted with symbols of Unity. But there were far too many people for the seats to accommodate. Soon the aisle was full. Uniformed marshals began to physically ram people onto the train. The people behind Katsuhiro shoved at him in turn, and he was jammed into one of the nests of seats. Already, eight people sat in a space for four. If anything, it was more crowded than the monorail cargo box that had brought him from the east.

He had been separated from the few people he had spoken to, but he recognised most of the faces as being from the green chit group. They scowled as he tripped on their feet. He was forced closer to the window by the pressure of the crowd. Just when he thought the air would be forced from his lungs and he would suffocate, the doors slid shut and the train pulled out. Held aloft on a counter-gravitic field, the train accelerated quickly, blurring the innumerable people outside into a single, heaving mass.

Light flashed, and the train sped outside. The great mountain of a space port dominated his view for a fragment of a second, huge, flat-topped and covered in lights. The maglev whipped past it before he got a proper look, affording him a view of a city he had never seen for himself, but every man, woman and child on Terra knew. The artful spires and bridges he expected from the holocasts had gone, replaced by buildings more fit for war. Not all had changed. He glimpsed the soaring Tower of Hegemon and the great dome of the Senatorum Imperialis, where giant machines stood guard. Fire, Titans, glory and doom – all gone in a heartbeat as the train plunged into the side of a hab-spire, and thereafter hurried past rockcrete pilings into roots of the earth that showed him nothing but the dark.

THREE

Survival of the species
Council of war
A further enemy

Grand Borealis Strategium, 13th of Secundus

The pit of the Grand Borealis Strategium shimmered with hololiths. False worlds hung in frozen orbits, each a copy of Terra pasted over with differing iterations of disaster. Slabs of text scrolled relentlessly down. Numbers indecipherable to the untrained circled around them in illuminated bands. Excepting the maps overlaid with their thousand blinking points of data, the displays were abstract. There were no vid-feeds or picts of the falling bombs. Perhaps the lack of informational immediacy contributed to the calm in the strategium. The hundreds of people on its many galleries worked so quietly that the noise of the bombardment was audible, muffled though it was by the bastion's thick walls and further tamed by aural dampening. Even so deep within the bastion, the air carried a charge from the ceaseless activities of void shields. Metal brought near metal generated leaping sparks. The cold plasmas of foxfire clung to hard edges.

Officers from dozens of organisations operated as a seamless whole, each responsible for a small section of the overall strategic picture, but though serenity was the order of the day, most of the personnel were well informed enough to piece together a broad view of the situation from the data cascading down the pit. The future of humanity was suspended on a thread. They all knew it.

Absolute concentration was a tonic for fear, for though all had faith in the Emperor's Praetorian there was not a mortal within the Palace walls who was not afraid. Those in the strategium could usually take comfort from Dorn's golden presence. They felt his eyes pass over them as he scanned the displays from his platform above the giant central shaft.

But at that moment, he was not there.

Thuria Amund was one among the many. An in-system traffic controller drafted in to aid the war effort, she considered herself a civilian, even though the demarcation between combatant and non-combatant had vanished under the needs of total war. Her specialisation was etheric monitoring, a narrow discipline in which she excelled. She watched the void to see where reality split to allow ships passage to and from the warp. Once upon a time, her station had been high above the world in a dedicated orbital, but that orbital was gone. Gutted of its original equipment to take a battery of Lord Dorn's guns, it was now almost certainly lost to the enemy. She was lucky, she supposed. Her grading was high, and she had been taken down to the nerve centre of Imperial command. Her less fortunate colleagues had found themselves manning the guns that replaced their equipment. They would have died where they had worked, deafened, choking on fyceline, attacked by warriors who were made to protect them, bewildered that the galaxy could turn on them so.

Thuria's new world was a tiny sliver of the strategic whole.

Sol's etheric monitoring network was gone, forcing her to rely solely on sensing machines that were situated directly on Terra. With so limited a source of input, her devices, like many others in the strategium, were practically blind. She did her duty as best she could, using what resources remained at her disposal to watch the place behind the sky for further enemy intrusion.

To her left, a bank of lights in neat, crescent rows blinked off and on in patterns only someone from her caste could understand. Slightly offset from them, a cascade of hololithically projected numerical data ran on, silvery as a waterfall, offering cross-checks and correctives to the pattern of the lights. Seven screens in front of her, all either gel or active glass, displayed dancing sines and swirling motes of abstracted fact. To her right, a tall cabinet, open at the front, contained an intricate device somewhat like an orrery, whose whirling spheres ran on tracks representing orbits not found in the material realm. The visor she wore projected more data directly onto her retinas, adding to and enriching the flow of information. Each instrument had its own sound, a soft, repetitive signifier of its function, either electronically generated or as a consequence of the motion of its mechanisms, such as the gentle clicking of brass gears emanating from the etherscope, or the pulsing, white-noise hiss of the holo-cascade. It was hypnotic, soothing away her concerns and aiding her concentration. The collective orchestra induced a meditative state, where the sleep she so desperately needed ceased to be so pressing.

The size of the Warmaster's fleets terrified her. The size of the warp rift they'd entered by more so. A child of the secular Imperial Truth, she started her career thinking of the warp as nothing but a passage through time and space; indeed, she had been taught so. Despite the hegemony's best efforts to enforce that point of view, rumours escaped into the population as the war dragged on, that the warp was not a simple place of energy, but a deadly ocean swimming with creatures inimical to humanity. She knew enough to guess the rumours were true.

Scrambled readings crawled across her displays, all sense ripped out of them. The warp rift was of such a size that it blotted every signal that Terra's limited, fixed-point ether-augurs might detect. In looking at it, even as neutral data, she was confronted second by second with what they were facing. She doubted she would see anything through the spikes of energy which crawled in jagged graphics across her immersion visor. She pleaded with gods she had been taught did not exist that the ragged static, full of screams and half-heard whispers, would go away, and her world would return to the placid sensibilities of understandable notification bleeps and mathematically sound ingress and egress plots.

She was not naive enough to believe that would ever happen.

Thuria spared what little attention she had to glance upwards from time to time, seeking Dorn's return, daring to lessen the opacity of the display in front of her eyes in case the son of the Emperor was hanging back a little in the shadows. Each time she was disappointed. She saw instead the sweep of the monitor banks curved around the strategium pit, stern supervisors, battle group liaisons, army officers and transhumans of half a dozen Legions poised to relay any information of import to their respective commanders. Members of the regiments from the Old Hundred predominated, but there were a multitude of others. They fretted near their stations, waiting for something to happen.

An air of tension so pronounced it bred a peculiar lethargy hung over everything.

When Dorn finally strode onto his observation pier, the atmosphere changed immediately. He arrived unannounced, which was unusual. Thuria found herself looking up when he arrived nevertheless, without being aware why she chose that moment to do so. The primarchs were like that, exerting an influence on the human psyche that at once drew and repelled.

The hundred metres between her station and Dorn's pulpit did not diminish the Praetorian's presence. If anything he seemed larger above her like that, his golden battleplate carved into planes of blue and silver by the upwelling of the hololight. Lit from beneath, his noble features appeared indomitable, his hair startling white. He was as hard and cold as his native world of Inwit.

As he surveyed them, his eyes passed over Thuria, and she felt herself diminished, as if he found her wanting, not for lack of effort or of skill, but simply because she was what she was: human, fallible and frail.

She remained dismayed and exulted when his gaze swept on. He finished his survey, and leaned forwards to address them.

'Servants of the Imperium. Loyal subjects of the Emperor. Believers in Unity,' he began. His voice resonated with something drawn from beyond mundane human existence, sending shivers up Thuria's spine. 'We come at last to the striking of the final hour. The Warmaster encircles the Throneworld. During the first thousandth this day, at one minute past midnight by the old reckoning, his bombardment began.'

They knew this. They'd heard the shells. Those making their way to and from the strategium for their duty shifts had seen them lighting up the void shields. They all felt the explosions shaking the world; they all suffered the crawling sensation in their brains from the active warp tech of the aegis. Another man, even another primarch, might have made a humorous aside to this effect, how obvious his statement was. Drollery was not a characteristic that factored large in Lord Dorn's make-up.

'We have planned for this moment. We have striven to anticipate the traitors' plans. We stand now upon the brink of annihilation, but do not despair!' He raised his voice. 'We do not seek to overthrow Horus' armies. We must only endure. Let the defences of Terra be the cliffs Horus breaks himself upon. Let him fritter away his power seeking our end, and then, when he is exhausted, and drained, and his strength bled away, shall the revenging blow fall and wipe his perfidy from the stars!' Once more he swept his eyes across the pits. 'Not all of you will survive to see that day, but know this – we stand as a race upon the precipice of extinction. It may seem that in the equation deciding the survival of our species your lives do not amount to much. But your efforts, though they may seem small to you, are vital, one and all. I call upon you now, in the Emperor's hour of need, to put away your terror, to seal up your dread, and exert every fibre of your being towards our inevitable victory! I am a primarch, made by the Emperor's own hand and yet it is for you and you alone, the men and women of the human race, that all this undertaking was begun. Ours is not an Imperium of gods or monsters as Horus would impose, but a state of unity to shelter and protect our species from all the evils of this universe and beyond. Think not of yourselves as the bombs fall. Think not of your survival as the enemy comes. Think instead of continuance, of persistence, of the endurance of mankind.' His voice rose again to great volume. Thuria had never heard a voice so pure, or so terrifying. 'Keep in mind the coming generations of humanity. Keep in mind the peace that will follow the victory. Hold yourselves true to your purpose, do your duty to your Emperor, and we shall be triumphant!'

There followed a moment of silence in which no human sound was heard, only the workings of machines. Then first one pair of hands began to applaud, then another, and another, until every man, woman and transhuman in the strategium was clapping and shouting. Jubilation overcame fear. For a brief moment, Thuria saw what victory might feel like.

Dorn nodded once in satisfaction, turned his back upon the shaft and departed.

Bhab Bastion, 13th of Secundus

The primary defence council met in a room already steeped in history. The Bhab Bastion dated from before the Great Crusade, before the Wars of Unification. How far back, no one knew for certain, nor was its original name or builder known. It was built for war, and when the architects of the Palace had come to remove it in favour of finer buildings, it had refused to die.

Dorn admired its tenacity, and so he had adopted it and adapted it to be his nerve centre. Such a place suited his temperament perfectly.

The Praetorian stepped into a room muffled with old carpets and tapestries of forgotten victories. Its wood and cloth were steeped in tabac smoke and the scents of ancient wines, faded perfume and dust. Beneath mellow glow-globes the four most powerful people on Terra, save the Emperor Himself, waited for him.

A pair of Imperial Fists Huscarls shut the doors behind their lord. The thick wood cut down the noise of the bombardment further, but could not silence it.

'Brothers,' said Dorn. 'Captain-general, Lord Malcador.'

The greetings between them extended no further than a few return nods. Sanguinius, Jaghatai Khan and Constantin Valdor were all armoured. Malcador sported his usual plain, green robes, but he had protection none of the others could boast. He alone sat at the room's central feature: a large, round wooden table scaled for giants. He perched upon a tall stool sized to bring baseline humans level with the top, and though he exuded an aura of power even within this faintly ridiculous chair, he was more drawn and ancient seeming than ever.

'The situation deteriorates,' said Sanguinius.

'It does,' said Dorn grimly. As he approached, a small-scale hololith of the Solar System blinked on. He joined the company, and they spread around the table.

'The last pockets of resistance on Luna fell two days ago. All our orbital forts and the sky fortresses adapted from the orbital plates are taken or destroyed. Horus has complete command of near-Terran void space. We are cut off.'

'You dealt with the orbital guns of the forts before they were overrun, I assume,' said Malcador.

'Rendered inoperable. In some cases we were able to convince the enemy to destroy them rather than take them. In other cases my Imperial Fists and Sanguinius' Blood Angels left nothing useable,' said Dorn.

'It took too long. We both lost many sons ensuring it would be so,' said Sanguinius.

'It is enough that they cannot fire upon us,' said Dorn.

'Regrettable that the tactics you employed at Uranus could not be repeated,' said Malcador. 'I suppose we were fortunate Horus fell for the ruse in the first place.'

Dorn shook his head. 'Horus would not. Perturabo's arrogance can be relied upon, if nothing else can be,' he said.

Only when he spoke of the hated Lord of Iron did his delivery take on a hint of emotion. 'But you are right, we cannot rely on the same tricks twice.'

'Neither can the enemy,' said Jaghatai Khan. 'Here we are up against the truth of will. No more running, no more manoeuvring. It is time for stone and steel to speak.'

'You sound eager for the fight,' said Sanguinius.

'Even the wind grows tired of running,' said the Khan.

'Stone and steel will speak,' said Dorn. 'Horus' armies are...' He paused, as if he could not quite believe what he was about to say. A flicker of uncertainty passed behind his eyes. 'They are almost incalculable in size. There are representatives from every Traitor Legion within the Solar System. He commands thousands of regiments of traitor soldiery, hundreds of Knightly houses, dozens of Titan Legios, which though they were diminished at Beta-Garmon,' he indicated Sanguinius, 'still outnumber our own. Now the inner-system blockade has been swept aside, the unified forces of the Dark Mechanicum are heading for Terra from Mars. We are beset on all sides.' He gestured at the display, bringing a section of Terra's high orbit into focus.

'We are at bay. Horus could destroy us a thousand times over,' said Sanguinius. 'A comet strike, asteroid bombardment, a concerted salvo from his guns only. Any one of a dozen methods would render Terra into rubble.'

'That is not his intent,' said Dorn. 'If Horus wished Terra blasted down to the smallest atomic component, it could have been done weeks ago. Terra is not his target, only his battlefield.' He pointed his finger at the globe turning in its shaft of light. 'Throughout all this war, one thing has concerned me. Why this rush? Why does Horus speed to confront us? Were I to conduct this war,' he said, in a way that suggested he had spent a great deal of time contemplating the matter, 'I would have delayed. Horus has left too many of our forces intact behind him. His initial strikes at Isstvan and Calth threw us into disarray, and weakened the loyal Legions, but we retain billions of men under arms from hundreds of thousands of untouched systems. He spent little time securing his conquests. I saw early a pattern emerging in his so-called "dark compliances". The planets he invaded were chosen deliberately to supply his advance. This was no war of conquest – everything he did was to facilitate this rush for Terra. There are many good reasons why he would do this, but the surest path to victory if he wished to usurp our father would have been a longer war, time spent to subdue the galactic east, circumvent Terra via the Segmentum Solar to dominate the west, and isolate the seat of Imperial government. While we reeled from his treachery, he could have redoubled his efforts to finish Guilliman off – instead he left Lorgar and Angron to fumble the attempt. Now he is here with Guilliman at his back. And yet even now he could win this war at a single command.' Dorn paused. 'He does not.'

'He will not,' said Malcador. 'He must confront his father. That is the purpose of this attack.'

Dorn nodded. 'This is the conclusion I came to myself. This lack of a decisive bombardment of the Throneworld confirms it.' Dorn looked at the Imperial Regent. 'You speak of the warp?'

'I do,' said Malcador. 'Horus wages a war that goes beyond the material realm. There are factors at play here that are beyond your understanding.'

'Attempt to explain them then,' said Dorn. 'Repeatedly Horus' use of sorcery confounds me. I cannot fight this war with such poor schooling.'

'My boy,' said Malcador wearily, 'you cannot understand

because matters of the spirit were not given you to understand by your father. I could explain them at length and you most of all would never comprehend. Do you not think if it were possible that I or your father could have explained them already, that you would have been told of the threat in the warp from the very beginning?'

'I deeply regret that it was not done,' said Dorn.

'The results would have been disastrous, believe me,' said Malcador.

'Not telling us was arguably worse,' said Dorn.

'Was it?' said Malcador softly. 'Very well. Let us take you, Dorn. You were made to command the material realm. Nothing in this world is beyond your grasp. But understanding of the warp would have eluded you. Being a man who desires mastery of all things, you would have been drawn to study it, and in doing so, you would have fallen. You are resistant to the dangers in the dark, but no one is immune.' He paused. 'Only one of you had the mettle to resist the whispers of the gods at the start. He was told.'

'Who?' said Dorn in surprise. 'I thought this was kept from all of us?'

'Which one could have known?' said Sanguinius. 'Jaghatai?'

The Khan shook his head. He was not so concerned as his brothers at his lack of forewarning. 'It was not I.'

'So much pain could have been avoided!' said Sanguinius.

Malcador fixed Sanguinius with a serious look. He seemed to grow, like a fire flaring in an unexpected breeze. 'Do not think for one moment that your trials would have been any less arduous had you known in advance. I know you have been tested, Sanguinius. There is space in the hells of the gods for more than one red angel.'

Sanguinius blanched, causing Dorn some dismay.

'Malcador,' said Dorn evenly. 'You overstep yourself.'

The Imperial Regent sank back into himself with an audible sigh.

'I am sorry. These are testing times. Even I have limits. You know all of you that you are as good as sons to me. I merely seek to make a point.' He looked to Sanguinius. 'Forgive me.'

'I understand,' Sanguinius said. 'Peace, uncle.'

'Who the Emperor told is not important. Even now it is better that you do not know,' said Malcador. 'To name the powers in the empyrean is to invite their attention. The knowledge alone is corrupting – that is all you need to know now, and far more than you needed to know then.'

'I still say more knowledge would have benefited us. I, for one, would never have disbanded my Librarius if I had known what we faced,' said Dorn. 'I upbraided Russ for his refusal to follow the ban of Nikaea. The Khan here and I have also exchanged words on the matter for his refusal to do so.'

'Father is not always right,' said the Khan evenly.

'Spoken as you were meant to speak,' said Malcador.

'Perhaps,' said the Khan. 'But perhaps also He should have looked beyond His intended uses for us, and should have trusted us. He is a distant father.'

'Look how his affection was repaid.' Malcador struck his golden staff upon the floor; the flames wreathing the eye at the top burned brightly. 'Fate builds to this moment. The war in the warp, the webway and the materium are facets of a larger struggle. Your brother understands.'

Sanguinius' mind went back unwelcomely to Davin and Signus, where he had faced raw Chaos in its many forms.

'I do,' Sanguinius said. 'Whether father made a miscalculation or not, the truth is we are where we are, fighting a war that is not solely of the flesh.'

'That is the only kind of war I know how to fight,' said

Dorn. 'These creatures from beyond, the nightmares that wrack the populace... How can I plan for that?'

'You cannot, but the war of bullet and blade must be fought, as must that of soul and sorcery,' said Malcador. 'You must perform your part. I shall perform mine when the time comes.' As one of the few men in all existence who could look into a primarch's eye without flinching, Malcador met the gaze of each of the three loyal sons in turn. 'All of you have your parts to play in this struggle.' He smiled sadly at Sanguinius, and the Angel looked aside. 'They are not the parts your father wrote for you, but you are well suited all the same – the Angel, the Praetorian and the Warhawk.' He gave them a father's proud look. 'Three champions. The Emperor and I have absolute faith that you can do this.'

The primarchs fell silent a moment.

'Faith will be insufficient,' said Dorn. 'Our vox communications are unreliable. The turmoil in the warp prevents astrotelepathy. We are alone. Whatever happens beyond the orbit of Luna we will be ignorant of. I anticipate that the fringe fleets will survive for several months yet. Among the last messages to reach us were communiques from Admiral Su-Kassen. The remainder of our ships have gathered in force, including many of your Falcon fleets, Jaghatai.'

The Khan inclined his head.

'In force by any measure but Horus'. His void assets dwarf ours. We should have retained the *Phalanx* here,' said Sanguinius, referring to Dorn's immense flagship, sent away under Su-Kassen's command to form the core of the fringe fleets. 'Alone, it would have bolstered the defences greatly. We could have dealt Horus a painful blow.'

'And then it would have been lost, along with every other orbital and ship,' said Dorn. 'We have insufficient strength to oppose the armada Horus has gathered around Terra. That is why I sent our remaining warships away. The *Phalanx* leads them until the time is right for them to strike.'

'That is not why you withdrew it,' said Sanguinius.

'I made my decision,' said Dorn firmly. 'It stands.'

'Very well,' said Sanguinius. 'But I am unsure that this strategy of keeping the *Phalanx* as an escape vector for the Emperor will succeed.'

'If Terra falls, the Emperor must survive,' said Dorn. 'We all agree that the Emperor, not Terra, is Horus' objective. The *Phalanx* represents our best chance of effecting His escape. Only my flagship has any chance of fighting in and out of the system to carry Him away. In all other cases, the perimeter ships will remain out of engagement range until Roboute approaches,' said Dorn. 'Su-Kassen's standing orders are to clear the way when the Eastern fleets break warp. Perturabo and his bastard sons have yet to come into the system's inner spheres. If he remains true to form, he and his Legion will be fortifying the outer reaches against Guilliman. We cannot allow any ring of iron they might deploy to delay our rescuers. Su-Kassen will break it.'

'What of Guilliman's strength? Have we any further word on his progress?' asked the Khan.

'None,' said Dorn. 'We must trust that he continues to push on Terra and that his forces have not been depleted. The Iron Warriors litter the fastest void routes like contact mines, and when all other obstacles are overcome, Roboute must break through whatever rearguard Horus has left in place at Beta-Garmon before he can gain the Solar System.'

'He will do so,' said Sanguinius surely. 'Horus brought most of his armies here. Roboute's forces are formidable. When I left him, he was busy sending orders that Ultramar and all the Ultima Segmentum be emptied of men. More forces flock to him on the way, including elements of Vulkan's and Corax's Legions we thought lost. When he arrives, it will be at the head of a force the near match of Horus'.'

'The Great Muster stole much from him,' said Dorn. 'He will miss the assets we lost there.'

'It is unlike you to express regret,' said Sanguinius.

'Not regret,' said Dorn. 'A fact. If I regret anything it is that the circumstances of this war force so many unpalatable choices on us. The Great Muster was costly, but necessary.'

'I did what I could at Beta-Garmon,' said Sanguinius. A little strain entered his manner.

'Do not be defensive, brother. I meant no insult,' said Dorn. 'You delayed the Warmaster. You bled him. That is what I asked of you. You did all that could be done. Every task we set ourselves now is about delay.'

'What of the others? Is there any word from the Wolf, or the Raven?' asked Jaghatai. 'Do Russ and Corax live?'

Dorn's lip curled at the mention of Leman Russ, primarch of the Space Wolves, prompting Sanguinius to speak quickly.

'None. The last I heard of Leman was during the campaign at Beta-Garmon,' said Sanguinius. 'Abaddon's and Alpharius' honourless sons had him at bay at Yarant.'

'But did they catch him or did he slip their net?' the Khan asked. 'And does the Raven survive?'

'We cannot be sure, but I do not believe either are dead,' said Sanguinius quietly. 'I think I might know were it so. My soul has become more sensitive of late.'

'Then good tidings for us if they live!' said the Khan.

'Alive or dead, they can do nothing for us here, as I said to Russ before he left,' said Dorn. 'Nor can the Lion.'

With a tired sigh, Malcador rose from his stool. His staff's light danced around the room.

'The Lion does what work he can.'

'His harrowing of the traitor home worlds is premature vengeance,' said Dorn. 'He should be here.'

'You have not seen what I have seen,' said Sanguinius. 'I know you fought a daemon on board the *Phalanx* not many days ago, but you have been insulated by your walls and your guns from the horrors that stalk the stars. What you witnessed is but a taste of the dark magics that upend rationality. This has become a war of sorcerers, like nothing we fought during the crusade. Every traitor world scoured of life by the Dark Angels is a blow to the plans of our enemies.'

'It is purely symbolic,' growled Dorn.

'Symbols have power,' said Malcador. 'Do you see how you fail to understand, Rogal?'

'Then where is the Lion now?' said Dorn. 'There has been no word since his destruction of Barbarus.'

'Who can tell? If we do not know, then the enemy does not either,' said the Khan. 'There is something in what Sanguinius says. I have faced the Neverborn myself. You know they do not follow the logic of our realm. They are wild. Mortarion's fleets have yet to arrive. Perhaps the Lion's activities can be thanked for that. If battle luck favours us, the Death Guard may never come.'

'Could Mortarion have had a change of heart?' wondered Sanguinius aloud. 'I am certain few of our brothers expected to find themselves allied with daemons. Mortarion least of all – you know how much he hates the warp.'

Dorn's eyes narrowed. He thought momentarily of Alpharius. When the twentieth primarch infiltrated the Solar System, he had spoken with Dorn, and what he said could have been interpreted as contrition. Dorn had not listened, and had slain Alpharius at Pluto, a fact he still kept from his brothers.

'None of them will change,' Dorn said. 'They are corrupt,

traitorous. All of them. We cannot save them, and they do not deserve saving.'

'I spoke with Mortarion in the ruins of Prospero,' said the Khan. 'His hatred of the Emperor goes too deep. He is fixated on our father's death. He will come.'

'So they will not have a change of heart,' said Sanguinius. 'Where, then, are the rest of our fallen brethren?'

'I have spent the night examining the disposition of Horus' fleet,' said Dorn. None of them had slept for a long time. Primarchs rarely did so, but all were wearied by their burdens. The hololith's light deepened the lines under Dorn's eyes.

'We know that Perturabo is here,' began Dorn. The map zoomed out to encompass all of Sol's system. Dorn gestured at a point of light. 'His last confirmed position was at the Battle of Uranus. We have no indication that he has come out of the First Sphere. If he follows his usual patterns, the Iron Warriors will be fortifying the Elysian and Kthonic Gates. That is not a task his pride will allow him to delegate, but his hatred for me is such that he will come to Terra eventually, if only to watch the walls I have built fall and name himself my better.

'Angron's flagship is here,' he said, his finger moving over billions of kilometres of the void, 'near the *Vengeful Spirit*, on the far side of Luna, where half of the traitor fleet waits. We must assume that where the *Conqueror* goes, so too does Angron. There were contradictory reports concerning the *Pride of the Emperor*, but they are numerous enough that we should also expect Fulgrim's presence in the coming battle. I suspect he is with Horus. Alpharius is unaccounted for.' Dorn ignored the look Malcador gave him as he spoke. It was patently obvious to the primarch that the old man knew Alpharius' fate. It was impossible to hide secrets from the Regent. 'Magnus is possibly dead,' he continued, 'though the opening of the in-system rift has all the hallmarks of his sorcery.'

'Magnus is not dead,' said Malcador.

'And you state this so surely how?' said Dorn.

'His soul is too bright a thing to hide entirely. It is known to the Emperor that his essence persists, and so it is known to me,' said Malcador. 'I am sure Magnus the Red marches with the Warmaster.'

'This news is poor,' said Sanguinius. 'I had hoped, if he survived, that he would stand aside from the conflict.'

'He took his punishment badly,' said Malcador.

'At least we can account for Curze,' said the Khan. 'Because you pushed him into the void, Sanguinius.'

'I have confirmed sightings of the *Nightfall* and perhaps a dozen or so other capital ships,' said Dorn. 'His sons are here even if he is not.'

'What of Lorgar?' asked the Khan. 'His Legion is large, but the numbers present in the Warmaster's armada suggest only a portion of his strength is here.'

'Is he, too, absent?' wondered Sanguinius.

'What is not known cannot be assumed,' said Dorn. 'If he is not present yet, it does not mean he will not come later, or that he is not waiting to ambush our brother Guilliman. We should prepare ourselves for both his and Mortarion's eventual arrival. For the moment, we must count ourselves fortunate that they are not here yet.'

'The others announce themselves,' said the Khan. 'They make displays of open challenge. Angron, riding upon the hull of his ship. Fulgrim's coyness is a statement – and if Magnus did not want us to know he was here, then we would not.'

'He hides himself only enough to show his presence,' said Malcador. 'His psychic might remains unbroken.'

'Fulgrim, Perturabo, Angron, Magnus. And not forgetting,

of course, the most treacherous of them all, our dear brother Horus. The Warmaster.' Dorn bit the title. 'Arch-traitor. Five primarchs, some changed by the things they serve, and in all likelihood a sixth on the way.'

'Six against three,' said Sanguinius. 'Where are the rest of those loyal to the Throne?'

'The Lion, incommunicado as always,' said Dorn. 'Roboute Guilliman, on his way. Corax, lost. Headstrong, foolish Leman Russ, lost. Ferrus Manus, dead. And Vulkan, dead. We are short of allies.'

'So six against three,' repeated Sanguinius. 'With two more coming.'

'Horus was always the most charismatic of us,' said the Khan drily.

'There are more of you than you think,' said Malcador.

Valdor, who until that moment had kept his own counsel, looked sharply at the Regent.

A sly look crept across Malcador's face.

'Vulkan lives,' he said.

The shock visible on Sanguinius, Dorn and the Khan's faces gratified the Sigillite, and he smiled like a conjuror pleased with the effects of a trick.

'I'm sorry?' said Dorn.

'What do you mean, Malcador?' said Sanguinius. 'I saw him dead upon Macragge. I witnessed his corpse borne away by his sons myself!'

'Vulkan's corpse is not like other corpses. The Salamanders took him back to Nocturne, where they were successful in restoring him to life. Vulkan has... certain abilities, as you all do,' said Malcador. 'You have your wings and your foresight, Sanguinius. The Khan has his questioning nature and his keen mind. Dorn has rectitude, his genius for voidcraft and his talent for building.'

'Vulkan was a smith,' said the Khan.

'His other gift is to be particularly durable,' said Malcador.

'He is not dead?' said Sanguinius, displaying neither the angelic expression of his earlier years nor the persistent woe he carried with him now, but instead a look of perfect surprise.

The Khan laughed. 'Outstanding!'

'Then where is he?' demanded Dorn. 'Is he coming here?'

Valdor and Malcador glanced at one another.

'He is already here,' said Valdor, slowly at first. 'He emerged through the webway before Lord Sanguinius returned. He stands guard over it now.'

'What?' said Dorn. The colour drained from his face.

'That was months ago,' said Sanguinius. 'And you tell us now?'

'What?' said Dorn again.

'He has been there since then. He is alive,' said Valdor.

'Why has he not shown himself?' asked the Khan, who alone of the three brothers seemed amused rather than angry at Malcador's secrecy.

'Like you, he has his role.' Malcador wrapped his hands around the black iron shaft of his staff. Its wreath of psychic flames flickered. Some of the age faded from his face. The man lived for intrigue. 'Tell me,' he asked the three, 'how much do you know of your father's project in the Imperial Dungeon?'

Eager to show he knew at least something, Dorn spoke first. His desire to reclaim some of his honour, if only in his own eyes, made the Khan grin more deeply.

'Our father left the Great Crusade to come here.' Dorn not so much spoke as recited the information. 'His intention was to create a bridge from Terra into the webway, the network constructed by the ancient eldar. Being neither of the materium or the immaterium, the webway is therefore free of the effects of both. Having entrusted the end of the Great Crusade to Horus, our father returned here to complete His work. Success would free the Imperium from reliance on the warp for travel and communication.' He paused. 'When He first told me this, so that I might guard Him while He worked, I thought it was a matter of improved efficiency. With what I now know...' He looked at his brothers.

'It would have shielded us from the powers that now attack us,' said Sanguinius. 'I knew little of this.'

'And I less,' said the Khan. They both looked at Dorn.

Dorn stared straight ahead. 'I am the Emperor's Praetorian. I must be aware of all threats, in order to protect our father.'

'Bravo, Rogal,' said Malcador. 'You were listening to Him. Though in point of fact, the webway is far older than the aeldari. They were merely the last to occupy it, before their own downfall. A fate we are coming dangerously close to repeating.'

'Why can I not see Vulkan?' said Sanguinius. 'I should have felt something, or seen something.'

'Your father shields his presence.'

The Great Angel pressed. 'Then why were we not told any of this?'

'Genuinely? The fewer who knew the better.' Malcador raised a hand to ward off Sanguinius' protest. 'It didn't matter who you were. Trust is not the issue. The enemy have unnumbered ways to discover what they need. At first, we had to keep the project secret to protect it from our foes, and latterly, because of the threat it represented.'

'What do you mean?' Sanguinius asked.

'Father failed,' said Dorn.

Valdor took up the tale. 'Disaster struck when He was

close to completion. Your brother Magnus, my lords, was
loyal, but arrogant. In his hubris, he used sorcery to warn the
Emperor of Horus' treachery. The sorcery he employed, that
he had been forbidden from, destroyed the wards around
the bridge, and all the foes of men came rushing in.'

'That is where Valdor's men were for so long when you
returned, my brothers,' Dorn said to Jaghatai and Sanguinius.

Valdor's handsome face rarely expressed anything as human
as emotion, but he appeared apologetic. 'The Emperor ordered
me personally to keep this to myself.'

'So Russ was sent to punish Magnus without reason,' said
Sanguinius.

'Not without reason,' said Malcador. 'But the chastisement
was never meant to be so harsh. We determined to despatch
the Wolf King to bring Magnus back to Terra for censure
for defying the judgement of the Council of Nikaea. Horus
manipulated the order.'

'Another secret that spawned disaster,' said Sanguinius.

'The Emperor has His reasons for keeping His plans His
own,' said Malcador. 'Only in this case, I agree. Leman's temper got the better of him, worsening the catastrophe, and
so two Legions that were loyal to Terra were taken from us,
one forced into the arms of the enemy, the other depleted
in strength, and so enraged Russ could not ignore honour's
call and went to fight Horus alone.'

'Many, many died holding back the daemon tide. But the
war in the webway is over, for now,' said Valdor. He looked
to Malcador for permission before continuing. The Regent
shook his head.

'Let me explain, Constantin,' Malcador said. He paused
to gather his thoughts before he went on. 'What none of
you know is that your father is trapped upon the device
He created to keep the bridge to the webway open. It was

intended to be a temporary measure, until the Mechanicum could stabilise the conduit. But all their work was destroyed. If He leaves the Throne now, the doors into the warp will open, and Terra will drown under a tide of Neverborn and all their infinite malice.'

'I thought Him at work to remedy the damage… The situation is far worse than I knew,' said Dorn.

'It is worse still, Rogal,' said Malcador. 'The Emperor is powerful, but His ability has limits. Vulkan waits before the gate as sentinel, in case the Emperor should fail.'

'Is this likely?' said Dorn.

'It is possible,' admitted Malcador.

'Does Vulkan have his sons at his side?' asked Sanguinius, still bewildered. 'Are the Legio Custodes with him, captain-general?'

'Vulkan stands alone,' said Valdor quietly. 'My warriors wait in the Inner Palace. The Ten Thousand lost too many in the webway.'

'What good can one primarch do against all the evil of the warp?' asked Sanguinius.

Malcador shrugged. 'What indeed? You have a point there, so I say that we had better win.'

The Khan leaned down to peer closely at Malcador. 'You are old, but you are cunning, for all your signs of frailty, Sigillite,' he said. 'Tell me now that you have something resembling a plan, that your agents in grey work for our victory, that your many wheels within wheels spin still to your design.'

'My Knights Errant are gone,' said Malcador. 'Their purpose and mission are elsewhere. You are the plan, you three. As of this moment, you know everything there is to know. Your father fights a war on a higher plane of existence, one that should have been mankind's to call his own, but which now seethes with the enemy. The battle here falls to you.

The game is set. No more subterfuge is possible. Your role is here, just as Vulkan's is to stand against the full force of Chaos should the Dungeon be breached. And Roboute's is to get here before we're all dead. You must hold these walls of stone as your father holds walls of spirit. Fight with your guns, and your sons, and all the many, many gifts your father gave you. Use them wisely, sons of the Emperor.' He looked seriously at them all. 'Use them to buy your brother and your father time.'

The magnitude of the task weighed on them all. Outside, the thunder of Horus' guns boomed endlessly on.

'Thank you, Malcador, for bringing our objectives into such sharp focus,' said Dorn. He manipulated the hololith via the neural linkages of his warsuit, bringing up a detailed map of the Palace and its many defences. 'It is time to discuss the practicalities of our survival.'

Grand Borealis Strategium, 13th of Secundus

Thuria Amund swept her tired gaze across her instruments for what felt like the millionth time.

The tinkling of a brass bell, one of three dozen suspended from the top of the ether-scope, broke her trance. She glanced up at it in time to see more start pealing. A rapid chime struck up from behind the bank of lights, then a more urgent alarm from the wall of screens.

'Sir!' she called to her supervising officer. In the profusion of lords, generals and aristocrats, all of whom held different ranks and required different modes of address, 'sir' was the safest option.

Alerted by the chiming, the man was already on his way. He frowned as he took in the warnings singing from Thuria's desk.

He summoned someone else. 'Contact Lord Dorn,' he said. He kept his eyes on Thuria's work station. 'Tell him I have direct confirmation that a new fleet has arrived. Possible identity, Fourteenth Legion. The Death Guard.'

FOUR

No slave
Arrival on Terra
The coming of death

The Vengeful Spirit, *Lunar orbit, 14th of Secundus*

'This place you have made here, Layak, I do not like it,' growled Abaddon.

The temple existed in no plan of the *Vengeful Spirit*, but it was but one of many changes the ship had undergone. As Horus' power grew, the Warmaster's flagship left behind the constraints of the materium, twisting itself away from its original form to please new shipwrights whose concerns were not those of human beings. Under their direction it became as mutable as potter's clay. Sections vanished. Huge parts of the structure heaved with pseudo-organic life. Areas resounded to screams that came from no human mouth. Adornments of spikes and grimacing statues grew overnight, then vanished the next day. Inconstant doorways opened into strange mirror-worlds where men were lost forever.

If logic were followed, the great black doors that led into the temple should have opened directly onto the void, but it was clear that logic had no place there, and that the temple was not on the ship. It lay in some place beyond the void and the universe that contained it, where the laws of physics did not hold true. An interstice between dimensions, perhaps, or a pocket of the warp, Abaddon guessed. The air was frigid, though the metal radiated a dangerous heat that bit at his flesh through his Terminator plate. High windows let in sickly light that gave no hint of the vast armada shoaling around the flagship, or of Luna beneath its keel, or of the stars, but showed an endless, curdled swirl of colours that hurt the eye and the mind to see.

Members of Layak's Unspeaking lurked in guard alcoves, all of them wearing armour as bizarrely decorated as their master's. Abaddon did not like the fact that Layak's men guarded it instead of his own. When Horus had ordered it be so, an ugly look had come over him, as if he tested his son, though to what end Abaddon could not discern. Like the vessel that carried him, the Warmaster was no longer what he had once been.

The chamber's air reeked of incense that was sweet at first breath, harsh with bitterness and iron scents on the second, foul on the third. A pool of viscous liquid so still it looked solid filled channels beneath the path. Shadows whispered between the warriors of the Unspeaking. They called to Abaddon, offering him power, wealth and glory as they probed his soul for weakness. Lesser men would succumb, but Ezekyle Abaddon had no weaknesses, and he scorned the voices' feeble promises as he did all the temptations of the warp. Contempt armoured him. His will was a sword against the dark.

'It is a throne room fit for the lord of the Primordial Truth,' said Layak.

'It is a prison,' said Abaddon. He looked upon his father.

Horus' face was swollen with power, its beauty lost beneath stretched skin. When awake, Horus still possessed the legendary charisma that made all men love him. When entranced like this, he was diminished, a hero past his best. It angered Abaddon to see him so, and tainted his love with pity.

'If Horus had not forbidden me from harming you, you would already be dead,' Abaddon said. 'I will hold to his word only so far, priest. Be careful what poisons you pour into my lord's ear. No order will prevent me taking your head if I deem the provocation sufficient.'

'The truth poisons no one,' said Layak mildly. He appeared as ordinary as he possibly could at that moment. When he worked his sorcery, hoar frost cloaked him, strange scents rose from him, blood oozed from his vox-grille. But though he was currently bereft of the aura of dark magic, corruption left its mark. The bladed design of his helm and the six eye-lenses arranged down its faceplate cheeks could have been a bizarre aesthetic conceit. Abaddon guessed they were not. He wondered what he would see when he finally slew Layak, and tore the misshapen helmet from his head.

'Your truth is subjective,' Abaddon growled. 'Horus rose to free us from one tyrant, not submit us to four. He fights with them. He will not be beholden to your masters. Your certainty is your weakness.'

'The Warmaster is not a slave,' said Layak, making no effort to hide his condescension. 'He is the champion of the Four. The power of the Eightfold Path is his to command.'

'I do not trust you, Apostle. I do not trust your words, or your faith, or your intentions.' Abaddon looked sideways at the Word Bearer over the neck ring of his Terminator plate. 'Know that the Warmaster does not trust you either, no matter what favour you currently have. You are a useful thing. When things no longer have their uses, they are discarded.'

Still infuriatingly mild, Layak replied, 'You have no idea, First Captain, what your father thinks or feels. You never will, until you allow yourself to worship as he does, and open yourself to the Pantheon.'

Abaddon grunted and continued down the walkway. His feet rang loudly from the metal and stone. Layak's footsteps dogged his own. Four others followed them: Layak's mute blade slaves, and behind them two of Abaddon's Terminator-armoured Justaerin, their weight shuddering the deck with every step. Layak's tread was the most grating, ever-present, following the First Captain everywhere he went. Layak would not let him be. Horus more than tolerated his parasitic presence; he hearkened closely to what Layak said. Once, the religion Lorgar preached was resisted by Horus. Since Lorgar's attempted coup and subsequent banishment, principles Horus had found distasteful before seemed acceptable from Layak's lying mouth.

It angered Abaddon that it was so. He did not like the faint streams of red, blue, pink and green energies that, now he drew closer, he could see racing around his unconscious genefather. He liked none of it at all. Horus was changing. He had fallen without warning, bleeding from the cut the dog Russ had given him. When Maloghurst the Twisted had brought the Warmaster back to them, it seemed to Abaddon that not all of Horus had returned.

More magic. More trickery. More weakness.

They halted before Horus. Infernal light bathed the Warmaster's face. Unconscious, he looked sickly, his face twisted by the powers of the warp, his handsomeness deformed, become lumpen and rough as the features of any narcotics addict or drunkard. His eyes twitched under swollen lids. His once full lips thinned to bloodless lines. A thread of drool snaked down from teeth that had become sharp. He was twisted, warp-touched – a bloated, swollen shadow of greatness enthroned. He seemed vast, like an extrusion of a hidden, awful truth greater than a man; but he was less than a man, when once he had been so much more.

Abaddon was reminded of the time Horus lay close to death on Davin, wounded by the anathame, before he returned to his sons with new vigour, and declared that the Emperor must fall. Then, Abaddon had felt a lifetime's anguish. But now...

Each time Horus fell, he came back. Each time he came back, he was diminished. Horus still believed himself master of his own destiny. To Abaddon it was clear he no longer was. By running to the lodges and heeding Erebus, Abaddon bore some responsibility for that, and the thought pricked him.

Layak hissed his quiet laugh. 'Oh, Abaddon. Does your love for your father waver? Do you see him vulnerable, and feel your regard curdle into disgust? He is not weakening, I assure you.'

Abaddon turned so that he fully faced the Apostle. 'Speak so of the Warmaster again and I shall kill you here.'

Servos whined as Abaddon's Terminators presented their guns to fire. Bolts racked into chambers. In answer, heat rose from Layak's blade slaves as they began their transformation in preparation for combat.

Layak laughed again. 'You speak words of loyalty, but your reactions betray you. I voice only your thoughts. He is the vessel of Chaos, the most high, the most exalted.' Layak knelt and bent his head. 'The champion of the Pantheon, but you think he is weak.'

'He is the greatest being in this galaxy,' said Abaddon, 'not the prophet of your so-called gods.' He stared proudly at the Warmaster, ignoring the worms of doubt in his mind. He wanted to act, now – to strike down the priest and remove his taint.

That moment would come.

'Is that so?' Layak's sextuple lenses flared defiantly. Abaddon's fingers twitched towards the massive combi-bolter mag-locked to his hip. His warriors tensed. Like their leader, the Justaerin would have happily seen Layak dead. They wanted the Unspeaking and all the Word Bearers away from their general.

The heat from the blade slaves grew. Their armour cracked, forced apart by bodies swelling underneath. Flesh boiled out of the rents in the ceramite. Their unclean swords leapt from their scabbards into waiting hands, where they lengthened, additional mass unravelling from smoke and darkness into heavy, unnatural blades of bone. Ash sifted from the heat shimmer cloaking them. Embers drifting from their bodies hissed in the black channels below the walk. They presented their weapons, hunching into combat postures far removed from the forms trained into them as legionaries.

With one gesture, Abaddon could condemn them all. He clenched his fists, and looked sidelong at his men. One gesture.

'You would slaughter me while I pay respect to your gene-sire?' said Layak. 'I saved your life, First Captain. There is a cost to that.'

'I saved yours too, if I recall. I owe you nothing.'

Layak raised his hand and twitched his fingers. The blade slaves stood to attention. The hell-light burning in their helm lenses dimmed, and their swords shrank away until they looked like any legionary gladius, and were sheathed.

Abaddon grunted dismissively.

'Your death would be an unwelcome distraction,' he said. He looked back to his father. The light of the energies racing around Horus' head played over the armour of the group. 'When will he wake?'

'He does not sleep,' said Layak. 'Horus' affinity with the warp grows by the hour. His powers swell. The Warmaster has gone into the past.' He clasped his strange staff in front of him and bowed his head. 'Pray with me,' he said, 'for your father goes to seek out the Emperor.'

Terra, the past

Having allowed himself the briefest glimpse of Terra's approaching orb, Horus kept his eyes closed during the whole of the descent. He wanted his first sight of the world to be the interior of his father's Palace, for that was where all the power of mankind was concentrated.

'I look to the future. The grey dust of today's Terra is the past.' That was what he told his companions when they asked why he closed his eyes. They smiled at his words. Horus had a way with men, to speak profundity laced with humour that did not lessen what he spoke of, but raised it up. When he joked, he mocked himself. When he teased his friends he did so more gently than he teased himself. He was humble in his confidence. To be in his company was to feel oneself his comrade, regardless of what station one might hold.

'The matter of Terra is greater than I,' he said, as the dropship started the shake and moan of re-entry. He settled into his restraints, nestling his great head in the padded brace. 'I want to see what will be, not what has been. Terra is old and used up, but it will be great again. The Palace of the Emperor is the centre of this change. From it, authority shall spread, uniting mankind as one people for the first time in thousands of years. Why would I look upon the ruin of what is now, when one day the world shall live again, and thrill to new life returned to it by the efforts of the highest power?

When my father's work is done, and all Old Earth's glories are restored, then I shall look upon it fully.'

'So long as it leads to a good fight,' growled the first of his companions, the largest and the strongest.

The other three of his four companions spoke their agreement. They relaxed and shut their eyes too. Always, men copied his example, out of respect, and love.

They fell through the sky in silence, rocked hard by pockets of denser air, until the thrusters ignited and burned to full, and the party felt themselves grow heavier. Landing claws spread upon the ground with loud rings.

The ship's roaring engines cut out, and were replaced by a noise greater still.

'My lord, they are shouting your name!' said the fourth of his companions, his voice pure as silver bells.

'Lead me to them,' said Horus, his eyes still closed.

The restraint cradle clacked open, and rose with a hiss. His companions took his giant hands in theirs, and guided him eagerly to the gangplank. Waves of adulation roared into the hold as the doors parted and the ramp fell, so loud Horus' ears sang and his warriors had to shout to be heard.

'They love you, my lord! They love you!' said his second companion.

'They do not know me,' said Horus.

'They love you anyway,' shouted the second. He was wise, his words considered, but there was an undertone of suspicion in his voice that resonated with Horus' own most guarded fears, and the primarch's smile wavered.

'Come, my lord! Come! Such life is in the crowd, such pleasure to be had,' said the third companion. 'A profusion of people! They call to you!'

The others were enthused by the jollity of the third, even the grim and growling first, and pulled Horus down the gangplank. The noise grew louder as he emerged from the shadow of the ship's belly and the people saw him.

'Open your eyes,' whispered the fourth sweetly.

Horus did so to the cheers of a million people.

The Emperor, his father, had prepared him as best He could for the sight of the Imperial Palace, but what Horus had taken for boastfulness he saw now was modesty. The Emperor's description of His plans had in no way encapsulated what Horus saw. Only half-finished, the Imperial Palace exceeded anything he had ever seen. Nothing on Cthonia could compare. Not even the great starships that had come for him and borne him away from his home came close in scale, or majesty, or ambition.

For only the second time in his life, Horus felt awe.

'Such vision!' he said.

'It is overweening,' said his second companion. 'His understanding of history's flow is simplistic, and His project will fall.'

'If it does, it will fall and rise again, as all things fall and rise,' said the third.

'It is beautiful!' said the fourth.

The first said nothing.

Horus glanced askance at him. The four were his brothers from Cthonia, warriors who had been with him since the beginning, but he found at that precise moment that he could not recall their names. The first had a warrior's ugliness, pitted and battered, his nose flat, shaved head scarred, forever on the edge of violence. The second was a scholar, waspish in temperament. Heterochromatic eyes looked calculatingly upon everything. His face shifted into uncertain shapes beyond the human form. Horus frowned. He did not know their names! The third was heavier than the rest, fully fleshed and jolly. Yet flakes of skin at the corner of his mouth and red rims around his eyes displayed an imbalance in his humours.

The fourth distracted him, slipping his slender hand back into Horus' own, and leading him deeper into the Palace. 'My brother! My lord!' he laughed gaily. This one wore his hair in elaborate knots, and coloured his cheeks. His eyes were bright with pleasure. 'They adore you!'

Music played from every quarter. Wafers of gold leaf fluttered from the spires either side of the road. The buildings were tall and beautiful, but every window lacked for glass. Columns waiting for statues were placed at fifty-metre intervals, until they ran out, and only sockets for their placing were visible. Not far from the processional way the marble cladding gave way to rockcrete, and the rich pavement stopped. Nothing was finished. Freezing wind whipped up the crimson standards, each flap and flutter drawing the eye to another incomplete artwork, or another tower swathed in scaffolding. The thin air carried multiple chemical taints blown up from the poisoned world. The whole place was a work in progress, yet the people within the unfinished walls cheered and roared as if they were already triumphant, ignorant of how very far they had to go to achieve their master's dream.

The road Horus and his four companions trod was of a gleaming stone, amber as a lion's eyes. Upon it was a purple carpet a kilometre in length. At the end, on a dais made with enough art and beauty to persist ten thousand years, though it would be demolished as soon as Horus professed his fealty, was a throne of gold. A double-headed eagle formed its back, its wings outspread, its claws grasping stylised lightning bolts which thrust jaggedly out over the crowds lining the way. It was preposterously sized. Horus himself, bigger than any two mortal men combined, would have vanished into its seat. But even though the being upon it seemed to be but a man and no gene-forged giant, he overfilled it, his presence spilling out in a blaze of light so glaring Horus had to narrow his eyes to keep walking forwards. His four companions hung back, afraid. Though they had seen the Emperor before and borne His presence bravely, this time they trailed after Horus like frightened children. He lost respect for them, there and then, that they never fully recovered.

Was that how it was? Something was wrong with all this. He had lived these events before, he was sure. The Palace had all the solidity of a memory, a spun-glass recollection perfect in every detail, as all his memories were, but nothing more than a fragile echo of time gone, never to be experienced again.

The four who accompanied him were the cause of the dissonance. The advisors who walked with him the day he came to Terra were not these four men. Those companions had been his first Mournival, beloved comrades from Cthonia who were too old to take legionary apotheosis, and who aged and died with disappointing rapidity.

It was right that these false friends should hang back. They should not have been there. Something in the light hated them.

Horus walked through the roaring acclaim, and his humility fled before it. So many shouts for a being the crowd did not know or understand, and never could. He was a weapon made by an oppressor. If his so-called father had commanded him, he would have killed every single one of them without a thought, and he would have made the massacre seem just. That was the truth of it.

The Emperor was anything but just. His achievements were founded on falsehood.

The Emperor was a liar.

Horus looked at the Palace again.

The towering arches were the expression of arrogance. The walls symbols of oppression. The very idea of Imperium was inimical to the freedom every man had held dear since the first examples of humanity dropped from the trees and walked out into the grasslands. The Emperor was a tyrant like every other tyrant.

'Can you not see what He is?' Horus shouted boldly. 'He brings you slavery in the guise of liberation.' But the words were not heard by the crowd. He could not affect the memory.

Time is a river. It flows only where it can. It is bound by laws as sure as that of gravity. Horus cheatingly followed the path of before like a man can return to a river's source and walk its length again. He remembered now. Events must play out as they did. Some beings, however, are timeless. Through the act of remembering, Horus escaped time's shackles. The Emperor's soul had never felt time's lash so heavily as other men, and so there, in memory, father and son met.

Horus' spirit walked out of step with his former self. He looked through the back of his own head as his past and present moved out of synchronisation. How naive he had been. How excited by this outpouring of affection. He had been taken in completely. He allowed himself to be angry about that.

Horus and his small party came to the foot of the steps. From the great chair, the Emperor stared down at him. There was imperious pride and triumph in His face as He looked upon His creation. But no love. Never that. From the vantage of the present, Horus looked back upon the Emperor's affection and saw it for a sham.

Back then, he had not known. Back then, he had believed.

Horus of Cthonia and Warmaster Horus knelt before the

man who would become a god – the first shaking with joy at reunion with his father, the second disgusted by himself.

Silence fell. From His high seat, the Emperor intoned, 'Horus of Cthonia! Do you swear fealty to me, your creator, the Emperor of Mankind? Do you swear to serve me faithfully, to bring the light of the Imperium to every world touched by the hand of our people, to protect them from the dark, to deliver them from ignorance, to give them succour when they are in need, to guide them where they falter, to save them when they are in danger...'

The Emperor went on with His list of pompous demands.

Warmaster Horus looked up while his weakling former self grovelled in the light. His mouth split far wider than a human's could, evincing a reptilian smile.

'Hello, father,' he said.

+It is not enough that you pursue me through metaphor and dreamscapes? Now you chase me down the roads of what has been,+ said the Emperor.

'I will chase you where I must, father,' he replied. His smile spread. 'You sound tired.'

Snow whipped past Horus from the shadows of a forest hidden on the edge of sight. Lupine shapes prowled behind him, panting hot breaths, eyes of red, green, pink and blue shining from shadowy faces.

+Be careful, Horus,+ the too-perfect voice rang in his head. +The past gives me strength. It has worn itself into the fabric of things, and cannot be altered. It is not mutable like the place you made your last attempt on my soul, and that did not end so well for you.+

Light flared. Horus was pushed back away from his former self as he ecstatically pledged to follow the cause of crusade. Behind the glare Horus saw another Emperor, a man in pain, bound to a seat He could not leave, holding back a tide of darkness while a lone sentinel waited, hammer in hand, before a sealed gate. And past that, a third version of the Emperor, fleetingly glimpsed, this one a corpse trapped within a machine grown monstrous around His throne.

The Warmaster laughed, and pushed back, drawing on the might of his allies.

'I was weak. Now I am not.' The light dimmed. 'The truth makes me strong.'

+False strength derived from false truths. As you draw it, it eats you alive from the inside. Drag upon their lies as much as you wish – you are not strong enough to come against me in this way, my wayward son, and you never shall be.+

The Emperor of the past continued to speak. 'Will you, Horus, first of my primarchs, stand by my side and shepherd humanity into a new era of prosperity and peace, where no xenos race might oppress us, and no fault of our nature undo us?' The Emperor stared at him with His rich, brown eyes, and it was the man of the past and the man of the moment combined when He spoke next. 'Do you swear this, Horus, do you swear it?'

Light swamped Horus Lupercal's form, and cast him from nowhere into somewhere.

The Vengeful Spirit, *Lunar orbit, 14th of Secundus*

An hour passed before Layak raised his head.

'He returns to us.'

The lights circling Horus sped faster and faster, grew brighter, burst apart and fled shrieking for the furthest corners of the hall, where they died in flickers of witchfire. A moment later, Horus stirred. His eyelids flickered like those of a stupefied man coming round, showing only the whites, and refusing to open fully.

'Horus.' Abaddon moved for his father. Layak's hand shot out and grasped his forearm.

'Do not touch him!' he hissed.

Frost spread over the Warmaster's black armour, turning the glaring eye on his chest milky blind. It melted as fast as it formed. The reactor buried within the Warmaster's battleplate whined with building power, and Horus lolled sideways with a groan, pawing at the arms of his seat for support.

'Father,' said Abaddon, appalled by the display of weakness.

Horus held up his hand to silence his son. The jointing of his Terminator armour prevented him from slumping far forwards, but his head hung within the cowl.

'Father,' Abaddon repeated.

'I am well, my son, do not be afraid,' said the primarch. He lifted his eyes to meet Abaddon's. In the dark they shone silvery, like those of a felid caught in a beam of light. 'You disgrace yourself with your fretting, First Captain. Nothing ails me. Far from it.'

With a sigh of armour motors, Horus Lupercal stood. Light danced along the claws of his armour as he activated them and inspected them, and skittered away to nothing when he shut them down. Abaddon relaxed. There was the man he had pledged to follow. There was his father. There was the future Emperor of Mankind.

'The Emperor is afraid. Our time comes,' Horus said. His huge head turned, taking in the party before him as if seeing them for the first time. 'Why do you disturb my meditations? Why are you not on your ship, Abaddon?'

'I wished to see you myself, my lord,' said Abaddon. Energy beat upon him from Horus' engorged soul. *Kneel*, it demanded. *Kneel before me*.

Abaddon would not kneel.

'I wanted to look at your face with my own eyes,' Abaddon continued, 'and ask you why, when Terra is within our grasp, do we delay?'

Horus stared at him. The weight of his regard pushed at Abaddon's being.

Kneel, the demand came again, this time fully voiced within his mind.

Abaddon's armour sighed as his muscles strained within his Terminator plate. He would not kneel!

'You wait too long, father,' Abaddon continued. 'Your armies stand ready for your command. Everything is in place. The last geno-temples of the Selenites are in our hands. All resistance has been purged from Terra's orbits. The bombardment proceeds as you ordered. Terra burns, my lord. But we wait here. We give our enemies time. We give them strength.'

'We are not yet gathered,' said Horus. Such power was contained in his words it scalded Abaddon's soul. 'You push at the bounds of your authority, my son.'

'I will not apologise, nor shall I beg your forgiveness,' said Abaddon. 'The Mournival exists to speak truth to you, and I do so now. We risk everything. Mortarion, primarch of the Death Guard, and all his Legion have broken warp and sail for our position,' he continued. 'You should know this, and be ready to act. Instead, I find you slumped on your throne. You allow yourself to be influenced by this priest. You waste your time in worship.'

'Careful, Ezekyle,' Horus said. 'I worship nothing.'

'Your forces are complete. We should begin our invasion now. Do not tarry, Horus. Strike the final blow.'

For dangerous seconds Horus stared at his son. Strange fires leapt behind his eyes, and Abaddon feared he witnessed the bonfire of Horus' soul consumed. In so many ways it was too terrible a sight to endure, but he held his father's polluted gaze.

Horus suddenly moved down from his throne dais, his vast bulk pushing past the lesser beings at his feet as he headed for the chamber door.

'Mortarion is late,' growled Horus.

FIVE

Bastion 16
Guilliman is coming
The first tower

Daylight District, inner wall, 15th of Secundus

Katsuhiro passed a couple of nights in freezing warehouses, an interminable wait that ended without any warning with an early waking, and they were packed onto another, less luxurious train.

An official ordered them off the train at a small halt and took them through to open service ways above the level of the wall. Winter winds threatened to blast the conscripts from the walkways, and they were urged to hold tight to the guard rails. Through streaming eyes Katsuhiro looked out. 'Wall' was a misleading term for what Katsuhiro saw, for the fortifications were a linear mountain. The wall walk atop it was as broad as a major highway, double sided with crenellations on inner and outer faces of such height that a secondary walk ran along each battlement to act as a firing step. From regularly spaced embrasures giant guns pointed outwards, with smaller pieces between. There were many towers visible in both directions, for the wall there was long and shallowly curved, allowing Katsuhiro to see dozens of kilometres, as far as the Eternity Wall space port to the north, looming large over the defences to block out the view thereafter, and further south, to where the wall was shrunk by perspective to a ribbon, and bent around out of sight.

Before the dizzying mass of the space port, a greater tower jutted skywards over all the others, oval in shape, even more immense than the wall, like a ship athwart the defence. This bore the largest gun he had seen – a macro cannon mounted in a spherical turret. Every minute, the gun barrel drew in and coughed forwards violently, vomiting a gout of fire heavenwards. Katsuhiro learned later that it was the southerly tower of the great Helios Gate, the major exit through that part of the wall.

A part of the plain beyond the wall was visible for a time as the conscripts descended. The ground immediately at the foot of the main defences was obscured by the fortification; further out Katsuhiro saw trenchworks and ramparts. Detail of the plain was lost to the haze of the edge of the aegis, though the violent light of shells hitting the ground flashed through, and he had a hint of a horizon foreshortened by the drop of the Katabatic Slopes to the south and east.

All over the Palace weapons fired skywards. Plasma, shell, laser and rockets roared towards the Warmaster's fleet. The counter-barrage was so loud that no voice could be heard, and their guiding official was forced to resort to hand signals, or shouted orders directly into the ear of the first man in the group, who passed them back up in a game of whispers. By the time the words reached Katsuhiro, halfway along the line of three hundred, they had lost all sense.

In some confusion the conscripts descended long staircases, exposed all the time to the wind and the roar of the guns, coming eventually to ground level shaken, frozen and half-deaf. The journey was long and nerve wracking, and Katsuhiro relished the relative quiet of the canyon street between the wall and the soaring Palace structures behind. It was but a brief respite. The group was rearranged, orders being more easily given there, and then led straight to a small postern guarded by legionaries in green. Few in the group had ever seen a Space Marine, and they stared at the giants as they shuffled past them. The legionaries ignored the conscripts as they passed between them through the gate.

A tunnel led steeply downwards, going through seven adamantium portals before taking a sharp dog-leg covered by emplaced heavy bolters. Then through more doors which groaned violently and flashed red lights at them when they approached, before the final portal opened onto the ground beyond the wall.

Again the roar of the guns battered the senses, and their guide led them wordlessly through a maze of trenches. They crossed paths with other groups, who emerged unexpectedly from the tangle of defensive ways before being led off to their own fates.

They passed a tall wall of prefabricated sections, going out through a triple gate guarded by a switchback approach. Many groups were using this way, and Katsuhiro's unit were forced to wait their turn in a side trench, where they jumped and moaned at every explosion spreading over the aegis overhead, and endured the impatient shoves of uniformed soldiers eager to get by.

A second, lower wall came soon after the first. It stood atop a recently piled slope of rubble that led down without the interruption of trenches to a final wall a few hundred metres further out. Of the three main lines, the last was the lowest, the defensive lip being only two metres above ground level, and the rampart running behind easily clambered onto from the back. They headed for this wall, then after reaching it turned north towards the Helios Gate.

By then it was snowing. Gentle at first, the weather gathered itself into a freezing storm that chilled them all and curtailed what visibility there was.

Cold and tired, the conscripts were gathered into a square among several dozen others collected at the outermost line, and introduced to their leader.

The commanding officer was an exhausted-looking man. There was nothing unexpected about that. Katsuhiro hadn't seen a fresh face for weeks, but their new leader excelled all others in weariness, pushing past to the unexplored realms of misery beyond. His skin looked to be ordinarily a light brown, but it had gone a haggard yellow-grey, like a blanket left too long outdoors. His black hair was plastered miserably to his forehead. His lips and nail beds were unhealthily pale. He gave the impression of being a man who had seen everything, and liked very little of it.

The pad of flimsies in his hand particularly displeased him. He scanned again the cheap bioplastek films, already disintegrating in the snow melting off his skin, then looked down with pouched eyes at the three hundred conscripts failing to hold a parade ground formation behind the revetment. He did not look impressed.

Katsuhiro was right at the front of the group, close enough to hear the officer's voice over the roaring of the attack. They were now some distance from the walls and the violence of the Palace guns, while the aegis stole a good amount of the noise of the enemy's bombardment along with its destructive power.

'Is this it?' said the man miserably. 'No officers? It's just me?'

'Sign here and here,' said the official who had brought the group down from the Palace.

'Ghosts of Old Earth, we're all going to die.' The officer made a depressed sound and scribbled at the form. Part of it came away on the nib of his autoquill.

'They're all yours now.' The official rolled up the disintegrating plastek and shoved it inside his coat. 'For Unity and the Imperium.' He made a full aquila over his heart before marching off down the rampart, where he disappeared into the snow. The officer pulled a face and fetched a vox-horn from his belt. Feedback squealed when he activated it.

'Right, you lot,' yelled their new officer over the thunder of the bombs and the moan of the wind. 'My name is Adinahav Jainan. I'm...' He held up the flimsies again. 'I'm an acting captain, lucky me. That makes me your commander. Do what I say, or you'll get shot.' He made an expression that could equally have been a scowl or a smile. He didn't have enough enthusiasm to form either properly. 'That is, I'm sorry to inform you, the full extent of military training that is currently available under the circumstances. You are all now members of the Kushtun Naganda, one of the Old Hundred, from Ind, not that you're worthy of the honour, and not that it matters any more anyway.' Pent-up emotions forced themselves up through his world-weary exterior, where they bubbled, briefly visible, on his face before draining away into a general lassitude. 'There was a time when that meant something. But at least you will all have the satisfaction of dying under a famous flag. Our role,' he said, raising his voice over a sudden upsurge in the bombardment's volume, 'is to reinforce the third line outworks,' he kicked the wall, 'near Bastion Sixteen.' He pointed down the line, where there was nothing visible though the whirling snow. 'You will form reserves to the very first line of

defence! More of that honour when we get there. Yes, I'm
afraid that does mean more walking. No, I don't have anything to shelter you from the weather. The sooner we get
there, the sooner you can get warm. We go at the pace of
the slowest. Feel free to beat a bit of speed into them. But
we do have a little bit of time.' He looked upwards. 'The
enemy won't be coming today.'

Katsuhiro gave a small sigh of relief.

'Don't get too excited,' said the thin man Katsuhiro had
seen cleaning his nails with a knife in the city. He leaned in
from behind and whispered into Katsuhiro's ear. 'Reservers
aren't for keeping back. They're for doing all the scutwork,
and if the enemy don't come today, they'll come tomorrow, or the day after.' His voice smiled, but his words were
meant to hurt.

'Shut up!' Katsuhiro snapped behind him. 'There's no
need to make it worse.'

'Got some teeth after all, eh?' said Doromek, who was a
file over from Katsuhiro.

'Leave me alone!' Katsuhiro said.

'Hey! Hey, you!' Jainan's amplified voice thumped into
Katsuhiro's ears. 'Yeah, that's right. You. Just so we're all read-
ing from the same manual here, talking when I'm talking
is definitely not allowed.' He patted the laspistol at his hip
meaningfully. 'Got it?'

Katsuhiro nodded.

Acting Captain Jainan sighed. 'Right then, this way.' He
turned off the horn and hooked it on his belt, then executed a lazy left turn. 'Quick march.' He stopped and held
out his arms when half a dozen of the new soldiers went
to the rampart to get out of the mud.

'Nope,' he said. 'I stay up here on this relatively dry prefabricated wall. The rest of you have to trudge through the

snow.' He straightened his snow-damp uniform. 'There has to be some privilege of rank.'

Their march north allowed Katsuhiro a little time to take in his new surroundings. The walls proper soared to improbable heights to his left. Though the spires of the Palace were far higher, from his position the walls hid nearly everything behind them, so huge were they. The outworks were tiny in comparison. Being stationed in the maze of walls and trenches that fronted the main fortifications was alarming. His fears increased as the thousands of conscripted men and women continued to pour into the complex, splitting and splitting again as they were directed down differing trench ways already ankle-deep in snow. His dismay continued to rise, while never hitting the peak he expected. There seemed to be no end to how much fear he could feel. It surprised him he was able to walk, or talk, or do anything, but he did, his terrified mind operating his limbs through a buzzing fog of terror. He felt numb inside and out. The bombardment pounded endlessly down. Millions of tonnes of ordnance exploded upon the Palace's shields every minute, their released energies stolen by the voids' displacement technology. The aegis must have been thinner out past the walls, not that Katsuhiro knew the first thing about military shielding, because periodically a shell the size of a heavy hauler would pass through and impact the ground beyond the last rampart, sending up a plume of rock splinters dozens of metres high, and shaking the soldiers on their feet.

'This isn't so good, is it?' said the thin man conversationally. 'I just love being cannon fodder. Isn't that right, darling?' he shouted at the woman from the station, who was a few ranks ahead. She scowled at him.

'I wouldn't call her darling, if I were you,' said Doromek.

'Why? She's a looker, I could do with a taste of that.'

'I know her kind, my friend. She'll kill you.'

The thin man snorted.

'I mean it,' said Doromek.

'Will you shut up?' said Katsuhiro, addressing both the thin man and Doromek. He was by now more miserable than he had ever been. Outside the city was even colder than inside. His hands were unfeeling claws clamped upon his gun. His teeth chattered. The snow had turned black with ash, and wind chilled the exposed side of his face so that it burned. The air was thin and oxygen-poor away from the Palace's atmospheric cycling system. Some provision had been made for this; every half-mile or so giant snakes of soft tubing emerged from the ground and whooshed thicker, warmer air over the outworks. The conscripts noticed these quickly, and ran between them, desperate for the heat and nourishing airflow, though the distances between caused them to flag, and their provision was meagre overall.

While approaching the fourth of these outflows, the thin man spoke again.

'This snow, you know it's toxic, right?' He jogged along-side. Katsuhiro was too breathless to tell him to be quiet. The man took his silence as interest. 'Void shields will stop fast things, or big things, and especially big, fast things, but small stuff like this, or slow stuff like an infantryman or a tank, it can't stop that. Rain or snow'll fall right through it. This is black snow. The Palace is covered in layered void shields so deep it'll take the enemy months to pound their way through. Everywhere else on Terra? Not so well provided. So what's falling on us is the vaporised remains of the rest of the world. It's full of rad and poison. Kill us all dead eventually, not that we'll last that long.'

'I think he said shut up, you. I'm asking the same,' said Doromek to the man, causing him to back off a bit.

'What's he mean?' Katsuhiro asked Doromek.

'It's a defensive layer thing,' said Doromek. Near the pipes the snow melted, and they splashed through freezing water running over the ground. He appeared bothered far less by the cold and the thin air than just about everyone else. 'They don't need to keep us safe. We're the first line of defence.'

'First line?'

An aircraft screamed overhead, making them all flinch and more than a few throw themselves into the muddy snow. A soft explosion thumped bare metres over their heads, prompting a lot more of the conscripts to scream and fling themselves down, Katsuhiro included.

'Get up! Get up!' shouted Jainan. 'It's just a bloody leaflet drop. Get up!' He jumped down from the wall, and hauled weeping conscripts to their feet. Those who were too tightly curled he kicked until they stood. 'Come on! Come on! Get up!'

Katsuhiro unclamped his hands from his head. A white sheet of paper floated face down in a puddle in front of him. He reached out and picked it up.

'Get up! Get up! Everyone, come on!' Jainan glowered after the aircraft. 'Bloody propaganda. Does nobody any good!'

On the other side of the paper was a poorly printed image of a warrior. A Space Marine, Katsuhiro thought at first, but closer inspection revealed it was in fact a primarch. A large 'XIII' was printed beneath him.

Lord Guilliman is coming, it read. *Stand firm and survive.*

'Lot of use, that,' Doromek said. He reached down. Katsuhiro clasped his arm. 'If he gets here at all, we'll all be dead.'

'That's right.' The thin man nodded sagely as Doromek pulled Katsuhiro to his feet. 'First line of defence. They'll keep the Legions back behind the main walls for the real fighting.'

'Then what are we for?' asked Katsuhiro, dreading the answer.

Doromek laughed ruefully. 'We're here to die, my boy. Soak up bullets. Cannon fodder, as our friend...'

'Runnecan,' the thin man said.

'As Runnecan says.' Doromek smiled sympathetically, attempted to scrape the mud off Katsuhiro, shrugged at the amount and gave up. 'The way this battle will play out is so – you see the batteries there, there and there?' Doromek pointed out the giant guns mounted upon the wall's towers. Flashes and rods of coherent light marked out the presence of thousands more.

'I can't really miss them,' said Katsuhiro.

'Now you're getting it,' said Doromek, and slapped him on the shoulder. 'There are lots more deeper within. Lord Dorn cut a thousand towers flat to take guns, guns and more guns. They stud every high structure, clustering most densely around the space ports, gates and, especially, especially, the Lion's Gate.'

'Yes?' said Katsuhiro tersely. They began to trudge through the mud again.

'Well, yes, obviously. My point is, no real attack can come down until those guns are taken out. If I were the Warmaster,' he said – Doromek's arrogance was astounding – 'then I would attempt to clear an area of crossfire, and begin to land my first forces. With men on the ground, the walls will be threatened. All this out here,' he swept his hand about, 'will come under intense attack. Some guns will fall, some guns will be reoriented to target the ground. The weight of fire will decrease. That will enable more ships to come down, then more, until the surface of Terra is crawling with the enemy, and the guns will cease to speak at all. But first, he has to get through that.' Doromek pointed upwards. 'The

Palace aegis. It'll last, but not forever. As soon as that starts to fail, then we'll see the real bombing start, and after that, the proper invasion.'

'So we're safe. For now?' Katsuhiro sneezed. Feeling in his toes and fingers was a fond memory.

'If by "now" you mean for the next few hours, then yes we are, safe as the Emperor Himself. Not that He's particularly safe at the moment.'

'We're all going to die!' tittered the thin man. Several of the conscripts within earshot were rigid with fear.

'You! Talkative man.' Jainan strode out of the rain. He alone out of the unit wore a rain cape, but it was thin and he was as cold and wretched as the rest of them.

'Yes, sir?' Doromek gave a coprophage's smile. The thin man grinned.

'I heard you, giving all these wretches the benefit of your wisdom. Are you a military man?' snapped Jainan. 'Don't lie to me. I can check. Save us the time and tell me now.'

'I was once,' admitted Doromek.

'And you are again,' Jainan said. 'Sir.'

'Indeed. Sir.'

'How many years, and what regiment?'

Doromek rubbed at his head. 'Atlantean Rangers. Fifteen years.'

'Role?'

'Sniper.'

'Good one?'

Doromek waggled his free hand. 'So they say.'

'Then how come you weren't called up in the early drafts?' Jainan's eyes narrowed.

Doromek shrugged. 'Lucky, I guess.'

'Hiding you mean. Well your luck's run out. You're my new lieutenant. Congratulations.' He stalked off back into the storm, hollering at the group to get a move on. 'And stop diving into the ground at the sight of every aircraft – they are all ours!'

'An officer? Me?' shouted Doromek.

'Don't get excited. Acting officer!' Jainan called back over his shoulder.

Doromek grinned at Katsuhiro. 'That makes you my first sergeant.'

They staggered on for another few hundred metres. A dark shape loomed out of the snow to meet them. Katsuhiro peered fruitlessly into the storm. The shape grew firmer with every step, until it stopped being a shape and became a great drum tower, a hundred metres tall and almost as wide across, set back some fifty metres from the outermost ramparts. Guns mounted in the walls tracked back and forth across the artificial plateau beyond the aegis. Lights shone through tiny windows in only one place, halfway up the front.

Doromek whistled. 'I guess that's Bastion Sixteen.'

Jainan's vox-amplified voice cut over the rumble of the Imperial guns and the muffled thunder of the bombardment.

'This is it. Follow me. Our section is to the south-south-west. Stay close. Don't get lost. There are uniforms, shelter, food and water waiting for you. Alternatively, you can blunder off into this blizzard and either freeze to death or be executed by the Marshals Militaris. I hear they are itching to shoot something. Your choice.'

Jainan strode away. There wasn't much option but to follow him.

Bastion 16, 16th of Secundus

Afterwards, Katsuhiro was not certain if it was the increasing noise of the explosions or the wailing klaxons sounding from the wall that woke him. Mercifully spared duty, he had fallen into a deep, sudden sleep atop a pile of sacks just as soon as he'd found somewhere to hide.

Tocsins blared all along the ramparts, wrenching him from slumber into nerve-jangling consciousness in the space of a single breath. He leapt up, flailing around. There were no formal barracks for the new members of the Kushtun Naganda. The storage bunker he found to hide in was unlit, and for a moment he forgot completely where he was. He'd lived in the same room for his entire life. Twenty-five years of familiarity sought to impose themselves upon reality, and he stumbled about, wondering who had moved his few pieces of furniture around.

The door opened, catching on poorly finished rockcrete with a squeal. Horrendous noise blasted in from outside.

'Out, out! The enemy are coming, the enemy are coming! Come on!' A wild-eyed man he didn't recognise beckoned frantically. He wore the badly made tabard that marked him out as a conscripted member of the Nagandan; this was the uniform Jainan had mentioned, and not the warm coat Katsuhiro was hoping for.

Who the man was, Katsuhiro never discovered. He found his rifle and ran outside.

The snow had stopped, and cold sunk its teeth deep into the mountains. Although Katsuhiro had been warm in the bunker his clothes were still wet. Winter hit him like a blow, so hard he almost missed what occurred. The sky above him was an eye-watering pattern of unnatural colours holding back an ocean of fire. Something squeaked and ground like ice on stone, then there was a tremendous bang, and the noise of the bombardment suddenly grew loud enough to shake the teeth in his head. There were people shouting all around him, but he could not hear a word they said.

Pulsed shocks of overpressure batted at him. The ground bounced like a drum skin. He staggered about in shock, half blinded by strobing explosions hammering the ground a kilometre distant.

Doromek was there, turning him around, pointing and shouting. It took three attempts before Katsuhiro heard what was being said.

'The voids have come down!' he yelled. 'The voids over the Palace!'

He followed Doromek's finger. He could see it then, a dark space over one of the wall's enormous towers. The edges of other void shields were visible thanks to the lack of the missing element, layered over one another in flat petals that pulsed like hearts with every impact. They held back their portion of the bombardment, but through the hole shells fell unimpeded, making it down to the ground and exploding all around the tower. Flames burst off the tower's sloped sides. Katsuhiro tried to ask if they would be targeted next, but nobody could hear him. Warning sirens sang over the explosions, audible only by dint of their shrieking pitch.

The huge defence laser that dominated the tower prepared to fire, the nested barrel pulling itself back with a series of businesslike metallic booms. With a defiant roar and cast of light the cannon uncoiled, hurling its response upwards. Whether the las-beam hit its target or not Katsuhiro could not tell, but at that moment the enemy appeared to notice the section was unprotected, and destruction speared from the night.

Five beams of collimated light slammed into the tower, their impacts tightly grouped, each coming in from a different angle.

Molten rockcrete and metal poured off the structure in torrents. The beams were persistent, and moved along, sawing at the tower. One punched clean through both sides of the building, bringing up a mushroom of fire from within the Palace before they all snapped off. Part of the parapet of the attached wall tumbled away, its sheared edges glowing with heat.

The gun pulled its muzzle in again, but its last roar had already been voiced.

A triple hit of high-velocity mass shot slammed into the spherical turret. Explosions rolled out over the defence works, each one louder than the last. Fire swept out in a hollow disc around the top of the tower, and when it receded the gun was a tumbling wreck, slipping from its moorings and taking the outer face of the bastion with it.

'Come on! Come on!' The man who had woken Katsuhiro ran past, his need to act dragging a score of his comrades along with him. 'The tower, the tower!'

They made impressive speed through the lying snow, though Katsuhiro saw they could achieve nothing and did not follow. Thin screams crept under the noise of the barrage. The heat of the molten rockcrete singed his face from so far away. In their need to do something, anything, the conscripts raced headlong into danger, while others stood rooted to the spot, weeping in terror.

More lance beams scored their way across Katsuhiro's eyes, coming this time from a lower angle. Half of them smeared away to blue light across the neighbouring void shield, but the rest hit the tower squarely, slicing it open down to the magazine. The largest, brightest fire Katsuhiro had ever seen boomed out, breaking apart the tower as it grew from nothing to everything, so big and loud it swallowed the whole of the universe.

Searing air knocked him flying, sending him skidding metres through the snow. Debris rained down around him, bringing more screams into the night as men and women were crushed.

Gasping for the breath that had been punched from his lungs, Katsuhiro staggered upright onto his knees and remained there, filthy again, his back chilled to the bone by the wind, his front warmed by the dying fires of the tower. Through phosphor-bright after-images burned into his retinas, he saw the tower was gone, a tooth torn out from the root. A single shell corkscrewed down on a spiral trail of fire, bringing up a last explosion. The air thrummed. His skin prickled, and the void shields flexed back into existence over the ruin, glowed like the cells in an insect hive, then faded out of notice. A few hits splashed upon the surface of the aegis. The bombardment moved off, on to test the next mighty bastion ten kilometres away.

Doromek found him again.

'The first gun falls. This is it now,' he said. 'They'll concentrate their fire like that, to take out the biggest anti-ship cannons we have. Little by little, they'll nibble it away, until there's nothing left to threaten their landing zones.'

'Landing zones,' repeated Katsuhiro dumbly.

'We're lucky,' Doromek said sardonically. 'I'd say they're clearing this area here. They're going to be coming right at us.'

SIX

Tears of an Angel
The Emperor's work
Fabricator General

Imperial Palace airspace, 24th of Secundus

Sanguinius flew under a ceiling of fire. His strong wings bore his armoured form easily over the sprawl of his father's Palace. Not for the first time, he marvelled at the artifice that had gone into the creation of his wings. Most winged creatures analogous to Terran vertebrates had keel bones to anchor their flight muscles. The ones that did not were gliders, not flyers; they could not beat their wings. For his own amusement Sanguinius had once calculated how far his sternum should project to allow him to fly if he had followed the same design as a bird. Two and half metres should have covered it. Yet he had a human form, with no grotesque deformities. Indeed, they called him beautiful.

Exactly how he was able to fly would have been impossible to determine without having himself dissected. His father never spoke with him about his wings. Sanguinius had often wondered if they were part of the Emperor's design, or were the outwards signs of Chaos' blight upon his soul. The servants of the Ruinous Powers had intimated as much to him.

'They lie,' Sanguinius said, through gritted teeth, his words torn from his mouth and left behind as he wheeled through Terra's tortured heaven.

If the Emperor had made the wings, Sanguinius assumed that a musculature of the most inspired design had been incorporated into his body. The wings were broad, and strong, and glorious to look upon. They lifted him and the great mass of his armour easily. He could control his great pinions as finely as fingers, tilting them individually this way and that to catch the air perfectly. When he moved his feathers so, air ran over the barbs like water over a hand. The sensation pleased him greatly.

Sanguinius passed comfortably between the blasts emanating from the Palace defences. His gift of prophecy was stronger than ever before as he neared his foreseen end. The fixed point of his death anchored his ability somehow, the coming seconds, minutes and hours unfolding more readily for him. He knew where each shaft of killing light would go before it cut the sky, and adjusted his flight accordingly. He saw shells spear upwards before they were fired.

Flying was a gesture of defiance. It was sad for him that it had often been so. On mutant-hating Baal before he was found. On Macragge, where he had flown in defiance of Guilliman's wishes. On Terra now, where Dorn said the same. Always, his brothers sought to ground him.

But he would not stay out of the air. How could any of the others understand him, when none could fly?

He hoped Horus could see him beneath the squalls of energy bursting on the aegis and know he could not be touched.

The Palace stretched beneath Sanguinius, immense in

scale, almost impossible to grasp as a whole. Dorn's defences came close to matching the Emperor's vision in grandeur. The Eternity Wall ringed the whole, stupendous in scale, thousands of kilometres long, hundreds of metres high, layers and layers of rockcrete, ferrocrete, plascrete and stone, the sloping fronts reinforced with adamantium. The metal alone equalled in value the combined wealth of dozens of lesser empires. In places the walls were stepped with multiple battlements marching up the outside. Hundreds and hundreds of towers punctuated its length, many topped with anti-fleet guns. Orbital batteries occupied bastions the size of hills behind them.

The Eternity Wall spawned many offspring, dividing the Palace into various wards. There was the Ultimate Wall, around the Sanctum Imperialis, and the Anterior Wall, which looped out from the Eternity and Ultimate Walls to form an outer bailey for the Lion's Gate, girdling the artificial mountain of the Lion's Gate space port as it did so. Each of the sections of the walls had their own names: Daylight, Dusk, Tropic, Polar, Montagne, Celantine, Exultant, and more besides, so many in number, though still few when divided among the overall length, so that each named section was dozens if not hundreds of kilometres long.

Laid out below Sanguinius were the spires and hives of the Palatine Sprawl. The Tower of Hegemon thrust contemptuously up at the enemy fleet, its existence vouchsafed by Skye, the last of Terra's great orbital plates, whose straining engines held aloft a treasury of transplanted guns.

Not far from Skye's anchor the giant dome of the Senatorum Imperialis managed to retain its dignity despite being swaddled in protection. This varied from technologically advanced foams and layers of dispersive and ablative materials to simple piles of sandbags filled with the dust of ancient civilisations. Further out he spied the Investiary, and though all except two of its monumental statues had been destroyed, they and the empty plinths around them were also covered over. These buildings and monuments were too precious, too evocative of the dream of Imperium to be taken down. Removing them would be tantamount to admitting defeat, even if only to keep them safe. But elsewhere, much of the beauty of the city had been trampled on by Dorn's fortification. Guns bristled on buildings never meant to take them, and what could not be weaponised had been torn down to make way for yet more guns.

Sanguinius circled over the ziggurat of the Lion's Gate space port, banking to avoid the immensity of the gate itself. Guarding the way to the Inner Palace and the sanctum therein, the Lion's Gate was the greatest of the Palace's many portals, an entire mountain refashioned into a fortification. A few dozen kilometres before it was the Ascensor's Gate, the largest of the Anterior Wall's six entrances. In any other setting the Ascensor's Gate would have been a monument to Imperial might. Before the Lion's Gate it was a child's model.

Diving fast under the constant thrum of the void shields, Sanguinius accelerated, and he powered by the space port. It was of such stupendous size that its flat top alone accommodated landing fields to rival the chief ports of a sector capital planet. Its sides held docking cradles large enough for major void-ships. Everything about the Palace was scaled for gods. Sanguinius had lived much of his life feeling the world around him to be small. There had been one or two occasions, mostly before the glory of cosmic phenomena, once even at the Fortress of Hera, where he had been humbled, but these things had a lesser effect than the Palace had. In the Palace, he was a mote before the majesty of his father's ambition.

He turned south-west. Hundreds of kilometres of ancient massif sped quickly beneath him, all built over by the Imperial capital. Mountains had been levelled and valleys kilometres-deep filled during the construction. Away from the Palace to the south, east and west, artificial plains, also geoformed from the most rugged terrain on the planet, reached for the horizon. They ended in the plunge of endless slopes, beyond which lay Kush and Ind. North, north-west and north-east the mountains reasserted themselves, their heads smothered in dirty snow. They were the sovereigns of this world once; now they appeared as supplicants, beggared by their usurper.

Cold winter winds blew from the heart of Eurasia. Sanguinius rode them through flurries of snow. Exulting in his flight, he forgot awhile the bombardment and the war. A fragile calm filled him, and the world shifted. Through his Emperor-given foresight, he saw another time as clearly as the present. The Palace had swollen to many times its size, outgrowing the walls, spreading beyond its original limits, devouring most of the Katabatic Plains and crawling up the sides of the mountains. What beauty it'd had was gone, yet it was not the ugliness of war, but that of carelessness and of neglect. He saw the familiar landmarks still, swamped by edifices of lesser quality. The Terra of his father was a greening place, a world of wastes seeded with oases and the glint of growing oceans. All that was gone in the future. Everything was grey, and oppressive.

Sanguinius let out a cry, and he fell uncontrolled before he mastered himself, and stretched out his wings again to catch the winds. The Palace as it was now, in his present, reasserted itself, though the vision continued to trouble him.

The Eternity Wall space port lunged heavenwards ahead. The second of the Palace's in-wall space ports, it was a giant ridge of metal fifty kilometres long, festooned with guns, crackling with void shields, its dry docks and berths enough to hold a subsector fleet with room for more besides. The grand capital craft could never come down from orbit, not without breaking their spines, but there, at the ports at the top of the world, smaller ships ordinarily confined to the void could venture to the surface, with all save the larger classes able to put in. But its honeycomb of quays was empty. Terra's naval might had been smashed asunder. What vessels survived hid far from Terra.

Sanguinius' eyes strayed to a sky crowded with enemy ships. He still maintained it was a mistake to send the *Phalanx* away.

He curved past the Celestial Citadel at the Eternity Wall space port's southernmost tip. A city unto itself, large as any hive, in better days it was the haunt of void clan emissaries, ambassadors from xenos powers, Navigator houses and naval dynasts. Before the war, the citadel's uppermost spires had extended beyond the atmospheric envelope and into space. In doing so, they had exceeded the reach of the Palace aegis, and so Dorn had cruelly cut them short, leaving truncated stumps a few hundred metres below the void shield barrier. It was predictably covered with ordnance.

Rogal Dorn did so love his guns.

Within minutes the second space port was behind him. Sanguinius wore his helmet to mollify his brother rather than for safety, but it gave him access to his battleplate's systems. Gauges on the faceplate display put his airspeed at well over one hundred kilometres an hour. He smiled for the pleasure of it, and reluctantly began to check his speed. He went into a broad spiral, circling down towards the southern tower of a gate straddling the Daylight Wall, that section of the Eternity Wall that faced east, into the rising sun.

Fast, faster, the rooftop sped at him. At the last moment,

he opened his wings as wide as he could, his primary feathers spreading like fingers. Wind tugged through his plumage. Minute adjustments no aircraft could make had him smoothly descending, landing upon the tower roof at a speed no greater than a fast walk.

Raldoron, First Captain of the Blood Angels Legion and Sanguinius' equerry, was there to greet him.

'My lord, welcome to the Helios Gate,' Raldoron said, and saluted. An Imperial Fists captain attended him. He too saluted in the Blood Angels' way out of respect for the primarch. A thick parapet, two-thirds the height of a Space Marine and punctuated with deep embrasures, enclosed the roof. Quad lascannons, sat upon turntables on sculpted podiums, were spaced around the giant macro cannon dominating the centre.

'Rise, captains,' said Sanguinius.

'How was your flight?' said Raldoron

'The winds of Himalazia always remind me of home,' Sanguinius said. 'Of the Wind River, on Baal Secundus, where I first tested my wings. The speeds I could attain there…' He let the sentence die.

Raldoron was wrong-footed. Sanguinius had rarely spoken of Baal since Signus Prime. His sight seemed fixed on the future, and the past forgotten.

'You are of the second moon, Raldoron. Did you ever fly the river?' asked Sanguinius.

Raldoron hesitated. 'No, no I never did, my lord. I always wanted to, but I never wore the wings.'

'Then I pity you,' said Sanguinius. 'Flight is the last pleasure left to me.'

Bereft of a suitable response, Raldoron changed the subject. 'This is Captain Thane of the Twenty-Second Company, Imperial Fists. He is designated watch captain for the sixteenth section of the wall.'

'Your company is of the Exemplars Chapter of the Seventh Legion?'

'It is, my lord.'

'Do you live up to your name?'

'We do, my lord,' said Thane proudly. 'There are no better builders in my Legion than our Chapter, and my company is among the best.'

'Propitious. You have some work to do here.'

Sanguinius strode past the captains towards an embrasure looking down the southern reach of the wall. He was tall enough not to need the secondary walkway running around the inside of the crenellations, but climbed it anyway to look. Some kilometres away, past the first tower after the Helios Gate, scaffolding surrounded a scar in the wall.

'We are working night and day, my lord, to plug the breach made by the collapse of the Dawn Tower,' said Thane.

'The repairs are nearly complete?'

'They are. The finish is rough, but the wall will hold. We cannot, regrettably, replace the tower.'

'There was a flaw in the void generators under that section,' said Raldoron. 'We are unlikely to lose another bastion soon.'

'This is known to me,' said Sanguinius. 'Flaw or not, the loss of that tower is only the first we shall suffer. The bombardment continues. The shields of the Palace cannot last forever.'

'What the enemy tears down, we shall rebuild, my lord.' Thane clashed his fist against his chest-plate.

Sanguinius turned to look over the outer defences. Besides extending the city's walls, Dorn had supplemented the fortifications with miles of outworks. Trenches and ramparts extended over the artificial plains in three parallel lines. Whatever had been there before had been bulldozed. Bastions, deliberately isolated from the lines, stood behind the outermost ramparts like pieces laid out for regicide. Though much smaller than the towers of the wall itself, they were still enormous at a hundred metres tall. Sanguinius followed the lines of radial trenches emanating from the wall proper, past the third and final line where they stopped, and on towards the point where the horizon, foreshortened by the drop in elevation down to the plains of Ind, cut the earth from the sky.

Past that point, the world was burning.

He saw, with a primarch's acuity, young forests aflame, and palls of dust cast skywards by the relentless pounding of the enemy's guns. There was enough firepower in orbit to tear Terra to pieces, but that was not the Warmaster's aim. It was as if instead he wished to wipe away every good thing the Emperor had done. Sanguinius recalled his glimpse of the sprawling mega-hive, and the grey, dead world around it. This was the birth of that grim future. He needed to distract himself from that realisation.

'The outer defences are fully manned?'

'As well as they can be, my lord,' said Raldoron. 'Mostly conscripts, with a stiffening of what's left of the Old Hundred – not many though. We have stationed only the most severely under-strength formations in the outworks. Veteran companies of Imperial Army over fifty per cent manned stand beside us here on the wall. As Lord Dorn ordered, no legionaries are stationed without.'

On impulse, Sanguinius unclasped his golden helm and lifted it from his face. His shining hair unwound and flew like a banner. The cold wind should have been refreshing, but it carried the smell of burning, and deprivation. He faced into the breeze and breathed deeply, his enhanced senses capturing a thousand scents that together told only of despair.

'My lord…'

Raldoron gestured hesitantly to his genefather's face. Sanguinius reached up and touched his cheek. As he brought his fingers away, he saw that they glistened with tears. He had not realised he was crying.

'Why do you weep, my lord?' asked Raldoron.

'I cry for the price of victory, my son,' said Sanguinius, and wept no more. He stopped the tears with an act of will, and his face chilled as they were dried by the wind.

Daylight Wall, Helios section, 24th of Secundus

Sanguinius spent the rest of the day on the Daylight Wall. There were extensive guard chambers beneath the Helios Gate's tower tops, but most of the rest was solid mass with few internal voids. Only the very centre housed further chambers, and these were small and hot, packed full of machines, men and servitors. Thane was keen to show the primarch the command centre, though it was obvious to Sanguinius he simultaneously wished his exalted visitor gone, for his presence distracted his men. Raldoron had little to report.

Sanguinius excused them both and walked a little way through the firing galleries of the Daylight Wall. These were occupied in the main by Space Marines, with a heavy presence of ordinatus tech-priests of the Adeptus Mechanicus autokrator, manning the many medium and smaller guns mounted within the walls. The baseline, unmodified humans in the galleries were all veterans of the Imperial Army, principally of the Old Hundred as Raldoron had said. Those at that part of Daylight were drawn from the well-armoured Anatol Evocatii, but he saw uniforms from a dozen others.

Privately, Sanguinius had misgivings about the conscripts outside the wall. They had been handed a death sentence.

As a man, he lamented their sacrifice; as a commander and a primarch, he appreciated Dorn's decision as ruthless pragmatism. When Horus' forces landed, it would be insane to throw away their better troops slowing his attack on the Palace defences, when pressed civilians would serve as well to tie up the initial landings. Everyone outside would perish. He could imagine the destruction to come only too easily. Better their elites were kept back for the real fight.

You care too much. Curze had said that to him once, before he had gone completely insane. It was a fair assessment.

Sanguinius passed through the Weeping Tower between the gate and the fallen Dawn Tower, amazing those working inside. Nobody expected to see a primarch within the Outer Walls. He apologised for disrupting their watch, and passed on. Most were Blood Angels, but Raldoron's Chapter was not much in evidence. As veteran Space Marines, the Protectors were held back further within the Palace. Besides a company from his own Chapter, Raldoron commanded a network of fifteen subordinate officers, and the Blood Angels Sanguinius met with were drawn from everywhere within his Legion. It saddened him that he did not know many faces. So many were young, new recruits speed-inducted by the Lunar genomancer Andromeda-17, Terrans in the main who had never seen Baal.

He reached the downed tower. The inner walkway stopped abruptly. Fresh rockcrete walled the passage off, and although Thane would doubtless bore fresh ways through, for the moment it was a stark reminder of what the walls would have to endure.

Sanguinius ran his fingers over the freshly cast false stone, and turned about.

His vox-beads popped into life. A priority channel, no override possible.

'Rogal,' he said.

Dorn's voice was clear in spite of enemy interference and the energies spilling off the void shields. *'Where are you?'*

'I am on the walls, at the fallen Dawn Tower, south of the Helios Gate.'

Dorn made a noise of annoyance. *'What are you doing all the way out there?'*

'The Dawn Tower is not the most easterly,' Sanguinius said, ignoring his brother's irritation. 'The name should go to the tower at the easternmost point of Daylight, surely?'

'What relevance does that have to anything?' Dorn said.

'I teach my sons that nothing is worth doing, if not done right.'

'I had not factored pedantry into father's gifts to you,' said Dorn, a little humour creeping into his voice.

'There is nothing else to occupy myself with,' said Sanguinius. 'I tell these warriors that I have come to oversee them, but there is little to oversee. Your Captain Thane has done an exemplary job.'

'Of the Twenty-Second? He is a good man,' said Dorn. He spoke to someone else, a terse order to redirect supplies. Dorn's life was fashioned from such details, delivered by silent messengers, absorbed, appraised, responses sent out in brief bursts of speech. He returned to their conversation. *'You should not put yourself at risk, brother. Stay off the wall.'*

'I am perfectly safe. We cannot hide in the Bhab Bastion until Horus drags us out.' He paused. Receiving no reply, he asked, 'What do you want, Rogal?'

'The Fabricator General wishes to speak with me. He says it is urgent, and it is not something that he is willing to discuss remotely. He insists on a meeting in person.'

'You wish me to speak with him in your place then?'

'If you would. I am somewhat occupied at the moment, and I think Jaghatai's manner would annoy him.'

Sanguinius laughed at Dorn's dryness. 'Very well. I will serve as your ambassador. Our men are in place. There is nothing to do but wait. I could do with the diversion.'

'*That is the nature of sieges, my brother,*' said Rogal Dorn dourly. '*Inside or outside the walls. There will be desperate escalade, but not yet. Waiting, waiting, and then a few hours of fury. Either they succeed, and we die, or they lose, and the process begins again. The passage of war for mortal men is measured in boredom punctuated by terror. Nowhere is this more true than in sieges.*'

'Your wars, perhaps.'

'*You are fighting my kind of war now,*' said Dorn. '*I shall tell the Fabricator General you are coming. Perhaps then he will leave me alone. Zagreus Kane is loyal to the Imperium, committed to the alliance of Terra and Mars, and a valued asset of our father. I am sure he is a genius in his own field of expertise, but he is no general.*'

Dorn sent a tight-beam datacast to Sanguinius' armour apprising him of Kane's whereabouts. '*Take a guard appropriate to your status,*' Dorn advised. '*Kane is proud, but fragile. He will require a display.*' With that, he bid Sanguinius good day, and cut the line.

'My brother,' said Sanguinius to himself, 'is growing curt.'

He remained in the passageway a few minutes longer, staring at the fresh rockcrete, his mind wandering, then sent word to Raldoron to arrange a small squad to meet him at the base of the wall along with transportation. He would not listen to his brother. Sanguinius had had his fill of pomp on Macragge. If he must arrive escorted, then he would do so minimally.

SEVEN

The conclave of traitors
Risks and benefits
For the glory of the gods

The Vengeful Spirit, *Lunar orbit, 24th of Secundus*

'You are displeased, First Captain.'

Abaddon scowled blackly at Layak. They walked dark corridors towards Lupercal's court.

'I told you to keep out of my head.'

Layak chuckled wetly. 'I am not in your mind, cousin. I do not need to be. You do nothing to hide your emotions. Your expression says everything your voice will not. You are unhappy. I say you would fare badly in a game of wagers.'

'This isn't a game, Layak,' growled Abaddon.

'Is it not? You think like a gamesman. Formulating moves, and counter-moves.'

'This is war,' said Abaddon irritably.

'I am not talking about the war out there. I am talking about the struggle in here.' He tapped his free hand to his primary heart.

Abaddon turned on his heel, fist clenched, bringing the

small group of captain, blade slaves and Apostle to an abrupt
halt at a junction in the corridor. Again the blade slaves
objected to his attitude to their lord, and cracks in the armour
flared, and their hands went to the hilts of their swords.

'Go on,' said Abaddon. 'Try.'

The blade slaves remained ready to fight. Warp light shone
from their helm lenses. Ash drifted around them like snow.

Chuckling, Layak raised his hand, fingers upright. He let
the gesture hang in clear threat, then shook his ornate staff.

The blade slaves removed their hands from their swords.

'I told you,' said Abaddon. 'Stay out of my head.'

'Having a little trouble with your priest, Ezekyle?'

Horus Aximand approached the group from the trans-
verse way, joining them at the junction.

'Lord Horus himself is my patron, Horus Aximand,' said
Layak. 'It is your brother here who is having trouble with
his faith.'

Aximand's ruined face sat badly on his skull, stretching his
once handsome features into an angry leer. They still called
him Little Horus, though he barely resembled their genesire any longer. The hilt of his famed sword, *Mourn-it-All*,
protruded above the top of his power plant.

'I grant they're annoying,' said Aximand. 'But we have
these Word Bearers to thank for the return of our father
to health.'

'Do we?' said Abaddon. He resumed walking. 'Where are
the others?'

'Kibre hangs around the Warmaster like a bad smell, as
is his habit. He will not leave Horus' side without being
dismissed. His brain has gone soft since Beta-Garmon and
Horus' return.'

Abaddon did not disagree. Horus' fall had shaken Kibre
to a pathetic degree. 'Tormageddon?'

'He does as he pleases.' Aximand's expression became more horrible as he frowned. 'But he will be at the court for this.'

'Then you are blessed,' said Layak. 'The Neverborn show you favour.'

'I'd rather he showed his favour somewhere I wasn't,' said Aximand.

'You should embrace it,' said Layak. 'You are champions of the Pantheon. The might of the warp can be yours, if you but reach out to take it.'

Aximand snorted through his misshapen nose. 'I'll pass. The blessings of your gods have been decidedly mixed of late. Guilliman breathes down our neck. The Warmaster makes no move on the prize. Is a blessed warlord forced to keep his generals apart for the harm they will do each other? This edification is to be conducted by hololith. Gathering his brothers in one place has become too much of a risk for the Warmaster,' Aximand continued. 'Angron, who by your estimation is probably very blessed indeed, rages at everything when he has control of himself, which is never, and when he does not, he has the unfortunate habit of butchering everyone around him.' He continued, the voice of reason emanating from his devil-mask of a face. 'Then there's Lord Fulgrim, who especially annoys Lord Angron. True to his nature, Fulgrim revels in Angron's ire, and goads the Red Angel for his own amusement, which puts us all in danger. That's not to mention the fumes around the Phoenician that choke the mortals who breathe them.' Aximand shook his head ruefully. 'Perturabo sulks on the fringes of the system. Mortarion approaches but refuses to answer any hails. Horus' grand army is riven by divisions at every level.'

'Indiscipline is our enemy now as much as time,' said Abaddon. 'This is what your gods bring us, Layak. Chaos,' he said sourly.

'Things were going so well,' said Aximand. 'Until you failed to catch the Fenrisian, Ezekyle. The Wolf, the Consul and the Raven at our backs. Time grows short.'

'So good then that you and Kibre kept everything working smoothly while I was about my supposed failure,' said Abaddon sharply. 'Horus cannot arbitrate every disagreement. The war will be won soon enough.'

'What if it isn't?' countered Aximand. 'Horus could allow you or I to do something about these divisions. But he won't – worse, he forbids any activity on our part. Something has changed. Horus has not been the same since Maloghurst brought him back.'

'Says the man who fought to prevent it, yet who wept tears of blood when our father returned from the dead a second time. Hypocrisy does not become you, brother.'

Aximand looked at his brother sternly. 'Mock me all you like, Ezekyle, I know you agree with me.'

Abaddon grunted. He did not disagree, but he would not add to his father's burdens by feeding Aximand's fears.

Lupercal's court was dark and forbidding. It was hard to remember how it was before Davin. A place of glory, where honourable men met to decide the fate of a galaxy; Abaddon assumed it had been so, rather than truly recalled it. The *Vengeful Spirit* stank of the warp's influence, and it cheated men's minds.

On the surface, not much had altered. The banners had changed along with their allegiance, but the same decisions were made there, the same tables and chairs furnished the room, and many of the same warriors attended. The real transformation was less obvious. It lingered out of sight, an unmistakeable taint that hung over the hall, and a coy scent that refused definition forever on the edge of sensing: hints of incense, burnt sugar and powdered bone.

The source of the unease was centred on Horus. Abaddon stared at his father. Again he was disturbed by what he saw. The Warmaster sat rigid on his throne, looking off into hidden worlds, not blinking, smiling knowingly, dull eyes oblivious to all that went on around him. The cracked skull of Ferrus Manus sitting on the throne's armrest had more presence than the Warmaster at the moment, staring with empty-eyed defiance over the gathering.

Kibre stood at Horus' left side at stiff attention. He and Abaddon had hardly exchanged words in the last few weeks. Tormageddon, the daemon wearing its third stolen body, attended at Horus' right. It wore a smirk that echoed Horus' distant smile. Elements of Grael Noctua remained in Tormageddon's warped features, but it was a dangerous illusion. Tormageddon's being was wholly alien. It was at best a temporary ally. Tormageddon was another threat, another warp foulness that poisoned Abaddon's father, twisting him away from what he had been, remaking him in the gods' image and robbing him of his will.

'*Ezekyle, Little Horus,*' Tormageddon greeted them. Kibre was slow to acknowledge their presence, looking between the members of the party before speaking.

'Brothers,' he said eventually. 'The Mournival is gathered.'

Aximand looked suspiciously at Tormageddon. Both he and Abaddon had a hard time accepting the daemon as one of their own, but as Horus decreed it, so it must be.

'For the final moves in this long war,' said Abaddon. He clasped arms with Kibre, then did the same with the daemon, doing his best to mask his distaste. Aximand greeted Kibre, but pointedly ignored the Neverborn.

A change came over the Warmaster as he returned from that other place his spirit so often went. His smile smoothed away, he grew in stature. Unease was replaced by calm. As

Horus looked over them all and blessed them with his attention, Abaddon caught a glimpse of the man he had known.

'My sons,' said Horus. 'The hour approaches.'

Horus rose from his throne. His presence was such that the Mournival struggled to remain standing, while Layak freely knelt. Horus had always possessed a preternatural charisma, but this was something else, a dark majesty that demanded all the universe grovel before it.

'My brothers!' Horus commanded. 'Hearken to me!'

One by one, cones of hololithic projection light leapt into being around the court, turning the shadows grey and filling the space with phantoms. Besides Horus, only the Mournival and Layak's group were present in the flesh.

First to emerge was Angron. The transformation wrought on him made Horus' change inconsequential. He was a red-skinned giant, the equal in size of the Pantheon's greatest servants. Huge wings of tattered black skin furled around his back. The cables of the Butcher's Nails, the archeotech device implanted in his brain when he was a slave, hung from his scalp around jutting horns in a tangle of metallic dreadlocks. Wild, yellow eyes stared from a face contorted forever with hate and rage, and his jaw worked around wolf's teeth. He paced with poorly contained rage, making the role of the imagists on his ship difficult. He swam in and out of focus, and often only his face remained visible. He gave voice only to growls.

Fulgrim was next, a purple-skinned, serpentine monster with four arms and a shock of ghost-white hair. Though he remained within the viewing field, Fulgrim was never still. Overwhelmed by his unnatural form as much as by his fidgeting, occasionally the hololith would fail completely, and present a jumble of white hair, serpent's body and mocking faces, interspersed with glimpses of other places alive with abstract horrors.

'*Hello, brother,*' he said, always on the verge of mockery.

Perturabo's image snapped into being. The Lord of Iron remained in the outer system, more distant that the rest, and consequently his image lacked the definition of the others. He flickered, but persisted like a bad memory unwelcomely recalled. Unlike his brothers, he retained his original form, too stubborn to give himself over to worship as they had.

'*I attend you, my Warmaster,*' he said solemnly.

Following Perturabo, Magnus the Red appeared, manifesting as a psychic projection that lent him a form of ersatz reality superior to the hololithic phantoms. When he walked, the air moved. Abaddon could smell his foreign scent. Despite the veracity of his image, it was a sorcerous falsehood that prickled at the skin and the soul. The cyclops wore the appearance of a crimson-skinned ogre clad in rich jewellery. Clothing himself in majesty he attempted to hide his true, altered form. He could not quite. The projection stuttered, showing some of the many faces Magnus favoured. Magnus had ever appeared in different guise, but masking what he had become seemed to tax him, and though he affected a studious air, all the expressions on all of his faces hinted at his pain.

'*Brothers,*' Magnus said. '*Ezekyle, Little Horus, Falkus, and to you Tormageddon and to the priest, I give greetings.*'

With the principal players in place, dozens of lesser images flickered into being. Some full bodies, others disembodied heads. The highest officers, the grandest marshals and most lordly of admirals, commanders of the mortal armies that gave Horus' forces so much of their size and might, and which outnumbered the manpower of the Legions hundreds of times over.

The Fabricator General's image appeared late among this crop, so large it swallowed several of the smaller phantoms.

Kelbor-Hal was finally free of Mars and took the place of his emissary Sota-Nul, who had been at Horus' side these last years. Abaddon thought it a change for the worse. Sota-Nul had been most useful, whereas the Fabricator General was inflated with a sense of self-importance. Abaddon doubted Kelbor-Hal knew how much his overweening pride offended the Warmaster.

Barely had the group gathered, when Angron launched into a familiar tirade.

'When do we attack?' He thrust his head close to the imaging equipment, reducing his communications phantom to a single, glaring eye. 'Why do we sit here in the void, when our weapons cannot harm our father? We must land, take the fight to Him with blade and fist. The God of Battle demands blood!'

Fulgrim let out a musical laugh. 'You may not believe this, brother Horus, but I am in agreement with our angry sibling. This bombardment is boring! Let my perfect sons run free – they will give you a swift victory.'

'Your peacocks will achieve nothing!' shouted Angron so loudly the audio-feed of his hololith shrieked with feedback. 'My Legion should be first. Mine! We are the chosen of war. Give me the order, brother, and end this cowardice!'

'Do you call the Warmaster coward?' said Fulgrim slyly. 'I say he bides his time for the Lord of Death to join us. Has Mortarion not yet arrived?' He feigned disappointment at the XIV Legion's absence.

'There is no word yet from his fleet, my lord,' Kibre reported. 'They approach, and will be here within days.'

'He was to be first on Terra. He begged you for the honour,' scoffed Angron. 'And he will not even speak! Give me the task, and I shall show you how ruin is made!'

Horus stared at Angron with a baleful eye. He allowed his brother to rant on.

'*We smashed aside Dorn's feeble defences,*' Angron said. '*We broke Luna in days. Why now do we slink around the Throneworld like curs, waiting for Mortarion, when victory is in our grasp?*'

'*We smashed Dorn's defences?*' Perturabo's leaden response simmered with anger. '*I, I, I! I broke Dorn's gates, not we. Your sons did not bleed to ensure our success. You gave no plan to penetrate the system defences. I delivered the Solar System to the Warmaster. You claim a role in a victory you were not party to. Do you forget that I had to drag you back from your orgy of bloodletting to rejoin our brother? Were it not for me, you would not be here. Fulgrim would not be here. None of you would be here, now.*'

'*You have done your part, little digger!*' Angron scoffed. '*Land the Legions now! Let me be the point of the spear aimed at father's heart. Cease this game. Bombardment is a weakling's ploy.*'

Perturabo stiffened, taking the comment personally, which was surely Angron's intention.

'*Attempt to land, and see how quickly father's guns tear you to pieces,*' said Perturabo.

'Silence,' said Horus. His voice was hardly louder than a whisper, but it brought immediate quiet. 'You will be silent now. All of you. All proceeds to plan. Perturabo, explain,' said Horus.

Angron snorted when Perturabo began. Horus cowed him with a glance.

'*Three things stand in our way,*' Perturabo began. '*The Palace guns, the Palace aegis and father's will, which keeps the Neverborn at bay. These problems cannot be resolved at once, but must be dealt with in order – beginning with the aegis. The bombardment patterns I have devised have revealed multiple shortcomings in the Palace shields. Between the hours I spend each day fortifying the outer reaches against our brothers' coming – tasks not one of you have taken upon yourselves,'* he grumbled, *'I have been examining auspex soundings of the void shield network.'*

'The priests of Mars designed the aegis, applying knowledge salvaged from the high days of technology,' said Kelbor-Hal proudly. *'You will find no weakness there.'*

'Then why do you not provide us with the information necessary to shut it down?' said Abaddon.

'Impossible,' said Kelbor-Hal. *'The control systems for the shields are as impregnable as the aegis itself.'* He was proud, a vain fool.

'Every wall has a weakness. Build it how you will, from whatever material you can – stone, iron or dancing light, I shall bring it down,' said Perturabo. *'The centre is too strong as yet to break. Ground operations will be necessary to collapse the network to the extent that direct landing or bombardment will be successful within the Palace bounds.'*

'Then let us be about it!' Angron howled.

Perturabo gave the chosen of Khorne a sullen stare. *'Against the success of such an action,'* the Lord of Iron continued, *'stand the following factors. Firstly, the shields possess a wide-range modulation, beginning at the lower reach against any penetration of objects above one half-gram travelling faster than two metres per second. Infantry might walk through this aegis, but slowly.'*

'Impossible,' said Aximand. 'Voids are no defence against close attacks.'

'These are not void shields as you understand them,' said Perturabo. *'The second factor against ground assault is the Palace's extensive anti-air and anti-orbital defences, and its air defence squadrons. Before a major landing can be undertaken, these must be weakened, or any force sent against them will be annihilated in the air.'*

'You spoke of weaknesses,' said Fulgrim. 'Then, pray tell, oh glowering, sulky brother, where they are.'

'The shields cannot be brought down from outside,' said Perturabo, continuing his lecture as if Fulgrim had not spoken. 'The Palace possesses an unrivalled void network consisting of multiple layers of lenticular fields. These differ from a standard voidal energy bubble, which forms a single skin defence around its ward in spherical or hemispherical configuration. The technology required to project stable lensing is exceedingly difficult to replicate, and at this scale practically impossible. Yet following the old patterns the Mechanicum succeeded. The Palace aegis networks consist of discrete elements, like a wall of shields, each an energy lens, each one overlapping the others enough that failure on the part of one reveals only a small hole, directly blocked below. By the time the lower lenses covering the hole are also brought down, the first will have been raised again. There are legions of Mechanicum adepts labouring beneath the Palace to keep the shields in operation. Multiple redundancy networks protect against failures up to full systemic levels. Power is provided by advanced thermal conversion beneath the Palace itself. It is a low-yield but stable energy source, and cannot be upset by magnetic frequency harmonics as a plasma reactor might be. The power supply cannot be directly targeted. Only the destruction of the planet itself would be sufficient to interrupt the flow of energy from the Palace vaults to the aegis.'

'Then let us set down and lead our warriors in glorious charge against the walls,' growled Angron.

'That would result in your total destruction, either on descent, or on the ground.'

'Cowards!'

'Be patient, brother,' said Perturabo. 'You will have your glory. The shields cannot be broken. They cannot be starved of power. But they can be weakened.'

An orbital vid-capture of a section of the Palace defences sprang up. The walls cut across the landscape neat as a draughtsman's marks. The Palace-city's giant buildings were models behind. The flattened coins of explosions displaced by void shielding blinked all over the defences, not touching the ground beneath.

'This sequence depicts a rare failure. Within the bombardment pattern I concealed several distinct targeting cycles to test various aspects of the aegis – modulation, raising speed, power absorption and displacement, displacement response time, displacement triggering velocity and others.'

'I provided all this information!' protested Kelbor-Hal.

'Consolidated datasets fall into false, idealistic patterns. Direct, practical experimentation is the only way I can be sure. The result of my test can be witnessed here,' said Perturabo.

Several shells and a volley of lance fire sparked off the shields. Suddenly, a gap opened over a tower, exposing it to fire from orbit that quickly toppled it.

'Alas, this small result was achieved only due to an isolated flaw in that part of the network. Augury readings suggest a chained failure in three series of void generatoria, quickly rectified.'

'Not so perfect, eh, Kelbor-Hal?' giggled Fulgrim.

'Note how quickly the shield is replaced,' Perturabo continued.

Over the burning rubble, the explosions changed back to toothless rounds of fire flattened on the shields.

'Then what are you proposing?' growled Angron. His head shook. His face twitched, but he held his temper. His display of control was impressive.

'From this response time, and the other measurements provided to me from the main fleet, I have determined that the voids can be weakened sufficiently to allow passage of medium- to low-velocity objects, around the fringe only.'

'Our brother has calculated a bombardment pattern of

surpassing genius,' said Horus. For a moment, Perturabo's stolid expression showed a glint of pride. 'We will unleash all of our fleet's firepower at these points.'

The vid-feed disappeared, replaced by a wider angle, tri-d view of the entire Palace. Equally spaced red markers blinked on all eight principal winds of the compass.

'The precision of Perturabo's attack will cause a serial weakening of the shield wall.'

'*Then it can be bombed,*' said Fulgrim.

'*The bombardment will not penetrate the final layer,*' said Perturabo. '*Rapid, high-mass munitions or zero to low-mass light speed energy emissions will still be displaced. However, the final aegis layer will be weakened sufficiently to allow a seventy per cent chance of successful passage to attack craft travelling at one hundred and fifty kilometres an hour or lower.*'

'*We can attack directly? What fine news!*' Fulgrim clapped with glee. '*I shall prepare my squadrons at once.*'

Perturabo nodded. '*Attack ships should prioritise void shield projection blisters and anti-ship weaponry towers, with secondary emphasis on anti-aircraft emplacements. Voids have one true vulnerability, that their projecting elements must be exposed. A large number are mounted on the wall itself. I predict an attrition rate of forty-five per cent attack ships lost, minimum. However, though the defences are formidable, we shall darken the sky with such numbers they will despair,*' said Perturabo.

'While the Palace defences are occupied by our aerial attack,' said Horus, 'we will begin first landings. By splitting the enemy's fire, we safeguard both attack and landing craft. Dorn will not want his guns destroyed, nor will he want our warriors outside the walls, but they cannot afford to lose their shields.'

'*I will prepare my warriors!*' bellowed Angron.

'*That brings us to the problem of the Neverborn,*' Perturabo said. He paused. '*Who will tell him?*'

'*You must find patience, my brother,*' Magnus said to Angron. '*The warp is in turmoil around Terra, but no daemon may set foot there. Our father's power holds back the tides of the empyrean. If you, I or Fulgrim were to attempt a landing, our souls would be torn from our bodies, and likely obliterated.*'

'Perturabo's genius shows us the first cracks in Dorn's walls. We must force another,' said Horus. 'Every drop of blood spilled upon Terra's soil weakens our father's power. The second blow will quickly follow the first. Once our allies of the warp have access to the mortal sphere, and the orbital defences of Terra are crippled, then the Legions shall attack.'

'*There is a way to limit our father's power.*' Magnus waved his hand, and a new image, far sharper than any hololith, appeared. Lines joined the eight points together into an octed superimposed over the Palace. '*Centre this upon the Palace, spill enough blood, then, and only then, Lord Angron, will father's might be contained, and you may set foot safely upon Terra. Shortly after, all the legions of Neverborn contained by eternity shall march forth.*'

'Sow the dragon's teeth, water the harvest with the blood of untold millions, and we shall come to you!' said Layak, quoting from obscure scriptures.

'We do not need the help of these unclean things, my lord,' said Aximand.

Tormageddon snickered. '*This is not your war alone, Little Horus. Greater beings than you have a stake here.*' He gestured to Fulgrim and Angron knowingly.

'It shall be as I decree,' commanded Horus. 'There is no need for the Legions to march yet. The Emperor will conserve His best troops behind His walls. We shall land our mortal followers all over the Throneworld. Every city shall be attacked. Every settlement burned. Let the lost and the damned tire His guns. Let the False Emperor know despair behind His mighty walls while His people suffer! And when the tide of blood is high enough and our daemonic allies are ready to infest Terra, the outer defences shall be broken, the guns cast down and the defenders left bloody and bruised. Then we shall unleash the true face of death. Lord Fulgrim, Lord Angron, prepare your Legions for ground operations. When the time is right, they shall follow in the wake of Lord Mortarion, this I promise you.'

EIGHT

Mandragora
A litany of complaint
Fabricator Locum

Daylight sector, subsection 99.4, 24th of Secundus

A clade of motionless skitarii Mandragora awaited Sanguinius. They stood at attention in the cold, red robes sculpted by
the wind, each cyborg aligned so precisely with his fellows
that they appeared to be lifeless objects rather than men.
No trace of flesh was visible; every surface glimpsed beneath
their uniforms was gleaming metal. Their eyes glowed a
steady green. In the spaces between their exposed, metal
ribs cogs spun. Tiny lumens blinked deep in their innards,
but the once-men themselves did not move. They showed
no reaction as Sanguinius clambered from the golden Land
Raider and his bodyguard of First Company veterans fanned
out to bracket him.

Kane was supposedly in the squat building ahead, around
whose seamless exterior the Mandragora arrayed themselves
in geometrical perfection.

'There is no way through, my lord,' said Galenius, the

sergeant of Sanguinius' escort. He was not a warrior the primarch knew particularly well, though his armour was heavy with honours.

'Be patient, my son. And be mindful of what you say. You speak on Legion vox, but be sure that the Adeptus Mechanicus are listening.' The new term for the Martian priests was still foreign to Sanguinius.

Beneath the muted crump of Horus' bombardment, silence of a sort held sway.

'This is an outrage,' said Galenius. 'Demanding your presence then making you wait!' He strode forwards. 'Move aside! Move aside I say, for the primarch of the Ninth Legion!' The Mandragora remained motionless as he paced up and down their front rank. When Galenius put his hand upon one of the warriors, he made no reaction, but nor did he move, and when Galenius attempted to push him aside, his torso moved but his feet remained locked to the floor. Galenius ceased his efforts to shift the cyborg, and the guardian of the Fabricator General swayed back into the regiment's uniform stance.

'Mindless,' said Galenius. 'Slaves.'

'Enough,' said Sanguinius.

Galenius stalked back.

'Doesn't the Martian know the enemy are at the gates?' the sergeant complained. 'This is no time for posturing.'

'Politics never cease, not even in war,' said Sanguinius. 'Maintain calm.'

'As you command, lord,' said Galenius. 'My choler gets the better of me.'

'Then perhaps I should have you transferred to Captain Amit's command.'

'You are not the first to make that suggestion, my lord,' Galenius chuckled. 'I sometimes think Captain Raldoron keeps me around to remind himself why he doesn't like Captain Amit.'

'That is a disloyal assertion,' said Sanguinius.

Galenius would not be rebuked, even by his genesire. 'As you said, my lord. Politics.'

Without warning, the Mandragora formation divided itself into two halves and turned inwards, so that the left-hand side of the legion was facing the right. A ripple of scarlet passed up their ranks as they took several steps back, opening a path to the cylindrical building. The clash of iron feet on stone echoed from the surrounding spires, then ceased as suddenly as it began.

'They have made their point. That is my invitation.'

'Squad Galenius, form up!' the sergeant commanded.

'Sometimes the best move in politics is to refuse the game in the first place,' said Sanguinius. 'You will remain here, Galenius.'

'As you so command.'

Sanguinius strode towards the building alone, the reflections from ten thousand sets of glowing eyes glinting off his golden armour. As the primarch drew near, the smooth surface of the cylinder split. Two great sections withdrew, sinking deep into the structure, then angled back and slid aside, opening a door onto an interior ablaze with light.

Five figures waited for the primarch. Four carried banners depicting the skull and cog of the Machina Opus. The fifth, ahead of the others, was obviously female. Upon the steps leading into the interior of the cylinder the delegation struck an imposing sight, until Sanguinius climbed beside them and dwarfed them with his presence.

'Greetings to you, son of the Emperor,' said the female.

'Well met, Ambassador Vethorel,' said Sanguinius. 'The architect of the solution to the Binary Succession. I am honoured to meet you.'

'The honour is mine, son of the Emperor.'

Vethorel was outwardly human looking, fair of face, though the subtle signs of suppressed ageing marked her flesh. She had few visible augmetics, and what were displayed were finely wrought to enhance her humanity rather than diminish it. Her voice was modulated to bring out pleasing, if unmistakably machinic, tones. She was the Martian ambassador to the Imperium, and therefore her modifications were cynically chosen to influence baseline humans. Nothing too deviant from the standard form, everything designed with Terran aesthetics in mind. Sanguinius appreciated the art of it nonetheless.

'Beautiful,' said Sanguinius.

'I… Thank you, my lord,' said Vethorel. Her eyes appeared human until she dipped her head. In the shadow of her hood they glowed with concealed bionics.

'The Fabricator General is here?' asked Sanguinius.

'He awaits you below,' said the ambassador. She bowed lower. Robes stiff with brocade circuitry rasped on the marble step. 'Magos Kane, most exalted, gives his humble apologies that he cannot greet you himself, but there is much to be done.'

Such as making a point about how important he is, thought Sanguinius, who was by now impatient with the charade. Outwardly he displayed nothing but a warm smile.

'Of course.'

'Please, I shall take you to him.' Vethorel held up her arm. Sanguinius stepped within the gates. They closed behind him.

Once Sanguinius was inside, the entire floor of the cylinder slowly sank, bearing him away down a shaft of gleaming plascrete to the heart of the mountains. When the lifter platform was well below ground level, three iris doors of adamantium hissed shut overhead, each of sufficient thickness to withstand a direct hit from a void-ship weapon. Strings of faint lumens recessed into the walls emitted a dim light. The plascrete gave way to melta-bored rock. The geoforming was recent, the cuts clean, yet already the deep earth wept out its moisture where the stone's grain had not vitrified fully under the fusion beams. Down there, the weight of Terra's history pressed in. The wars of men seemed distant and unimportant.

Like the Grekan bard Orphee, Sanguinius descended into the underworld.

The lifter was made for Titans, and the shaft stretched up and up. He could have flown if he had chosen, yet still a stuffy claustrophobia pressed on him. His wings twitched. He felt caged enough to remove his helmet, and expose his face to the chill, moist air.

The lifter platform came to a slow halt twenty minutes later. A huge tunnel, lined with skitarii of the most elite legions, stretched off for a kilometre or more, where the tunnel terminated in a huge cavern.

'This way, please,' said Vethorel. She walked beside Sanguinius, her bannermen following at a respectful distance.

The sounds of hymns and rhythmically striking tools echoed down the way. The work of the tunnel was less smooth than the shaft, for the lifter had intersected with older workings. The ground beneath the Palace was riddled with caverns, mostly artificial, delved out in humanity's long, uneven history. There the new tunnel cut through the past. The walls were pocked with dark openings, some blocked and pale with fresh rockcrete.

'Kane commands significant resources,' said Sanguinius, gesturing at the legions to show he had noticed the Fabricator General's efforts to impress him.

'These are the personal guard of the Fabricator General, augmented to the highest degree, their wills subsumed utterly to the command of the Machine-God,' said Vethorel. 'As you know, appearances must be upheld, even if they can be deceptive. Much of the Adeptus Mechanicus' might is lost. We shed an empire's worth of blood holding the webway for your father, and so many of our kind pledged for the Warmaster.'

He expected the reply Vethorel gave him. Even with the issue of the Binary Succession resolved, and the Mechanicum become the Adeptus Mechanicus, the war strained relations between Terra and Mars to the limit.

'When this war is done, my father will set all to rights,' said Sanguinius.

'To the Machine-God we pray,' said Vethorel. 'We ask only that the Omnissiah be permitted victory so Mars might be restored to us.'

Diplomatic, but she is unconvinced, thought Sanguinius. *Does Rogal know the depths of their dissatisfaction?* he wondered.

'Yet we remain mighty. Ahead you will see more of Mars' manifest power,' Vethorel added.

They passed into the cavern. Multiple tunnels radiated from it, like spokes from a giant wheel. In the spaces between the spokes, runs of alcoves were carved, each housing a god-engine of the Collegia Titanica.

The cavern was larger than Sanguinius expected, capped with a huge dome of raw rock ribbed by plasteel and flying rockcrete buttresses that rested on columns the size of towers. Alone, these physical supports were insufficient to hold back the weight of the mountains and the Palace atop them, and between the architectural matrix shimmered the telltale blue of structural integrity fields.

Thousands of tech-priests laboured in this subterranean world, attended by an army of servitors and thralls, all of them hard at work upon the Titans. Giant machines, dwarfed by the war engines they attended, ground back and forth across the cavern. The floor sprouted forests of machinery. Tangles of cables ran everywhere. Despite the enormous volume of air the cavern contained, the place was thickly redolent of oil, incense, hot metal, cooling ceramite and all the myriad scents of technological worship running at a high gear.

'Behold, one-tenth of all the Legio Titanicus' strength upon Terra.' Vethorel swept her arm around the dozens of machines being serviced. 'This cavern is one of several such facilities. Within them, the priesthood of Mars labours night and day to restore what god-machines we possess, for although this may appear a potent assembly, my lord, it is a fraction of our former strength.'

Vethorel turned her gaze upon him, and Sanguinius was shocked to see the hatred burning through her diplomat's mask.

'Be careful here, my lord,' her tone took on a steely edge. 'Despite your successes at Beta-Garmon, many of our magi believe that the campaign was a mistake. So many god-machines lost. I am sure you understand.'

'I do,' he said, 'and I thank you for your warning.'

She bowed, and her voice reassumed its former gentle beauty. 'The Fabricator General awaits you there,' she said, pointing to a large, many-legged vehicle whose flat back sported a bewildering array of mechanical arms, all of them in motion. 'I will take my leave of you, my lord.'

'I thank you again,' Sanguinius said, but Vethorel was already walking away, and she did not look back.

Amid the thickets of constantly moving mechanical arms, Zagreus Kane rode the machine upon a dais. It was edged in brass and big enough to accommodate his tracked body along with a dozen of the most exalted magi of the Adeptus Mechanicus. The machine moved no quicker than walking pace, allowing its busy upper limbs to perform their tasks. Sanguinius caught it easily. He ignored the glares of hostility emanating from the tech-priests he passed.

Kane made an elaborate pantomime of speaking with his chief advisers in a torrent of binharic. Sanguinius understood the machine speech, though no being without extensive mechanical alteration could hope to speak it. Kane said nothing important. His whole purpose was to force Sanguinius to wait. Despite his show, when Kane deigned to turn his attention onto the primarch, he seemed affable enough.

'I am grateful that you came to see me, Lord Sanguinius,' said Kane. His advisers shuffled away, indifferent to the Angel when they were not openly hostile.

'How could I not? You are the master of the Adeptus Mechanicus, ruler of the Martian Mechanicus Empire, and one of the most powerful beings in the Imperium. I am but a primarch, a tool of war. I thank you for receiving me.' Sanguinius bowed.

Kane's internal mechanisms chattered. 'You always were one of the most gracious of the Omnissiah's sons, but we are honest men, you and I. You are the son of the Emperor, glorious by holy design. I am merely a quester after knowledge. My appointment to this position is an accident of circumstance. It is I who am grateful. If I were as important as you say, my messages would have been acted on with more speed. The Praetorian could have come himself, but Lord Dorn does not answer me.'

Sanguinius stepped to Kane's side. The slender, diffident technocrat Sanguinius had first met years before had gone. Kane wore his enhancements lightly in the past, but he had evidently changed his way of thinking, for now he was more akin to a small tank than a man, his heavily modified torso sitting atop a set of tracks, and his human face buried beneath a dozen individual augmentations.

'Lord Dorn sends his apologies. He asked me to come only because he is busy.'

'Gracious again, Lord Sanguinius. The truth is he does not rate my abilities as a military commander. I am an irritation to him. He sees me as a block on his ability to command, because the armies of the Adeptus Mechanicus answer to me and not to him directly,' said Kane. 'Please, if you are about to, do not lie to save my pride. I know I am no general. The knowledge may be acquired, but talent cannot easily be engineered. Kelbor-Hal unfortunately is far better versed in the arts of war than I. I was always more concerned with creation than destruction.'

'A finer sentiment for the best of men,' said Sanguinius, and meant it.

'Alas, not in these times,' said Kane bitterly.

Kane had once been a gentle man. War reforges all it touches, thought Sanguinius, not always for the better.

'You are loyal to the idea of concord between Terra and Mars, and to the ideal of human unity,' Sanguinius said. 'If you will not accept my first compliment, then know that this second attribute is far more valuable than any other you may possess.'

Kane touched no controls nor gave any audible commands, but the legged machine stopped and its multiple arms froze. Plasma torches blinked off. Cargo was deposited smoothly on the floor. The arms folded back and locked into position. The machine's legs rippled in series like a millipede, turning it around, and with a soft lurch it set off again at greater speed.

'That is so,' said Kane, 'but there are many thousands of adepts in this hall, and a good portion of them believe we of Mars have sold ourselves cheaply to the Imperium of Terra.'

'Someone might tell them that we live through times where every hour brings difficult choices.'

'Oh I have. They are aware,' said Kane. 'I make those choices for them. I understand why it must be this way, even if they do not. I believe this is for the best.' Something clicked repetitively deep in Kane's chest. 'The Omnissiah's vision is the will of the Machine-God. I truly believe this. It cannot be realised if Mars and Terra remain divorced. In all alliances there must be compromises.' He turned his head to look meaningfully into Sanguinius' eyes. 'And sacrifices.'

Kane referred to the massed engine battles of the Garmon Cluster that saw hundreds of valuable Titans destroyed, but Sanguinius felt the words as a knife twist in his guts, as if Kane referred to him and knew the awful truth that he would not last out the war.

The Fabricator General returned his attention ahead, to the side of the cavern where sixteen god-engines in the mottled white and green of the Legio Solaria underwent the attentions of their wardens.

'What I think and believe are only two strands in the data stream of our new adepta's collective opinion,' Kane went on. 'There are still those among us who doubt your father is the Omnissiah. To many of my people, I will forever be only Fabricator Locum, a lieutenant to the true ruler forced into the role of the Fabricator General, and my elevation a gross modus unbecoming.'

'Your followers are loyal,' said Sanguinius. 'That is all that matters for the time being.'

'To Mars, they are loyal,' agreed Kane. 'Unquestioningly. They abhor Kelbor-Hal and all his works. They lust for the forbidden knowledge of Moravec, but unlike our estranged kin in the so-called New Mechanicum they are wise to its dangers. Men are not meant to blend the essence of the warp with that of the materium. Nor should they dabble in the evils of the Silica Animus. The last loyal Titans of Mars wait for Lord Dorn's order to walk, and they anticipate the summons with righteous fury knowing it may be their last. They will fight and they will die for the cause. But if you were to ask me whether the magi are loyal to Terra's Imperium, then the answer might well be different.' Kane paused. Mechadendrites extruded themselves from his shoulders and slipped back inside in a peculiar display of discomfort. 'We have to win this war, and we need to win convincingly. At the moment our aims are the same. The destruction of Horus and his traitors must be accomplished. But I need your word that the interests of the Martian Empire will be addressed fairly when this is all done, or we may end one war only to begin another. I tell you, you must make your father listen.'

'Or what will happen?' said Sanguinius hotly. 'Did you call my brother to threaten him? You will find me no less disdainful of such tactics.'

An angry noise blurted from Kane's innards. 'It is not a threat. It is the truth. Who else am I supposed to speak with? The Emperor is locked away. Politics do not go away because the enemy has come.'

'I have had my fill of politics,' said Sanguinius.

'I have had my fill of war,' said Kane. 'No man can expect the life he wishes for, even less demand it be the way he wants.'

Conversation ceased until the platform's rattling legs clattered to halt, and they stopped.

'Forgive me,' Kane said. 'I spoke more angrily than I wished to. I did not contact Dorn for this discussion. In point of fact, I sincerely believe he is already well aware of how things stand. I see you, and I see someone to spend my frustration on.'

'That is understandable,' said Sanguinius.

'What I contacted him for was to convey some news that may be of use to us all.' Kane gestured up at a Warlord Titan ahead. It had been badly damaged, and was cocooned in gantries, scaffolds and sheeting. On floating platforms and crane lifts, dozens of repair teams were busily at work. 'This is *Luxor Invictoria*, the command Titan of the Legio Solaria. This is all that remains from that proud order.' He pointed out the handful of machines around it.

'I recognise it. It fought at Nyrcon City. I thought it fell in battle.'

'It did, but where the Titan survived, the Grand Master of the Legio did not.'

'Who has succeeded her?'

'Her nominated heir, who fought on Beta-Garmon Three, at the Carthegia Telepathica.'

Luxor Invictoria emanated more than the diffuse awareness of an electric soul. Its eye-lenses seemed to be looking at Sanguinius with human intelligence. 'He is within the Titan now?' the primarch ventured.

'She. The princeps is the daughter of the last Grand Master. All members of the Order Solaria are of the XX gender designation, as is the custom of this particular Legio. Her name is Esha Ani Mohana Vi. Great Mother of the Imperial Hunters, though hers is a murdered brood. The Legio Solaria is a shadow of its former self. It is not alone in being so.' Kane bleeped sadly. 'But who she is is not pertinent. What she saw is. She is why I wished to speak with Dorn. The new Great Mother was badly injured, and has only recently awoken from therapeutic coma. I am sure you will find her tale as intriguing as I did. This information will prove uplifting to the morale of our soldiery, and may prove to be of even greater use than that.' Kane glanced up at the primarch. 'Replace your helmet, my lord. This is a conversation that should be conducted privately. I have enjoined Esha Ani from sharing her story, until you and your brothers have decided what should be done with it.'

Understanding that information was both the coin and the vitae of the machine priesthood's domain, Sanguinius bowed his head. 'We thank you, Fabricator General, for your gift.'

Sanguinius sealed himself back within the private world of his battleplate. With his vision closed in and overlaid by sensorium data, the sense of claustrophobia returned, and he yearned once more for the sky.

An incoming vox request chimed in his helm, appended with the Titan's ident code.

Sanguinius opened communications. A voice whose softness was at odds with the giant plasteel being spoke directly into his ears. And yet, despite the voice's humanity, Sanguinius knew he was talking, in a real sense, with the Titan itself.

'*My Lord Sanguinius,*' Esha Ani said. '*I am grateful you are here, for there is something I believe you need to know.*'

'I thank you,' he said.

'*Before I do,*' she said, '*please know that I stand with you and your brothers. Many of our kind bear ill will towards you for the losses our Legios took. I do not. I understood the need. I pledge now that if you have uses for my Legio, you have but to ask.*'

'Again, I thank you,' he said.

'*Then it is done. An oath to you. Now, my story.*'

And then she told him how, on the slopes of a nameless mountain, she had witnessed Horus Lupercal fall.

* * *

Sanguinius emerged from the subterranean fortress to find the Mandragora gone, leaving his men alone on a windswept plaza that seemed vast now it was empty. The bombardment patterns had shifted. Whereas before every void shield sparked with displacement, now it was the edges of the city, around the walls, that bore the brunt of the attack, ringing the fortifications with fire, but leaving the sky over the Palace clear. Clouds churning with thermal vortices and dancing with lightning caused by the brutal ionisation of the air were now visible over much of the Palace. The wind switched about constantly, conflicting gusts battling one another and twisting themselves up into short-lived whirlwinds. Snow melted to rain by the bombardment spotted his face.

Sanguinius wasted no time crossing to his transport. His men filed in behind him without a word. The doors clanged shut, and the Land Raider lurched as its tracks bit the road.

'Dorn,' Sanguinius voxed. Cogitators in the Palace comms network heard his voiceprint and opened a priority channel to his brother.

Rogal Dorn responded immediately. '*Sanguinius,*' he said. The vox crackled in time with the lance strikes slamming into the outer shield network. '*Be quick. Events proceed.*'

'I see the enemy has altered his attack patterns.'

'*Horus has finished testing the aegis,*' Dorn said. '*They fire now in earnest.*'

'Then I shall be brief. I have news, from Kane. There is a princeps of the Legio Solaria who, while close to death, saw our brother Horus on the mountain of the Carthegia Telepathica.'

'*That is only news if something of note occurred,*' said Dorn.

'It did,' said Sanguinius. 'She saw Horus survey the battlefield as a conqueror, then fall suddenly, though no blow was struck. A wound opened in his side with no identifiable cause. She saw it clearly. His aides panicked, and bore him away by teleportation.'

Dorn was silent as he digested the information.

'If this is true, then Horus is not invulnerable, as some have suggested.'

'Perhaps it is evidence of Russ' success. Maybe the Wolf bit,' said Sanguinius. 'It could be that Horus is wounded still. That spear of our brother's…'

'This is supposition,' said Dorn. 'Though if Russ did manage to wound the Warmaster, and the injury troubles him still, it would explain why our forces at Beta-Garmon were able to withdraw as easily as they did.'

Sanguinius remembered the bitter fighting to get out of the doomed cluster. Denial of communication cost them dearly. Isolated battle groups were annihilated piecemeal. Millions dead, millions more scattered beyond hope of returning to Terra, and the rearguard he set to cover the retreat of the IX and V Legions lost.

Nevertheless, Dorn was right. It had been easier than it should have been.

'This changes nothing,' said Dorn. 'Horus is here. If he was wounded, we must assume he has recovered.'

'I can only agree. I suggest we do not allow this information into wide circulation. Fabrication will fill the gaps in the story. Rumour may grant Horus additional power – to recover from Russ' attack, surely he must be omnipotent.'

'That is one interpretation.'

'It is the one we should worry about,' said Sanguinius.

'We shall discuss this later, if needs be. For the moment our plans are unaffected.'

'Agreed, brother,' Sanguinius said, then ventured, 'It may have been a mistake for you not to attend on Kane yourself. The magi chafe. Every other utterance is of injustice. They blame me for the loss of their god-machines. Kane alluded openly to the possibility of war between Terra and Mars if their grievances are not addressed.'

'*I am aware of their displeasure,*' said Dorn. '*Unrest will last only until they are committed to the fight – thereafter they may vent their anger on the foe. The presence of our mutual enemies will cement our alliance until the battle is won, and it is far from won. The time is now. We have detected large manoeuvres within the blockade fleet.*

'*The enemy is about to attempt his first landing.*'

NINE

Beastherd
Faithless
Ground assault

Herdship, Traitor fleet, Terran near orbit, 25th of Secundus

For too long, you have suffered!'

The Apostle's voice rang over the vox-speakers, fighting with the rising bleats of the herd. Azmedi strained to listen. Comprehension was slipping away into animality. He considered the part that listened his human half. The other part, the beast part, jerked against the leashes of shame. Soon it would break free and consume his reasoning mind, but for now he could still understand.

'You have been cast out and consigned to the fringes of ten thousand worlds, fit only for the noisome places where pure-bloods will not go,' the Apostle said. *'You are the lords of ruin, for ruins are all you have ever had to call your own. The citizens of the Imperium, those upright tyrants who shun you, have another name for you, a shameful name, a name that is soaked through with their contempt.'*

Azmedi didn't need to hear the word. It was uttered the

moment he was born to his horrified mother, and chased him out of the bright places into the haunts of freaks and criminals. There the word had been shouted again, and he had been driven further on, despised even by other creatures who bore the stigma of mutation.

The word. The Apostle was going to say the word.

'No! No! No!' Azmedi shouted, his speech losing its shape, becoming a warbling, caprine bleat.

'Beastmen,' said the Apostle. The hold erupted with shouts and cries; there were those who raged, but most voices cried out in despair. 'They call you beastmen.'

There had been Imperial iterators, down in the deeps where Azmedi had found his own kind, who had come to teach their secular religion to every branch of mankind, no matter how devolved, in mean schools they carved out of compressed, hive-bottom junk. The Apostle's words evoked those lessons, fifteen years ago. So long, for one of his kind. The lives of the beastkin were short.

'In the beginning, when man left the world you will soon conquer, he had but one form. Many places moulded the genome of our species, and one form became many!'

Azmedi's breaking mind reeled with the sermon. His memories intruded into the present, words said to him, words that were more than sounds on the air, but chains to bind him.

'Homo sapiens variatus,' the smiling man had said, as if that explained everything.

'Others retain the name of human, but not you. Not you!' the Apostle railed. 'Your dignity was taken from you. You were decreed as less than human, abhuman, mutant. Undesirables on worlds you called home for hundreds of generations! The Emperor meddles with mankind's form, and they call His monsters heroes, yet you – you, the rightful children of change – are branded beasts!'

There were those who tried to follow the rules. There were those who tried to understand. There were those who tried to atone for the sin of being born. It made no difference. All Azmedi's kind were hated. Though their forms were no more aberrant than other human strains, their appearance evoked folk-memories of devils and they were treated accordingly.

'*If a man is treated as a beast, then he becomes a beast!*'

The beastmen roared out their pain. They locked their horns and butted heads. The hold reeked of droppings and rage.

'Beasts!' shouted a beastman close to Azmedi.

'Beasts!' bleated another.

The cry spread through the herd, until the hold shook with stamping hooves and the chant of 'Beasts! Beasts! Beasts!' The Apostle's sermon rose in volume to compete.

'*But to the Pantheon, you are holy beings! You are pure! You are the children of Chaos! You are the living example of mutability! Go out! Go out into the fire, and cast down those in thrall to the False Emperor! Trample His works beneath your feet, wet your horns with the blood of unbelievers!*'

'Beasts! Beasts! Beasts!'

The stink of aggression filled the world. Azmedi's nostrils flared to breathe it in. He resisted joining the call for violence until the very last. His senses reeling, memories of oppression crashed upon him in waves, threatening to drown his sanity in misery and injustice.

He would not drown. He wanted to remain a man. He wished to stay human.

He could not.

His muzzle shaking, Azmedi opened his mouth and threw back his horned head.

'Beasts!' he roared. His human mind sank into rage.

There were two colours to the world: red and black. All

other hues existed to be drenched in the former or cast into the latter. The first came with violence, the second with the end of life. There was nothing in between blood and death.

Azmedi welcomed such oblivion, for there was no pain there.

When the clamps released the herdship from its carrier, and the nose pitched down for the desperate rush to Terra, the beastmen were already fighting each other.

Loman's Promise, *repurposed fleet tender,*
Terran near orbit, 25th of Secundus

The butt of Hanis oFar's lasgun was made of hyperdense plastek. Scratching an octed into it was incredibly hard, and had become boring well before he had finished the initial cross of the eight-pointed star. Hanis had a reputation for doggedness to uphold, and so kept at it, dragging the sharpened end of his mess spoon back and forth, cursing when the plastek crumbled and the edges roughened. It wasn't something he enjoyed, but there was precious little else to do.

He'd long since blocked out the smell and constant noise of five hundred men living in close proximity. What he couldn't cope with was his tiny little sliver of private space being invaded. When the blanket that separated his cot from the next man's was tugged back, he stabbed himself with the sharpened spoon and swore colourfully.

The nervy figure of Fendo stood in the gap. Behind him the rest of the regiment, what was left of it, went about the mind-fraying tedium of shipboard life – arguing, smoking, fighting, sleeping and swearing.

'For the Warmaster's sake,' grumbled Hanis. He sucked at his cut hand and yanked at the curtain with the other.

Fendo wouldn't let him close it. 'We're going in,' he said.

Hanis oFar scowled at Fendo's moronic face. He was the kind of man who wore a look of slack-mouthed wonder ninety per cent of the time. He gaped at everything, a tendency that had only got worse since he'd embraced the Eightfold Faith. It was the less intelligent ones who had done so first, and Fendo was right at the front of the queue.

'We're going in,' said Hanis flatly.

Fendo nodded encouragingly.

Hanis sighed. He shook his wounded hand and pressed a rag to it. 'We're not going in. Whispers promising battle have run through these barracks over and over again. We haven't gone in.' He took away the rag. Blood dripped into the unfinished octed on his gun, and he scowled.

'But we are this time, Hanis. I heard.' Fendo scratched around the octed branded onto his cheek. The flesh around it was still inflamed weeks later. It didn't seem to bother him. 'Everyone's talking about it. *Everyone.*'

'Is this the same everyone who said so last time?' Hanis picked up his spoon and recommenced work. The edge cut more smoothly now it was greased with blood.

'Come on, Hanis!' Fendo implored.

'Get lost, Fendo, I'm busy.'

'I see! I see!' He pointed at Hanis' work, only now noticing it. 'The masters will be pleased. You take the mark!'

'Don't get excited. I'm not fool enough to do that to myself.' He jabbed the spoon at Fendo's brand, then hunched back over his weapon. 'I'm just doing this so I'm not singled out. And because I'm bored.'

'It doesn't matter why you're doing it, just that you are! The gods, Hanis. They'll watch over you, protect you. They care! The Emperor lied to us – there are gods. They want our worship. They can make you powerful!'

Hanis looked past his comrade into the wider hall. *Loman's Promise* was a fleet tender. The Thernians had lost most of their transports three years ago and since then the cargo hold had been their home. 'Look at this place, Fendo. It's cramped, smoky and always either too hot or too cold. The air is hardly breathable, we've barely enough pots to piss in and next to nothing to eat. I'd say if the gods granted wishes none of us would be in here.'

'They look over me.'

Hanis blew out a curl of plastek. He must be getting the hang of carving, because it was getting easier.

'Fat lot of good it's done you,' said Hanis.

Nothing could dent Fendo's idiotic ebullience. 'If you believe that, why are you fighting the Emperor?'

'I'm fighting for the Warmaster, not for these so-called gods of yours.'

'Why? They're gods. The Warmaster's just a man.'

'*Just a man?* You're such an idiot.' Hanis had a flash of the one time he had stood near the Warmaster, ten years ago, before the civil war. In the wake of 63-10, Horus had walked among the regiment, stopping to talk with men at their fires, easy with them, sharing jokes and giving praise. Hanis had been too dumbstruck to address this giant as he strode by within touching distance. He remembered the moment as clearly as if it were happening again. The sheer presence of Horus had deformed Hanis' life, like a star's mass bends space. Everything before and after was rendered meaningless. Some of his comrades had been even more affected. A couple never recovered. Not Hanis. When Horus had gone by, he had known with absolute certainty that he would follow Horus Lupercal wherever he went and whatever he did.

'He's not a man,' muttered Hanis. 'He's much more than that.'

'Well then, lad!' said Fendo, his overfamiliarity prompting another scowl from Hanis. 'Best get ready, because you'll
have the chance to prove your worth to him soon.'

'No, no I won't!' The spoon sliced through the plastek.
After only a couple of minutes, he suddenly had all eight
arms done. He started on the arrow tips for the ends. 'There's
not enough of us left. What kind of threat could the Thernians present? Eh? We've hardly got sufficient guns for every
man. What are we going to do, throw our empty ration packs
at the enemy?' Hanis shook his head. 'Mark my words, he'll
send in his Legions first – we'll be left to mop up.'

'I know you're wrong.'

'And I know you're–'

A klaxon sounded twice, cutting Hanis dead.

The vox crackled on. *Attention all Thernians. This is not
a drill. Prepare for immediate combat deployment. Prepare for
battle. I repeat, this is not a drill. We have the honour of securing the beachhead.* Their commanding officer's voice wavered
with pride.

'That… that was the colonel!' said Hanis. He frowned. 'I
thought he was dead.'

Fendo nodded, his idiot's grin spreading wider.

'We're going in?'

Throughout the bay every man froze, looking up dumbfounded as if the gods themselves had spoken to them, and
would do so soon again.

'By the Four,' said Hanis.

Suddenly, all at once, the hold exploded with activity.
Everybody was shouting. Everybody was moving. Tatty uniforms were thrown on. Battered flak armour shrugged over
worn jackets. Guns were snatched up. Crude amulets yanked
off hooks and slung about necks.

'But how… how are they going to get us down there?' said

Hanis. We've got no landers. This ship can't put down! Are we going to be transferred?'

The ship answered his question with a shudder. The background noises of the vessel changed, the grunting whoosh of its plasma thrusters sounding loud, even over the racket of excited men. A faint push upwards told Hanis which direction they were going.

'No,' he said, afraid now. 'No, they're taking the tender down. It's not made for it! We'll crash! We're all going to die.'

Fendo's smile turned wicked. Before that moment, Hanis had never really noticed just how ugly the man was.

Traitor fleet, Terran near orbit, 25th of Secundus

All across Horus' fleet the landing ships departed.

From the carriers and the troop transports, the hulks and the freighters, from vessels of every kind pressed into service by Horus' armada, a hundred thousand craft set out. Among them went vessels never intended to leave the weightlessness of the void. Sinking determinedly, they pierced the upper envelope of Terra's dirty atmosphere, bellies glowing with compressive heat as smaller ships plummeted past in a race to the surface. They descended among a hail of mass fire and the discharge of ten thousand lances. The boiling fires around the Palace were visible from Luna, while overworked void shields sparked lightning that crackled from one side of the planet to the other. Outside of the Palace's protective fields, tracts of Terra burned under heavy bombardment. Dust pillared the heavens. Ash flew streamers in raging stratospheric winds. Every city, every settlement, was under attack. Most possessed their own defences, but none compared to those guarding the Palace, and several hives already burned, as giant pyres that lit Terra with a hellish glow. Debris had yet to occlude the sky completely, though it was only a matter of time before the atmosphere was choked by the ejecta of so many impacts. Steam boiled from young seas. Regenerating vegetation burned. Wherever there were settlements, buildings were reduced to craters and people to ash. Nothing was spared, no matter how insignificant. In his desire to make his father suffer, Horus punished the human race.

Into this maelstrom went the ships. Terra's guns gave fire as soon as Dorn judged the drop formation set. The guns of the Palace targeted anything on a downwards course. Once the landers were past the protection of the larger ships' shields, they were immediately at risk. Smaller ships were atomised. Larger craft were crippled to plummet blazing through slate-grey skies. The warp around the Throneworld boiled with souls snatched from their mortal housings, and yet still the Warmaster's ships came, thundering through the air by the thousands. So many were obliterated, but the forces of Horus were so immense that each one lost was but a grain of sand removed from a desert.

When the void was thick with this flotilla, and the gunners of Terra spoiled for choice of target, then the hangars of the fleet opened, and uncountable fighters and bombers rushed out. Their engines burning at full capacity, they raced down between the landers as swift as arrows, each locked upon a goal, their bomb bays filled with ordnance and cannon magazines stacked with shells.

Their mission was to break the teeth of the Imperial Palace.

TEN

A soldier's duty
Bright Hawks
Flight at last

Eagle's Watch rapid deployment hangar,
Eternity Wall space port, 25th of Secundus

We wait. That is a warrior's primary task. Our duty calls for read-
iness to fight, the ultimate result of which is sacrifice, but before
death comes the wait. The wait lasts and lasts, and sometimes
is never done. Equally it can cease at any moment, and life fin-
ish in the fire. An airman therefore must be two things above
all else. They must be fearless, and prepared at all times for the
end, but more than that they must be patient, or the waiting
will drive them to despair.

Sat at her small desk, Aisha Daveinpor reread yesterday's
words in her diary. Her pencil was poised over the day's new
entry as it had been for three minutes, but she could think
of nothing new to add. The bombardment had gone on
for nearly two weeks, and her squadron hung on the very
edges of their nerves waiting for action. Sleepless nights led
to tense days. The repetitive duties demanded of any soldier

helped fill the time: flight readiness checks, kit checks, cleaning, tidying and so on. They formed a fortification of duty around her emotions, but as the bombardment wore on with its ceaseless, gut-rumbling pounding, it eroded those walls. Trepidation crept in through the breaches, and fear snuck in behind. She wasn't frightened to die – she had become resigned to death a long time ago. A useless death terrified her, however. While her squadron was grounded she was useless, and as much at risk as any civilian.

A useless death, she wrote in her diary, *is the worse death of all.*

The words looked stark on the white of the journal page, and she almost crossed them through. Instead, she threaded the pencil back into its loop and snapped the small book shut, and left it upon her table.

Her status as an Aeronautica pilot gave her a good-sized room; being a squadron mistress gained her a little more space. Her quarters even had a window. High up on the side of the enormous Eternity Wall space port, it had unrivalled views, the sort a rich man would pay a planet's ransom to possess. On fine days she could look out across the Palace, taking in a slice of the northern aspect, over the Daylight section of the Eternity Wall, and the mountains beyond.

That's what she saw in normal circumstance. Fire was what she saw then, reds and golds and orange, shot through with the multicoloured lightning flicker of void shield discharge. The Eternity Wall space port's great bulk projected high over the fortification it was named for. The top of the port scraped the underside of space. As such, the Palace aegis rose around it in a sloped blister of energy.

The fire was a few hundred metres from her window. If she angled her head, she could see down towards the ground, past the docks and wharfs projecting from the sides of the port. The top of the wall and the towers she could also see, before the downturn of the aegis cut off the view of the world beyond and screened it with fire. The chrono said it was night, but for weeks the world had endured perpetual firelight.

She left her quarters. The 198th Squadron barracks were plain yet neat. What the pilots themselves didn't keep in order, their unit servants did. Corridors of plain grey rockcrete decorated with a single yellow stripe at waist height made up the majority of her world. Breaks in the colour told her where she was. There were scores of barracks in yellow sector, and they all looked very much the same.

The corridor terminated on a balcony overlooking hangar one. Half her squadron was housed inside: eight one-man Panthera-class fighters including her own ship, *Blue Zephyr*. Like the corridors, the hangar was plain but for yellow striping. Their banner hung limp on the wall over the entrance, machines underneath wrinkling up the number and the common name of 'Bright Hawks' stitched into it. Hazard striping stencilled directly onto the floor took up much of the space, especially around the fighters' individual standings, and at the ends of the two mag catapults that propelled the craft out of the hangar. With two more catapults in hangar two, all of the squadron's sixteen ships could be in the air within minutes, and at full burn in the void ten minutes after that. Right then the fighters were silent, their canopies covered with tarpaulins dogged tight, except Yancy Modin's ship. She sat in the cockpit fiddling with her guns while their tech-priest checked the tracking of their swivel mounts.

Aisha leaned on the gallery railing, and stared at *Blue Zephyr*. There weren't many ships like the Pantheras in the Imperium. They were among the best, advanced technology laid into every part; rumours had it that the Emperor Himself had a hand in their design, and why not? They were the front line of the Palace's airspace defence.

'The best pilots in the segmentum, and we've been sitting on our behinds for weeks,' she muttered to herself.

'Getting itchy to fly, ma'am?'

'Flight Master Dandar Bey,' she said, accepting the mug of recaff he held out to her. He was her second-in-command, and led flight two of the Bright Hawks. 'I'm always itchy to fly.' She made a sorry little noise. 'I should never have accepted this posting. No action for years, always bloody waiting.'

'I don't think you want to fly in that, ma'am,' Bey said, nodding out at the firestorm through the hangar entrance. He'd told her where he was from, somewhere on Terra warm enough to give him rich brown skin and matching eyes. He never looked unhappy, even when he was. Thoughtful was the most miserable emotion he displayed.

'I'd fly in that quite happily,' she said. 'Better than sitting in here.'

'Aren't you supposed to stamp down on that kind of talk? Keep our morale up?'

She snorted. 'What are they going to do? Relieve me of command? Not right now, my friend.' She sipped her drink and pulled a face. 'This is bloody awful.'

'Thank you, ma'am,' said Bey.

Aisha looked out past the end of the mag catapult ramps; metal piers that looked to be supported by nothing, they ended in thin air, past which was the ceaseless roil of explosions. It was a view she was growing tired of.

She was about to open her mouth and ask the question she did every morning, 'Do you think it will be today?' when klaxons stopped her.

'*All squadrons report to launch bays. All squadrons report to launch bays.*'

The lumens snapped off. Rotating ready lights spun up to action on the walls. Emergency lighting came on.

'Is this is a drill?' Bey said.

'It better bloody not be,' she said. The klaxons barked on and on. Men and women were streaming into the hangar from all sides, followed by stolid servitors moving to prepare the Pantheras for takeoff.

'*All squadrons prepare to launch,*' said the voice.

Outside a flight of golden aircraft sped by.

'The Legio Custodes are up!' said Bey.

She grinned savagely, and put her recaff down by the railing's footing. 'Then it's not a drill,' she said.

A clangour of sirens rose wailing over the Palace, outcompeting the sound of the bombs.

The crews tumbled into the ready rooms, wrenching open their lockers and flinging on their flight gear. In a ruckus that hid how orderly they were, they were suited and sprinting to their war machines in moments.

Aisha shouted the ground crew out of the way and sprang up the ladder hooked into *Blue Zephyr*'s fuselage, then shouted at them some more to clear her path for takeoff.

'Get the ladder off! Get me into the air!'

They'd been drilling this for months, they should be faster.

All around hangar one, engines coughed into life and began pre-ignition burns. The rotating tables they sat on turned them towards the hangar slot. Small trucks were guided forwards to the first two ships, and munitions locked into place. Aisha checked her chrono.

'Point two slower than best!' she yelled into her helm vox. 'Hurry it up!'

More ships were streaking past the hangar, disgorged from similar facilities all over the Eternity Wall space port. She keyed in her vox to strategic-level communications.

'Squadron Mistress Aisha Daveinpor ready for launch,' she said.

'*Scramble immediately,*' came a terse reply. '*Engagement coordinates incoming.*'

'Understood. For the Emperor.' She switched channels to the squadron net. 'Into the air! Now! Now! Now!'

Her own clusters of missiles were loaded up. By then, the first two Pantheras were angling their jets, pushing up from the ground on cushions of shimmering air. They hovered forwards and let the mag catapults take them. Running lights on the short runway spars turned from red to green, and the ships were hurtled out of the port. The second two were close behind, the third pair rising. Aisha adjusted her helmet, kissed two fingers and pressed them against the pict of her husband pinned to her ship dashboard. She'd not seen him for five years. That didn't stop her loving him.

Her hands danced over a dozen switches. Displays came on in a crescent in front of her. Easing up the stick, she fell into line between the third pair of aircraft, and waited her turn for the catapult.

Third pair were out, shrinking to the size of birds before punching through the voids and into the maelstrom.

Then it was her turn. The ship wavered on its own backwash, the scream of engines magnified by the hangar. Red light, red light, red light. Her foot hung over the burner pedal.

Green light.

The mag catapult took her ship in its fist and hurled her like a javelin out over the Palace. She slammed back into her seat with force, and pressed hard with her suddenly heavy foot.

The burners roared at full power. *Blue Zephyr* and its companion *Leo* shot out at near-maximum speed from the sides of the space port. The sprawl of the Palace was a blur. The world was a crush of acceleration weight and a glare of fire.

'*Bright Hawks flight two, in the air,*' voxed Bey.

'Bright Hawks flight one, in the air,' she responded.

Blue Zephyr shot through the voids into a world of flame.

Mass projectiles dumb and explosive, laser lance beams thick as hive spires, nova cannon shot, plasma streams and plasma balls, weapons of such potency as could level a world slammed into the aegis of the Palace, and Aisha flew straight into it.

'Bright Hawks, fall in.' She gritted her teeth. There was no time to say anything more complicated than that. The vox was a shrieking mess of conflicting voices and interference cast out by the bombardment.

'*Bright Hawks, converge attack point–*' Her controller's voice broke up into squealing as a particle beam sliced down from orbit, cocooned by an invisible magnetic coherence field that incidentally blotted out all nearby vox-comms. Her displays danced. She got a snatch of her squadron on the disposition screen coming into formation, only for them to break in every direction as a lance strike punched through the middle. The graphics flickered out. When they came on, one of her ships was gone.

'Curse it, Bey! Bey! Get them moving!'

No reply came over the whooping of energy weapons ionising the air.

Suddenly, they were through the worst of it, racing across a patch of sky over the central districts clear of weapon strikes. The dust-laden heavens writhed with lightning. Visibility was down to a few kilometres. Through the haze of dust and smoke and the witchfire glow of the aegis, the Palace was a set of unguessable shapes spitting fire into space.

Thousands of aircraft were in flight from every division of the Imperial war machine. True starfighters raced beside purely atmospheric craft. Legion attack ships of white, red and yellow fell in with Aeronautica wings, while the rare, bulbous pursuit ships of the Legio Custodes glinted between. Communications cleared enough for Aisha to organise her squadron, and for orders to come down from high command within the Bhab Bastion.

'All air defence units prepare for engagement.'

Augur screens lit up with a solid mass of contacts. As fast attack ships, the Pantheras arrowed upwards ahead of the flocks of fighters, ready to take the fight up into the void if need be.

When her prow was pointed heavenwards, Aisha saw it would never come to that.

The traitor's air fleet filled the sky.

ELEVEN

Thernia's last glory
Rage of beasts
We hold

Loman's Promise, *Katabatic Plains airspace,*
25th of Secundus

Loman's Promise shook all the way down. Men who had been full of excitement minutes before screamed in terror. The engines roared like dying, angry things. Metal screamed and tore. Subsystems gave out in showers of sparks that lit fires among the regiment's possessions. The temperature within shot up, the terrible howl of tortured atmosphere wrenched at the hull. Smoke billowed from open doors, rolling over the ceiling like a monster out to suffocate them. Alarms blared from every quarter, mocking the screams of the men. The racket was tremendous, but the noise of the enemy guns crashing outside was louder, and growing worse the further they fell.

A deafening bang stole Hanis' hearing. The ship tilted hard to the fore, sending an avalanche of men and upended objects cascading on top of one another, destroying the little comforts they had made for themselves. Hanis' arm was

wrenched behind him. A man sat on his head. He fought
his way from a tangle of cots and blankets. Water and the
contents of chamber pots sluiced over them. He felt he was
drowning. He punched and fought with his comrades in his
desperation to be free.

He crawled out of the tangle and saw the ship had righted
itself as he struggled. Now the floor sloped only a little, but
a fierce wind was shrieking through one of the doors, pulling the smoke out after it, and the noise of the enemy guns
pounded all the louder.

'We've been hit, we've been hit!' someone was shouting.
He was one of the few not reduced to shrieks. Hanis staggered as something punched the vessel hard from beneath. A
musical strike of shrapnel chimed somewhere, then another
hit, and another. He leapt back as a searing blue beam of
las light stabbed up from the deck, blasting apart a man not
four paces from him. Three quick bangs announced more
impacts, a deadly display of light leaping from the deck to
the ceiling, gone before he could blink.

A man holding the stump of his severed arm out before
him ran past.

The ship wallowed, slipping across the sky. The lumens
blinked and went out, and the hold flickered with the strobe
of weapons fire outside, let in by breaches in the hull. Terra's
atmosphere screamed at them. For the first time in his life,
Hanis breathed the air of mankind's home world.

It smelled of burning metal.

The last few seconds were a confusion of blood and terror and light. Projectiles clattered off the hull, now coming
from the side as well as from below. Hanis dropped and
curled into a ball, his teeth clamped tight.

The loudest crash of all lifted up from the deck, the engine
roar ceased, then all was still.

He looked up. Dancing light shone through a rent in the hull. Dead men lay about. The wounded wept and groaned.

The loading gates at the end of the hull, gates Hanis had seen opened only once before, gave out a sorry wail. Of the four warning lumens around them, only one worked, and it flashed twice before failing with a small pop. The mechanisms struggled against crumpled metal to pull the doors open, giving up halfway.

Battle light flooded the room. Hanis saw through the gap onto a scene of utter carnage. Ships powered down from the sky aflame, vomiting hordes of men upon an artificial plain when they landed. Beyond them were the towering walls of the Imperial Palace, and beyond those the soaring spires, all sheltered by glowing rounds of interlinked void shields. Guns spat out a wall of deadly energy and shells into the Warmaster's hordes, while substantial outworks sheltered an opposing army ready to kill any who made it under the skirts of the aegis. Fighter craft of both sides duelled over the battlefield.

A regiment vanished in the conical explosions of a minefield.

Flights of loyalist aircraft swept down, strafing the landers.

An enormous plasma cannon immolated a hundred men in a single shot, leaving only molten stone behind.

A ship exploded hundreds of metres in the air showering burning bodies and fuel over the armies beneath.

Everywhere he looked, there was only death, death and more death.

The ship rocked again. The defenders on the walls had detected life within.

Shouts came from the corridors outside the hall. The regiment's last officers entered, shock goads in their hands. Mercilessly, they laid about the warriors still alive.

'Up! Up! Up!' they yelled.

Hanis needed no encouragement. He looked around for a weapon and, amazingly, saw his own gun with the octed carved into the stock looking up at him. He smiled at it as if it were an old friend.

He stumbled on Fendo's corpse as the men were rounded up and bullied into ranks facing the door. Their colonel led them from the front again, like he had on 63-10, when the regiment won its colours from Horus himself. Looking on the Palace filled Hanis with a sense of rightness. All his life had led to this moment.

The colonel had no inspiring words. He did not need them.

'For the Warmaster!' he said.

'For the Warmaster!' the Thernians responded.

Whistles blew, and the Thernians commenced their last charge.

Herdship, Katabatic Plains airspace, 25th of Secundus

Azmedi no longer knew words.

Gas flooded the transport hold as the herdship came down. It smelled bitter, but by then he was past caring, and with its inhalation the last of his reason fled. The Apostle's voice never stopped as they fell through the air towards the ground, though his words meant nothing to Azmedi now 'slaught filled his lungs. The ship slammed down hard, staggering the passengers, then ramps blew from their mountings, the explosives that tore them free slaying a score of the beastkin too close to the door.

They needed no encouragement to charge. Azmedi understood nothing. His thoughts were a single sheet of red. With the rest of his kin, he hurled himself from the ship, falling five metres to the ground. He stumbled, but did not fall, and rushed away into the storm of fire and destruction. From half a dozen ramps other holds emptied, and a horde of beasts ran out.

The pounding of the guns could not frighten him, only quicken the racing of his heart. His feet were arranged like a beast's, with powerful haunches and elongated feet with the ankle held high off the floor, so that he ran on the single toe of his hoof. Such physiognomy gave the beastkin great speed, and they outpaced the pure men and the mutants pouring from their own landing craft. Azmedi ran with the wind, his mane flowing behind him, his swollen tongue lolling from foam-flecked jaws. There was a glow ahead that writhed and shifted. He ran full pelt into it, felt it try to rip him in two, but he forced his way through and out of it, and emerged on the inside of the Palace aegis.

Ahead was the third defence line, prefabricated sections half buried in crushed rock. Sheltered by their defences, a thousand men waited, lasguns resting on the lip, ready to open fire.

At three hundred metres they let fly. Beastkin to the right and left of Azmedi fell bleating, tumbling madly such was their speed, before they came to a broken rest dead on Terra's soil. Azmedi roared, his eyes rolling. Racing through the hedge of las light towards the line he howled out his pain and his hatred. Men had denied his humanity. Men had trodden him down. Now it was his turn.

A burning shaft of light branded his shoulder, filling his flared nostrils with the smell of singed hair and his own roasted flesh. He barely felt it, but ran on, gathering himself as he approached to jump. His abhuman legs bunched to hurl him over the rampart in a leap no standard human could match. A dozen more of his kind were behind him.

He came down atop a terrified man. In his hand Azmedi clutched a simple maul, a threaded bar with a nut the size

of a man's fist screwed onto the end. Shouting wildly, his
cries more bleats than words, he smashed the man's helmet in with a single blow, destroying the skull beneath.
Wrenching out the weapon, he turned quickly, sending the
dead man tumbling off the firing step. A pure-blood stared
at him, eyes disgustingly large in his flat face. He swung his
lasrifle around. Azmedi battered the bayonet aside, dropped
his head and launched himself forwards. His horns buried
themselves up to his forehead in the man's gut. Azmedi
thrashed them around madly in the soldier's innards, yank-
ing ropes of gut out when he tore back his horns. The man
screamed in agony. Azmedi stamped his face in with one
kick, and raced on.

By then, more beastkin were flooding onto the rampart,
leaping over the piled stone and the rockcrete. They had no
formation, no discipline, only years of hurt amplified by the
combat stimms pumping through them. The savagery this
alchemy summoned was more than enough. The conscripts
panicked. The volleys they fired were poorly coordinated
and badly aimed. Azmedi was shot again, but though devo-
lution had robbed his kind of man's wits and longevity, it
had made them tough. Several hits were needed to bring
the beasts down. Even when mortally wounded, they fought
with undiminished wrath, dragging their killers into the
warp with them.

Azmedi shrugged off the hit as he had shrugged off the
last. Feeble bayonet thrusts were no match for his strength.
His broad fingers wrenched weapons from trembling hands.
His maul crushed ribcages, smashed heads, caved in faces,
broke limbs. All along the rampart, the hordes of the Warmaster were coming over, widening the opening made by
the beastkin. Units of turncoat Imperial Army added their
firepower to the beasts' rampage. Setting up position on

the forwards-facing portion of the defences, they began to attack the second line with heavy weapons and concentrated lasgun volleys. Seeing the third line broken, the officers on the second line ramparts some three hundred metres away ordered their troops to open fire on the rear of the third. As reinforcements raced along the second line, the weight of this exchange grew in intensity. The beastkin were caught. The remaining conscripts suffered more. Azmedi hauled a man from his feet, and carried him screaming as a shield against the loyalist fire. Soon he was out of the worst of it, still running purely on instinct, charging with his dwindling herd into the next company of soldiers.

He cast aside his now dead human shield. Lifting his head to the sky he roared and roared, until the self-hate he had carried all his life was all spat out, and murder took its place.

Daylight Wall, Helios Gate command centre,
25th of Secundus

'Sir, we have a breakthrough in sector sixteen, three kilometres down from the commanding bastion.'

'I can see it,' said Raldoron. He watched from the relative safety of the Helios Gate as the first section of the outworks was breached. 'Move reinforcements outwards from line one to two. Form firing lines between three and two.' He performed a quick mental calculation. At the rate the enemy were pushing out from their breaching point, they did not have long. 'One kilometre north of Bastion Fifteen, five hundred metres south of Bastion Sixteen.'

'This is insanity,' said Maximus Thane. 'I have never seen a battle like this. They fight without care for themselves.'

'I do not believe there has ever been a battle like this,' said Raldoron.

Above the aegis, fighters duelled, numerous as enraged wasps. The bombardment thundered into the energy shield, but as yet it was holding. Out on the plain, countless ships were setting down under heavy fire. More than half were brought crashing to the earth before they landed. None of them came down undamaged. They landed dangerously close to the wall. With the Katabatic Slopes to the south and east, and the mountains of Himalazia in every other direction, they did not have much choice, but it was a costly strategy. Thousands upon thousands of guns scoured the plains before the outworks. There was no time or space for the enemy to form their own camps. They landed, and they attacked, if they did not die first.

'None of our traitorous brothers show themselves,' said Thane. 'Horus has a multitude of expendable mortals. This is sickening work.' He looked down onto the outworks, where flashing storms of las-fire marked out points of intense conflict. 'All the more so because we must wait here, while the men and women we were made to protect sell themselves alone.'

'We must remain here. This attack is a ploy.'

'That worries me,' said Thane, gesturing to the aerial battle. 'Theoretically, the aegis is invulnerable. But the Warmaster would not launch such an attack if there was not a way through. There are many heavy attack craft within his flotilla. I say they are waiting to breach the shields and attack our emplacements.'

'We know the shields are not perfect,' said Raldoron. 'There are flaws. Perturabo works for the Warmaster. If anyone can find a gap in the defence, it will be him.'

Thane's voice turned angry at the mention of the Lord of Iron, but he did not dissent. 'All over Terra, down they come,' said Thane. 'The dispossessed, the spurned and the deluded run raging into the full force of Rogal Dorn's guns. They die by the million, but still they come. Horus has no regard for these creatures he hurls at us, but though they are expendable to him, they will not be wasted. There is reason behind this insanity.'

'So then,' Raldoron said, 'we watch, and we wait, and we slaughter the enemy on the plain. When they draw nigh to the wall, that is the time for the Legions to fight. Until then, we hold.'

TWELVE

War in the air
Blue Zephyr
Shield breaker

Imperial Palace airspace, 25th of Secundus

It was like no flying Aisha had ever done. The airspace was a conflicted mess of shock waves that turned every manoeuvre into a bone-jarring fight with turbulence. Compounding the problem were energetic wave fronts. Electromagnetic discharge disrupted her instruments, forcing her to rely on her own, dazzled senses, while gravitic disruption from exotic weaponry flipped ships over and sent them crashing down to oblivion against the aegis.

Amid all this, Aisha's wing managed to kill. *Blue Zephyr* stabbed a swift enemy with lascannon flash, blowing out an engine. It spun out of control into the path of an incoming plasma stream before it could recover, and was vaporised.

That kill under those conditions would have been the highlight of any of her previous battles. In this fight, it was barely remarkable.

'Enemy Raptor, stooping low, on the tail of Ninth Legion fighter.'

'I see it.' Aisha barely heard Yancy. A blurt could have been an affirmative from Accinto. Most of the vox-net was a smear of crackles and whoops; nevertheless, two of her ships peeled off and down, Yancy's jinking to avoid a missile strike hurled at her from a higher level in the battle sphere. Missing her, the missile contacted the shield and vanished in a flash of displacement light. Yancy and her wingman blasted through the backwash, gaining on the enemy craft tailing the Blood Angels strike fighter.

Aisha lost them after that. She had her own problems. Proximity alerts bleeped all round her cockpit. Aisha swore, flicking switches to bring a wireframe image of her tailing foe slewing around crosshairs that blinked every time he came close to locking on. Luckily for her, that part of her ship's tech was robust enough to withstand the energies boiling around her.

'You've got a friend down there,' Bey voxed.

'I see him.' Aisha yanked hard on her stick. The ship fired thrusters down its port flank, sending it screaming sideways out of her pursuer's fire arc.

'Do you want me to help?'

'No,' Aisha said. *Blue Zephyr* bounced through a violent thermal rising off a low-yield atomic strike. Flames flashed over the cockpit. Rad counters clicked like maddened insects.

'Only way is up,' she said, heaving back on her flight stick. G-force pushed her into her seat, smoothing back her skin until her lips peeled back. The world turned upside down. Through the upper part of her canopy, the Palace aegis flashed and writhed. Then the loop was complete, she was up and over, jinking through screaming shell-fire, coming down hard on the tail of her pursuer. Seeing she'd given him the slip and manoeuvred behind him, her foe threw his craft about, trying to shake her, but her wingman boxed him in with a stream of blue-white las light.

Now it was the turn of her targeting reticule to blink. It turned green and her instruments shrilled.

'There's a cliche to be said about hunters and the hunted,' she said.

Las-beams pulsing at an eye-watering flicker chopped through the firestorm, puncturing the wing of her foe in a row of holes as neat as a tailor's stitch. The wing flapped loosely, then tore off. She put a double hit into the fuel tank as it spiralled away, just to be sure.

The explosion was lost in the greater inferno curling over the aegis.

She was already hunting for her next target when something caught her eye. A tight formation of ships was coming down from orbit perpendicular to the shield. The bombardment around them had a precise, neat patterning and beat. As she watched, the outer layer of the shielding gave out with a sparkling dance, but there were two more layers beneath, at least.

The formation continued its plunge.

'What are they doing?' she breathed.

The first of them, a pair of escort fighters, smeared themselves to nothing on the aegis, the remains shunted into the empyrean by warp tech. She expected the same fate for the three bombers coming behind, but an instant before they hit, a dozen lance strikes battered at the shield. Collimated light shafts wide as road tunnels pummelled the voids. Her augurs shrieked. Her visor dimmed to compensate for the glare, but she found herself half-blind. When the lances snapped off she had flown near, five hundred metres and closing, and saw that more bombers were hurtling towards one, precise point. One exploded into pink fire on the voids, but the others punched through without harm. She saw them pull up steeply once through, chased by anti-aircraft fire over the Palace as they split up.

'Shield breach! Shield breach!' she reported. 'Daylight Wall anterior, sector sixteen.'

Bey responded. *'Not just here. Five points on this section alone.'* He stopped speaking, his engine noise increased, and he swore. *'Hang on. Someone's trying to kill me.'*

'Be advised, fighter control. Some kind of anti-harmonic fire pattern, weakening the aegis,' said Aisha. *Blue Zephyr* screamed through the bombers streaking down from space, dodging through them, firing as she went. 'They'll be going for the void projectors and anti-air cannons.'

'Noted, Blue Zephyr. Freedom granted to pursue.'

Aisha grinned wolfishly. This was more like it! 'Five years sitting behind lines. A great reward for being a good pilot – now I finally get to fly. Wing one, form up, follow me in.'

Four ships answered her call. Three of her squadron were dead, and she hadn't even noticed.

'You can't follow them down!' voxed Bey. *'There's no space. The flight ceiling is too low. If you come back up through the void shields, you'll be caught in the bombardment.'*

'It's days like this that made me want to fly. Hold position here, Bey. Help the Legions hold the ships back from the holes. I'm taking flight one down with me.'

Thrusters firing all over her ship, she powered upwards, weathering a fusillade of solid shot from enemy fighters, flipped over, and dived down at the aegis. Her wing, expert pilots all, stayed in perfect formation with her all the while.

The surface of the aegis rushed at her. The upper shield kept rising, only to be torn down over and over again. The taxed lower layers remained up, but wavered forever on the edge of existence at the sort of strength that might – *might* – permit her craft through. There was no telling if it would work; the aegis made no distinction between friend and foe, but operated solely on esoteric calculations of mass and velocity and dimensional interface.

She flicked a look at her husband's picture.

'You always told me I was reckless,' she said. 'I guess you were right.'

Blue Zephyr hit the aegis. The stick jerked in her hand as three layers of void shields attempted to hurl her bodily into the warp, but they were stressed, feeble, and she powered through to the other side.

The ground was alarmingly close.

'Up we go!' she shouted. Again the push of force on her body threatened to squeeze her into unconsciousness. Implants in her chest cavity squirted chemicals into her bloodstream, and she fought off the blackness.

More enemy aircraft had got through than she'd expected. They were wasting no time, emptying their payloads of missiles at the towers and wall tops, aiming especially for the flattened spheres of void projectors and the larger anti-ship cannon emplacements.

Explosions bloomed in fiery chains along the Daylight Wall.

'Targets of opportunity,' she voxed. 'Split up. Let's put a stop to this before it gets out of hand.'

Her flight divided instantly, each Panthera chasing after a separate target. Aisha upped her thrust and shot after a pair of Reaper ground attack craft. Their missiles spent, they were turning inwards, pounding the roads and marshalling yards behind the wall with unguided bombs.

She used one of her precious stock of air-to-air missiles to knock the first from the sky. The other lumbered aside as its companion plummeted down and crashed into the side of a hive spire. Aisha drew a bead on it, and fired her lascannons, but the pilot anticipated her move. He turned hard, and her beams seared past, scorching up the ground.

'Dammit, dammit, dammit!' she swore, accelerating after it. The bomber was slow, but the pilot was good. He took the Reaper down, close to ground level, using the tangle of spires and canyon streets to stay out of her firing line. She searched overhead, but there wasn't enough room to climb to come down on top of her target without flying right into the bombardment. In such close confines, her speed was of no use.

She chased the Reaper down one of the Palace's immense processional ways, jinking to avoid fire from its tail gun. Her own shots were spoiled by her evasions. In the end, the pilot's luck ran out. She dived down behind him, coming so close to the ground her jet wash shattered windows, and fired up beneath her prey. His attempt to get out of her way saw him clip a starscraper, and that sealed his fate. The craft tumbled viciously from the sky, exploding on impact.

Her exultation was short-lived. She didn't dare wonder how many people had died when the bomber hit the ground.

There was no time for mourning friends, never mind people she'd never met. She pulled up *Blue Zephyr*, and swung around to head back towards the wall. At her speed it was a flight of seconds, but in that time there was space to see three things of dreadful note.

The first, Yancy's ship blasted apart by a trio of enemy fighters.

The second, dozens more bombers punching through the weakened shields.

And the worst, innumerable bombs plummeting unhindered where the void blisters had been cleared, striking home on the defences with all the wrath of armageddon.

'A woman's job is never done,' she whispered, and accelerated *Blue Zephyr* back into the fight.

THIRTEEN

Three lines
Abhuman
Spawn of Chaos

Palace outworks, Daylight Wall section 16, 25th of Secundus

'They're coming, they're coming!'

Men sprinted past Katsuhiro's position. They were on the outside of the rampart line in full view of the enemy, but didn't seem to know or care. The noise alone was enough to frighten a man out of his wits. The Palace's peripheral shields were giving out, allowing the enemy munitions to strike the earth. Attack craft strafed the outworks on their way to the walls. Destroyed, the enemy ships were as much danger to the defenders as they were flying, crashing down and cartwheeling over the muddy ground before exploding. The carcasses of landing craft, many on fire, hid the plain. Others poured out an endless stream of hateful creatures that ran at the parapets. Gunfire from the walls scythed them down by the thousands, but they came on, replenished by more ships, and more, landing among the wreckage of those downed earlier. Debris rained from the sky constantly, a hail of grit and metal splinters that pattered off Katsuhiro's helmet, some big enough to kill a man.

A hand gripped his arm, pulling him back from the parapet edge.

'Hold the line!' A veteran in full uniform grabbed him and spun him around. 'That way! That way!' The man slapped him hard. In his dirty face his eyes seemed big as saucers, and full of fear.

'Three lines! Make three lines!' Jainan had found a handful of veterans like himself, and they kicked, swore and shoved the conscripts into three wavering ranks stretching between the third and second rampart lines. Katsuhiro couldn't keep his eyes forwards. His head rolled around on his neck of its own accord to look out at the plain, as if some perverse part of him was drunk on the destruction, and wanted more. Bastion 16's guns were turning from the front, pointing right at him.

'Three lines! Three lines!' screamed Jainan. 'Three lines, damn you all! Get your guns up!'

Whistles shrieked impotently over the boom of guns.

A few more routers were racing across the firing ground between the third and second outwork rings. When they encountered Katsuhiro's company, they shoved their way through, spreading consternation. Some of them were caught, slapped, turned about. One cannoned right into a veteran, knocking them both flying. The fleeing man was up first.

'Stop! Stop!' shouted the veteran.

The runner sprinted on.

Katsuhiro heard the rasp of metal on leather as the veteran pulled out his laspistol, sighted down the barrel, arm straight, and dropped the man with a single shot.

'Any one of you cowards runs like him, you'll die the same. Now, three lines!'

Another company was running up, this one a little better disciplined than Katsuhiro's own, with a third on their heels, enough to fill the space between the two outermost defence works completely. All of their officers were shouting, whistles blowing, voxmitters blaring.

The fleeing men petered out. A sparkle of crossfire was working its way down the killing field towards Bastion 16 as soldiers on the second line fired on the enemy who had overwhelmed the third and were advancing down the gap. A dark mass was moving towards Katsuhiro. He squinted, not quite able to make out what was approaching.

'There's the enemy,' said the man to his right.

'Oh no, oh no, oh no,' said the man to his left.

'This is a fine mess,' whispered Doromek from behind. The hard woman was close by him. She gave them both a black look. Katsuhiro had not yet seen another kind on her face.

Faces pale with fear looked out at the enemy. Black figures emerged as individuals from the group, but the flickering battle light made it hard to pick out details.

Jainan pushed his way in front of his company and turned to face them.

'Look!' he said, pointing behind him to the running mass of enemy. 'They are coming for us because people like you lost your nerve and abandoned their positions. Our lords and masters, up there on the walls, are turning their guns upon the overrun sections. If you do not hold, if you do not stand and fire in a straight, Emperor-beloved line, then you will die, because if those monsters don't kill you, our own side will. And I for one do not wish to die today!' he bellowed. 'You will not let me down. You will hold in three lines. The first line will lie prone. The second will kneel, the third will stand, and you will not move, you will not run. You will work your fingers upon the triggers of your guns until they bleed. You will fire until your power packs are empty, but most of all you will hold your ground!' All up the line of soldiers, similar speeches were being delivered to other terrified conscripts. 'If you do not, then we're all dead, not tomorrow, but now, right now.'

Jainan pushed his way back through the troopers, drew his pistol and blew his whistle.

'Lines, assume position!'

'First line prone!' bellowed the veterans, kicking those that did not obey.

'Second line kneel!'

Shaking, slowly and in poor order, the conscripts obeyed. Katsuhiro, who was in the second line, knelt in the mud. Cold seeped through his trousers.

He noted then that the enemy were running unnaturally quickly towards them.

Bastion 16's cannons opened up, flinging bright lines of tracer fire over the conscripts' heads.

'Oh no, oh no, oh no,' the gibbering man continued to say.

'Present arms!' yelled Jainan. His veterans relayed his orders again, and held their lasguns unwaveringly on the enemy. The conscripts did rather less well. Their unfamiliar weapons wavered in quaking hands. The firestorm was creeping down the kill-zone as the troops stationed on the second line continued to fire, each section opening up as the enemy neared. It was short-lived display. As it ran, the horde attacked the ramparts, some of them leaping over in single bounds.

Katsuhiro blinked. He couldn't believe what he was seeing. No men could jump so high.

His weapon shook in his hands.

A sharp crack sounded over his head. Doromek was firing already.

'Wait for the signal, acting lieutenant!' barked Jainan.

'Not likely,' said Doromek. 'I was a sniper. Let me do my thing. I can drop three more before you give the order. Or you can shoot me.' He fired again without taking his eye from his targets. 'What a waste that would be.'

The enemy were close enough to see properly. A hundred metres away, no more. They were beasts in the shape of men, long-muzzled creatures with curled horns and manes of coarse hair. They could have been xenos, but Katsuhiro knew instinctively that these were a twisted offshoot of his own race, and they disgusted him.

'Open fire!' bellowed Jainan.

The holding force obeyed. A volley of gunfire erupted from all three ranks, then a second. Raggedly at first, then with greater coherency, the regiment put out a torrent of las-beams in time to the shriek of whistles.

Five volleys, then the enemy were upon them. Each of the beasts took three or four shots to put down. Goat-headed monsters leapt up and crashed down among the men, their hooves stamping heads flat, their primitive bludgeons smashing bones with every swing.

Promptly, discipline broke down. The line wavered, then collapsed. Those who fled were laid low as they turned to run. Those who fought were barged aside, cast into the dirt, gored and smashed.

Katsuhiro found himself face to face with one of the creatures. Its mouth sported sharp tusks alongside flat, grazer's teeth, all slicked with bloody foam that dribbled down its face and off its wispy beard. Its eyes were wide, wild, but human-looking, among the only features it had that were. Sharp horns jutted from its forehead, slathered in gore. It snorted at him, and swung its maul.

There was a split second in which Katsuhiro could react.

One side of it was death, on the other life. Deep inside Katsuhiro something gave way like a dam; a flood of rage swept aside his passive, former self.

Launching himself from his kneeling position, he rammed his bayonet into the creature's gut, shouting into its face as he did.

The creature fell backwards, voicing a wordless, agonised scream halfway between a human cry of pain and an agonised bleat. Katsuhiro leaned his full weight on his lasrifle, twisting the weapon about, as the mutant howled and clawed at the gun barrel.

Its head shook, a fat blue tongue flapped out of its mouth, and it was dead.

Katsuhiro yanked out the blade. The mutants were slaughtering the conscripts. A beastman ran at him, hands held out to throttle. Katsuhiro brought up his gun to fire, but the thing's head disappeared in a mist of blood and bone that splattered across him and stung his face.

The lines of men were thoroughly disrupted, and pushed back from where Katsuhiro stood, leaving him isolated. Smoke from burning void-ships occluded the field of battle. The fur of the beast things had caught fire from the heat of the las-beams, so that some of their dead were ablaze, putting out greasy blue fumes. Combatants leapt into view and were stolen away again by the fog of war. Blue and red las light blinked through the murk, sometimes nearly hitting him. He walked backwards, alert, searching for his own kind. Strangely, he was not frightened. His body sang with adrenaline.

A sheet of smoke rolled back like the curtain of a proscenium, revealing a bloody play. The conscripts were pushing back against their foes, whose number, despite their hardiness, had dwindled. More fire came in from the second line, cutting into the rear of the mutants. But more were on the way.

A heart-stopping wail cut through the brume. Giant shapes lurched through the smoke, bursting through it, and suddenly there were other things pressing the line of men, huge mounds of quaking flesh that shuddered forwards on twisted legs. They were as slow as the abhumans were fast, but seemingly impervious to las-fire. Behind them pairs of savage men herded the things forwards. Half wielded arc whips crackling with electric force, sweeping them about their heads to crack against the shambling creatures' flanks. The others worked chains whose hooked heads were buried in the creatures' flesh.

One of the things lumbered into a knot of men, where it flailed at them with a multiplicity of freakish limbs. Skinless arms shot from sucking apertures, spined with hooks and claws that ripped at flesh. A man was snatched up by a barbed tentacle, whirled about and hurled away with a cry. Men screamed desperately as it coughed wetly and vomited acidic bile to blind their eyes and melt their skin.

These new foes defied description. The first wave had been mutant abominations, but their form was stable, they were of a type. The things facing them now were nightmare composites. They made no sense to look at. They were not xenos or laboratory beasts, but chimerical horrors made of disparate body parts carelessly stuck together. Their physiognomies should not have allowed them to live. But live they did, and move, and kill. They were all different, united only by their complete disparity of form and the horror it kindled in Katsuhiro, for these things too were of human stock. Human heads lolled on boneless necks. Human eyes peeped from fanged orifices. Human tongues screamed lunacy from multiple mouths.

A wailing monster came past him. Katsuhiro stumbled backwards out of the way, managing to fire, but though his beams did no more than brand its skin, it felt the hits, for its single, furious eye swivelled to look upon Katsuhiro, and its course changed to approach directly.

One of the thing's handlers saw him, and flashed a grin full of metal teeth. He, too, was deformed, another mutant, albeit of a less gross sort. He yanked hard on his cruel reins, causing the beast to howl from a dozen mouths and increase its speed.

A las-beam flashed past Katsuhiro, taking the handler in the face. He fell, dragging at the chains and causing the beast to turn to the side. The second handler extinguished his arc whip and ran forwards to disentangle his comrade from the chains. A second las-round smacked into his thigh, and he swore loud enough for Katsuhiro to hear. The beast heard too, turning immediately on its injured tormentor. A vertical slit opened bloodily down its front, exposing quivering teeth and a writhing knot of tentacles. These darted out, snatched up the handler and dragged him whole and screaming into its gullet.

At that moment, the hard-faced woman moved in to attack. She moved so fast, Katsuhiro didn't recognise her. Only when she slowed to step on the mutant's swollen foot and launch herself up did he see who it was. She tossed something into the beast's mouth – a grenade, Katsuhiro realised a moment later – and kicked away from its chest, her foot narrowly missing the mucus-dripping maw.

The creature moved with surprising speed to catch at this new morsel, but the woman was away. The grenade exploded inside the mutant, rupturing its flesh and sending it into keening throes. It was mortally wounded, but still lived, flopping around in pain, thrashing its limbs with deadly ferocity. The dead handler whipped around on the end of his reins.

Katsuhiro shouted, and discharged his gun into the thing's single eye. It exploded with the first hit, but he did not stop firing until the mutant was lying on the ground, body heaving its last.

He stared at it. He had never seen anything like it. He had no idea things like that even existed.

A hand caught his upper arm gently.

'Nice job,' said Doromek. 'It's time to get out of here.'

'Did you see that?'

'See what?' said Doromek.

'The woman… She did this. She killed it.'

Engines grumbled behind the combatants. Large shapes were heading through the smoke.

'You know,' said Doromek, 'it really is time to get out of here.'

Whistles blew far back towards Bastion 16. Officers and their veteran bullies were shouting for everyone to retreat. The surviving knots of infantry gladly obliged, making way for three huge tanks coming to the battle. Anti-personnel weapons in sponsons tracked down to draw a bead on the enemy, their targeting augurs shining red in the battlesmoke.

Without realising it, Katsuhiro was running, following Doromek and the stream of men falling back from the attack. Though retreat had been called, there was no order to the withdrawal, only mad, headlong flight.

The high grey sides of the tank flashed by him, and he saw another line of infantry, this one of regular troops, properly provisioned with uniforms and winter kit, waiting in neat ranks and ready to fire. Hands pulled him through to the back even as las-beams flashed out.

He fell in a heap behind the line.

A moment later, the tanks opened fire, belching choking, acrid smoke over the infantry lines. Heavy bolters and stubbers rattled into action, drowning out all noise with the roar of micro-rocket motors and the detonation of miniature warheads in flesh. Katsuhiro got himself up, turned around to see the mutants being torn apart. All the large abominations fell to the fighting vehicles. The few lesser abhumans that got past the tanks were shot down by groups of infantry. Doromek was firing rapidly but calmly beside him, taking the things through the eyes or mouth, or hitting them squarely in the heart. When he fired, they went down, their toughness no protection against his accuracy.

The last of the abhumans fell dead. The tanks ground forwards, their blocky rears vanishing into the maelstrom of smoke and fire, still discharging their guns.

'Cease firing!'

Jainan's voice was a lonely coherent sound in the racket.

'They've gone!' someone shouted.

A ragged cheer went up from the conscripts. The regulars remained quietly vigilant.

'What were those things?' said Katsuhiro.

Doromek was efficiently changing out his power pack for a fresh charge.

'Mutants. Abhumans. Beastmen, one of humanity's more degenerate subtypes.'

'But the others, the big ones, what were they?'

Katsuhiro locked eyes with Doromek. He could have sworn he saw a flash of consternation before the man's flintiness returned.

'Honestly? I don't know.' For a moment he seemed like a different man, then he smiled and slapped Katsuhiro's arm hard enough to make him wince. 'You survived your first battle. Well done.'

Jainan strode past them. 'It's not over yet. Everybody back to the ramparts.'

Doromek called something after the captain, but it was drowned out by the whistling boom of incoming ordnance and the angry buzz of overstretched void shields.

The enemy was bombarding their section again.

Daylight Wall, Helios Gate, 25th of Secundus

'The breach of the third line of sector sixteen has been contained, only just. We have minor breakthroughs in two other places in our section.' Thane's report was delivered in unhurried, stolid style, typical Imperial Fist. Raldoron's auto-senses dampened the cacophony of the attack, allowing him to hear his counterpart. *'They will soon be dealt with. How looks the situation from the wall?'*

Raldoron was on the wall walk over the gate. He cast his eye across the sweep of the battle. Only a fraction of the invasion force had made it to Terra alive, but the Warmaster had managed to land millions of men even so. They surged through the wreckage of their transports, a black tide of hatred, battering at the ramparts of the outworks.

Aircraft roared over the gate. Cannons clattered at them.

'We still have enemy fighters and bombers making it within the aegis envelope,' said Raldoron. 'The shielding here has taken severe damage. I have contacted the Adeptus Mechanicus to request repair teams be sent, but many of the projection discs are destroyed, and I do not know if they will be able to accomplish much. Over the Palace, the aegis is holding, but out here, past the foot of the walls, it won't be long until it fails.'

Raldoron turned his gaze towards that part of the battlefield where the enemy had broken through.

'Traitor army units have taken up position outside sector sixteen. We cannot let them dig in. I recommend immediate purgation fire from the wall defences.'

'*I concur,*' said Thane.

Raldoron paused while three more fighters screamed overhead, firing on each other, too loud for his auto-senses to screen out.

'I will send the order,' said Raldoron, when they were past. 'Let this be on my conscience, as commander of the Helios section, Daylight Wall.'

'*Then I shall return to my duties here,*' said Thane. '*My thanks, brother.*'

A macro cannon volley got through the peripheral shielding, slamming into the plain just beyond the outworks and killing hundreds of traitors. It wouldn't be too long before the enemy could breach the voids more reliably, and rain death down on the fortifications directly. Raldoron doubted the aegis would fail completely for some time, but it had already been weakened. Eventually, they were going to have to trust in Lord Dorn's walls alone.

Raldoron called his aides to him, and had them relay his command that the Palace open fire on the outworks. The bombardment would cost loyal lives, but from up there on the wall, he could see there was no viable alternative short of sending out the Legiones Astartes, and that had been expressly forbidden.

The guns were opening up as he opened channels to the other captains under his command. His kind were not made to sit and wait behind walls, and he found the duty onerous. Twenty companies, Imperial Fists as well as his own Blood Angels, looked to him for guidance, his purview covering a two hundred-kilometre stretch of the Daylight Wall.

He was in the process of hunting one of his subordinates

out through a tangle of vox-relays, when one of his aides shouted out a warning.

'Attack run!'

A void fighter was coming in at a steep dive straight for the Helios Gate. As Raldoron looked up, its cannons fired. Rockcrete burst in high cones as it strafed the wall walk. The First Captain flung himself out of the way, his battleplate ringing off the parapet as he hit the ground. The enemy fighter made a single pass and sped off southwards, loyal interceptors in hot pursuit.

Raldoron clambered to his feet, armour motors grinding. His two aides were dead, their armour shattered and the bodies inside pulverised by direct autocannon hits. The blood stirred his emotions, and he stared at it for too long.

He tore his eyes away, looking instead towards the third line of the 16th outwork section, now under fire from the Palace walls. Piece by piece, they would lose ground. It was happening faster than he had hoped. He could move inside, but he refused to hide in the Helios command centre, when he could see the battle far better from the walls.

He opened a vox-channel to his Chapter command cadre.

'This is First Captain Raldoron,' he said. 'I require a new nuncio vox-specialist and logistician immediately at my position.'

FOURTEEN

In support of betrayal
I am Alpharius
Not in vain

Palace outworks, Daylight Wall section 16,
contested zone, 25th of Secundus

Myzmadra found it easy enough to slip away from the skirmish down the third line towards the overrun zone. The attack was coming to a close, and a heavy quiet took hold where the roar of distant voices and munitions blended into an avalanche rumble, threatening but far away. Shouts were coming from the second line, so she kept to the ramparts of the third, out of sight in the drifting smoke. She was more than capable of moving unseen when occasion required.

Explosion flash lit up the devastation, the harsh light more disorienting than illuminating. Dead abhumans lay strewn across the killing zone between the third and second lines, their bestial faces still twisted with the rage of battle. She almost pitied them; she knew little of their kind, but what she did told a sorry tale of a rejected human offshoot, not quite debased enough to kill out of hand, but too different

to be afforded dignity. The rank chemical smells of fren-
zon and 'slaught rose from them, the foam around their
muzzles another telltale sign of combat drug administration, but she doubted they needed much encouragement
to kill. The Imperium promised peace and advancement for
all mankind, except for those it didn't. Creatures like these
lived lives of abject misery.

Lies upon lies.

The baseline human corpses she saw were of both loyalists and traitors, not that those terms meant anything to
her. Allegiance hadn't spared either side the savagery of the
abhumans. Both traitor and loyalist had been ripped into,
and showed signs of cannibalism.

She passed through a platoon of dead traitor soldiers. On
the line, the loyalists spoke of scum and dregs, but despite the
symbols of dark gods sprayed onto their equipment and the
fetishes hanging from their kit, these were professionals from
once loyal regiments. Scum wouldn't undertake such a suicide
mission; you needed discipline for that kind of sacrifice. You
needed belief in the cause.

Activity on the second line was increasing, risking her
discovery, so she skidded down the outer face of the rampart. A shell had come down at the foot of the wall, laying
out men and body parts in a pattern of gory regularity. Her
eyes caught on the stock of a lasgun on the fringes of the
crater. Upon it was etched a crude octed, painted red with
recent blood.

The icon was a blasphemy in a world that was supposed to
be beyond such things. Myzmadra didn't believe in Horus'
cause. He was a puppet of awful powers. She didn't think the
Alpha Legion believed in him either, though they hid their
purpose behind a hedge of deceit. The Alpha Legion could
be trusted to be untrustworthy, that was all. It was enough.

In her experience, that was about as much assurance as any human being could get about anything.

After the Battle of Pluto, before the Legion had cast her and Ashul back out into the void, she'd prodded at the legionaries. Myzmadra wasn't likeable, but she was good at getting people to talk. Legionaries, however, were not people. She'd exerted herself, she really had, asking why they fought and received the same answer she always did, if she got any answer at all.

For the Emperor.

They said that to her over and over again. Even when their actions could only be construed as being directly contrary to the Imperium's survival.

For the Emperor.

She'd heard that maybe a dozen times, which was a lot, coming from so secretive a group.

Maybe she was being foolish, but she chose to believe it.

Her thoughts went back to the first time she'd heard it.

'For the Emperor.' He'd said that to her, when she was recruited. Alpharius, he said his name was, but they all said they were him. Was he Alpharius? Was he the warrior who fought at Pluto, truly? Maybe they all *were* Alpharius. There were stranger things in the universe now than a Legion of clones.

How long ago was it? A decade? Fifteen years? Time was one of those bedrocks of civilisation that didn't have anything sensible to say once you interrogated it. Time was like money, a convenient, mutually agreed fiction. It wasn't real, not in the way people thought. It was a human construct. A collective delusion.

Nobody liked to hear things like that. When she was young, she'd said that and similar once too often. Finding her opinions unwelcome, she'd tried to go as far away from humanity as possible, fetching up in the back end of nowhere on a planet that was itself at the back end of nowhere, cosmically speaking. Out there, in the dry maquis, there was nothing to do but scratch a living and drink. She did the former desultorily, and the latter with great enthusiasm.

She still didn't know why she'd been chosen.

One night, exactly when was not important enough to remember, she returned from the local taverna to find a stranger in her tatty hab-module. There were precisely one hundred and fifty-nine people in her village and the scorched hills around about it. As soon as she saw the silhouette of her visitor in the dark of her living quarters, she knew he was not one of them, primarily because none of her neighbours were warriors of the Legiones Astartes. He was big, even for one of their breed, perched precariously on one of her chairs. His knees were too far off the ground to go under the table, and he had arranged it so it was in front of him, with the only other chair she owned set aside for her to sit upon. Despite his incongruous size, he somehow contrived to be unobtrusive, a trick all the Legion seemed to have.

Intelligent eyes glinted in the depths of a camouflage hood. Throughout their entire meeting, he did not take it down.

'Lydia Myzmadra,' he stated. He didn't ask. She had her gun in her hand before he could blink. That seemed to entertain him.

'Shoot me if you like,' he said. 'If you do, you will never know why you came home to find me in your hovel.' He looked around, finding great amusement in the piles of dirty clothes and the unwashed utensils spilling from the sink. 'A reduction in circumstances, for a woman of your background. I doubt your family would be impressed with your living arrangements.'

'My family's none of your damned business,' she said. She waved the gun barrel at the door. 'Out,' she said.

He remained where he sat. His smile hardened, just a little. 'Let me rephrase what I was saying before. You can try to shoot me. I will kill you.'

'Who are you?' she said.

'I am Alpharius,' he said.

Her gun lowered a fraction. 'The twentieth primarch? Don't be ridiculous.'

'Whether you believe me or not is irrelevant, it is how you will address me,' he said. 'Otherwise "my lord" will do.'

Could it have been him? So many of the Legion looked like their genesire.

'What do you want with me?' she said.

'Straight to the meat of the matter.' He appeared pleased. 'My Legion likes people like you, Lydia.'

'Nobody calls me that,' she said. 'Not ever.'

'We like competent people. We like people who get things done. People we might use.'

'Who says I want using?' she said.

'Please,' he said. He held out an enormous hand. The skin tone was unusual, coppery to the point of metallic. 'Sit.' Despite his politeness, it was not a request. She obliged, but kept her gun up.

'I am looking for someone Terran-born, but who is not too attached. Someone who believes in what the Emperor is doing, but not the way it is being done. Someone who suspects that things are not what they have been told.'

'What are you talking about?'

'You're not frightened, are you?' said Alpharius. Once more, he was pleased. 'The psychological effect of the presence of legionaries on some mortals can be overwhelming. It's worse for we primarchs – I've seen people piss themselves when I walk in the room. But you don't care, do you? You'd shoot me, right now, if you didn't want to know why I was here, and you see my threat is good, that you'll die if you try, so you're not rash. You don't panic. That's good. That's very good.'

'Get to the point, or get out of my house.'

White teeth grinned in the shadow of his hood. 'Very well. The Imperium is doomed. Horus Lupercal, the Warmaster, will fall under the sway of forgotten gods and betray the Emperor. This will happen in a few years. The fate of the galaxy and everything within it is at stake.'

She snorted. 'Nonsense. Is this some kind of test?'

'No.'

'You're going to stop him then?'

'Not exactly. If Horus loses,' said the man who called himself Alpharius, 'the Imperium will be crippled. It will allow these gods to prosper, to the extent that they will eventually overthrow the laws of reality, leading to a catastrophic blending of the warp with the material universe.'

'Surely that would happen if he won?'

'We have… sources that tell a different story. Should Horus win, humanity will burn itself out in an orgy of violence, fatally weakening these entities, these gods.' He made a face at the word. 'Please be aware I use the term loosely. Eventually, it will allow for their destruction, saving all reality. The Emperor has known of these things since the beginning.'

'He lied?' she said. She wasn't surprised.

'Perhaps with good reason,' said Alpharius with a shrug. 'His design is to keep mankind safe. The primarchs, Unity, the Imperium, all of that, but He will not succeed. In trying He will make the problem worse. Apocalyptically so.'

'If you know this now, why don't you stop Horus? Why don't you warn the Emperor?'

'The events cannot be stopped. Even if they could, the result would be the same, or similar – they would happen a few thousand years later, and that is the end of the universe. In simple terms,' he added.

She waved her gun at him. 'What's this got to do with me?'

'We need people to help us. I would like you to help me.'

'Marvellous. Assuming this is all true, why would you tell me? How do I know you're not lying?'

Alpharius shifted. The chair, comically small under him, creaked dangerously.

'Most of the people I speak to don't hear the truth. Some of them believe we are working against the Emperor because we wish to rebel, or that we hate Him, and because they hate Him and wish to rebel themselves they are only too glad to join us. We tell people what they need to hear. Everyone has a lever. For most, it comes down to money or power, or a combination of them. Most people are simple. But someone like you craves neither money nor power. You had both, and walked away from them. Only the truth will do for you. You want to mean something, Lydia Myzmadra. I am offering you the chance to spend your life in pursuit of the worthiest cause of all – the protection of...' He paused, and smiled, as if they were sharing a private joke. 'Of everything,' he concluded.

She laughed at him.

'Let me put this another way, Myzmadra,' he said. 'You are alone, destitute and in danger. You are very far from home. The unification of humanity passes people like you by. You are the kind of person who looks in at society from the outside, never part of the group, always ill at ease, because you can see how foolish other people are, how quickly they are duped, how fast they take on beliefs they know to be false in order to construct a comfortable reality for themselves.

You know instinctively how much they overestimate their understanding of the world. You sneer at their optimism, because you feel only despair. You laugh at their troubles, for their woes are small and pathetic when set against the unfeeling sweep of time. You condemn them for their friendships, because you see betrayal in every smile.' He leaned forwards. 'But what really hurts you, is that you long to be like them, for you know you are no better, that your intelligence might be greater, but ultimately it is as limited as theirs. You know enough to know you know nothing, so you yearn for their society, their delusions and their ignorance. You are tormented, because you understand too much, but comprehend far too little.'

'Riddles and lies,' she snorted.

'It is the Emperor who lied. Calculatedly, and regrettably.'

He was right. She despised her race. She supposed that he expected her to blanch and stammer, and deny it all, or become angry. Once she might have done, but she was too jaded for all that. Not very much later after their meeting, she realised had she evinced any one of those reactions, she would have died at that table.

'And your point is?' she said. With her free hand, she picked a splinter from the wood. Her sharp fingernails were perfectly manicured even then, out there, in that hole. 'I'm not the first woman to look at the apish herds of humanity and hate them for what they are, or to hate myself for being one of them. I came to terms with it.'

The stranger looked around her hovel with a smile on his copper face. 'It seems you have. You've done very well,' he said sarcastically.

'What does it matter to you?' she said. 'Space Marines aren't renowned for their psychological insight.'

'Contrary to popular belief, we weren't all made the same,'

he said. His smile widened. 'Our Legion looks for people with particular qualities. You have them in abundance.'

She raised an eyebrow at that.

'Contrary to popular belief,' he repeated the words so exactly it could have been a recording, 'the Legions have different roles to play. Ours was designed for intelligence and counter-intelligence roles. Infiltration, subversion and propaganda – all the dirty, dark sides of human interaction. Other Legions pull triggers, we pull levers. Illusion,' he said mockingly, waggling his fingers in front of his face. 'Misdirection.'

He looked down. Her gaze followed his unconsciously.

A pistol had appeared on the table between them. Small for him, it would have required both her hands to hold it steady. It wasn't one of the inelegant signature weapons of the Legiones Astartes, the blocky, barking death dealers they bore. It wasn't a boltgun, but a slender, alien thing. It looked quiet.

Details. It was deadly whatever it was, and he didn't need it. She could have run, right then. Fast as she was, she wouldn't have made it out of the room before he grabbed her and broke her neck. She wondered if he'd enjoy it, or if he'd be disappointed in her, or if her death might be used in some way, to make a point to someone else in some other place.

'So,' she said. 'Tell me if I understand correctly. The Emperor's most loyal son is going to rebel, having fallen under the sway of gods we've all been carefully taught don't exist, and you want to help him to win in order to deny said, non-existent ancient gods the opportunity to overrun all of existence.'

'That leaves out a lot of the nuance, but that is the basics of it, yes,' he said.

'And this will result in the extinction of mankind?'

'Sadly, but certainly.'

'So if I act on your behalf, I will die,' she said.

'If you choose not to, you will die in the next few minutes. If you join us, you will die eventually, but I promise
you will not die in vain. Nobody that serves us does.'

'Are you rebels?' she asked, incredulously.

'No,' he said plainly. 'I wish there was another way. Either
humanity dies now, and the universe is saved, or it dies later,
and every living, breathing, thinking thing that exists in this
reality will perish in torment.'

'Then why would you do this?' she asked, genuinely curious; although her death might have been seconds away, it
was worth knowing, just for a moment.

'There are other powers in the world besides these gods.
They are not exactly benevolent, but they are not evil.'

'That's not an answer,' she said. 'Why do you do it?'

'For the Emperor,' he said simply.

That conversation was the most she had ever heard any
one of them say.

She lifted her gaze from the octed carved into the gunstock.
Above the clouds, night was falling; under them darkness
was kept at bay by the bombardment. The world was orange
from the shelling of the breached outwork sector. The aegis
shone a lurid purple. Hugging the shadows, she made her
way to her destination at the very edge of the zone being
fired on by the walls.

There was a turret half a kilometre on, a small version of
the outwork bastions that were themselves small versions of
the Palace towers. Dorn's fortifications had a fractal nature,
each part a smaller reproduction of the greater parts, all
interlocking, covering and supporting each other. From this
simplicity of design arose complexity of defence.

There were four dead officers in the turret command

centre. Their suite of rugged equipment was functioning, but offline, the screens for the cogitators blue fuzzes. Myzmadra was skilled with such devices, and soon had them dancing to her tune. She was sifting through the dataloom when a noise outside had her facing the door, a looted laspistol in her hand.

'I thought I'd find you here,' said Ashul. He stepped through the door, his gun cradled in the crook of his arm. He carried it as if he'd always had it, as if it were a child. 'Did you find anything useful?'

She nodded, keyed the cogitator off then put several shots through it. 'I've found tunnels under the bastions. They present opportunities.'

'Opportunities worth dying over? You were lucky. Chances were that you'd be shelled by Dorn before you got here.'

'We have to seize what resources we have. It's worth a little risk.' She shook her head. 'All this care and attention the primarch Dorn goes to, and these fools have all the data I need copied onto their unit cogitator.' She went through the bodies, checking jewellery and pockets for cypher keys and signum identifiers. 'Anyone could have found it.'

'Anyone did,' said Ashul. 'I thought we were done with this,' he added after a pause. 'After Pluto. When they sent us back. I thought, what more could they possibly want from us?'

'You're never done, Ashul,' she said. She pocketed an ornate ring and a data wand. 'Not with them.'

'The name's Doromek currently, better use it,' Ashul said absently. He looked out the door. 'There will be men here soon. They're regarrisoning this section now the enemy have been forced back. You need to leave. It'll raise awkward questions if you're found here, and you'll be executed if they find those keys on you.'

'Let me worry about that,' she said. 'It's you that should leave.'

He shook his head. 'I'm supposed to be here. I'm acting lieutenant. I volunteered to scout ahead, on account of my proven skill set.' He smiled humourlessly. 'It is my sworn mission to retake this turret. I count it accomplished.'

She scowled at his joking. 'You're making too much of a show of yourself, and you're too close to that trooper.'

'Katsuhiro? He's harmless. We might need him, and others. You said it, we have to make use of the resources we have, and we don't have very many right now.'

She gave him a black look. 'When you've finished playing hail fellow well met, why don't we see about doing what we're supposed to be doing?'

'I get a bit tired of hanging back all the time,' said Ashul. 'And it's working. I'm in now. We'll find life a lot easier if I've got influence. Jainan listens to me. He needs me.'

'You should stop it. You're losing focus. You're drawing attention to yourself.'

Ashul shrugged. 'Attention sometimes works.'

'Be careful.'

'We're going to die,' he said.

Myzmadra gave him a tight nod.

'But not in vain,' she said.

FIFTEEN

Rage and decay
First Captain
Sword arm

'Dorn defies us! The walls should be broken, the streets red with blood. Attack, attack, we must attack!' Angron's growls rang across Lupercal's court. Drool ran from his snarl, vanishing into nothing as it fell outside the imaging field.

'Walls cannot be shouted down,' Perturabo said, his voice the ringing of a leaden bell. *'You have lost your patience with your sanity.'*

'He's not insane,' said Fulgrim sweetly. *'Are you, dear brother?'*

'Do not allow this snake to address me!' roared Angron.

'Cease your yapping, hound,' said Perturabo. *'This is a gathering of intellect, not animals.'*

'Speak with me in person and we shall see who is silenced first!' roared Angron.

'I bested you before, and will do so again,' said Perturabo levelly.

Angron let out a howl of outrage that shook the air.

Abaddon glanced at his genefather's empty throne. Horus was late to the meeting.

'For the Warmaster's sake, Ezekyle,' hissed Kibre. 'Do something.'

'Someone has to,' said Aximand, as the primarchs goaded each other. He made to step forward.

Abaddon grabbed his brother by the arm. He shook his head, his face a warning. Aximand shrugged and stepped back.

'I'll do it.'

'Suit yourself,' Aximand said.

Abaddon stepped forward, but did not speak. He stood in the midst of the primarchs and disdainfully watched their bickering.

'Oh, Angron, my dear brother, your howling grows tiresome,' said Fulgrim. *'Where is Horus?'* He appealed to the room. *'If anyone can get Angron to quieten, it is he.'*

Angron sneered. *'Nothing is more important than–'*

'Do be quiet, Angron,' said Fulgrim. *'There's a good fellow.'*

For a moment Angron stared, wide-eyed with affront, then his face swelled with apoplexy, and he screamed in anger. *'I will not be quiet! I am the chosen of Khorne! You will heed me. You will–'*

'I have heard enough. Cut Lord Angron's audio-feed,' Abaddon said. Adepts of the True Mechanicum working in the background complied. The Red Angel was left a silent, raging ghost.

'Look at how weak you have become,' Abaddon said in disgust. 'Lord Perturabo, you sit at the edge of the system pronouncing your genius and implying no one heeds you. This behaviour is not worthy of you.'

'Do not provoke me, First Captain.'

'Be quiet a minute, or you will find yourself further goaded,'

Abaddon snarled. 'You, Fulgrim, and you, Angron, have whored yourselves out to the gods in the warp.'

Angron raged in silence. Fulgrim tittered girlishly. Abaddon glared at him. Fulgrim pulled a lewd face.

'Where is your majesty, where is your purpose? We stand at the threshold of victory, and you threaten everything with your bickering,' said Abaddon. 'You posture, you rage, you question your Warmaster's orders. It is he who has brought you here. It is he who has ensured your power grows. It is he who made all of this possible. I have seen the brats of decadent nobles behave with more decorum and sensibility.'

Fulgrim clapped all four of his hands slowly. *'So brave, so noble,'* he mocked. *'So bold. The son grows while the father fades. How proud of you he must be.'* Fulgrim leaned closer to the lens capturing his image. *'But careful now, little Ezekyle,'* he purred dangerously. *'You are mighty, but you play in the court of the gods. You cannot murder us as you did your birth father. You do not have the stakes to wager in this game. Back away, small man, and we might let you live.'*

'Do you think Horus would allow you to kill me?' Abaddon said, pacing around the circle of hololithic phantoms. 'He could obliterate you all, any one of you, utterly. You are slaves to your passions where you are not slaves to your gods. Horus is above you, and he is above the entities you worship.'

'Our brother would not put the life of his son before that of his brothers,' said Perturabo. *'You go too far.'*

'Tell that to Lord Lorgar,' said Abaddon. 'Banished, lucky that Horus did not tear him limb from limb. Be careful that you do not further test my father's patience – it is not inexhaustible.'

'Well said,' Aximand muttered under his breath.

'Abaddon. Never speak to me in that way again,' warned Perturabo. *'I am not as indulgent as my brother.'*

'And nor am I,' said Fulgrim.

The door to the court opened and Horus strode in, more alive and vibrant than he had seemed the last time, Abaddon thought.

'Captain Abaddon is correct,' said Horus. 'You disgrace yourselves.' The court trembled at his words. 'Listen to my chosen son as you would to me.' He walked to the centre of the room and rested one of his great talons on Abaddon's shoulder. 'He is my sword arm.'

'What kept you, brother?' asked Fulgrim. *'Why do you call us here and keep us waiting?'*

'I commune with the powers who guide my hand, and strive to ensure our victory in their realm as in this. They say this, that Abaddon is right! You gather power to yourselves and become pathetic for its excesses. Cease your arguments, or face the punishment of your patrons.'

Fulgrim's never-still form flickered. For an instant his perfect, monstrous face was transformed into a mask of terror, then the image blinked, and his mocking smile returned.

Horus paced up to his throne, the Mournival making way for him. His huge bulk shook the court, and he sat. 'Angron,' he said to his brother's image. 'Can you hold your peace for a few moments?'

Angron snarled silently, but nodded.

'Return his voice to him,' Horus commanded. 'You may speak, favoured of Khorne.'

'Brother,' said Angron, remaining calm only by dint of the most immense effort. *'Why do we not attack?'*

'Events proceed as planned,' said Horus. 'I am in control of our strategy. Do you not trust me?'

Horus' unnatural charisma reached across the void, dominating his brother. Angron looked aside in furious shame.

'Yes, my Warmaster.'

Horus swept his gaze around his siblings' images. 'The time has come to enact the second phase of the invasion. Ambassadress Sota-Nul, attend us.'

A hololith unlike the others manifested beneath the apex of the dome. Technology blended with warp magic rendered Sota-Nul in perfect verisimilitude that exceeded even the projections of Magnus. Around her was a constellation of eight smaller images, subsidiary to hers, though each also perfect, and presenting the full gamut of Mechanicum insanity. Every one of these nine tech-adepts had begun life as human beings; now few of them remotely resembled their original form. They had eyes of glass, tentacles, grossly enhanced bodies, multiple arms with tools for hands, exposed innards of glowing glass tubes, all swathed in the black of the New Mechanicum.

Thin lines of silver light linked them into an emblem akin to a compass rose: the octed of Chaos.

'*We are the nine,*' they intoned, their mixed voices of warbles, twittering databursts and synthesised humanity a jarring electronic chorus. '*Nul, Protos, Duos, Tre, Tessera, Pent, Ex, Epta and Oct.*'

'*No Fabricator General, brother?*' Perturabo asked, a sly tone entering his doleful voice.

'Kelbor-Hal is a loyal and trusted ally,' said Horus. 'But Sota-Nul served me well while the Lord of the Mechanicum was penned on Mars. Her acolytes have delivered many marvels to me. Sota-Nul heralded my armies and successfully enjoined several forge worlds to side with us against the slave master of Terra. Her warp tech eases our communications, and reduced our reliance on the cursed Erebus' warp flasks. Ardim Protos found a way to bind the souls of daemons to our Titans. Axmar Tre uncovered the archeo-tech hoard of Periminus. Each one of them has exceeded my demands. Each one of them is a magos of rare talent. Kelbor-Hal shall oversee the ground operations of the forces of Mars, as is his right, but it is to Sota-Nul we turn now to ensure the next phase of the invasion is successful. The Nine Disciples will ensure our victory is swifter and sweeter than it could otherwise be.

'The aegis is sufficiently weakened to permit a larger assault to begin,' Horus continued, addressing the whole room. 'Our attack craft destroy more of their defensive batteries with each sortie. The numbers of their own defence squadrons dwindle with the hour. The efficacy of the Palace outworks is broken. All over Terra, our loyal armies conquer and burn. Now we must take the fight to the walls, and open the way for our allies from the empyrean. *Then*, Angron.' Horus extended a claw at his brother. 'Then you may set foot on the soil of Terra, as may you, Fulgrim. Sota-Nul's acolytes will land their arks upon the surface as eight points of the octed. We shall begin the work of besieging the Palace in earnest. Siege camps shall be established, the arks will be fortresses to oppose the walls. Under their protection, the siege masters of the Mechanicum will establish defences and deploy their engines to break the fortifications.'

Perturabo growled with outrage. *'That is my purpose! You said that I would be given the honour of breaking Dorn's fortress. You do not listen to me, brother. You dismiss my ideas. You do not let me attack the sun of Sol itself to bring this to a speedy conclusion, or to break Terra into rubble. You wave away my plans of planetary Exterminatus. You keep me at arm's length, and now this insult? Dorn's humbling is mine to accomplish!'* His famed temper boiled quickly once provoked, and before he had finished he was shouting.

'I did,' said the Warmaster evenly. 'I meant what I said.

You will have your turn, Lord of Iron. The Mechanicum will prepare the ground for your Legion, so that your genius may be set to work with minimal distraction. Your task on the system fringe is done. Return now. Begin your plans for the contravallation of the Palace.'

Perturabo calmed, reassuming his dour manner like iron plunged into a quenching barrel.

'I have my plans prepared already,' said Perturabo pettishly. *'Dorn cannot stand before me.'*

'When will the Legions land?' said Angron.

'My orders remain as they were. No Space Marine is to set foot on Terra yet,' said Horus.

'A legionary attack will draw out the defenders,' wheedled Fulgrim. *'Let my children out to play, most lordly brother. We can destroy at will, and weaken the Palace defences. I am bored!'*

'I have a role for you. One you will enjoy. Like all the greatest pleasures, it must be deferred a while. Until then, the bombardment continues,' said Horus. 'If we feed our legionaries into the fire piecemeal, we will all burn. The attacks on the walls must be complete, total and overwhelming.'

'What of my Neverborn legions?' said Angron. *'What of this witch's hex that keeps me from battle?'*

Zardu Layak stepped forwards.

'Not him! Hold your tongue, priest. Where is Lord Magnus?' Angron bellowed.

'Yes, Magnus. We would take his word on this subject, not that of this… groveller,' said Perturabo dismissively.

'Let Layak speak,' Horus commanded.

The primarchs fell to grudging quiet.

'The Emperor shields Terra,' said Layak. 'But He cannot do so forever. Blood flows in such torrents upon the Throne-world that it calls across the barrier between the warp and the material realm. Souls flee their bodies in crowds, every one wearing at the fabric of space and time.' He rubbed his fingers together. 'Each death sees the servants of the Pantheon push harder on the veil. When the weight of slaughter is great enough, then they will be called through in their multitudes. By my god-granted vision I see vast legions of the Neverborn ready to take to the field. The door is creaking. The latch rattles. We lack but a key.'

Perturabo was the first to grasp the strategy, and nodded in understanding. *'If father's dogs attack the siege camps, they will spill more blood, and aid the coming of your allies. If they do not, then the Mechanicum may raise engines by the dozen to break the walls. Dorn will see this, but he will have no choice.'* A rare smile broke across Perturabo's features. *'He will have to fight it either way, and give you victory whatever his choice is. A bridgehead of blood!'* To his brothers' amazement, he began to laugh.

'Then I shall land first!' said Angron enthusiastically. *'I shall come at them, and cleave their bodies!'*

'You will not,' said another. A familiar voice, a quiet, rasping, sullen growl, but changed, thickened with phlegm. *'I claimed the task. My Legion will be first to attack the walls, as I pledged to the Warmaster months ago.'*

Mortarion, primarch of the Death Guard, entered through the grand doors of Lupercal's court. This was not Mortarion as his brothers remembered him. He was changed, like Angron, Fulgrim and Magnus, lifted by the Pantheon and given new form. Always among the tallest of the primarchs, he had grown further, his famine-spare frame pushed to great height. Tattered moth's wings furled on his back. The scythe *Silence* had grown with its master, become as long as a vox-transmission pole. Mortarion appeared sickly, his face scarred by disease and his eyes milky with cataracts. Fluid wept from craters in his dirty armour, while all around him swirled a dense, stinking fog.

Where he passed the door guard, Abaddon's Justaerin fell heavily. Black fluid leaked from perished seals and bloody phlegm coughed from their breathing grilles. The sounds of armour closing itself against the environment filled the room, but it did no good. The Terminators suffered in the grip of sickness. Mortarion continued forwards, felling Horus' elite by his very presence.

'Back away from him!' Abaddon commanded. 'Seal the room!'

Atmospheric cyclers ceased turning. Machines bleeped out tones of compliance. Still the Lord of Death marched forwards. Kibre began to cough behind his mask. Aximand took several steps back, his face greening as he fumbled on his helm. Layak dropped to his knees, singing praise in the ear-burning tongue of his worship, but he too struggled to breathe Mortarion's miasma. Of them all, only Horus, Torma-geddon and Abaddon were left unaffected. A stench wreathed the Lord of Death that defied any kind of description. Human senses lacked the capacity to experience it in fullness. So foul, so pungent with rot and sickly life was it, that it triggered Abaddon's omophagea, and he tasted a bouquet of miseries sublime in their variety. It shocked him to his soul that he could breathe. He looked to the others choking on Mortari-on's foetor, and yet when the primarch approached Abaddon, he inhaled easily, though the stench appalled him.

Mortarion stopped a few feet from his brother's throne. Pearlescent eyes stared down into brown, both afire with inner power that was not of the material realm. His breath-ing was laboured, rattling in his lungs so that each exhalation sounded like his last. Puffs of reeking corpse-gas jetted from Mortarion's mask.

Aximand and Kibre dragged themselves back, behind the throne, crawling as far as they could from the corrupted primarch. Retching grated from Kibre's voxmitter as he vomited into his helmet. Aximand pulled himself into a corner, managed to roll onto his back, and lay there stupefied.

The Lord of Death slammed the ferrule of *Silence* upon the floor hard.

'My Warmaster, I heed your call.'

With those words he knelt. The height his transformation had bestowed meant that he was as tall as the seated Warmaster even when he bowed.

Abaddon suppressed a sneer. Such weakness. The Lord of Death had traded his position as a lord of men to become a slave of the gods.

Angron paced in and out of the field of view of his holo-emitter. Fulgrim giggled. Perturabo glared.

'My brother, we welcome you,' said Horus. 'Rise.'

Bones popped as the Lord of Death stood again. *'I come to fulfil my promise and lead the assault upon the Palace.'* His voice, once a pure bass, was a hoarse whisper.

'You are greatly gifted by our patrons,' Horus said, taking in his brother's transformation. 'You will not be able to set foot upon Terra.'

'I have patience. My sons will go before me to prepare the way. They are ready,' said Mortarion. *'We bring new weapons for an old war. My warriors have transcended the limitations of mortality. Nothing can harm them, while I have seven plagues for you to unleash upon Terra. Let the unseen soldiers of bacillus and virus reap the foe, and add their deaths to the total, and when the tally pleases Father Nurgle, then I shall descend to the Palace, and take my vengeance upon the False Emperor.'*

'Do you see?' said Horus. 'You all must wait, but not for

long.' He raised his voice to address them all, but stared
Angron in the eye. 'The second phase of the invasion begins
tonight. Once the Mechanicum begin the construction of
their siege engines, then Mortarion's Legion shall be given
the honour of being first upon Terra.'

'*No!*' shouted Angron. '*No! It should be me!*'

'It is my will,' said Horus, 'that the Death Guard attack
first.'

SIXTEEN

A new pattern
The bombardment continues
Sea of mud

Palace outworks, Daylight Wall section 16, 1st-13th of Tertius

A new pattern was set. For two weeks after the first landing, the enemy attacks followed the same routine. Swarms of enemy bombers and fighters descended from orbit while the fleet pounded the void shield periphery. Somehow, the exact mechanism was beyond Katsuhiro, the enemy got through, and while the ships in orbit hurled their fury at the ground, the attack craft bombed and strafed everything they could. Every attack saw the aegis lose efficacy, so that each successful raid inflicted more damage. The shields over the Palace proper were inviolable; not so those around the edges. The trench lines took a pounding. Kilometres of works were obliterated, along with the men and women guarding them. The nature of the landscape before the Daylight Wall was transformed. The perfect flatness of planed away mountains was upheaved, and new peaks and declivities carved by orbital attack. Quakes shook the ground as the planetary crust was disturbed.

All the while, the enemy landed more of his troops. They came down as regular as the tides, rising up across the twisted landscape to break against the fortifications in spumes of blood. Though it was cold at such an altitude, the stink of spoiling flesh infiltrated everything.

The sun was gone, hidden by clouds of ash black as the sackcloth of myth. Winds laden with corpse dust blew from far-off cities. When the visibility was good enough, they saw the funeral pyres of distant hives.

Spring approached. The energy poured upon Terra caused a rapid warming, and snow turned to rain, even at the top of the world. Freezing mud clogged everything. Watered now by blood, the ground reeked horribly. The recruits fought in the clothes they had been drafted in. Nobody had anything to change into, nor was there water to wash. They became a dirty tribe, skulking behind their broken ramparts in the shadows of the Imperium's greatest fortress. Whatever their original skin colour they were remade in a single shade, caked in grey dust, red raw eyes startling in their filthy faces. Dust coated the whole world. Their clothes took on the hue of the ground, the fortifications, the downed ships. Everything was the same colour, everything smelled the same, living and dead.

A lucky few were given coats to stave off the cold. Katsuhiro was not among them. To begin with he cut a hole in the middle of his blanket and wore it over his head as a poncho. He was never warm, even when the dead provided him with a padded jacket and trousers more suited to the climate. All were bloodied, and covered in excrement and rotting flesh. He had ceased to care. The cold was a worse killer than the guns. Battle was an infrequent peril. The cold was persistent.

Sometimes, it rained a toxic slime of pollutants from the

burning cities. When it stopped, it left behind a metallic
stink. Those who dared to drink the rain perished. Some
tried for lack of water – thirst and hunger tormented them
all – but after a time, some drank the water purposefully
in order to escape. The rain brought other dangers. When
tech-adepts and their robotic guardians paced the outworks
on their inscrutable tasks, rad clickers rattled loud as hys-
terical ravens.

'We're all dead,' Katsuhiro said, to no one in particular,
one night when they tried to snatch some rest. His teeth
wobbled in his gums. His hair was falling out. 'The question is when.'

'That's the question asked the moment you were born,
boy,' said Runnecan. He was one of the few Katsuhiro knew.
He never learned many of the others' names. The conscripts
hadn't made much of an effort to get to know one another.
Death took most before familiarity could set in.

Sleep was only ever taken in snatches. Watches were four
hours long. The enemy could come at any time, and did.
Katsuhiro's time was filled with terrifying battles repuls-
ing hordes of raving traitors, sheltering from the bombs, or
engaged in backbreaking manual labour repairing the fortifications. Their efforts were overseen by tech magi, not the
VII Legion as the conscripts hoped. At least sometimes the
Martians lent their servitors or constructs to the task, though
machines and cyborgs were just as likely to stand aloof while
sentient men worked themselves to death.

Daily, trench networks spidered out from nexuses like
Bastion 16, bridging shattered sections of the original rampart system, or breaking up the kill-zone between the lines
into defensible boxes. Sometimes they looped out into the
plains to create deeper zones of defence for the bastions, or
incorporate lumps of wreckage into the plan. Remarkably

quickly, Lord Dorn's original circles of defence were remade, but as soon as they were done, the enemy did his work again. Trench lines were smoothed away, along with the lives of those within, and the digging started anew. Constant attacks broke up the stone of the geoformed plain, but although this eased the cutting of trenches, it churned flesh into the mix, making the work abominable. The walls of the networks were mortared by the remains of the dead.

Such things Katsuhiro saw in those two weeks. A lifetime's supply of fear and awe packed into a terrible winter. There were rains of debris that created an optimist's wealth of shooting stars; each wish Katsuhiro made was not to die. Sometimes, huge elements of sundered craft made it down from the heavens, or entire vessels cut burning wakes overhead. Once, a capital ship, its back broken, fell on the Palace. It appeared suddenly through the ash cloud, its burning lighting up the land. It plummeted towards the Palace centre, disappearing from view behind the monumental walls moments before impact. They expected the worst. Men stood from their defences pointing. A voice called.

'The Emperor has fallen!'

The detonation that followed could only confirm their fears. A brief sun rose in the west over the Palace, vaporising the Warmaster's falling ordnance and half blinding the conscripts with its brilliance. For a second a searing false day bled all colour away, then winked out, leaving after-images in the eyes of its witnesses, and the rumble of thermic shock rolling over Himalazia's distant peaks.

'The Emperor!' someone whispered.

Further down the line people were weeping.

Yet the Palace guns fired on, punching glowing holes through the pall of ash smothering the sky, and the Warmaster's fleet returned the same, while the aegis danced with purple, pink and blue arcs of discharge as it had for days and days.

'The Emperor lives, so do you. The shields took it!' shouted one of Jainan's veteran bullies. He moved down the line, shoving people back to the wall. 'No danger! All mass and energy gone into the warp. That's the aegis' job or we'd all be dead a thousand times already. Back to your stations. The war's not over yet.'

Indeed it was not.

Sometimes, hours passed with no attempt made on sector 16. Its bastion heart fired ceaselessly, one small part of the Palace's endless array of weaponry. Three macro cannons with limited traversal studded its outwards-facing walls. The rearmost portion was free of guns, to prevent their use against the fortifications should it fall to the enemy. Between these iron-collared behemoths, the slimmer barrels of lascannons protruded, and neat stacks of heavy bolters in vertical series. The top was crowned with anti-aircraft weaponry, whose quad cannons, each as big as super-heavy tank barrels, banged endlessly away. Their distinctive chattering became the background to Katsuhiro's life, so constant and unvarying that he only really became aware of them when they stopped firing briefly to cool.

Behind Bastion 16 were Bastions 15 and 14, offset from the outermost tower to provide the greatest amount of cover. Bastion 14 made the transition from active defence to blackened stump sometime around the end of Secundus, taking a direct hit from orbit that sent its magazines up in a pyrotechnic display. Bastion 15 went soon after.

Katsuhiro lost track of the date. It seemed to him that time flowed differently on the line. Life became a series of horrifying incidents interspersed by periods of exhausted terror. If he had been familiar with the old Catheric myths, Katsuhiro would have thought himself in hell.

Despite all the privations and loss of liberty the rebellion had incurred on Terra, and the sorrow and the death of hope for man's future, the war had been far away. Now he was living it.

Thus was the pattern of the siege set, until, inevitably, it changed.

SEVENTEEN

Blood and skulls
Father's wrath
Five of Eight

The Conqueror, *Terran near orbit, 14th of Tertius*

The *Conqueror* shook to the steady beat of its guns. Since arrival in orbit over the Throneworld, they had not ceased. Overseers worked their gunnery crews to death. Weapons fired to the point of failure. Reports that the magazines were running empty went unheeded.

The Legion did not care. The World Eaters could not hear the booming of cannons. They did not feel the decks vibrate. Their skulls sang with the sawing song of the Butcher's Nails, and that obliterated all other sensation.

At being denied the spear point, Angron had lost all vestiges of restraint. The Legion agreed with him.

Violence had been endemic on the *Conqueror* for years now. The thralls knew to keep themselves apart and seal themselves away where they could, lessening the effects of the great massacres that had come after the Thramas Crusade. With little to spend their rage on, fights broke out between rival squads of legionaries, staining decks that were already black with mortal vitae with transhuman blood. Those particularly afflicted were brought under control only with much bloodshed, which provoked more. Others made for the embarkation decks and the lesser hangars, eager to be off the ship in defiance of their orders to remain aboard.

Angron could not be restrained again as he had been before Ullanor. He strode his vessel as a pillar of living rage. The deck plates shook to his tread. The air trembled to his words. Where he went, lives ended, but when he learned his sons attempted to depart the *Conqueror*, his rage could finally no longer be contained, and his rampage cut a bloody swathe through his Legion.

'None shall depart!' he roared. *'I go first! None shall take skulls on the Throneworld's soil before I!'*

Khârn ran in his genefather's footsteps. Where the daemon primarch trod, the metal smoked. Heat as much as anger radiated from Angron. Mortals ran from him. Those that did not fell convulsing, bleeding from their eyes, or else attacked one another in awful outbursts of violence.

'Khârn, I have reports of a demi-company attempting to breach hangar nineteen, not far from your position.'

'Hnnnh,' Khârn swallowed bloody spittle. 'We are nearly there, Lotara,' he said. 'Angron knows.' Speaking with the shipmistress calmed his fury a little, but not much. He struggled to concentrate.

'That is not good.'

'I... I... hnnnh, I would agree,' Khârn finally managed.

'You will not land before me!' Angron roared, and sprinted ahead. *'I will be first!'*

'I must go.' Khârn swore, and ran after him. Angron pulled ahead easily. His sword was ready and trailing black vapours.

Khârn caught up as the primarch was slaughtering his

way through a hundred World Eaters. The fools had been throwing themselves against the hangar doors, despite all of them being sealed at Khârn's order. The heavy portals were scarred with melta burns. The disobedient company had made little headway before their father arrived to punish their presumption.

Angron's lessons came at the edge of his sword, and all were fatal.

'You dare? You dare!' Angron roared. He cut one of his sons in half from helm to crotch. The sword wailed as it swung, blood boiling from its edges. Always huge, Angron had grown to immense stature since his change, dwarfing his sons. He caught one up in his left hand, his fingers easily grasping the Space Marine's chest, and slammed him repeatedly into a wall. Armoured fingers prised at Angron's grip, but nothing the World Eater did could free him.

'I will be first upon Terra!' roared Angron. *'You are not worthy! It is my honour! Khorne demands it! The Blood God decrees it! You shall burn in lakes of fire for your temerity!'*

Several hacked at the primarch's limbs. The blows his brass armour did not turn aside sunk only a little way into his daemonic flesh. Sprays of scalding ichor hissed over the primarch's assailants, blinding those without helmets. His skin rippled around the wounds, closing them quickly. Angron ignored those who attacked him, and continued to pound the warrior in his fist against the wall.

'Traitor!' roared Angron. *'Usurper!'*

The ceramite cracked, followed by the warrior's ribs. Blood gushed from rupturing flesh. The primarch cast his dead son aside, and turned his blade upon the others.

Angron would not rest until everyone in the corridor was dead. Khârn tried to think of how to calm his primarch, to bring his rage to manageable levels, but the answer eluded him. His own reason was drowning in a tide of blood. The Butcher's Nails pounded into his skull. The smell of spilt vitae excited his senses. He swallowed a mouthful of saliva, suddenly conscious of a flood of it streaming down his chin. Before he lost himself entirely, he reopened communications with Lotara.

'Seal decks eighty-four through ninety, portside of the spinal way. Every entrance.' He could barely speak. His vision swam. He wanted to fight. He needed to kill. With heroic effort he growled out his orders. 'Order this deck cleared. Dispatch suppression teams to all other hangars, ship-wide. Lock them all down. Prime remote weapons to kill on sight. No one leaves this ship. Angron will slaughter us all if anyone tries. Seal all portals on this deck except forwards gate nine. Open all doors leading to the lower decks beyond. If Angron wants to keep fighting, he can do it among the thralls.'

'Confirmed. No one runs from the Conqueror,' Lotara said. 'What about you? Khârn?'

Khârn could no longer hear. Words belonging to something else forced themselves out of his mouth.

'Blood for the Blood God!' he roared, and joined battle at his father's side.

Ark Mechanicum Pent-Ark, *Terran near orbit, 14th of Tertius*

Clain Pent's Ark Mechanicum took its first orbital breach with good graces. Spherical and of a mass similar to a large asteroid, it was not designed for such a landing, but it was not the first void-ship to break Terra's atmospheric envelope during the siege, and it would not be the last.

Pent's lair was situated right at the centre of the vessel, in an armoured sub-sphere that could be ejected in the event of the ark's destruction. It was a ship within a ship, equipped with its own void shields, drives and external weapons systems. Throughout the descent, Pent's metaphorical hand hovered over the activation codes in the ship's infosphere.

He had his own clade of lesser servants. Some of the disciples of Sota-Nul, such as Ardim Protos, had no followers of their own, whereas the likes of Illivia Epta kept legions of them. For Pent, eight followers were sufficient. Not too many to control, enough to be useful, and with the additional bonus of flattering Nul through imitation. The eight of them served him as ship crew, engineers, advisers, agents and all other things.

<Great magos,> said Acolyte Penta-7, who hunched low over the auspex scopes cramming the forwards portion of the command dome. <The Palace Androcline Battery has acquired us as a primary target. Defence lasers cycling to fire.>

<Blind their augurs,> Pent blurted. He used direct voxwave communication, always. The body he wore had a mouth, but it was not his own. Pent's preferred disciplines were those of biomancy and cybertheurgy. He kept a stable of bodies of his own design to wear. He'd chosen his current one for its combat efficacy. It was large, heavily muscled, being vat-grown from abhuman gene stock, and heavily modified with bionics. Not that he intended to do any fighting; he wore it for appearance's sake.

Outwardly, he showed no sign of fear. Within his suit of flesh, it was a different story. Pent was little more than a brain in a jar hidden in the armoured chest cavity of his host. He had no face of his own to display worry or similar emotions, while that of his temporary body was immobile. Pent found joy in manipulating biological matter, but he saw no need for the humanity in them; the biological was merely another form of machine. The face had been cured upon the skull and painted brightly so that it looked like a carnival figure, and in whose permanently open mouth Pent's glowing sensor array hid. But a magos can betray himself in other ways than an unguarded scowl or frown, and Pent kept a tight rein on his external links in case an involuntarily expelled data packet revealed his dismay.

<Maintain void shields at maximum intensity. Increase displacement index to highest value.> The command, delivered as electric pulses, was transmitted instantaneously via augmitter wired into his host's vestigial brainstem. The ship shook when the order was executed. Air is remarkably hard and hot when encountered from the void, and the shields treated it as they would any other threat, shunting it partially into the warp.

The violence of the reaction was alarming. The ship dropped by sudden degrees as the voids annihilated huge pockets of atmosphere, and accelerated into the lacuna, then decelerated abruptly when air rushed back in.

An outside observer would have seen Pent in his grotesque body and his eight servants, all augmented to more or less horrific degrees, working quietly but for a gentle bleeping passing between them. The peacefulness of the data exchange belied the ferocious argument it conveyed.

<I respectfully demand that the void opacity matrix be reduced to allow free passage of air,> spoke Acolyte Penta-1.

<The terse nature of your request denies protocols of respectful behaviour,> rejoined Acolyte Penta-2.

<Penta-1, regardless of respectfulness and appropriateness of irony in delivery of honorific, has valid concerns,> said Penta-5, who was female once, but had transformed herself

into a waving shock of metal tentacles arranged around a metal box. <Current accelerative/decelerative forces risk terminal hull compromise.>

The ship lurched to the side. External gravity was taking hold, throwing the grav-plating's effects out of true. Miniature gravitic vortices tugged at the adepts' black robes.

<Hold course and current void parameters,> commanded Clain Pent. <This I so command. Atmospheric void shock is preferable to atomisation by ground battery fire.>

Attacks from the ground were coming in hard. Machines sang their hosannas of alarm as the first of the void generators burnt out. Immediately, servitors detached themselves from deep-set alcoves and clomped off the bridge to enact repairs. Pent reviewed the damage in his internal data-feeds. They were wasting their time.

<Quaternary void generator burn out,> buzzed Acolyte Penta-3. <Time to next ground volley, zero point nine seconds. Primary, secondary, quintenary void generators holding. Tertiary nearing collapse.>

By the time Penta-3 had finished, the next hit slammed home.

<Blind their augurs!> demanded Pent. Fear suppressant swirled into the fluids of his cerebrarium, dulling the panic.

<Negatory,> responded Acolyte Penta-7. <Augur clouding ineffective. Palace noospheric security network impenetrable. Enemy cogitation reaction time superior to *Pent-Ark* data illusion capability.>

Pent's brain twitched. Well-protected noospheres were the bane of the Mechanicum's war. He cursed the day Koriel Zeth had conceived them. Though the one at Calth had been easily corrupted, the slaves of the Emperor had learned quickly. When any lesser system could be subverted, a noosphere on guard was nigh impossible to breach.

Like Dorn's walls.

He was reminded there would be no lesser systems in the battle below, whether in the warp, the materium or the electronic ether world of machines. They were assailing the Palace of the Emperor Himself.

Another thrill of fear, more deeply felt this time, shook his amygdala. He really ought to have it removed.

<Bring us down more quickly!>

<Confirmation,> said Penta-4. Thrusters fired on the upper surface of the ark, pushing it faster into Terra's churning atmosphere.

There were no windows on the *Pent-Ark*. They were weaknesses. Pent was in full agreement with the primarch Perturabo on that. Views of the exterior were displayed via hololithic representation and pure-data displays comprised of abstract symbols. Less dramatic to view, perhaps, but so much more efficient.

<A second battery has locked on to your vessel, oh great eminence,> Penta-7 reported.

So unfair, thought Pent. The ark ships of the other seven disciples were also coming down, and all of them were screened by fleet assault. Why was he being singled out? He would petition the lords of the warp for more favourable luck after they landed.

<Predicted intersection of plasmic streams in four, three, two, one…>

If they landed.

The *Pent-Ark* shook, flinging the adepts about in their restraints. The reactors warbled at having to increase their power output, but the ship stabilised.

<Damage minimal,> Penta-7 reported.

<Shields holding,> Penta-3 added.

<Incoming wideband datapulse,> Penta-2 code-blurted.

<Infiltration attempt by Throne-slaved Mechanicum. Releasing data-jinn. Thwarting.> A pause of several microseconds had Clain Pent fearing the worst. He'd always had an active imagination. During battle that was a curse.

<Thwarted,> Penta-2 finally reported. <Ongoing interference from external Throne-slave sources. Cogitation efficiency compromise at thirteen per cent. Holding.>

<The ship nears the landing zone. Preparing for impact reduction.>

'Show me Terra. I wish to see our target.' This time Clain Pent spoke aloud in the standard Gothic, his rasping voice emanating from a voxmitter stapled to his host's flesh. An indulgence, but it seemed appropriate to the occasion.

<Compliance,> Penta-2 responded.

The middle of the room vanished, replaced by a view of the ground. The last streamers of ash cloud smothering Terra's skies wriggled past the external augurs, giving Pent a view of his destination. He was looking directly down, but the image was presented vertically, so that it appeared, from Pent's point of view, as if he were running towards it. Back when he had such things as a vestibular system, effects like that had made him feel mightily nauseous. Thankfully, such weaknesses were far behind him.

As a biologian, Pent was apt to draw comparisons with fauna. From above, the Palace resembled a chelonian beast. He saw the inner precincts, isolated from the main body of the city behind the edifice of the Lion's Gate, as a head extended on a neck. Being roughly circular and several times larger than the Sanctum Imperialis, the other Palace districts resembled the great shield of a turtle's shell.

The impression was fleeting. The *Pent-Ark* was coming down to the east, near the Helios Gate in the Daylight Wall, and on a parallel with the Eternity Wall space port. As the ship neared the ground, perspective shifted, and Pent's view of the Palace as a whole was lost.

Thousands of fires burned on a cratered plain fronting the eastern walls. Defensive lines wriggled their way across the terrain, like the marbling of fat in meat. Flights of attack ships from both sides swarmed thickly over the battlefield.

<There, the Daylight Wall,> he said, his thoughts highlighting the fortification on the hololith. Thread-thin from that altitude, it was rapidly thickening into significance.

Idle curiosity led him to superimpose old orbital views over the scene – first, the old Himalazian mountains and valleys, then over that the artificial plain the Emperor had levelled around His sprawling creation. After millions of years of stasis, the area had gone from the natural repetition of geoforms to rigidly imposed order to the void-ship graveyard in less than a few centuries. The plains were shattered. The corpses of fallen vessels were scattered everywhere, and the tides of armies moving over the land stained it black.

Lower they went. The augurs flashed with every hit upon the shields. His acolytes burbled their status reports, but Pent paid them little attention. Instead his view was fixed upon the actions of the Palace aegis. It shimmered under the bombardment, revealing its complex, cellular structure. Far superior to standard void shielding, it was one of a kind. If Pent still had a digestive tract to call his own, his mouth would have been salivating at the prospect of learning its secrets.

But first the aegis had to fall. He was proud to be playing a part in that.

The wall grew larger and larger under the ship's keel, perturbing Pent with its scale. Then that moved off to the left as they came down. The Katabatic Plains filled the holo side to side. The sights of individual skirmishes became clear, rapid, chaotic exchanges of las light slashing across blackened ground, and the flash of explosions like flowers on bare earth.

More impacts were troubling the ship now as smaller weapons drew a bead on it. The void shield arrays chimed constantly. Large hits shuddered the shielding still, taking down two more of the *Pent-Ark*'s layered protective fields.

<Landing cycles initiated,> intoned Penta-4. A great shaking took the craft. Pent saw individual men on the ground briefly, before the vibration blurred focus away from the augurs, reducing the ventral view to a brown smear.

Bringing down a ship the size of the *Pent-Ark* was no small feat, and deleterious to its physical condition. It would likely never ply the void again once it set down, but the sacrifice of his personal ship was nothing compared to what Clain Pent would gain should the Warmaster be victorious.

Screaming alarms forewarned of imminent arrival on Terra's soil. Thrusters roared and the bombardment intensified, taxing the vessel's shielding hard.

Clain Pent gritted the memory of teeth.

<Touchdown complete,> Penta-4 announced, when the screaming of the thrusters seemed about to break open the world.

The ship settled. The engines cut out. The thunder of battle reasserted itself as the dominant noise.

Pent drew himself up. Now was his moment.

<Prime all automata. Redirect shield focus. Divert reactor power to shield generators.>

His acolytes worked fast, both physically and within the sacred world of the machines. The void shields were realigned, clamping hard onto the earth, and extending outwards to cover an area around the ship emanating two hundred metres out from its hull.

<Prepare external portals.>

<Automata awoken,> reported Penta-2.

<Tech thralls active,> added Penta-1.

<Machine-spirits awakened,> said Penta-5.

<External portals primed for opening,> said Penta-3.

Pent's grotesque body leaned forwards, huge hands gripping the railing around his command pulpit.

<Execute.>

The sides of the *Pent-Ark* opened like petals. Ramps slid out from housings. Armoured doors opened.

The servants of the Order of Nul marched out.

At seven other equidistant points around the Palace, the same procedure was undertaken by the rest of the disciples of Sota-Nul. Their ark ships put out a stream of cyborgs and semi-autonomous mechanisms, forbidden machine intelligences and things motivated by essences of darker sorts. They began working as soon as they walked off the ships, ignoring the weapons fire that punctured the void shields of their transports and shot them down, neat and as orderly as ants. Though each device had a governing mind of its own, be it human, machine or otherwise, all were slaved to the will of the Machine-God, as enacted by the eight. Under the disciples' direction they began the next phase of the Warmaster's plan.

Such variety there was among these creations. Giant, armoured earth-moving machines came out first, beginning to heap up high banks of stone extending from the sides of the grounded arks as soon as they emerged. Teams of noo-linked servitors armed with melta-cutters followed behind, burning tunnels into the stone to house command centres, and carving trench networks behind the banks. Machines and prefabricated sections of buildings were wheeled out, their erection commencing before the fusion-smoothed ground

had cooled. Among them went heavily armoured adepts and
followers of the myrmidon creed, who strode the battlefield
with arrogant disdain for the fury the enemy threw at them.

Weapons fire from the walls zeroed in on these fledging
networks, but in doing so they took pressure off the mortal
servants of Horus, allowing ragged hordes of traitors deeper
into the outworks. After weeks of attacks, the outworks were
much disrupted, and though the arks set down close to the
outermost perimeter, much was in ruin and there was little
resistance to be found there.

Physical defences were the least of the New Mechanicum's
assets. Within two hours, the framework of siege camps was
in place, and growing outwards. When the excavators reached
the limits of the arks' void shields, more machines rolled
out from the innards of the craft. Some bore giant shields of
adamantium, others energy mantlets of varying type. They
moved in precise order along newly carved roads, stopped,
turned at forty-five degrees and presented their fronts to the
enemy walls.

<Our passengers inform us that they are about to activate
their defences,> said Penta-5.

<See to it their mechanisms do not disrupt out own shield-
ing,> Clain Pent ordered.

<Compensating,> Penta-3 said.

A few hits struck the hull as the void shields were recali-
brated. Now was a moment of vulnerability. Through senses
integrated with his ship, Pent felt the beat of activating
power supplies radiating from the outside.

The pulse built to a crescendo. Clain Pent cackled as the
energy mantlets of the Ordo Reductor sprang into life across
the siege camp and a wall of roseate light leapt between
the machines.

He glanced inwardly to his datacore, running a critical

mind over the plans contained therein. The Ordo Reductor would be piecing together their grand cannons very soon, but he had his own work to do, a project of such ambitious scale he was daunted by it. Monumental engineering was required, and sorcery to bind an appropriately powerful soul.

He watched the energy screens extending further out from the *Pent-Ark*. Soon, behind them, his grand work would begin.

EIGHTEEN

We are symbols
Grounded Angel
A subterranean break

Eternity Wall, 3rd-7th of Quartus

Forethoughts of death afflicted Sanguinius more often as the days passed. The vision of Horus, standing over him in leering triumph, leaked into his waking hours.

Dorn had little time for him, and when he sought out the Sigillite for company he was nowhere to be found. Consumed with foreboding, the Great Angel sent himself out upon a tour of the walls. He did not tell Dorn. He had no wish to hear another lecture about keeping himself safe.

'I am more than a symbol,' he had said to Dorn.

'Your value as such should not be underestimated,' Dorn replied.

'Then I should put myself to use and be seen on the wall.' He would be gainsaid no further, and left Dorn fuming.

Dorn was right. All of them were symbols, and though he hated the role his father had placed upon him and which

Guilliman had exploited, he took upon himself the bur-
den of humanity's hopes again. This time he did not fly. He
went on foot, surrounded by all the ceremony his position
allowed so that the people would better see him.

Azkaellon insisted they stay upon the walls and not venture into the city wards.

'The streets are not safe,' he said. There was unrest throughout the Palace, the worst in the outlying districts close to
the walls. Food and water were scarce, fear was in plentiful supply. Privation did the work of ten thousand enemy
operatives, tying down troops to watch civilians when they
would better serve the defence on the walls.

Eventually Sanguinius relented, and they stayed out of
the city on the perimeter defences, where the Angel might
be seen by the populace from afar, and the warriors of the
Legions stood at guard with predictable discipline.

He set out with a dozen standard bearers, both imag-
nifers and signifers. The serried banners of the IX Legion
made an awe-inspiring sight in ranks behind the primarch,
and the winged figures of the Sanguinary Guard swooped
overhead, weapons ready. Their wargear glinted in the fires
of the bombardment, but there was more – an inner light
that shone from the primarch, so those who saw him said.
To these lucky witnesses, the Blood Angels appeared as a
procession of demigods passing along the walls. Wherever
Sanguinius went, memories of sunlit dawns were kindled,
and people remembered better times, and hoped that those
times might yet return. The arbitrators and enforcers of each
city block he passed reported a calming of mood, and a ces-
sation of violence that lasted several days.

His procession took him many days, past several areas
facing various siege camps of the Dark Mechanicum, but in
time he found himself staring down the Daylight Wall, on

that section overlooked by the heaped massif of the Eternity Wall space port.

Sanguinius' stride was the speed of a legionary's jog, which was the speed of an unmodified human running, so they travelled many kilometres in a few hours, and by the closing of the day, by which point Sanguinius had been on the Daylight Wall for seven hours, they had covered nearly a hundred, and so made their way through lesser league-castles to the Helios Gate.

The party headed directly for the command centre at the tower's heart. A thousand men and women laboured in a modest recreation of the Grand Borealis Strategium. Emergency lumens saturated the spherical room with threatening red, and though thousands of hololiths and other displays provided illumination of other hues, they were too weak to banish the bloody glow.

Once more Raldoron greeted him.

'My lord,' he said.

'The section where the first tower was brought down has been repaired?' the primarch asked. His eyes went to screens showing the enemy siege camp on the horizon, aglow with active shielding and flashing with the work of construction.

'Thane's men did as they pledged,' said Raldoron. 'Truly, they can work miracles with false stone. The wall there is plugged, and the walkways reconnected. They have repaired most of the damage so far inflicted on my section, my lord, while Salamanders repair ruptured power networks and bring guns back to life. It is good to see our kindreds working together. I thought not to see the like again, there has been so much suspicion bred between Legions.'

'But there is still damage.' Sanguinius did not criticise. There was damage everywhere, worst on the far north of the Dusk Wall on the opposite side of the Palace, where a score of major towers had been reduced to rubble by arcane energy cannons, and the wall only held at great cost.

'Eighty-seven way castles from the five hundred in my protection are damaged, four lost entirely,' said Raldoron. 'The Helios Gate comes under protracted attack with each aerial foray. The aegis here is failing. Every attack sees more void blisters scoured from their mountings, though the Emperor's squadrons make them suffer for it. I fear what Horus' Martian lackeys have in store for us behind that energy screen.'

'We have been lucky thus far,' said Sanguinius. 'The walls are holding past Dorn's more optimistic estimates.' He ran his gaze over the displays, away from the live feeds covering the siege camp. 'The outworks less so,' he said, gesturing to the images of scarred, twisted lands where trenches, walls and men had been only a fortnight before. 'The enemy continue to test our defences, and taunt us with their intent.' He pointed at the shimmering energy fields of the siege camp. 'This is a ritual. The Palace is the epicentre. I imagine whatever they plan will be fuelled by blood.'

All the Blood Angels present had been at Signus, and at Davin. What had been consigned to the realm of impossibility was now a matter of course.

'Sorcery must be accounted for strategically like any other factor of war. We help them by fighting, we lose if we stand back. We are damned if we do and damned if we do not.'

'An ancient saying,' said Raldoron.

'But apt,' said Azkaellon.

'The conscripts fight bravely,' said Raldoron. 'They hang on, and repulse the enemy every time, though they dwindle in number daily and I am forced to order the wall guns activated more frequently to bombard compromised sections. I regret we cannot go down to aid them ourselves, but I understand my orders,' he added.

'Lord Dorn forbade me from fighting outside the walls,' said Sanguinius. He turned his sad, noble eyes onto his equerry. 'He did not forbid us to venture outside.'

'My lord?'

'Let us go down outside the wall. I want to go among them. I want to see the troops. I want to tell them their heroism is valued.'

'There is no attack at the moment,' said Raldoron thought-fully, and no enemy near the gate, but the bombardments come without warning.'

'There are other considerations.' Azkaellon stepped in front of his primarch. 'There have been mutinies on the line.'

'You suggest that I, a son of the Emperor, have something to fear from my father's subjects?' Sanguinius said.

'You are not immortal, my lord,' said Azkaellon quietly. As Sanguinius' death approached, all the Blood Angels had a foreboding that their lord might leave them soon. They felt it in their hearts and in their humours. Azkaellon's words hung over them, like the dying echoes of a funeral bell.

'Nothing truly is.' Sanguinius smiled sadly. 'But I do not die today. Gather additional legionaries if it will make you feel easier, Azkaellon, but I am going outside the wall.'

Palace outworks, Daylight Wall section 16, 7th of Quartus

Katsuhiro was there when an angel came down from the distant heights into the mudscape of the outworks. He arrived without warning, passed among them like something from a dream and was gone before they could acknowledge his reality.

Sanguinius was gold and he was glory. Familiarity can lead a man to accept the worst circumstances as normal. In the blood and the destruction, where flesh was pounded into the pulverised stone, Katsuhiro had forgotten what purity looked like. In the person of Sanguinius he was reminded.

The first Katsuhiro heard were shouts of amazement, and he looked back from no-man's-land to see a soft glow, then Sanguinius himself. He stood behind the broken rampart in full view of the enemy. There were snipers in the drop-craft wrecks, but he forgot them.

The guns on the walls were firing, aimed at the siege camp and the contravallation that grew day by day around the city. Counter bombardments answered from the enemy lines; the orbital batteries had not ceased, nor had the fleet bombardment, and shells periodically broke the flickering voids to blast up craters among the defensive lines. The roar of the siege was at its worst, save for those times the foe made direct attempts on the outworks, when all became a bedlam of flashing light and terror.

A hush descended. Though the guns continued to fire, their violence was somehow lessened by the primarch's presence.

Men and women fell to their knees as Sanguinius passed along the line. His entourage of aides, standard bearers and the gold-armoured and winged elite that guarded him were almost as affecting as the primarch himself. Grumbles were silenced. Fear ebbed. Filthy hands reached out to touch the Lord of Angels. His warriors moved to push the soldiers back, but Sanguinius raised his hand, just slightly, and the guards moved away. A female soldier was the first to dare to hold out her fingers to his wings. The feathers twitched, but Sanguinius stood firm, and allowed her to caress him.

Another person came forwards, then another, until a crowd was around the Great Angel, arms radiating inwards like worshippers from less enlightened times stretching for their idol.

Sanguinius was uncomfortable, Katsuhiro could see. The primarch kept his perfect face as neutral as he could, but it was there in the set of his lips, and the way he looked upwards, away from the supplicants around him. Like all the rest, Katsuhiro was captivated, and moved towards him, his feet dragging through the mud of their own volition. The Angel's radiance touched Katsuhiro. He felt a peace in his heart, a calmness in his mind and a stilling of fears. The aches and chills that sickened him were alleviated briefly. For a moment, he felt whole again.

Surrounded by the dirty and the desperate, Sanguinius shone as pure as sunlight reflected from snow.

Then it was over. The light dimmed. The Great Angel's guards moved forwards and, gently as they could, pushed back the weeping crowd so Sanguinius could address them.

'Be brave, children of Terra,' he said. 'Your courage and your fortitude are most needed in this war, and I, on behalf of my brother Rogal Dorn, and the Emperor of Mankind, thank you.'

With those words he moved on, his crimson-armoured sons marching in wary perimeter. Their boots were smeared with the muck of the field, but Sanguinius was pristine, or so it seemed. He was as much a vision as a solid being, and as a vision he was untouched and untouchable by the filth of the mundane world.

Katsuhiro watched him go, joy and awe overwhelming him.

'You there!'

A man with a sergeant's rank insignia stitched to his civilian clothes accosted Katsuhiro. The man was trying too hard, probably angry at his own awed reaction to the primarch. Not one man had continued his duties while Sanguinius was there.

'Stop your gawking. Captain Jainan is looking for volunteers.' He looked Katsuhiro up and down. 'A little small, but I think you'll just about do.'

* * *

Jainan was sick. Katsuhiro was not the only soldier feeling ill. A host of minor ailments had swept through the defence force. Coughs, colds and digestive complaints to add to the misery of rad poisoning. Nothing immediately fatal, but every sickness wore down the resolve of the men and women in the outworks, making their condition that little more insufferable, and every misery increased the chance that they would run. But Jainan was genuinely afflicted. He was propped up in a makeshift bed occupying the shell of a bunker. Part of the roof had been blown in by a direct hit. The gap was covered over with corrugated sheeting. The walls were blackened. Katsuhiro couldn't stop looking at the marks. Much would be the soot from incinerated human bodies.

It was shelter, and Jainan needed it. His eyes were red and puffy, and his nose ran. His skin had turned an even unhealthier stage of grey. Sores spotted his mouth, and his breath was rank; though Katsuhiro was never nearer than an arm's length away, the stench of it filled the enclosed space.

Katsuhiro arrived to find Doromek, Runnecan and the woman present. She and Doromek were drawn with hunger, but less afflicted than the others.

Jainan coughed before he spoke. A light tickle that grew into heaving, rib-punishing hacks. When it subsided, he spoke quickly, in case it began again.

'Acting Lieutenant Doromek here has come up with a worrying possibility. There are tunnels... There are...' He ran a hand over his face. 'Doromek, you explain.'

'I'll keep this simple,' Doromek said, shifting his gun on his shoulder. 'There are supply tunnels under the battlefield running out from the second line to the bastions. Some of them have been opened by bombardment. They might give the enemy a way behind our lines. I think we should check them out.'

Jainan's eyes closed. 'You're a good man, Doromek, a real find. There we have it. I need someone to go into the tunnels to see what's left. To…' He swallowed. His pale lips trembled. 'To see if they're a risk.' He was struggling to speak, and coughed again. Through spluttering breath he managed, 'Dismissed. Be about it,' before he curled in over himself, a bowl was brought and he bent double to vomit up a stream of red-streaked phlegm.

'What's wrong with him?' Katsuhiro asked Doromek. 'It's not rad poisoning, is it?' he added. They all suffered that to a degree. Anti-rad pills kept the worse effects at bay, but Katsuhiro lived in terror of the day they stopped working.

'Nah, it's the camp sickness,' Runnecan said.

'What do you know about it?' Doromek said. He strode easily through the mud. The woman, Myz, he'd heard Doromek call her, was even more assured. Thin-faced Runnecan scampered, rodent-like, his small feet pit-pattering. Only Katsuhiro was struggling, needing to wrench his boots from the sucking ground with every step.

'You've never been in a war before, Runnecan,' said Doromek.

'I have. I've fought on five worlds for the Emperor.'

Katsuhiro looked at him in mild astonishment.

'I was born hive scum, and I am hive scum, but I was a soldier in between,' Runnecan said proudly. 'I've seen people get sick, all the time!' He sniggered. 'Then they die.'

'Nasty little piece of work,' Doromek said. 'You are a hive rat. In this place, awful as it is, we have medicine. That's the reason why you're not all dead from rads yet.'

'They're stopping the rads but what about everything else? The medicae aren't doing any good!' said Katsuhiro.

'Do you know, Katsuhiro, I like you but you take forever to catch on. *Exactly*, the medicae aren't doing anything. These sicknesses are coughs and sneezes and upset bellies. Nothing any anti-viral or bacteriophage shouldn't stamp out. But they're not working.'

They were walking away from the front, towards the second line. Bastion 16 loomed large to their right.

'Is Horus using germ war on us?'

'Now you're getting it,' said Doromek. 'Could be.'

'I feel dreadful, why are you still healthy?' Katsuhiro said.

'Natural resilience,' Doromek said humourlessly.

'Be quiet, all of you,' Myz snapped. She pulled ahead, heading for a gap blown into the second line. Twisted lengths of plasteel reinforcement writhed up like briars around the breach.

'Why do you let her speak like that to you?' said Runnecan. 'If my woman spoke to me like that, I'd give her a hiding.'

'That attitude explains your lack of female company. She's not "my woman". I barely know her.'

'I think you do,' said Runnecan slyly. 'I think you know her much better than you're saying.'

Doromek grunted. 'What can I say? I lose my heart to pretty faces. That's as far as it goes. I know her about as well as you do.'

'What did you think of the primarch?' asked Katsuhiro, trying to find something positive in the day.

Doromek shrugged. 'How did he make *you* feel?'

It annoyed Katsuhiro that the question was turned around on him, but he answered anyway. 'Joy, awe.'

They headed down the slope of the crater. Filthy water puddled the bottom. As they skirted it, Doromek glanced back.

'That's not all is it? Come on now, we're all comrades here. Be honest.'

'I feel… sad,' said Katsuhiro uncomfortably. 'Hollow.'

'Insignificant?'

Katsuhiro nodded. They walked into the network of trenches between lines two and one. Large sections of it were collapsed and abandoned.

'They do that. Them and their sons. I ask myself why the Emperor created them,' Doromek said. Myz was well ahead, and he spoke more freely when she wasn't listening in. 'He always said they were to protect us, and that men would take over when they were done. But why make something so powerful, so beyond humanity?'

'Oooh, that's treason that,' said Runnecan.

'Shut it, you,' said Doromek.

'He's right, Runnecan,' said Katsuhiro. 'I don't know what to think any more. I felt insignificant when I saw Sanguin- ius.' He fell quiet for a few paces. 'This is their war,' he said quickly. 'We're just in the way.'

Doromek nodded. 'That's about the size of it.'

The aegis thrummed painfully overhead. A shell pierced the energy membrane and dived murderously for the ground, scattering troops with a terrifying howl. It bored into the mud and stone a few metres ahead of the first line and det- onated, lofting a section of the outwork ramparts upwards with a searing flash. Katsuhiro and the others hit the ground the instant before it struck. He kept his hands over his head as debris pattered everywhere.

They got up. Men were screaming. New corpses waited to be carted off by servitor orderlies to the funeral pits. Kat- suhiro looked on helplessly at a screaming man clutching the ragged stumps of his legs. There was nothing he could do. Doromek was already walking on. The others followed. The screaming had stopped before they'd gone a hundred metres more.

Myz was over by a small, isolated bunker at the end of its own run of trench.

'Get a move on!' she shouted.

'I thought this was your idea,' said Katsuhiro.

'It was,' said Doromek. 'Truly.'

'I thought you said she wasn't your woman,' Runnecan said unpleasantly.

'I told you, she's not,' said Doromek, and jumped into the trench.

A small plaque over an armoured door proclaimed the bunker Nexus Zero-One-Five. Myz did something to open the lock, and the four of them descended into the dark under the battlefield.

A short spiral staircase brought them out into a tunnel just wide enough for two men to walk abreast. Cabling hung in long sweeps from loops set into the ceiling. The tunnel was made of precast ferrocrete sections, but if it had been laid straight, it no longer was. Deformation of the battlefield by the bombardment pushed the tunnel out of true, in some places forcing the segments apart and allowing water to seep in. As a result, a stream of dirty water, ankle-deep and polluted with bodily fluids, ran along the bottom, collecting into deeper pools where the tunnel sagged. The tunnel shook every now and then when a shell or energy beam made it through the aegis. The ground transmitted the vibrations well, and down there, without other distractions to the senses, hits on the earth seemed more frequent than they had above.

Doromek consulted a map. Myz paid particular attention to it, then pointed off down the tunnel. The pair of them disappeared around a kink in the line. Katsuhiro made to follow them, but was stopped by a grubby hand.

'Did you see that?' said Runnecan. 'She had a cypher wand.'

'So what?' said Katsuhiro grumpily. His bones ached with his fever and the rads. He welcomed the quiet under the battlefield. He wanted to lie down. Standing still made the aching worse.

'Where did she get it from?' said Runnecan.

'I don't know – Jainan?'

'Then why didn't he give it to Doromek?'

'He's not thinking clearly, he's sick.'

Runnecan gave a smile partway between sympathetic and patronising. 'Listen, I know you don't like me very much. You think I'm underhive scum, and I am. Because of that, I can see something odd is happening here. Those two know each other, trust me. There's something going on here. I–'

Footsteps splashed back towards them.

'Come on. Stop hanging back. We'll need your guns if there are infiltrators down here,' said Doromek.

'I bet you will,' muttered Runnecan.

'Coming,' said Katsuhiro. 'Just catching our breath, that's all.'

They followed the tunnels as best they could. A little way beyond the kink was a crossroads. The western line went half a kilometre towards the walls before terminating in another staircase leading back to the surface. The northern line had taken a direct hit, and was open to the sky. A surprised sentry posted to keep soldiers from hiding down there challenged them. Doromek told them of their business and they quizzed him as to the state of the tunnel beyond.

'All gone in,' he said. He had a nigh-impenetrable accent. 'All pounded flat, far as the Helios Gate.'

Doromek thanked him.

'Back this way, lads,' he said.

Myz said nothing.

Back at the crossroads they turned east, away from the wall.

Katsuhiro couldn't decide what the tunnels were for. They were too small to move many troops or munitions, or to shelter men from the bombs. They could have been escape routes, he supposed. He asked Doromek what he thought, but the veteran muttered something he didn't catch.

'Lines for power, for water,' Runnecan said, pointing to the bundles of cables hanging down. 'And yes, probably so the officers can run away, and not die with the rest of us.'

Neither answer satisfied Katsuhiro, but no other was forthcoming.

Eventually they arrived at a wall in the tunnel. The power lines disappeared through a plasteel plate stencilled with a large numeral sixteen.

Doromek shook his head. 'Nothing the enemy can do with these,' he said. 'Too small, too short, too fragmented. I declare myself satisfied.'

He rolled up his map. 'Come on, back to our posts. Our little excursion is over.'

It took little time to retrace their steps. As they reached the bottom of the iron stair, Katsuhiro paused.

'Something's changed.'

'Shh!' Doromek had his head cocked to one side.

'I tell you, something's changed!' said Katsuhiro.

'It's the shells,' said Doromek.

The noise of the bombardment was so ubiquitous that it took a moment for Katsuhiro to register they had stopped. The tunnel wasn't shaking.

'Shhh! Do you hear that?'

'What? What do you mean? I hear nothing,' said Runnecan.

'Exactly.'

'The bombardment. It has really stopped? Oh thank the Emperor!' Katsuhiro forgot his aches, and forced his way up the stairs. Runnecan was right behind him, and they hurried through the door together.

Outside the sky had ceased to burn. Rolling ash clouds filled the air. Although the Palace guns had not relented flinging their cannonade towards the heavens, without the shelling from orbit the battlefield felt quiet. Katsuhiro's ears rang with the lack of noise.

All down the line cheers fluttered from lips pale with tiredness.

'They've stopped!' said Katsuhiro, letting his lasrifle dangle from its straps so he could grasp Runnecan's skinny arms. The hiver smiled back at him.

'They have!'

Myz pushed past, eyes on the heavens. Doromek shook his head pointedly.

'I'd stop that if I were you,' he said.

'But it's stopped!' said Katsuhiro. Excited chatter rose from the soldiers. More and more were looking upwards. Only the veterans, few in number, remained stern and watchful. That should have informed Katsuhiro something was about to happen, but hope outdoes sense in every contest.

'They've stopped bombing, because they're coming at us again.' Doromek put his face between Runnecan's and Katsuhiro's.

'So?' said Runnecan. 'We beat 'em back half a dozen times! Let them come.'

'No, no, no,' said Doromek with a cruel smile. 'If they're not firing, it's because they don't want to hit their own troops. They've not minded about that before, have they? Stand ready, boys. They're going to have another go, and I don't think they'll be sending cannon fodder this time.'

NINETEEN

Ride of the ordu
Information
Siege work

Palace outworks, Daylight Wall section 16, 7th of Quartus

Sanguinius was still outside the wall when the bombardment ceased.

The Blood Angels recognised what this meant before their helms rang with urgent communications.

'Legionary spearhead inbound across all sectors,' Azkaellon relayed. 'Father, you must retire behind the walls.' He looked upwards. As yet, no drop pods pierced the ash clouds.

'What example will that set to our brave defenders?' said Sanguinius distractedly. His attention was on the wall, not on the void. He was so intent on the stretch between the Helios Gate and the Dawn Tower that several of his men followed his gaze to see what so fascinated him.

'My lord…' Azkaellon began. He waved forwards the Sanguinary Guard to shield the primarch.

'We remain. My brother will need me,' Sanguinius said, his voice still distant.

Azkaellon looked at Raldoron.

'What do you foresee, father?' Raldoron asked quietly.

'A need for assistance. The White Scars come.'

The scream of jets cut through the boom and thwack of the Palace defences, high and pure, an orchestra of a thousand engines: Land Speeders, jetbikes, gunships and attack craft. Over a narrow frontage of the defences, between two lesser towers to the south, a storm of white shapes dropped precipitously off the wall, then raced over the outworks towards the siege camp facing the Helios Gate. As soon as the threat registered, guns on the contravallation began firing again. Though their first volleys smacked harmlessly into the aegis, the White Scars were heading courageously into a solid enemy barrage.

Sanguinius smiled as his brother roared by on an oversized jetcycle and tilted stubby wings in salute. Mortals ducked, so close to the ground were the White Scars flying. Once they were past the final line, they flew lower still, their contra-grav sending up sprays of debris and their plasma jets heating the air into a dancing shimmer. On and on the stream of attackers went, a thousand warriors in white, all mounted, all shouting melodic Chogorian war cries. At the edge of the aegis they split into multiple flights, hugging the ground, dodging between the wrecks of ships and armoured vehicles from earlier days of the fighting. Starbursts of shrapnel detonated among them, swift lasers slashed out, unseating some of the ordu, but the mass flew on, accelerating towards the enemy line until they were jinking blurs. The kilometres between besiegers and besieged were covered swiftly, and they were soon in range, firing their guns, the gunships pulling up to draw the enemy's attention, loop around and attack targets of priority. One exploded under a withering hail of hard rounds. A few moments later, the siege line shields buckled under massed fire, and soon after that the first enemy cannon died.

Sanguinius watched transfixed.

'He fights with such elegance,' the Angel said.

'He was ordered not to attack?' asked Raldoron.

'He is the Khan of the ordu of the White Scars Legion, the Warhawk of Chogoris,' said Sanguinius. 'One might as well attempt to chain the wind.'

'The enemy will be with us soon,' said Raldoron. 'What are your orders, father?'

Azkaellon consulted with distant command nexuses.

'My lord, we must return within the walls. The Death Guard are arriving in force. A third of their Legion is bound for the Palace battle sphere alone.'

Sanguinius looked skywards calmly.

'Bring me my helm and my weapons. Retire our colours behind the walls. We fight.'

'You are at risk!' Azkaellon said fiercely.

Sanguinius responded with the disturbing mantra his sons had heard all too often of late. 'I do not die today,' he said, 'and if I do not aid my brother on his return, he will. I have seen it. My sword, my spear! Man the ramparts alongside these brave warriors of the Imperium.'

His helm was brought and Sanguinius locked it into place.

'It is time at last for the Ninth Legion to fight.'

Grand Borealis Strategium, 7th of Quartus

'My lord, the Death Guard drop assault will be on the ground within five minutes.' The officer stood to attention, not daring to meet Lord Dorn's eyes. 'Here is a cartograph of their projected landing zone. The larger part is divided into seven groups bound for the Palace, but there are numerous smaller detachments headed for locations all over Terra.' A cartolithic map blinked on close to Dorn's observational pulpit.

Dorn knew all the map had to tell. He guessed the enemy's intentions well in advance, and read the actualities of their attack, seeing them in the dance of numbers streaming through the hololiths before the strategium's machines or his subordinates could collate them.

'Keep monitoring. Notify me of anything out of the ordinary. Compare projections with the developing situation. Miss nothing!'

The officer swallowed.

'My lord, there is more. We have large numbers of loyal light grav-attack craft departing the Palace, sector fifteen and sixteen, around the Helios Gate.'

'What?' Dorn's stone-hard face turned suddenly to look at the officer.

'It is the White Scars, my lord. They are making a sally.'

'Where is the Khan?'

'He is leading them. I am sorry, my lord, we had no warning, and have made all attempts to urge him back but–'

Dorn silenced him with a gesture. 'Strategic overlay, Daylight Wall, central quadrant,' he commanded. An overhead representation blinked into view in the strategium shaft.

'My lord!' another officer shouted. 'More White Scars battle groups are departing the Palace, sections 1,004, 320, 87 and 2,400.'

Dorn summoned more cartographs.

'He's going for the siege camps. Damn his impetuousness. Aerial command!' he barked. 'Get our fighters into the air now. Split six squadrons off from interception missions to cover all White Scars fall-back corridors, but concentrate efforts on sectors 15 to 16. Prepare to aid my brother's retreat – if he plays his usual game he will strike hard and make for the Palace. Ensure he returns intact.'

'My lord, if he doesn't?'

'Then he is on his own,' growled Dorn. Alarms bleeped from numerous stations in the Borealis Strategium. 'By the Emperor, get those fighters up!'

Palace outworks, Daylight Wall section 16, 7th of Quartus

Jaghatai Khan's jetbike surged under him with a leonine growl as he accelerated out past the contravallation. At the head of a hundred jetbikes, he burned out across the broken lands beyond, and swung back on another attack run. The defences were well planned, with outwards ramparts against the possibility of relief forces coming to the Palace's aid, and although the rearward guns were fewer in number than those facing the Palace, they mustered a considerable firestorm against the White Scars.

The Khan rode with three brotherhoods. They crowded the air, their jinking paths taking them so close to one another he could hear the snapping of pennants over the battle's roar. He took in a massive amount of information from the battlefield; he did not possess Sanguinius' ability to see the future, but his mental powers lent him near-preternatural reflexes. A slight movement on the parapet was enough warning for him to swing his jetbike a few degrees, avoiding the lascannon aimed at him.

His sons, though skilled, were not as gifted as he. Many were blasted from the sky. Some died in flight, their mounts consumed with fire, their armour shattered. The lucky ones tumbled from smoking saddles, rolling on the shattered ground with a born horseman's grace to come up firing. Some dozens were forming up in ad hoc squads to continue the fight on foot.

An eye-blink later the Khan was back over the enemy siege line. The shields protecting the camp were not as sophisticated as those making up the Palace aegis, and the light vehicles slipped through them with little more than a flurry of sparks breaking over their prows. The Khan banked hard down the trench, and sped along directly above the foe. Hundreds of Dark Mechanicum tech thralls turned their weapons around, too late, too slow. Rotary cannons in the nose of the Khan's jetbike whined up to firing speed and sent twin impact lines down ahead of him, shredding metal and flesh to ruin. He drew his tulwar, keyed on the power field and, with a kick on the control pedals, sent his jetbike arrowing down with a scream of overtaxed engines.

'For the Emperor!' he roared. 'For Unity, for the Imperium!'

Such was his speed that he could have wielded a switch of wood and it would have cleaved his enemy down. When the tulwar struck the enemy, they exploded in showers of oily blood.

'Onwards, my ordu! Onwards!'

Dozens of jetbikes followed him, the bolters mounted on their fairings spitting death. Mass-reactives pulverised the foe's servants, leaving them to hang as bloody shreds on the guns they operated. Land Speeders dipped from the sky, targeting weapons emplacements, turning them to slag with roaring fusion beams. Living beings hit directly by the terrible weapons were vaporised. Those only clipped suffered horrific deaths as the vapour within their cells was atomised, and their organs exploded with sufficient force to rupture their plasteel casings.

'Death! Death to the traitors!' Jaghatai called, his war cries broadcast over his Legion's vox-net. His khans' answers were loud with laughter and jubilation. Too long had they skulked behind the walls. The wind had them, filling them with its rushing power and lifting them up with its strength.

Their target was ahead, one of eight Mechanicum arks beached around the Palace. Enemy activity was the greatest around these vessels. Huge machines were in the process of assembly. Part covered though they were by tarpaulins and armoured sows, Khan recognised breaching cannons with shield-bane technology made to bring down the aegis, and other things – huge frameworks of stupendous size. He frowned, not quite believing what he saw, and set his augurs to record everything.

'Primary target,' Khan said. Their time was running down. The window of opportunity afforded by the pause in the bombardment would close as soon as the Death Guard made planetfall. 'Execute and withdraw,' he commanded.

Around the ark ship, the siege line broadened into a large space flattened by machines, and protected by turrets, energy screens and physical obstacles. The dark arts of technology were much in evidence. Arcs of crackling power whipped up to catch White Scars riders, leaping between them to bring three or four down at once. Actinic light burned from eye sockets as warriors were consumed within their armour while systems shorted out in their machines, dousing their jets and cutting off their contra-gravity fields. Clamp mines leapt up in fountains of dirt, riding short-burn jets to home in on their prey, where powerful magnetic locks slammed them home before they blew. Men fell on burning jetbikes left and right. The Khan dodged as the wreck of a Land Speeder plunged down in front of him. Beneath the black sky all was fire and energy light of startling colours, blue, purple, red and gold.

The ark ship was heavily guarded by Legio Cybernetica troops. There were siege robots there, huge things approaching the size of Imperial Knights. These remained inert, but their smaller brothers and sisters fired upwards. Radium bullets fizzled past. Volkite beams sliced the air. Still the White Scars came on.

His men ignored the robots and the cyborgs firing on them, but broadened their formation and peeled apart, the greater portion of them heading for the shield generators protecting the camp. The first were laboriously shattered by bolter fire, but as the shield weakened, missiles and weapons shot from the Khan's circling fighters streaked down, impaling more shield generators, and bursting them apart.

Jaghatai himself rode amok through the crowds of enemy, his tulwar held forwards at the charge in the manner of a cavalryman of Chogoris. A battle automaton swiped at him clumsily; he separated its head from its body. Another fell back with a glowing line cut through its torso. Limbs flew. His rotary cannons fired until they clicked dry. Bullets rattled musical holes into his vehicle's fuselage, and he jinked away, finding himself herded towards a wall of advancing war machines by lines of converging bullets. He slewed around, coming into a long, sweeping sideways turn, using the jet-bike's bulk to knock three of the robots to the ground and, gunning the engines, immolate their screeching data master with a wash of plasma burn. He hardly decelerated before he was away, ducking as the machines fired after him.

Fighter craft were shrieking overhead now, dropping bombs and missiles onto the siege camp. A line of fire raced along the ground, and a mighty detonation shook the air as chained explosions detonated several energy mantlets.

'Daylight Wall sections thirteen through sixteen, hear me. Jaghatai Khan, primarch and lord of the White Scars ordu, commands you. Priority target, these coordinates. Open fire on my command.' He didn't wait for confirmation.

'Sons of Chogoris!' he voxed. 'Break free, return to the walls!'

As suddenly as they had attacked, the White Scars disengaged. Jetbikes swooped upwards, corkscrewing through deadly patterns of las-fire. On the far side of the siege lines, Thunderhawks touched down only long enough to rescue some of the warriors who had lost their machines, before blasting back upwards again. As they fell back, they fired, until their guns were pointing towards the Palace, and they showed their jets to the enemy.

'Wall sections thirteen through sixteen, open fire now.'

The White Scars passed through a hail of ordnance heading out. Explosions boomed behind them, cutting off the fire that chased them.

Jaghatai Khan opened his throttle and raced ahead of the wind.

The depleted soldiery of the outworks watched the sky. Despite impending peril, their nerves were steadier than they had been in weeks. For the first time, legionaries fought with them. The Blood Angels were few in number. Sanguinius called no more of them down from the lofty walls. He seemed distracted, not like Katsuhiro had imagined a primarch.

That was a small thing. There was a primarch on the line, *a primarch*, and though he kept to the top of Bastion 16 with his closest aides and glorious bodyguard, conscripts felt new resolve at Sanguinius' presence. If they looked up, they could glimpse him shining behind the ramparts. He was a spot of golden hope in the blackness cloaking Terra.

Sanguinius put his legionaries out to strengthen the defence around Bastion 16. The mortal soldiery he also commanded closer to the tower. Even tired and ill, the conscripts found a new energy, moving with purpose they never had before. For the first time, under the gleaming green eye-lenses of the Space

Marines, Katsuhiro felt like a real soldier, and the thoughts of inferiority he had earlier in the day were swept away.

All of them felt that way. All of them, except Runnecan. The little man dogged Katsuhiro's footsteps. Often cocky, his confident air had given way to unease.

'I don't think he's up to any good.'

'Who?' said Katsuhiro, who was focused on the White Scars' attack upon the siege camp. With the bombardment halted, he could hear the discharge of their guns clearly over the wastes. 'Sanguinius?'

Runnecan spoke a name, but it was drowned out by a cheer erupting along the line as a series of explosions ripped through the distant camp, and the darting hornets of the Khan's Space Marines swarmed towards the beached warship.

'What?' Katsuhiro said.

'Doromek! Doromek! Listen to me!' Runnecan was wild-eyed now. 'All that trudging around in the tunnels. Why? Where did she get that cypher wand from?' He shook his head and huddled lower. 'They know each other from before, I seen it. They do.'

'She can fight,' said Katsuhiro, recalling Myz killing the giant mutant.

'Exactly!'

'But that doesn't mean anything. Maybe she's like him, a soldier. There are people in that Palace who can kill in a million different ways.'

'Yeah, there are, and they're in there, not out here. We're out here because we're not even soldiers, we're nothing! Do you really think someone like Doromek could avoid the draft, even now? And how come she's not piped up about her handiness with a blade? They shouldn't be here!'

'It's a mistake,' insisted Katsuhiro. 'Someone's bound to slip through the cracks.'

'Right,' said Runnecan darkly. 'But did they slip or did they creep through?'

That made Katsuhiro look round. 'What are you saying?'

'There are traitors everywhere, my friend.' Runnecan sighted down his gun towards the siege camp. 'There are–'

Once more, an explosion stole his words, this one much bigger. The White Scars fighters and gunships were pounding the encampment. The shields flickered, then gave out. Immediately, the White Scars pulled back, buzzing up in a flurry of white glints to race home. All along the line the remainder of the conscripts cheered.

A ripple of pops crackled across the sky, insignificant to the conscripts, but a warning sound the legionaries knew well.

'Stand ready, warriors of the Imperium,' said one of the Blood Angels. He was metres away from Katsuhiro but his vox-amplified voice carried far, strong, pure and proud. 'The enemy are coming.'

Nervous faces glanced skywards. Hundreds of bright dots were hurtling down through the sky, bursting through the cloud layer with violent speed. Ahead of them came a storm of attack craft.

From the Palace dozens of defence wings raced up to meet them.

The guns all along the section of the wall to Katsuhiro's back redoubled their barrage, and the siege camp was lost in a storm of fire. The White Scars hurtled through the flames as if the furies of the warp themselves were at their backs.

It was after that point that everything descended into anarchy.

TWENTY

Death among us
Spearhead
The Angel and the Warhawk

Imperial Palace airspace, 7th of Quartus

'Get it off my tail!' Aisha screamed.

She yanked the stick of *Blue Zephyr* hard, sending the Panthera into a bone-crushing curve to escape her pursuer. Enemy ships were all over them. A dual-pilot Stiletto fighter exploded at her left, taken out by the Legiones Astartes ship gunning for her. Bright tracer fire streaked by. The fuselage made a dull clang as a lascannon beam clipped her. She shot out a hand to silence screaming systems and reroute power away from damaged circuits, snatching it back just as quick to the stick.

'Old gods of Old Earth,' she snarled. 'If any of you are still out there, give me a little grace.'

The battle sphere was a tempest of metal, hard light and fire. Fighters of dozens of different marques duelled over the Palace walls and the outworks, while through the storm of flame and ships the drop pods of the traitors punched like iron fists. Aisha's mission was supposedly to destroy as many pods as she could before they touched down, but they were denied even the most unlikely shot by the enemy air armada, which protected the pods with furious tenacity. Her own auspex returns and what little sense she could make from flight control's messages suggested larger landers were coming in, almost certainly laden with heavy equipment. Such slow-moving beasts were meat to *Blue Zephyr*, but they were even better protected. The enemy were everywhere, over everything, flights and flights of them, and now they had an additional Legion's worth of air support to bolster them. The Imperial defence squadrons attempted to block enemy craft from penetrating the outer rings of the air defences, but some were bound to get through, and although most of them died in clouds of fire before they got far over the city, a handful wrought havoc, unleashing clouds of incendiary bombs. Phosphex fire had a special shine all of its own. Glaring magnesium white, it filled canyon streets with a deceptively beautiful light as it ate through metal, rockcrete and flesh with equal voracity. There were poison smokes and acid fogs and other vile weapons deployed. Gas blanketed a part of the outer city. Heavier than air, it sank down through ventilation grilles and fractured pavements to smother the people hiding below the Palace.

None of that would matter to her any more if she couldn't shake her pursuer.

Orders screamed in her vox-beads along with panicked calls for aid. The enemy was throwing more and more craft into the fight, and with the air defences already damaged and their own numbers whittled down by every engagement, the loyalist squadrons were suffering. Gunfire flashed over her cockpit. She heaved *Blue Zephyr* to the side, and burst through a streamer of flame, almost slamming into a Fury void-fighter spinning out of control across her flight path. A quick jerk of her stick sent *Blue Zephyr* skipping over it.

Still the legionary craft came.

She got barely a glimpse of it, it was so fast, but she'd seen enough to get an identity: a Xiphon interceptor, XIV Legion, one of the few machines she'd ever been afraid of facing in combat. Streams of missiles burned past her, shot with terrifying rapidity by the interceptor's rotary launchers. She was getting boxed in by the pilot. Where she dodged the missiles, lascannon beams waited for her. He was closing in on the kill, and she was running out of options.

'I'm coming! I'm coming!'

Aisha almost cried out with joy when she heard Dandar Bey's voice. *'I've got him. Hold your course. I'll free you up, get you back into it.'* He swore. *'This is a mess.'*

The fire from behind broke off as Bey joined the deadly game. Aisha caught another glimpse of the Xiphon; its green-and-white heraldry was dirty, and its engine exhaust an unhealthy black, but it flew true enough, breaking off its pursuit of her to dodge Bey's counter-attack. She immediately reacted, pulling herself up. Although she loved her ship as dearly as she did any person, she cursed *Blue Zephyr*'s comparative lack of agility as it sped out wider than her foe.

'I've lost him! Aisha, watch out, I can't see him in all this–'

There was a brief growl on the line, then nothing but static. So little to mark a man's death.

Aisha climbed. She found the Xiphon and opened fire with all her armaments. The Xiphon plunged down in an evasive dive impossible for a baseline human to tolerate. She couldn't follow to finish him, and knew it was going to come again behind her.

'Bright Hawks, Bright Hawks! Squadron Mistress Daveinpor requesting immediate support.'

Nothing came back. She glanced at her unit markers. Half her ship lights were red. Another blinked from green to mortis glow as she watched. There was a garbled message from somewhere, then nothing but the howling of interference and the half-heard shouts of orders blasting over the vox-net.

She was on her own. Warning signifiers bleated that the Xiphon was lining her up again. Gritting her teeth, she pushed *Blue Zephyr* into a punishing dive, penetrating the weakened aegis and coming down behind the walls of the Palace. An obvious manoeuvre, but designed to goad her foe to follow. She yanked up a few hundred metres above the deck, skimming fast down burning streets. The Palace was taking damage directly now. The aegis still held back the worst of the orbital bombardment, and doubtless would for months more, but Palace airspace was dense with enemy attack craft that rained down bombs on everything. She punched through a firestorm, narrowly avoided a toppling spire. All the while the Xiphon was closing. The pilot chanced a few lascannon volleys, herding her again like livestock to the slaughter.

An opportunity presented itself. A bridge ahead, grandiose, huge, typically Imperial. Her auspex was a welter of confused signals, but she knew it was there, in the poison fog and fire. She hoped only that her foe did not.

Accelerating as fast as she dared, she lessened her evasive movements, luring the Xiphon closer. Rockets stormed past her cockpit. Las light flashed by.

The bridge was there, somewhere.

She misjudged. The bridge, ablaze from end to end, burst from the gas almost too suddenly for her to react. She pulled up to nearly vertically, making *Blue Zephyr* scream in machine pain.

The Space Marine, for all his gifts, could not avoid the unexpected obstacle. The Xiphon slammed into the bridge and burst out the other side as a wingless stub in a shower of broken armourglass and masonry.

She took a breath, then another, and banked back round.

There was enough time to register three more fighters closing in on her from three separate directions. From that position, there was no escape.

Her fingers stretched out to the pict glued to the instrument panel. They did not reach her husband's face before *Blue Zephyr* was torn to flaming pieces.

Palace outworks, Daylight Wall section 16, 7th of Quartus

Ahead of the drop pods a brief but widespread bombardment of shells detonated over the outworks with soft, floury bangs. As they did not hit the ground, they seemed no threat at all, but then the defenders saw a paint-burst spread begin its rapid sinking, and they understood the danger that these bombs posed.

'Gas! Gas! Gas!'

Whistles blew. Men shouted. Though millennia old, gas was still a much feared weapon. An attack by the very air induced an atavistic response deep in the limbic system, a fear of drowning, of suffocation, a fear common to all creatures that must breathe.

Runnecan swore in fluent underhive gutter slang. A thousand hands went for cases at belts. The Space Marines salted among the lines remained impassive, protected from all environmental harms by their power armour. Katsuhiro was nervous of the Space Marines, for all the awe he felt. He had never wanted to be one, but at that moment he envied them their protection and their lack of fear.

Though the conscripts had started out poorly equipped, the rate of attrition was so high that by that time most of the troops on the outworks had some form of protection against the poison, a gas mask at least, looted from the dead if not assigned to them personally. Katsuhiro fell into the former category. He had no training in how to use the mask he'd acquired, and nearly didn't manage to get it on. In his panic he yanked on the straps all wrong and got the mask twisted about. A brown fog sifted around him as he struggled. He smelled acrid chemicals, then, mercifully, he managed to pull the mask down to cover his face. Stinging eyes made him fear the worst, but they stopped streaming after a moment and his breathing steadied.

Katsuhiro's hearing was muffled by the mask. The gas mask had an unpleasant, rubbery smell. The odour of gas stuck to the back of his throat and irritated it, but he couldn't spit, and he swallowed his gathering phlegm down repeatedly, until he felt nauseous.

The cloud, now a rich mustard brown, closed in over the troops. At first all he could hear was his breathing, in and out, roar and hiss with the click of the mask's simple purifier. The gas thickened until Runnecan was a grey shape, though he was only a couple of metres away.

False calm descended, peaceful and poisonous.

A man, blood running from blinded eyes and blistered lips, burst from the fog. Katsuhiro fired reflexively at him, missing in his fright. The man was clawing at his face, his screams turning to gurgles. His shoulder clipped Katsuhiro hard as he ran by and the gas swallowed him again.

Screaming came out of the fog. Not all of the troops had gas masks. Many that did couldn't work them, or had equipment that was damaged. They ran about in terror. One with greater presence of mind turned over bodies for a gas mask, finding one, slipping it on just in time. Two men brawled over a mask neither had any hope of donning. Others tried to run, but fell, screaming froth from burning throats.

Time slowed. Katsuhiro moved as a man underwater. Images of horror appeared as sheets of gas shifted like weeds in currents, each waft of poison opening a curtain on another scene of suffering. It seemed to go on forever, as awful things do, though according to Katsuhiro's chronometer less than two minutes went by.

The screams died as men died. Vapour drank the sound of the wall guns, squeezing them down to subaquatic thumps. Laser flash dispersed by the gas turned the rolling clouds into alien thunderstorms of yellow and brown lit by red lightning.

A roaring scream sounded right over Katsuhiro. Glaring yellow appeared overhead, and a wash of heat blasted the poison fog aside. A huge metal ovoid bore right down on him. He was frozen, sure he would be crushed. Other men, revealed by the backwash of the descending pod, were close to breaking, but a giant in red stood among them, his bolter ready, shouting.

'Stand firm, servants of Terra!'

Their panic quelled, they held. A storm of tracer bullets ripped around the vehicle, puncturing it many times. Half its thrusters went out, and it tilted over, hurtling off into the wastes beyond the third defence line.

It was only the first.

A drop pod assault was an intentionally terrifying spectacle. The pods fell so fast they seemed to be upon the verge of destruction, only firing their retro thrusters at the last minute to slow their descent from fatal velocity. They smashed into the ground with a force that would kill an unmodified human outright, even one lucky enough to wear power armour. The noise they made was tremendous, like containers full of scrap metal slammed into rock. Explosive bolts went off in crackling bursts, and the huge petal doors fell down with metallic booms. There were hundreds of them, suddenly, crowding the sky, jets roaring, some exploding. The fury of the wall guns was cutting over the third line, streaks of bullets and las light almost close enough to touch, and all the roaring added to the havoc.

More soft thumps overhead. More gas floated down. Different colours, copper-oxide greens and heavy yellows, powder reds and blues. Electromag munitions blew, filling the fog with crackling energy that earthed on the ceramite of the Space Marines in crawling displays of lightning.

'Stand firm!' roared the Space Marines, their deep voices pushed into inhumanity by the harshening of helmet voxes. 'Stand firm!' they shouted, and no one dared run.

Katsuhiro had only an impression of the warriors disembarking from their pods before the thickening gas hid them all. Again so much transpired in so short a space of time, seconds maybe, but fearful years crawled by.

He saw nothing in the murk, but the Space Marines' autosenses penetrated it easily, and they called out once again.

'They come! Ready weapons! For the Emperor!'

The Space Marines brought up their bolters to their shoulders and opened fire.

There were perhaps two dozen Blood Angels on that section of the rampart, nothing compared to the massed thousands who had fought on alien worlds the length and breadth of the galaxy, and yet the report of their bolters firing even in such thin numbers struck Katsuhiro with terror. They barked like hellhounds out of ancient myth, each round the equal of another age's cannon shot.

Bastion 16's guns raked past the rampart's front. Katsuhiro saw large shapes collapse. The wall guns still fired over their heads at the drop pods. So much noise.

The first of the enemy legionaries came out of the gas in a line, their own bolters firing.

A human voice bellowed along the rampart. 'Troopers of the Kushtun Naganda! Present arms!'

Two men down from Katsuhiro a soldier was hit in the shoulder by a bolt-round. When the mass-reactive detonated, the man's torso from his right shoulder to his hip ceased to be. A mist of blood joined the fog. The end of his left arm was blown clear; the right arm and the head, connected by shredded bridges of tissue, collapsed inwards.

'Ready!' the human officer bellowed.

Katsuhiro rested his gun on the rampart's lip. Though the men were sheltered by the fortification, in most cases only their heads exposed, they were still being hit, still dying. The Blood Angels knelt, but they were so big their chests protruded over the defence line. Bolt-rounds blew on their armour, taking out chunks of metallo-ceramic from the plates. The enemy were targeting them in favour of the lesser men. Incredibly, so it seemed to Katsuhiro, one of the crimson angels fell, his chest a bloody ruin.

'Aim!' the officer roared.

Katsuhiro did his best to ignore the carnage among his fellow defenders. He'd played his part in repelling six assaults upon the defence line; he'd been bombed; he was ill, hungry, cold and exhausted. But he had not yet faced Traitor legionaries.

He struggled to draw a bead on the warriors coming to kill him. Just aiming at them seemed profane, somehow, a final inversion of how things were meant to be.

Then they came from the fog, and terror showed a new face.

They wore green-and-white armour adorned with images of death. Where the Blood Angels were crimson and glorious, these beings were debased, though they wore the same wargear and had been created the same way. Their battleplate was filthy, and streaked with dirt and rust. From their vision and breathing slits oily fluids dribbled. Black smoke poured from the exhaust vents on their power plants. They shuffled forwards without the Blood Angels' grace, while preceding them was a stench of sickness, the collective illness of a hospice ward in time of plague distilled. They were dead men walking, and yet they would not fall.

Autocannon rounds, bolts, lascannon shots and explosive shells fell among them. Armour shattered on their bodies. But if they dropped, they climbed back up. Katsuhiro saw one riddled with dozens of hits from the loyal Space Marines. Only when a bolt punched through his helm and detonated in his skull did the filthy giant collapse to his knees and pitch forwards into the mud.

Katsuhiro drew a bead on a warrior advancing without his helmet. He was getting close, close enough to see wild, lidless eyes in a face as drawn as a skull and a black-lipped mouth forever set in death's humourless grin.

'Fire!' the officer ordered.

Katsuhiro squeezed the trigger. Hundreds of las-beams flickered through the fog. His own shot scored clean black through the slime weeping from the monster's armour plates. But the guns of the mortals were of little use against legionary battleplate. Lucky shots to eyes and softseal joints might do some harm, but such wounds were nothing to the corrupted legionaries.

A battle cry went up behind the advancing traitors, and foes more suited to Katsuhiro's gun emerged.

Through the gas, the lost and the damned charged the line again.

Jaghatai Khan's ordu were nearing the wall when the gas shells choked the sky. Dirty smoke rushed out, so thick his jetbike engines coughed when the intakes sucked it in.

Guns boomed on both sides. He raced between the tracks of death, his auspex picking out the features of the ground in pulses of lurid green. The Khan was blessed with the best eyesight that could be engineered into a human being, and marvellous wargear to enhance it, but in that murk he was half-blind. Drop pods screamed past him, blasting shafts into the gas that closed quickly.

He was close to home when a haywire shell, cast down from orbit to blind the Palace's machine eyes, exploded right by his jetbike. A pulse of electromagnetism so violent it made his armour scream shut down his engines.

Like a javelin cast by the thunder gods of Chogoris, Jaghatai Khan's jetbike plunged down. Its golden prow ploughed poison mist, then earth.

The Khan leapt free at the point of impact. He rolled twice, using the momentum of the fall to launch himself back to his feet, where he skidded to a halt, tulwar poised to strike.

He stood ready, every sense alert in the muffled battle zone. His warriors sped overhead. Guns coughed gently. Interference crackled in his helm, his communications useless in the electromagnetic bombardment.

Then they came for him.

The Great Angel watched the gases of the Death Guard envelop the defence lines, retreat momentarily under the blast of drop pod rocket motors, then surge back in, engulfing the top of Bastion 16 and banking high against the Palace walls. Throughout he kept his eyes forwards, following his brother's progress. He watched the haywire shells crackle, and saw the Khan plunge into the gas banks as more drop pods screamed down from on high.

'There,' he said. He pointed with the *Spear of Telesto* into the gas. 'The moment is at hand. Our foe blinds our communications, but you must find me. My brother, my brother! To the aid of my brother!' he shouted.

Without waiting for confirmation from his men, Sanguinius spread his wings and threw himself from the top of Bastion 16 into the deadly fog.

TWENTY-ONE

Khan of Khans
Courage's reward
Brothers at war

Palace outworks, Daylight Wall section 16, 7th of Quartus

The Khan was alone and the enemy saw immediately what a prize was within their grasp. Hundreds of Mortarion's sons closed in from the fog, boltguns blazing. His armour sparked with impacts; for the moment it withstood the assault, but even his panoply was not immune to concentrated fire. The Warhawk lived by one rule of war above all others, one learned the moment his adopted family were slaughtered by the Kurayeds, and borne out in his war against the Palatine on Chogoris.

Attack was the strongest form of defence.

The Khan fought with silent fury, charging into the ranks of the Death Guard with his tulwar spinning in a blurring figure of eight. He crashed into them without slowing, his sword cutting them down. Ceramite was atomised by the blade's disruption field. Viscera spilled onto the earth. Polluted blood showered him.

Through his armour filters he smelled the corruption upon Mortarion's sons. Theirs was sickness of flesh and soul. They fought slowly, without the finesse of other Legions, but the doggedness they were known for had been intensified by their fall into darkness, and no matter how many he killed they pressed at him without cease.

In the thick of them he was safe from the firestorm they unleashed; hand-to-hand combat was on his terms, not theirs. The Death Guard favoured disciplined lines and over-whelming close-range fire to bring down their enemies, taking whatever they received in return with grim stoicism. The Khan refused them their preference, leaping among them, barging down ranks before they formed. He fought unpredictably, throwing off the offensive of his foes, who rightly guessed he wished to regain the Palace. Though he rushed them and pushed them back, or cut diagonally through their forma-tion, always the pattern of his movements took him closer to the defences; if he was forced to take fifty steps away from the walls to throw them into disarray, he would take fifty-one back.

His fury would have inspired a thousand bards had any been able to see it. The fogs made his fight a lonely strug-gle. Hidden from all knowledge he faced the Death Guard alone, his vox and locator beacon jammed by haywire ord-nance. The enemy died by the dozen, for not one was the match of a primarch. But though he fought like a god of old, he was but one being against an army, and not even the sons of the Emperor were tireless or supplied with infinite battle fortune.

The first cut to break through his armour came after his fortieth kill. A son of Mortarion lunged at the back of his knee while he was engaging four to the front. The weapon he sought to slay a primarch with was a simple combat

knife, but perseverance pushed it through the armoured rib-
bing of the joint seal. The Khan felt the blow as an angry,
hot sting, and the attacker paid for the injury with his life.
The Khan smashed backwards with his tulwar's pommel,
his Emperor-given strength caving in ceramite perished by
rot and the greening head beneath. He bellowed in anger,
slashing across at transhuman chest height to drive back
the assailants to his front. Three of them died in a storm of
disruption lightning, their innards laid open to the chemical fog. A fourth lost his left arm, a fifth took a blow to
the head that spun him around and knocked him down.
The Khan would have finished him, but he was reaching
instead for his damaged left knee, trying to pull out the knife
lodged in his suit. At the first attempt his fingers slipped off
a blood-slicked hilt made for hands smaller than his. His
second attempt was foiled by a renewed attack.

The knife penetrated seven centimetres into his flesh, no
more, interfering minimally with the bones of his joint. He
had suffered far worse from deadlier weapons and fought
on. Trusting to his engineered physiology to blunt the pain,
he pressed forwards, but as he did so, he felt the strength
running from his body along with his unstaunched blood.

Another Death Guard died, then another. Explosives were
raining down on him now from the enemy side, seeking him
out, as the XIV Legion shelled their own troops in their lust
to slay a primarch. The Khan wondered if Mortarion saw
his battle there, and grimly ordered his death whatever the
cost to his sons. There was a soulless pragmatism to the act
typical of the Lord of Death.

The fog swirled with the rain of fire, lifting to reveal a
horde of warriors in dirty white and green. A hotness spread
from the piercing knife, infecting his blood with a fever.
Incredulous, the Khan fought still, but the touch of worry

grazed his heart. Never in all of his days had he been ill, but he instinctively recognised disease in him. He was human, after all, on some distant level. His bones ached like ice, and his flesh blazed like the forge. Sweat dripped from his brow. He looked around at his brother's corrupted sons, and wondered what awful pact had been agreed to make them so, and give them the power to sicken a primarch.

'Mortarion! What have you done?' he shouted.

There was no answer.

His body warred with the infection of the knife. Wellbeing came and went as the knife's poisons overcame each trick his engineered physiology deployed. He scrabbled for the knife again as fought, his great tulwar burning through the air to obliterate yet more of the traitors, but he could not take enough time to pull the knife free. It was so firmly embedded, and too delicate for his fingers to easily pluck out.

A surge of bile rose in his throat. His limbs shook. He was slowing. The enemy were gathering closer, like the pack hunters of ancient Earth's steppes, closing in on the great beasts of those times.

His next blow was weak enough to be turned aside. Arms clad in algae-green gauntlets grappled with his forearm. With a bellow of anger he wrenched himself free, and stood for a moment unmolested, before they surged forwards, hacking and stabbing with more diseased weapons, and dragged him down.

The Khan of Khans ends his days, he thought, not upon the sea of grass in one final, glorious charge, but dragged down and butchered in the mud.

They wrestled with him, their filthy knives dragging grooves into his ceramite. They tried to get at the joints in his arms, groin, legs and neck, crawling on him like vermin. He threw them off, once, twice, but the third time was an exhausted heave. His body burned with disease, and his strength left him.

A creature of unclean gods – they were no longer the Emperor's work – brought forwards a huge, rusted axe for the executioner's stroke.

'I am Jaghatai Khan!' he shouted, the passion of his words driving them back. 'I am Jaghatai Khan, loyal son of the Emperor, and I have ridden well.'

The axe swung up to its apex, and hung poised on the cusp of descent. It never fell. The legionary bearing it fell backwards, his headless corpse pulled over by the weight of his weapon.

Jetbikes cut through the gas, and the air was filled with the sound of engines and Chogorian voices.

'The Khan! The Khan! To the Khan!'

A warrior of the ordu leapt from his steed, the speed of his fall turning him into living ordnance that ploughed through the grimy ranks of Mortarion's brood. The warrior was brought to an end as he attempted to rise, hacked apart by a flurry of rusted, dull blades, but he had done his work; his genefather was free.

The Khan erupted from the pile of Death Guard, his tulwar flaring again with the lightning of its energy field. This time, he firmly grasped the knife hilt sticking from his leg. This time, he wrenched it free.

The source of contagion removed, his body redoubled its efforts to purge the sickness. The disease fought with a traitor's hate to undo his cellular biology, but the light of ancient knowledge shone from every curl of the Khan's genecode. Defeat was inevitable.

Still weak, still shivering, the Khan went back on the offensive.

'My ordu! My ordu! To me! To me! Chogoris calls! Ride to me!'

Flights of jetbikes streaked overhead, twin boltguns tearing into the foe. Putrid organs ruptured in rusting armour, and they fell. Land Speeders banked around, vaporising the Death Guard with their meltaguns, and hammering them to pieces with heavy bolter fire.

Now the sons of Mortarion turned their attentions outwards. Away from the Khan, they formed their lines and opened up, weight of fire accomplishing what aim could not. Jetbikes were shot from the sky to gouge tracks of flame and blood into the horde. Warriors punched from the saddles were pinned down and slain.

The Khan abandoned his dancing feints and misdirection, pushing instead directly for the wall.

The fog parted.

Between him and the Palace, a company of Death Guard formed three lines, all presenting bolters. Some fell to bolt or shell fire from the wall, but their ranks closed up as each warrior died. Behind them seethed Horus' damned mortal followers in uncountable number, most half-dead from the gas already, but driven on by hate.

He presented his sword, saluted them and prepared to die.

'A rush into the jaws of death, snatched free, to plunge therein again at will,' he said. 'I greet death with a smile on my face.'

Sanguinius' voice sliced through the muffling fog as if it were not there.

'My brother, my brother! To the aid of my brother!'

Katsuhiro snapped off shot after shot. Leaving the Traitor Space Marines to the attentions of the Blood Angels, he downed mutants, sickly men and turncoat army soldiers. When the call went out, the Blood Angels looked out into the gas, following something he could not see. They stood from the wall as one, and leapt over the sloping rampart.

'Drive them back!' roared their sergeants. 'Into them, for the Emperor! For Sanguinius!'

Caught up in their bloodlust, the Nagandan conscripts rose alongside the Blood Angels and charged after them. Katsuhiro ran behind a line trooper of the IX Legion, snapping off opportunistic shots and jabbing with his bayonet. The Blood Angel smashed his way through the lesser humans of the enemy, his fists alone enough to slay the rabble with single blows. He saved his bolts for his traitor kin.

'The primarch! I see the Khan!' someone called.

Horus' wretches parted for a moment, and Katsuhiro saw a line of Death Guard forming up ahead. Raised above them on a pile of corpses was a giant in white, another primarch, the Warhawk himself.

The Khan was utterly different to his brother Sanguinius, yet fundamentally the same. Like the Great Angel, he was forged of high science and lost arts. Like Sanguinius, he inspired dread and awe in Katsuhiro in equal measure. But where Sanguinius recalled higher, more refined creatures than men, and so inspired humanity to excel, the Khan was a being of caged lightning. He was a storm's fury poured into the shape of man. Where calmness and a near-holy beauty radiated from the Angel, the Warhawk was a restless wind that filled Katsuhiro with the need to rush forwards, to charge through the enemy, to ride them down and never stop moving, to doubt all, to know all, to laugh and live fully through the best of times and the worst of times, and then at the last to greet death with a defiant smile.

'To the Khan! To the Khan! For the Emperor!' the Blood Angels shouted.

They pressed forwards again, the poison fog and the swirl of combat obscuring the fate of Jaghatai Khan. Katsuhiro speared a man covered in weeping sores through the throat with his bayonet, and hurled back another diseased specimen with a shot to the chest. Many of the enemy had no protection against the gas and were dying as they fought. The traitorous soldiers of the earlier landings had been replaced by wild-eyed lunatics with sigils of their evil religion burned into their skin. There were people of every desperate sort, hive-dregs, mutants, abhumans and others of the lowest positions in Imperial society. Katsuhiro had wondered how anyone could turn on the Emperor, but confronted with the hatred he saw in the eyes of these savages, he gained an inkling that the dream of Imperium was a nightmare for some.

The damned came at them in large numbers, forming a buffer between the Death Guard's line and the Blood Angels. The IX Legion fought with terrifying ferocity, but their way was blocked no matter how many they slew. Katsuhiro's world closed to a few square metres delineated by the faces of the foe, time measured not in seconds but in kills. He saw but barely registered light blazing through the gas. The Blood Angels roared the name of their primarch, 'Sanguinius!' and pushed the enemy harder. Katsuhiro and his fellow mortals were sucked deeper into the horde in their wake, embattled, sure to die, until the last line parted, and the enemy dregs fled back into the fog. In reward for his courage, Katsuhiro was privileged to glimpse two of the Emperor's warrior-sons fighting side by side.

Light shone through the gas, and Sanguinius was there; bright and devastating as a cometary impact, he dived from the heavens into the enemy's midst. In one hand shone his golden sword, in the other he wielded the *Spear of Telesto*. The sword felled traitors with every blow, but the spear's arcane technology was particularly deadly to the tainted Death

Guard. With each blast from its gilded head, the Death Guard writhed and gave inhuman squeals, and melted in its rays.

'For the Emperor!' Sanguinius called, and saluted his brother.

Behind his filth-smeared mask, the Khan grinned and replied, 'For the Emperor!' and joined his brother's slaughtering.

Battle cries went up, and through the gas a mixed group of Blood Angels, White Scars and human soldiers came, cutting through the crowds of men and mutants. Jetpacks howled, and golden, winged warriors thumped down behind the Khan, forming a perimeter. Together, back to back, the primarchs fought until the Death Guard were reduced to a tattered handful who slipped away into the gas clouds.

Gunship engines thundered from the direction of the Palace.

'We must depart now,' Sanguinius told his brother. 'They will return.' Already the shelling was picking up pace around them.

'Not quite yet, my brother,' said the Khan, pushing past his guardians.

'What are you doing?' yelled Sanguinius, but followed after the limping Khan.

'My jetbike. I must go to it and inload the images I gathered. The haywire wiped my armour's datacache.'

'They are returning, my lords!' a Blood Angel shouted. The crackle of boltgun fire began anew.

'Then fight them off. I need only seconds,' said the Khan. 'With this we shall know our enemy better, and beat him all the more soundly.'

'This is unwise, brother!' Sanguinius shouted, loosing off a blast from the *Spear of Telesto*.

'Nothing in war is wise. Violence is not wisdom. Do you believe I went over the wall merely for glory?'

'It had crossed my mind you might be bored.'

'Hold them back.' The Khan's laughter turned into coughing.

'Something ails you, brother?'

'A poisoned knife,' he said.

'They poisoned you?'

'Sorcery brought the sickness. Do not fear, the effect is dwindling, but I trust you to strike off my head should my loyalty appear to waver.'

The Khan reached the wreck of his machine and heaved it over. Lights still shone on the instrument panel, and he punched them rapidly. A status bar appeared on the main display.

'They are returning! Hurry!' said Sanguinius. He raised his spear. A cone of noiseless light snapped out, taking the lives of three Death Guard who approached. More were behind, and Sanguinius leapt at them, sword whirling.

A Thunderhawk set down close by. Others whooshed by overhead, their boltguns swivelling as they tracked priority targets in the murk.

'Exload complete,' the jetbike's cogitator intoned.

'It is done,' said the Khan. 'I have what we need.' He stumbled. His wounded leg was still weak.

'Then we go!' Sanguinius shouted over the howl of the engines. He plunged his sword through the chest of a traitor, kicked another back and reached out to steady his brother. Together, their armour dulled by rotting blood and mud, the pair of them boarded the Thunderhawk as Blood Angels fired from the ramp, blasting back the enemy. The Khan limped inside while Sanguinius stood on the ramp and loosed a pair of final blasts from his marvellous spear.

Surrounded by explosions, the gunship took off into a sky crowded with ships. They were harried all the way back over the wall, where a combination of the aegis and the defensive guns drove off their pursuers.

Sanguinius turned away from the open ramp only when they were over the city. 'Did you see what has happened to them?' he said. 'Mortarion's sons are diseased. Were it not for all I have witnessed, I would not have thought it possible for a legionary to become so afflicted.'

'Despite that, brother, they are more resilient than ever.' The seated Khan dragged off his helmet, revealing a pale face drenched with sweat. 'They have sold themselves to the so-called gods of the warp,' he said. 'Mortarion has fallen far. Once the staunchest opponent of sorcery, he embraces it fully. Truly these gods play with us. They love irony very much.'

Sanguinius arched an eyebrow at the Khan. 'You do not look your best, brother.'

The Khan shivered. 'I do not feel it, but now we return within the walls, the disease appears to be withdrawing quickly. See the blade that infected me.'

He held up his left hand. Still clasped in his fist from when he had torn it from his knee was the Death Guard's combat knife. Beneath its coating of primarch's blood it was pitted with rust, and the edge was dull, yet it exuded a sense of peril. Black venom dribbled from the blade over the Khan's fist, evaporating in the air before it hit the ground.

'An evil thing,' said Sanguinius.

They passed some threshold over the Palace, and the knife blade suddenly crumbled into dust, and the venom boiled away, leaving only the filthy hilt, toylike in the Khan's immense palm.

The brothers shared a look.

'Curious,' said Sanguinius.

'Our father's doing, surely,' said the Khan, marvelling as the hilt collapsed into nothing. A smear of his drying blood gritted with grains of rust was all that remained of the weapon. 'His protection is strongest over the Palace. That is the only explanation. This is a blade of the warp, and He is proof against its witchcraft. The toxin, too, has gone from my blood. I feel His presence, as a cool wind soothes a burn.' He looked up at his brother. 'My equilibrium returns.'

He fell silent for a moment, then said, 'On Prospero, Mortarion tried to sway me to Horus' cause. He spoke of the truth and of Horus' rightness, and of our father's lies.' He clenched his fist. 'I was the most critical of father's designs, but now I see the truth, and it forgives all mistakes on His part. The warp is nothing but madness and corruption. Our brothers lose their minds one by one. When we face Mortarion again, we will fight a facet of a greater evil, a puppet, and not the proud warlord he once was. This troubles me greatly.'

Sanguinius' wings twitched.

'I cannot recall a time I did not feel troubled, my brother,' he said.

The primarchs retreated into the gunship and it rose from the battle with furious noise, carrying the sons of the Emperor away from immediate danger. The golden guardians of Sanguinius rocketed after the ship, the jet turbines set between their metal wings screaming like fighting birds.

'Fall back!' A transhuman voice boomed from the fog. 'Back to the defence line!'

Katsuhiro and the few conscripts still alive fled gratefully. The Space Marines let them run by, holding off the enemy with steady bursts of fire while they escaped.

Chaos ruled on both sides. The conscripts had gone into the fog of gas in poor order, and came out with none at all. But the Space Marines fought with incredible discipline. The swirl of battle had thrown them together. Red-armoured and white-armoured legionaries stood shoulder to shoulder. To an outsider, it would not have been apparent that most had never fought together before, but the ad hoc units worked smoothly, covering one another as they fell back, squad by squad, to the defence line.

The baying of barely human traitors mocked the retreat, but there was no doubt who was victorious. Hundreds, if not thousands, of lesser mortals blanketed the muddy field, with scores of giants in dirty white strewn among them. There were islands of bright red and cleaner white too, as well as swift contra-gravity mounts burning on the ground. Nevertheless the balance was in the loyalists' favour.

It was a hollow triumph. They had come only a short way from the ramparts. Soon Katsuhiro found himself scrambling over broken chunks of rockcrete, only belatedly realising he had reached the third line. Amid the devastation he found an intact landmark, a numbered comms tower, its mast lights still blinking, and made his way back to his station.

Shells continued to scream down, all of the explosive variety, but he was too exhausted to duck, and left his fate in the hands of the universe. The adrenaline gone, his sickness returned with a vengeance, and his limbs shook. As he made it back to his company's section the poison fogs began to part. He heard engines in the thinning mist, and saw armoured giants falling back. Tired warriors of his company slumped onto the few intact stretches of rampart left. There were more corpses than living men, and that included Runnecan.

Runnecan lay on his back staring up at the sky, not far from where he and Katsuhiro had begun the battle, not having made it off the wall. There was no sign of what had killed him. His gas mask was still in place. No claw or knife cut had opened his body. A mass-reactive would have left a spread of meat, but though he was unmistakably dead he looked unmarked.

Katsuhiro knelt by Runnecan's side. He had never liked the man, and the loss he felt took him by surprise. For some reason he pulled off the other man's mask, and wished he hadn't. Runnecan's ratty little face wore a disturbing expression of horrified surprise.

Footsteps crunched to a stop behind him.

'Now that is a spot of terrible luck,' said Doromek.

Katsuhiro twisted around. The effort required was immense. The mask he wore was poorly designed. His breath had fogged the lenses, and the front pulled to the side as he turned, cutting his vision down further.

Doromek peered down. He was unmasked, and munching on a piece of bread gripped in one bloodstained hand.

'You can take that off now, you know,' he said, nodding at Katsuhiro's gas mask. 'The air still stinks, but the gas is not concentrated enough to harm you any more.'

Hesitantly, Katsuhiro reached up, unclasped the gas mask and pulled it off over his head. It slithered on his sweat in a repulsive fashion. The cold of the mountain air was a punch in the face, and the smell of the gas nauseating, but he gulped it down gratefully, glad to be free of the hood.

'Thank the Emperor,' said Katsuhiro. 'The Emperor protects.'

Doromek gave him a curious look. 'You're not one of them, are you? The worshippers?'

'I...' said Katsuhiro. 'What? I just heard it somewhere.'

'Well,' said Doromek, 'the Emperor had nothing to do with this. Space Marines and blind chance saved the day.'

'Where have the enemy gone?'

'Back,' said Doromek. 'They'll reinforce the siege camps. They achieved what they set out to do, I expect. They brought up some artillery under the cover of the fighting, lobbed some shells over the walls.'

'Why?'

'Beats me,' said Doromek with a shrug. 'But they'll have a reason, you can be sure of that. I never knew legionaries do anything without a reason.' Doromek smiled at him. 'You were pretty brave, weren't you?'

Katsuhiro dropped his eyes, letting his gaze settle on Runnecan. 'Leave me alone.'

'Suit yourself,' said Doromek. He dropped a packet of bread by Katsuhiro's side and left. 'Don't get too comfortable,' he called. 'The third line's had it. We'll be pulling back behind the second soon.'

Katsuhiro watched until Doromek had gone. When he was out of sight, he grabbed Runnecan. Rolling him over made him grunt with effort. The dead were always heavier than he expected, and in his weakened state shifting the body was almost too much for him. Runnecan's open eyes disturbed him, and he was gladder than he should have been to pitch him over face down into the mud.

What he saw next was worse.

He remained staring at Runnecan's back for a long time.

The wound that had killed him was a las-burn, neatly placed in his back, right over his heart.

TWENTY-TWO

Bloodhunt
The price of glory
An unworthy son

The Conqueror, *Terran near orbit, 7th of Quartus*

Khârn's presence terrified the bridge crew. Lotara's armsmen stiffened when he entered, holding their weapons down but ready. The sound of his tread clanging slowly off the deck made the deck officers cower. They could smell the blood caked onto his weapons. They shivered at the clink of the chains that bound them to his armour. Let them tremble, he thought. Let them fear me.

Lotara Sarrin feared him too, but she was brave enough to face him. The ship and crew were ragged. Maintenance went undone. Whole areas of the command deck were dark. Machines spilled cabled entrails onto the deck. The smell of blood was ever-present. Dust lay thickly on abandoned stations. The crew's uniforms were filthy, and there were far too few of them on the bridge. Murder whittled them away. Sarrin too was dirty and unkempt. The blood print honour she bore on her uniform was lost beneath a hundred other stains but she, unlike her ship, was still proud.

She had been waiting impatiently for him and got up to speak to Khârn as soon as he approached her command throne. 'We have a big problem,' she said, as he reached her.

Khârn swallowed thickly. 'Hnnnh,' he grunted. He forced his panting breath into the patterns of speech. 'No greeting, Lotara, no inquiry after my health?' His voice was an intoxicated slur. Controlling his urge to violence took all of his concentration. The longer they were in orbit, the harder the Nails pounded, and the louder the whispered demands in his head were that he spill blood. Command was an unwelcome distraction. He had to fight.

'I don't have time for your attempts at humour, neither do you – not if you want to see this war out and not die at the hands of your own father,' she said. She was rake-thin, worn out by the struggle to impose some order on her ship. 'Do it,' she ordered one of her officers. 'Put it on the hololith.'

Khârn's hands flexed impatiently around the haft of *Gorechild*. The axe was never away from his hands. He'd rather lay aside his limbs. 'I do not have time for, hrrrrnh… for this… for this either.'

'Make time. Look, listen, damn you, Khârn. Wake up! Look at what you have done.'

A cylindrical projection sprang on. Blood red from top to bottom, it appeared to be malfunctioning. It was not. An awful roaring emanated from the audio projectors, accompanied by screams so thin they were barely audible. A huge, inhuman hand swept by, taloned fingers spread, slashing downwards. A tumble of limbs and gore spread across the floor.

'And?' said Khârn. The Nails thumped softly in his skull at the display, tempting him to indulge in a similar slaughter on the bridge. The crew left were below half-strength. All of them knew what he was capable of. They expected him to kill them. Why should he disappoint? His forefinger twitched towards the switch that would send the mica dragon's teeth into a blur. He estimated he could cut down twenty of the bridge crew before they raised a single gun against him. 'The mortals die. The legionaries do not.'

'Angron is rampaging through the thrall decks!' Lotara said. 'We've too few men left. We can't afford losses. Not like this.'

He imagined taking her skull. She was physically weak, but her efforts had sent millions of men to their deaths. She would be a worthy offering to the brass throne.

The idea horrified him, only a little, but enough to make him force his thoughts back under control.

'He'll kill them all, I'm sure, and we have a more pressing problem.'

'Explain,' breathed Khârn, a dangerous, throaty whisper.

'Since you shut him down there, Angron has been butchering his way through the ship. He is getting dangerously close to the enginarium. If he gets in there and slaughters the transmechanic clades the whole ship could go up. Or he'll get bored and find his way up here, then you'll have to fight him.'

Khârn stared at the image. Angron's daemonic face swung into view. A yellow eye squinted into the vid augur. A giant fist followed, punching it into nothing and sending the projection cylinder into a fuzz of static. He would fight Angron. He could.

'Cut the feed,' Lotara said. The projection cylinder winked out. 'Can't you stop him? We have come this far. I don't want it to end before we have the chance to fight.'

'My father is doing what he wants,' said Khârn, swallowing

a mouthful of coppery saliva. 'Nothing can restrain him. He will not go back into the vault. He has become too strong to contain. I... I...'

Blood. Angron spilled blood. A voice in his head demanded to know why Khârn did not.

Lotara took a step closer to him.

'Khârn? Khârn! Listen to me!' she snapped.

'I am listening,' he said, with difficulty.

'Khârn, I know this is hard for you,' she said gently. 'But I know you can hear me and that you understand. Angron has to be stopped.'

Khârn looked down on her. His pulse thundered in his brain, each beat of his hearts a terrible agony. 'You were his favourite. He gave you the blood mark himself, and you want to lock him away. Our father wished to be first on Terra. He was on the verge of rage anyway. Seeing Mortarion's Legion sent in before ours is an insult. We are fortunate he did not leave the *Conqueror* to attack the Death Guard.'

'This is not a good situation,' she said.

'He is contained. You sealed him in as I ordered. Let him alone. He can do little harm where he is.'

'That is little harm?' she said. Her face wrinkled in disbelief. 'Little harm does not encompass the slaughtering of our tech cadre and the resulting reactor death.'

'What do you suggest?' said Khârn. He looked at her through a red haze. Sarrin was renowned for her cool head, but she too was feeling the effects of Angron's influence. The crew had suffered the attentions of the Legion for a long time. He thought it likely they would soon turn on each other as the legionaries had. 'We are changed, Lotara. This ship is a crucible of rage. The pull to violence in my mind is so strong that the slightest faltering of concentration will see a scene on this command deck similar to the one below.' He moved. The chain binding his weapon to his wrist clinked. Lotara's gaze flicked to the head of the great axe. 'I think now of how much pressure would be required for me to crush your skull, how many shots your armsmen will have time to fire before I cut them down. Let Angron vent his fury on the thralls, better them than more legionaries. I can spare no more thought for the matter.'

She shook her head. 'No, no, if this is allowed to go on, we are all dead. We have to either confine him or get him off the ship. Only you can do that. You have to pull yourself together. Snap out of your bloodlust, Khârn. Help me!'

'If he attempts to land on Terra, he will die,' said Khârn. 'So say Magnus, and Layak and the other mystics. Insufficient blood has been offered to the lords in the warp. The Emperor denies the Neverborn access. Not until Terra's soil is damp with vitae will the gates open for their kind.'

'Daemons,' she said harshly. 'How has it come to this?' She looked at him fiercely. 'How did this happen to you?'

'They are our allies,' he said. 'Angron is blessed by the gods in the warp, and he is still my genesire.'

She nodded and massaged her forehead. 'He is still Angron, I know. He is in there.' She snapped her gaze back up to his face. 'Do you wish him to die?' Privation and time had aged her so much while he remained strong. She would be dead in not so many years, he thought, if she managed to survive the war. A poor end for such an accomplished killer. Better to die a warrior's death, in battle. He could offer her that honour.

'He might survive the detonation,' she said. She was speaking quickly, aware Khârn's thoughts were drifting. 'Will he survive an attempt to reach Terra? Do you want to find out?'

Khârn shook his head slowly.

'Then I have an idea. The *Nightfall*.' She was gabbling now. She had a limited period while Khârn would remain calm.

'The Night Lords,' he said dismissively.

'A few weeks ago, I received some intelligence,' she said. 'From the Twentieth Legion. They told me there is some kind of prison made for a primarch on the *Nightfall*. If we can get them to take Angron, it will keep him occupied for a while. Long enough until the time comes for him to land.'

The Khârn of old would have interrogated her as to how the Alpha Legion gave her this message, and why, but such finesse of thought was beyond him now, lost under an ocean of blood.

'How?' he said. It was all he could manage to say.

'You'll have to do it,' she replied. She rubbed her hand over her face again. 'You'll have to do all of it. The arrogant dogs won't answer my requests for communication. They might listen to you.'

'Might,' said Khârn. His sense of self floated on a sea of red, threatening to sink at any time. He could taste the blood. Hear the screams.

'Yes, curse you!' she snapped. 'Might! It's the best chance we have. Send the message,' she commanded. Her hololith master nodded and began to direct his few remaining serfs. A floating orb coasted down from the ceiling near to Khârn, ready to capture his image for transmission.

'I did not agree,' said Khârn, his voice dreamily murderous. In his mind's eye he saw Terra burning, and bodies falling before his axe.

'Another damn thing we don't have time for,' she said. 'Send my request again to the *Nightfall*. Inform them Lord Khârn, Eighth Captain of the Twelfth Legion, equerry of the primarch Angron, wishes to speak with their leader.' She turned her attention back to Khârn. 'There's some treacherous whoreson in charge now. No sign of Curze. Sevatar I have heard is dead. Khârn!' she said.

His attention drifted back to her. 'Who will I speak with?'

An acceptance chime tolled from the hololithic communications station.

'My lady, I have their assent.'

'Activate the projection field,' she said.

The hololithic phantom of a youthful-looking Space Marine stood upon the deck, life-size. He was unusually flamboyant in appearance for one of his kind. The long, pale hair draped over his shoulders was more characteristic of Fulgrim's warriors than Curze's, and his armour gleamed, sub-surface projection plates making it squirm with lightning effects. He lacked the skulls and fetishes of bone worn by his brethren. Most striking were the vertical black ovals tattooed over his eyes, and the large sword strapped to his left side. Khârn recognised it as a weapon of the warp. He growled instinctively. A weakling's weapon.

'My Lord Skraivok, the Painted Count,' said Lotara, bowing. 'Might I present to you the Lord Khârn, equerry to the primarch Angron, master of the Eighth–'

'Yes, yes,' said Skraivok, waving his hand. 'Your minions relayed all this. Besides, who would not recognise the great Khârn! Such a reputation.' He clucked his tongue. 'My, my, Eighth Captain Khârn, what an unexpected pleasure.' Everything about the Night Lord howled with insincerity: his posture, his smile, the tone of his voice. 'What can I possibly do for so vaunted a warrior as yourself?'

'I want a service from you,' said Khârn bluntly.

Skraivok laughed. 'How very forwards! You are not speaking with some fame-dazzled captain. I am the commander of the Night Lords in this warzone, perhaps leader of the Legion itself.'

'By what right?' said Khârn.

Skraivok gripped the hilt of his sheathed sword with his left hand. 'By right of conquest. I thought you might respect that.'

I have never respected any Night Lord, Khârn managed not to say. He wanted to challenge the captain to a duel right there. Enough of his wits remained under the punishing thump of the Nails that he refrained.

'Battle is what we are made for. If you have triumphed, then I will speak with you.'

This seemed to satisfy Skraivok.

That's better. I don't want us to get off on the wrong foot. Now, to business. This service, whatever it is it will cost you. Times are not what they were. Nobody gains the Night Lords' aid for free. I have a price in mind, depending on what you require, naturally.

This fool offended him. The Butcher's Nails pounded harder in his skull at the affront. Khârn managed, somehow, to keep his voice level.

'First tell me something, Painted Count. I have heard rumours about your vessel. Before we bargain, I must know whether they are true.'

Skraivok's eyes narrowed. *'What rumours might they be?'*

'That in your flagship is a prison for a primarch.'

The Night Lord's face crinkled with humour. Starting around his eyes in the depths of his tattooed stripes, his smile was entirely dark in nature. *'Don't tell me. You're having trouble with your transcendent lord! Favoured of Khorne, or whatever this god's name is. I suppose that is what happens when one hearkens to gods. You wish me to take that monster aboard my vessel?'* He smiled condescendingly. *'My my, what an interesting proposition.'*

'This is getting us nowhere,' said Khârn. 'Cut communications before I decide to go and cut off his head.'

'No, wait!' countermanded Lotara, holding out her hand to stop her communications officer. 'Forgive me, Lord Skraivok. Khârn is much troubled by his father's predicament. At least, let us know if it is true. Is there somewhere upon the *Nightfall* that might hold our lord until it is time for him to join the battle? Does this prison exist?'

'A prison? No,' said Skraivok. *'It is more than that. It is a labyrinth, devised by Perturabo himself to torment Vulkan. As you might imagine, it is ingenious and deadly in design. The Drake was one of the Emperor's more intelligent sons.'*

'How do you know this?' growled Khârn. 'How do I know you speak the truth?'

'Mostly because I was put into it,' said Skraivok.

'You escaped?' said Khârn. 'You. Then it is not fit to hold a primarch.'

Skraivok smirked. *'It'll hold your primarch. He is a mindless monster. I did escape, but I confess I had help. The labyrinth will hold your lord. Not forever, I imagine all those little traps and dilemmas will slow him down not at all and he'll simply batter his way out, but it will occupy him for a time.'*

'How long?' asked Lotara.

'Long enough,' said Skraivok. *'The moment approaches when he will be able to manifest on Terra, does it not? That is the Warmaster's plan.'*

'And how do you know that?' said Khârn neutrally. The Nails burned into his hindbrain. He did not like this Skraivok. He was pompous, melodramatic, playing the villain's role like an actor.

'As I said, I have help.' Skraivok's hand twisted around his sword's leathern grip. He thought a moment. *'I will do it,'* he said. *'We will take him. But I require something from you in return.'*

'What do you require for this service?'

Skraivok's unpleasant grin spread wider. *'This will surprise you, but I want something you have in great supply, Lord Khârn. I want glory, and you have so much of that I am sure you can spare me a little.'*

* * *

Khârn passed through heavy blast doors from the upper
levels of the ship into the abattoir of the thrall decks. The
doors were multiply layered, and strong. Even with his mind
half-drunk on the lust for blood, Khârn saw the irony inher-
ent to those doors. Angron had spent his youth as a slave,
fighting for other slaves. His anger towards the Emperor
sprang from his inability to save his fellows, yet he became
a master of slaves himself, and wary enough of them to keep
them under tight control as brutal as that meted out by his
former owners. As time had passed and the Legion degen-
erated, the doors had provided a little safety to the abused
multitudes of the crew. This part of the ship was one place
where Khârn's brothers could not easily go.

The decks had been in a terrible state even before Khârn
shut Angron in. Now, they were close to ruinous. The lumens
were out. Sparks spat lethargically from severed cabling.
Bodies clogged every corridor of the thrall decks, not a single
one of them entire. The whole warren of workshops, service
ways, barracks, food halls and conduits stank – that nauseating battle reek of spilled guts and fear. Viscera festooned
the walls like celebratory flags. Scraps of flesh spattered every
surface. Khârn paused and swung his head around, tasking
his auto-senses with a deep sweep of his immediate surroundings. Boosted by the ship's internal auspex, his helm
senses scried fifty metres in every direction, providing him
with an accurate cartolithic display of the area – a long
way in the convoluted bowels of a void-ship. Among the
maze of corridors he found not one sign of life. It was so
quiet. In the dark there he could feel the *Conqueror* itself.
The machine soul of the battleship had grown fierce with
the spilling of blood. It was watching Khârn.

None of Angron's victims could have put up much of a
fight. Where the bodies hadn't been smashed into a pulp

by the primarch, Khârn saw only wounds to the rear. They'd died running.

The sight could not disturb Khârn, he who had slaughtered civilisations. For years now blood and death had ruled the corridors of the *Conqueror*. Angron had despatched him below decks to kill three hundred thralls himself, to build a throne from their skulls. Even so, the extent of Angron's massacring stirred disgust in his flinty heart. There was no honour in this, no skill, no *point*, only butchery for the sake of killing. Blood must be spilled, their god demanded it, but there were better ways to make sacrifice than this.

He stopped to let his cartolith update. This part of the vessel had never been legionary territory, and he would be lost down there without the map. More pressingly, he did not know if Angron's otherworldly form would register on his battleplate's auto-senses. He had no desire to stumble across his genesire unprepared. He shifted his grip on *Gorechild*, his axe. Its teeth glinted. His thumb hovered over the activation stud.

'My lord!' he called into the darkness. 'It is I, Khârn!'

The drip of blood and creaking of cooling machinery replied.

Mag-locked to his thigh next to his holstered plasma pistol was a teleport beacon. There were no armourers left in the *Conqueror*'s ruined workshops, so Khârn himself had fastened a heavy, barbed spike to the shaft. Khârn hadn't checked the homer mounted at the other end. Its ready light blinked when activated, but he had forgotten how to run the checks needed to ensure it definitely worked, another part of his past drowned in the ocean of blood filling his soul. Either it would perform, or he would die according to the will of his god. He paid it little attention, letting it bump along the ground as he prowled through the under-decks.

Each turn of the corridors, each open door, showed him
the same bloody ruin. The steady blink of the teleport homer's ready light flashed on thousands of lifeless thralls. The
dead were scattered everywhere. In places they were reduced
by Angron's ferocity to thick slurries of gore where recognisable body parts were few and far between. In places
the primarch's sword had cut into the walls, and there the
wounded metal shone with dark light.

Khârn passed a spur corridor leading to the upper decks
closed off at the far end by an armoured door. According
to his cartolith, the corridor was over fifty metres long. He
could not see to the end, for the corridor was packed by
the standing dead. The bodies nearer the main way were
smears of red. Further into the crowd, the thralls' wounds
became less severe, until, about ten metres in, they exhib-
ited no sign of physical harm. The mortals had crushed
each other in their panic to escape, creating a press so tight
that Angron could not get to them all. It had done them
no good, for they had suffocated.

Khârn grunted at the sight and moved on.

He neared the enginarium section and several possible
routes of escape for the primarch. Blast doors leading out
to the lower embarkation decks and stores were scarred by
accidental cuts. Evidently Angron had been focused on his
quarry or he would have sliced his way out there. No mortal material could stop the otherworldly blade of Angron's
sword for long.

Shortly after, Khârn emerged onto the observational gallery of a long, hexagonal hold. The walls were punctuated
by four sets of doors down the sides, also hexagonal, and
surrounded by hazard striping splashed with blood. Corpses
lay about like storm-tossed leaves. When he descended stairs
to the hold floor, his feet splashed through deep puddles

of blood. The hold had been exhausted of supplies some time ago. Thralls had set up tents in the corners and more elaborate homes in empty containers, turning it into an ugly shanty town. If they sought sanctuary there, it had done them no good. Their bodies were sprawled over the wreck of their possessions.

'Lotara,' he voxed. His voice was obscenely loud in the confines of his helm. 'Lotara, this is Khârn. Have you any sign of him?' The vox-beads hissed in his ear. 'Lotara?'

The vox clicked. *'Khârn. We've lost him.'* Lotara's voice was faint.

Khârn stopped walking.

'Where?'

'Before he reached the enginarium. He's gone to ground. We can't find him on any of the augurs. Most of the internal systems are out. We're…'

Lotara's voice dropped out in a burble of static dominated by the pulsing of an electromagnetic heart. He was so close to the reactor it interfered with the vox. Its beating sounded uncannily like the throb of the Nails.

'Lotara?' he said.

Her voice reasserted itself over the pulsing hiss. *'The vox-relay downdecks must have been compromised. Shielding around the reactor blocks signals from outside. You could try to find a hardline.'*

'I see none,' Khârn said. 'Will Skraivok be able to receive my notification?'

'Keep your vox-channel open to me,' said Lotara. *'I will relay the order when you have him.'*

'Do not trust the Night Lord,' said Khârn.

'This is the best chance we have. Stop your father, or our war is over.'

Khârn left the channel open, and moved on again.

* * *

More holds came and went, all emptied long ago. The dried-up corpses of past rampages lay black in the corners. The pulse of the reactor on the open vox-channel grew louder. The temperature rose. Khârn reached the edge of the thrall decks and stores, beyond which the enginarium sections began.

In a hold half a kilometre long, he found his father.

Khârn felt the primarch's presence as a great warm patch of rage welling up from the dark spaces between stacked cargo containers. In the hold, a place of silent cranes and dusty supplies, Angron's fury was as obvious as a volcano spewing lava. But exactly where the primarch was, Khârn could not say. Every avenue dividing the supply stacks was a potential ambush site. He could not fight his father and win. When Angron was united with his Legion, many years gone by, he had killed every captain sent to speak with him apart from Khârn. None of them had fought back. Khârn vowed to defend himself this time, but even so he would die. Though he was renowned as the greatest warrior among the Legiones Astartes, even Khârn could not beat Angron before his transformation. Now, infused with the power of the warp and sharing the God of War's infinite rage, Angron was practically invincible.

Khârn unhooked the teleport beacon and proceeded in a crouch with his axe ready. He did not need to fight to win, only long enough to tag his genefather with the device.

The sooner it was done the better. There was no honour in skulking around in the shadows.

'Father!' he called. 'Father! It is I, Khârn!'

His amplified voice echoed through the hold.

'Father!'

Something huge moved way off in the dark. Khârn turned around while his auto-senses struggled with the echoes in their attempt to triangulate the movement.

'Father!'

'Khârn,' Angron's voice rumbled from the dark, so low and powerful the deck trembled. *'Why are you here?'*

'I have come to find you, father. The *Conqueror* is at risk. We can afford no more deaths among the crew.'

Angron laughed. *'Khârn, Khârn, Lord Khorne demands blood and skulls. Do you not hear his cries? Blood and skulls.'*

Khârn felt a stir of unease. He heard the whispers. The words remained elusive, but the furious insistence that murder be done and blood spilled was clear enough. He feared hearing what the words would say. He knew that enlightenment would come in time.

'I do not hear him, my lord,' said Khârn.

'You will. He values you, my son.'

Heavy footsteps thumped deep in the stacks. Knocked chains jangled.

'These slaves are unworthy offerings for the Blood God, but you, Khârn… Your skull will make a fine gift.'

Angron came out of nowhere. Khârn barely had time to twist aside from the blow of his unholy sword. The blade, longer than Khârn was tall, embedded itself in the deck. Green fire sheathed it, eating into the metal. Khârn leapt back too late. Angron's backhand clipped him, sending him noisily into the side of a cargo container. Khârn's bulk pushed a deep dent into the metal, and he struggled to get out before Angron wrenched his sword free and whirled it around at his head. Khârn fell forwards from the dent just as the blade hissed through the air, splitting the container's side wide open. Plastek-wrapped packets bounced off the floor. He pushed up with his legs, parrying the next blow with *Gorechild*. The impact jarred him from head to toe, and he reeled back down an avenue between the containers, turned, and ran.

Angron pounded after him. Khârn slipped into a dark space, and eluded his father.

He leaned back against metal. Both his hearts thundered. The Butcher's Nails sang their melodies of pain into the meat of his brain, urging him to fight.

'*You stole my axe, Khârn,*' Angron growled. '*You took my weapon from me. Now you steal his favour. Khorne's eye strays from me to you.*'

'I serve only you, my father,' Khârn called.

'*You serve me by hunting me in the dark?*'

'Only to bring you to the battle, my lord.'

Angron snarled. Khârn risked glimpsing down the avenue. Angron strode past, a monster from myth: horned, huge, red-skinned, nostrils twitching as he sniffed out his son. Blood stink and anger washed off him in hot waves. He was mighty, but his god-given gifts had robbed him of all art other than killing, and Khârn remained hidden.

'*What battle would that be?*' Angron rumbled. '*The battle against tedium as we watch Mortarion's sons fight where we should? The battle against my brother's arrogance? Horus defies Khorne. Khorne demands we fight for him now, yet the Warmaster keeps us caged.*' Metal squealed as he upended a stack of containers hundreds of tonnes in weight as if they were empty card boxes. The boom of them falling to the deck took a long moment to die. '*I am the avatar of rage. The power of the warp runs through me, my son. I will not be chained like a dog any longer, not by the Emperor, not by Horus, and not by you. You are a fool to come here. I will kill you. There will be blood, there will be skulls. Khorne cares not whence the blood flows!*'

Angron threw over another stack. Khârn used the cover of the noise to run out unnoticed behind his father. Angron's whole upper body heaved with each breath. Leathery wings flexed. Every movement he made revealed a towering anger barely contained. Khârn recognised the condition in himself.

Khârn ran, *Gorechild* in one hand, the unwieldy spear of the teleport homer in the other. Gathering all his strength, he leapt, the fibre muscles in his battleplate sending him high. He crashed into Angron's back, and buried the teleport homer deep in his father's searing red skin between the shoulders where, even with great determination, the primarch would struggle to knock it loose.

Angron's reaction was immediate and furious. He roared loudly, spinning around, knocking Khârn back. Khârn landed heavily, and scrambled up, while Angron's hand came up, scratching at his back, but though his black nails brushed the teleport homer, it refused to be dislodged.

'You have no honour! Attacking from behind.' Yellow eyes blazed. *'No true son of mine would stoop so low. We are warriors! We face our enemies. We look them in the eye before we take their heads for the skull throne! You are weak, all of you, slaves to my father then slaves to me. I should have killed you that day you first came to me. You are weak!'*

Khârn backed away. The urge to throw himself into battle with his father was crippling his mind. 'Lotara, now!' He spoke through a mouthful of blood. Fluid ran down his nasal passages from his bleeding brain and drooled from his lips and out of the open vent of his breathing grille. 'Lotara! Lotara!' he snarled. 'Now!'

Static replied. Angron was on him. He jumped, wings spread, half gliding, half falling towards his equerry. All sign of recognition, of humanity, was absent from the primarch's face, subsumed by the need to kill. His black sword hissed through the air, bringing a thin scream from reality as it too was wounded.

The Butcher's Nails pounded in time with the thumping

of Khârn's hearts. 'Lotara…' he managed, but the nails sang louder, and his words snagged in his throat. Roaring, he dodged Angron's swing, and surged forwards, gunning *Gorechild*'s motor as he cut down towards his father's knee. The primarch kicked, sending Khârn hurtling sideways and cracking his breast-plate. He drew his plasma pistol as he rolled out of the way of Angron's stamping foot. A return swing of the sword took off part of Khârn's pauldron. Sickly sweet smoke boiled off the damaged ceramite. He rolled again, too far gone into anger to feel the stab of his broken ribs. The plasma pistol whined as it charged. *Gorechild* blocked another punishing blow. Black sword locked with dragon's teeth. Ligaments tore in Khârn's arm as his father forced his weapon down towards his face. *Gorechild*'s engine screamed, the tooth track locked on to the edge of the daemon primarch's blade. Priceless mica dragon teeth smoked as daemonic fires ate into them.

'*You are disappointing, Khârn,*' said Angron. The sword was closing on Khârn's face. Angron grunted with the effort of forcing down the blade. '*I thought if any of my sons could test me, it would be you. I was wrong. You are weak.*'

'And you… Hnnh,' Khârn fought to speak. 'You have lost your mind, my lord.' The plasma pistol let out a ready note. Khârn brought it up and fired it point-black into Angron's face.

The heat from the plasma stream seared Khârn's face within his helmet. Angron roared and reeled back; his eyes cooked to steam and his cheeks stripped back to smoking bone. Khârn pushed himself up, playing the pistol across his father's chest. The gun let out a warning, but Khârn fired until it overheated and vented superheated coolant all down his arm. Red lights flashed by its charging coils; the gun was useless. He disengaged the power feed and threw it aside. Angron staggered back, crashing into a pile of containers that crumpled like paper under his weight.

Angron roared and thrashed in agony, but already the damage was being made good. Eyes swelled like moist fungal fruits in empty sockets. Charred flesh swelled with rehydration, skin closed over deep burns. Veins and nerves spread across exposed bone, followed by muscle and fat.

'You cannot beat me! You are as unworthy as these pathetic slaves!'

Khârn readied himself. His muscles burned. *Gorechild* shook in his weakened grip.

'Father,' he said in a drool-soaked growl. 'I do not wish to fight you.'

'You have no choice,' Angron bellowed. *'There is only war.'*

The black sword hurtled down again. Khârn could not block it, he knew, but held *Gorechild* ready to deflect the blade, and prepared the blow he would land before he died.

Angron's roar battered at Khârn.

Lightning skittered all over the daemon primarch. Wisps of corposant streamed off his body in a white fog. Then, with a clap of air rushing suddenly into a vacuum, he was gone.

Khârn fell down. His right hand refused to work, and he wrestled his helm off with his left, vomiting blood copiously onto the floor. The Nails hammered at him relentlessly.

'Kh…?' The vox-beads in his ears rattled with the reactor's angry beat. *'Khârn? Khârn? Can you hear me? Are you still alive? Khârn? The Night Lords have the primarch. Khârn?'*

Khârn coughed. His enhancements and armour were working in tandem to repair the damage to his body, and where they could not, to numb the pain. He sat down, legs out in front of him.

'Khârn?'

'Hnnnh,' he said. 'You took… you took your damn time.'

* * *

The Nightfall, *Terran near orbit, 7th of Quartus*

Angron appeared in a blaze of teleport light. His sword was still chopping down and it smashed into the deck of an unfamiliar room. He wrenched the weapon from the metal, ready to slay his son for the greater glory of the Blood God.

Khârn was not there.

Angron growled. His rage was checked for a moment. The ship smelled strange, its sounds were different.

He sniffed the air. He was alone.

A single portal led out of a featureless heptagonal space. Through this he ventured into a cylindrical corridor. A gate slammed down behind him as soon as he was through. Small laser emitters rolled from apertures in the wall and onto tracks cut helically into the tube. The emitters snapped on, their beams constant and razor-thin, and spun themselves into a whirling vortex.

The door behind Angron squealed forwards, pushing the primarch towards the lasers. One stung his skin, then a second, until he was forced into them and they scored his flesh with a netted pattern that would have cut his original body into chunks. They merely pricked his warp-formed flesh.

Angron snarled, brought up the black sword and smashed them all into oblivion. He strode forwards through the smoke of destruction and into the next chamber, where another trial awaited him.

That too he overcame with the sharp edge of his sword.

TWENTY-THREE

Senatorum
Infernal allies
Kinder powers

Senatorum Imperialis, 9th of Quartus

The Senatorum Imperialis had the capacity to accommodate thousands, having been constructed for a vision of civilian rule that would allow voices from all parts of society to be heard. It would never come to pass. Rows and rows of empty seats stared down as blind witnesses to the small gathering on the dais at the very heart of the chamber. No meeting had taken place within for months, and the space had been given over to refugees. They had been removed for a while, and now waited patiently outside in the cold under legionary guard, but their possessions remained behind, heaped on benches made into beds where lords were meant to sit. The smell of cooking and chamber pots lingered.

The last council of the Senatorum Imperialis was done before the invasion fleets arrived. Voluntarily it had ceded control to the three primarchs, yet the High Twelve in particular still had great influence, and many responsibilities.

It had been the Khan's idea to call them back together, just this once, a show of unity between men and demigods.

Upon the dais of the High Twelve, the Ruling Council of the Hegemony of Terra were gathered around their table of fossilised redwood. Twelve men and women, Malcador as their chairman – the once-rulers of an empire under siege. Dorn, the Khan, Sanguinius and Constantin Valdor stood at the edge of the dais, slightly out of the light, allowing the Council their moment of remembered authority.

'Thanks to the actions of Jaghatai Khan, we have a better understanding of what the enemy intends,' said Malcador. He pointed to the holo-captures the Khan had made, which floated before the gathering over the table. 'Lord Dorn and the others thought it best we were informed, and for that we are thankful.'

'What are the enemy's intentions? What is that?' Jemm Marison, High Lady of the Imperial Chancellory, asked.

'That is clearly a siege cannon,' Zagreus Kane said irritably. He was still new to his role as Terran potentate and had yet to master some of the gentler arts of diplomacy. The others found him abrupt, though preferable to Ambassador Vethorel, whose brash tactics in creating the new Adeptus Mechanicus had left her disliked. 'The type is quite distinctive. It is shield-bane technology of the Ordo Reductor, a most holy and terrible knowledge. Kelbor-Hal's traitors are working against the Palace.'

'It will penetrate the aegis?' asked Simeon Pentasian, the dour Master of the Administratum. Though all on the Council had renounced governance of the Imperium while the crisis lasted, he worked as they all did in his own sphere of influence, attempting to keep the failing city running while the enemy gathered outside.

'It has a better chance than a less specialised weapon,' said Kane. 'It is far from certain to do so. The aegis is strong.'

'There are eight siege camps around the Palace. I assume all of them contain similar weaponry,' said Chancellor Ossian, of the Imperial Estates.

Malcador glanced at Dorn.

'That is the case,' said Dorn quietly.

'I had my Legion survey five of the sites,' said the Khan. His armour appeared grey outside the area of bright light shining on the table. He moved fluidly, worryingly reminiscent of a predator outside a campfire's glow. The members of the High Twelve present peered nervously at him. 'All of them have similar machinery under construction. I chose to overfly the camp facing the Helios Gate myself, because of the tower collapse on that section early in the bombardment.'

'It is reasonable to assume they will make a determined attempt to break the wall there,' added Sanguinius. He appeared distant to the Council, as if his mind strayed beyond mortal affairs. 'They have concentrated their efforts on the Helios section of Daylight, and to the north, at the Potens section of the Dusk Wall.' His wings shifted, wafting air over the Council that carried sweet scents from a better place. Again they moved in their seats uncomfortably.

'Then why have they not fired their guns?' asked Marison.

'The cannon must be assembled, my lady,' said Kelsi Demidov, Speaker for the Chartist Captains. She was gentle with Marison, who though expert in her own field lacked breadth of knowledge.

'The weaponry of the Ordo Reductor is generally apocalyptic in scale,' said Kane. He chose a deliberately mechanical voice for the meeting, but could not hide his irritation at explaining the obvious to Marison. 'It takes time to prepare.'

'I am aware,' said Marison huffily. 'We're all aware of that.'

'Well,' said Kane. 'There are other strategic considerations, of course.'

'We have nowhere to go,' said Bolam Haardiker, Paternoval Envoy. *'They do not need to rush.'* That day he carried his own nuncio system. None of them had their usual servants in attendance.

'Let them dither!' said Pentasian. 'Every moment they waste building their weapons is more time for Lord Guilliman to make his way to Terra and to our rescue. Is that not the case, Lord Dorn?'

'There is another reason why they are taking their time,' said Malcador, before Dorn could answer. As Imperial Regent, Malcador was leader of the group. Though his title was more one of ceremony while martial law was in place, he was the only man the primarchs would still defer to. 'These bombardments, this wasting of life has to have a purpose. Do you think Horus Lupercal, conqueror of half the known galaxy, once most favoured of the Emperor's sons and appointed Warmaster by Him, has lost his mind?'

'I had hoped so,' said General Adreen, the Lord Commander Militant of the Imperial Armies. 'It would make him easier to beat.' His comment drew a ripple of gallows laughter from his fellows.

Malcador didn't laugh. 'Thus far we have not seen Horus' infernal allies upon the field. We are fortunate, the Emperor is powerful, and holds back the wickedness of the warp. But every drop of blood spilled on Terra's soil weakens His grip on the energies of the empyrean.'

'Daemons,' said Nemo Zhi-Meng, Choirmaster of the Adeptus Astra Telepathica. 'He speaks of daemons.'

The lords and ladies looked at one another uneasily at his use of the word.

'These beings exist,' Haardiker said, his nuncio set smoothly

translating the clicks and whispers emanating from his mutant throat into Gothic. *'We Navigators know them of old. They serve the entities that name themselves as gods.'*

'Well don't look so surprised,' said Pentasian sharply to the others. 'We've all heard the reports. We've spoken to eye-witnesses. Do not let the name frighten you – they are extra-dimensional xenos, nothing more.'

The primarchs did not correct him. Better that the High Lords thought that way.

'They could come in... here?' said Marison, glancing around the vast building.

'Maybe. Eventually,' said Malcador gravely. 'The Emperor's power is not infinite, and certainly long before the enemy is able to manifest his wicked allies within these walls, His protection will be weakened sufficiently that the barriers between the materium and immaterium will be broken through elsewhere on Terra. Then we will have to face daemonic creatures fighting alongside Traitor legionaries, besides all the misguided masses who follow the Warmaster.'

'I can't quite believe it. In all this, you know,' Sidat Yaseen Tharcher, Chirurgeon General said. 'Magic. Sorcery.' It was hard for him. He was a scientist to the core.

'The dark side of the warp,' said Malcador. 'You all understand, I am sure, that the full extent of the truth is still not to be shared beyond the higher echelons of government. We discuss these matters here among ourselves. They are not to be disseminated further.'

They agreed, some more than others.

'Why did He lie about this?' said Ossian abruptly.

'A lie of omission is not the same as outright untruth,' argued General Adreen.

'The Emperor's omissions are not as awful as some say. The warp has changed,' said Nemo Zhi-Meng. Few shared the reach of his vision, and he was apt at seeing past the surface of things to grasp truths others did not. 'Powers move in the deeps of the empyrean that were quiet before. Awareness of them gives them strength. His instinct to shield the human race was the correct one – for the same reason we should not spread this news. Knowledge of the false gods gives them strength. It makes them real. In a certain way of looking at it, until recently they did not exist except as whispers, nightmares and half-myths.'

'We are not here to discuss the motivations of the Emperor,' said Malcador firmly.

'True, true,' said Pentasian. 'But still.' He gave a weak smile, wholly out of place on his miserable face. 'Nightmares, witches, warp entities. All the old legends coming true.'

'Please, Lord Dorn, present your strategic analysis,' said Malcador.

Dorn stepped forwards fully into the light. His golden battleplate flashed resplendently, dazzling the High Lords. Although the dais raised the table well above the debating floor, Dorn was of sufficient height that he could meet their eyes when standing on the ground, and when stood next to the table as he was then, he dwarfed them. The brief illusion of the Council's authority was shattered. Any who witnessed the scene could not doubt who was the true power on Terra; this son of the Emperor, with his brilliant white hair and his golden panoply, was the embodiment of the Imperium.

Dorn cast his eye over the High Lords. Most looked down, afraid. A couple met his gaze with difficulty. 'There are further problems the Khan's reconnaissance has brought to light,' Dorn said. 'You see these structures here?'

'Buildings?' said Demidov. 'Fortresses?'

'Siege towers,' said the Khan.

Murmurs of disbelief went around the twelve.

'They are immense,' said Adreen. 'Is it possible? Will they even function?' He addressed this last question to Kane.

Kane fell into a contemplative silence. 'Yes,' he said eventually. 'Nullification of mass by contra-gravity devices and structural binding with integrity fields would enable such large objects to be motivated without becoming unstable. They are tactically impractical, and of limited use, but they could be built.'

'We have indications of other, similar siege engines under construction in the other camps, but none so far advanced as these. It is clear to us that soon the enemy will make an attempt on the walls by the Helios Gate,' said Dorn.

'You are bombarding them, of course?' said Zhi-Meng.

'I will come to that. First, enemy landing zones,' Dorn said, pausing after announcing the subject. A projection of Terra came into being, huge and grey, over the table. 'The enemy has made planetfall at over three hundred separate locations around the globe.' The hololith displayed enemy concentrations as blotchy purple. 'Most of this is speculation. There are no precise figures for enemy numbers. Terra's orbital network is either destroyed or in enemy hands. These figures are collated from information gathered from other hives where possible. In most cases, it is impossible. Supposition is our only tool.

'Siege camps.' Again, Dorn paused. 'Eight siege camps ring the city, all established behind defence screens. Overhead voids, layered power shields, ion shielding, while their smaller constructs go about protected by atomantic sheaths. Using the camps as a base, the Dark Mechanicum has begun work on a line of contravallation to encircle the entire Eternity Wall. They are under constant bombardment from the Palace, but this will only slow rather than stop them. The

shielding prevents our direct targeting of their siege equipment until it is ready, and moving against the walls.

'Enemy troop strength. We have downed thousands of their
landing craft. Nevertheless, several million troops of varying
quality are now encamped outside the walls. However, these
forces are of little concern. Other landing zones, out of range of
the Palace guns, have been set up further back in the Himalazian massif. These landing sites are by necessity far from us,
but we can be sure that reinforcements are marching from
them already. What intelligence we can gather shows higher
quality troops moving from these sites on other Terran cities.

'Space ports. Horus has secured a number of landing fields
across Terra. Near the Palace, Damocles space port is under
constant attack. For now it holds, but it will fall. As it lies
outside the aegis, most of the structures in the Damocles
zone have been destroyed, including the Black Ministry. Our
warriors have done what they can to compromise Damocles
port's usefulness, but even damaged it will offer the Warmaster a safe landing zone for Titan Legios and other heavy
formations close to our main defences.

'Aerial theatres,' he continued relentlessly. 'We have no
control of the void. Our fighter forces dwindle with every
sortie from the Warmaster's fleet.

'Aegis strength. The aegis holds at close to one hundred
per cent strength over the central districts and the Sanctum
Imperialis, but on the periphery we have less than forty per
cent efficacy. This is falling daily. Before long, the outer walls
will be open to attack from above, and when that occurs
they will be breached.'

'The shields will hold,' said Kane.

Dorn looked at the Fabricator General. 'We face five primarchs. One among them has uncovered and is exploiting
weaknesses in the aegis network. My guess would be Perturabo.'

'Or Kelbor-Hal,' said Kane.

'Perturabo was made for tasks such as this,' said Dorn, staring at the Fabricator General with certainty. 'The bombardment patterns bear his mark as surely as if he had fashioned them in steel and struck them with his die. The aegis will fail under his attack. The walls will then begin to take bombardment damage. This will happen soon.

'Palace outworks.' Dorn returned his gaze from Kane to the hololith, dismissing the Fabricator General's quibbles. 'The outworks are close to collapse. Greater than one half of the conscripts and other formations committed to their defence are dead. I will shortly give the order to abandon the third line, and fall back to the second.'

'The bastions still hold,' said Adreen.

'While they do, we can keep the enemy away from the Palace defences. I anticipate the next major attack will come soon in an effort to clear the outwork towers from the field,' said Dorn. 'This may be accompanied by the first serious attempt on the Eternity Wall. If it does not come then, it will come soon after.'

'This is a ritual,' said Constantin Valdor. He was almost as commanding as the primarchs, but being better known to the Twelve, they were not as afraid of him. While the Emperor's sons spoke, he kept his own counsel, and that was something Dorn encouraged. In earlier days, when the primarchs waged the Emperor's war among the stars, Valdor's voice had great influence on the Senatorum. His silence spoke volumes on the primarchs' authority now that they ruled in their father's stead.

Valdor stepped next to Dorn to point at the hololith. 'Eight camps at varying distance from the Palace. Draw a line from each, and the lines intersect over the Sanctum Imperialis. These desperate attacks by low quality troops against the outworks are not serious attempts. They are sacrifices.'

'Not long ago, we might have overlooked the possibility,' said Dorn, 'but the captain-general has it right. Though the Warmaster erodes our outer perimeters, the strategy is sub-optimal.' He pointed at two siege camps, one directly north of the Sanctum, the other to the south-west. 'For example, the walls here and here are weakened, yet the enemy establishes his camps kilometres out from those points. It is unmistak-ably a ritual arrangement.'

'My lords,' said Valdor, 'Horus is taking our choices from us. If we do not attack, we allow them to build their siege works unhindered. If we attack, we add to whatever blood magic they are planning.'

'But are they truly involved in ritual? How can we know?' said Marison disbelievingly. 'Not one of us here is a sorcerer.'

'I know it is hard to believe,' said Malcador gently, 'but by these means, the traitors will bring their creatures against us. The forces we see now are only a fraction of what we will eventually face.'

'For the time being, there are other problems to occupy us,' said Dorn. 'Until three days ago, we were at least being spared the attentions of the Traitor Legions. The Death Guard have put down all over the globe. Their preference for biological and chemical warfare remains as it always was, and the efficacy of these weapons appears accentuated by their recent change. I have notification of plague from every corner of Terra.'

'What has happened to them? What are these reports of mutants and other abominations in the ranks of the Trai-tor Legions?' Ossian inquired.

'A number of the Legions have given themselves over com-pletely to the so-called gods of the Pantheon,' said Dorn. 'The first we heard of these creatures were unstable mem-bers of the Word Bearers. We now know these warriors were Space Marines whose bodies were inhabited by warp entities.'

'Them again,' said Pentasian. He took a hefty gulp of wine. In the old days, he had only ever drunk water.

'This practice has spread to other Legions, notably the Sons of Horus,' said Dorn. 'Other malformities among the enemy ranks are caused by exposure to the warp, both intentional and incidental, and deliberate mutilation.'

'We've heard all this, but reports about the Death Guard are particularly disturbing,' Ossian said. 'Lord Khan's images and pict-capture from the walls show...' He peered at a dataslate in front of him. 'I don't know what they show. Diseased warriors. Fouled weapons. How can they fight?'

'The answer lies in the warp,' said Dorn.

'I saw them first-hand, as did Sanguinius,' said the Khan. 'They are diseased, as you say, but somehow this makes them more durable.'

'Have we any samples to investigate, corpses, remains?' asked Demidov. 'Perhaps Tharcher's hospitallers might be of help?'

The Khan shook his head. 'Do not ask for such things to be brought into the city. My Apothecaries wished to examine the dead. I was unwilling to take that risk. Any examples close to the walls I ordered burned. They managed to infect me with something,' he said, and his disbelief was clear to all. 'The Emperor made us proof against all disease. I have never been ill in my life, until this week. We cannot risk sickness of that potency getting into the general populace.'

Tharcher nodded. He was a precise and reserved man, his ageing face pocked with blister-scars. On initial impressions, he looked nervous but the scope of his intellect was apparent too from his quick movements, and his large eyes held reservoirs of compassion.

'That is for the best,' Tharcher said. 'Even so, the Palace has not been spared. Disease runs rampant through the outer districts already, thanks to Mortarion. It is getting worse.'

'Although on first examination the Death Guard attack on our outworks appears wasteful of men, their objective was to get close enough to the city to bypass the aegis with their artillery,' said Dorn. 'Short bombardments from near range covered by their infantry engaging with our outwork forces, followed by immediate withdrawal. Their aim was to introduce disease vectors into the civilian population.'

'Of what sort?' asked Ossian.

'Diseased corpses, living tissue riddled with bacteria, infected human waste matter, viral agents in suspension that aerosolised on detonation of the munitions,' said General Adreen. 'They were inventive.'

'They succeeded,' said Tharcher. 'Our medicae facilities are already overrun. Thousands are sickening. People are dying, and I expect many more deaths soon. Most of these diseases, though severe, are treatable under normal circumstances, but our staff are overstretched and we have insufficient medical stockpiles. Malnutrition is exacerbating the problem.' He looked to his fellows. 'Our populace is weak. I have taken the step of quarantining the areas within the walls that have been affected, but in a place such as this, with so many crammed into so small a space, no quarantine can be watertight. I cannot guarantee the core districts will escape disease. For the moment, the enforcers and the militia raised to assist them are shooting quarantine-breakers on sight. Unrest is increasing. The sickness will get through.'

'The people are frightened. Martial law has increased the incidence of rioting,' said Harr Rantal, Grand Provost Marshal of the Adeptus Arbites. 'My men are stretched thin. Only an hour ago, there was a concerted effort to break out of the fiduciary subzone of sector twelve. Five hundred and seventy civilians dead, twenty enforcers killed or seriously injured, one arbitrator dead. These events are occurring so frequently they're in danger of becoming statistics.'

'Civil unrest and disease must both be brought under control,' said Dorn. 'By any means. This picture we provide for you is a grim one, but we have gathered you together again because it is going to worsen. The enemy will begin attacking in earnest. Once that begins, Horus will attempt to break through the Eternity Wall until he is successful. We will hold it as long as we are able, but we shall be forced to fall back to the inner defences.' Dorn gave them a grave look. 'Listen to me as I say again this *will* happen. The civilians have to be moved before then, or they will perish.'

'What do you wish us to do?' said Pentasian wearily. 'If we bring them further in, they will carry their diseases to as yet clean districts. We've had this problem before. Do you remember? Our final Council meeting?' He looked at the other lords, who nodded and muttered their agreement. 'We struggled to screen them then. We cannot screen them now,' said Pentasian. 'They once numbered in the thousands. Now there are millions of refugees within the outer city. We have nowhere left to put them. They can't all live in here.' He gestured around the hall.

'Millions of people, Lord Dorn,' said Ossian. 'Leaving aside the time it will take to vet them all, and the men we do not have to do it, we will then have further overcrowding. Every quarter of the city is full of refugees. There is not enough space. Tension will increase. It is bound to.'

'I trust to you to see it done,' said Dorn. 'You have no choice. The other alternatives are to leave the civilians to their fate, or to actively cull them. I assume none of you wish to give either order.'

The High Lords looked uncomfortably at one another.

'Yes, well.' Pentasian said. 'We shall see what transpires.' He cleared his throat and massaged the bridge of his nose, then poured himself some more wine. 'That leaves the question of the rest of Terra.'

'With the bulk of the Legions at the Palace, the enemy is having an easier time of it elsewhere,' said Sanguinius. 'Over the last three days, since the Death Guard began their landing, we have received reports of four major population centres falling to the Warmaster, including Lundun, Noy Zaylant Hive, Neork and Brasyla. Millions are dying. The diseases outside the Palace are already killing. They are far more virulent than the ones we see here.'

'The Emperor shields us from such witchcraft,' said the Khan. 'I experienced the effect myself. As soon as I passed within the walls, the sickness left me, and the knife used to infect me disintegrated.'

'The Emperor protects,' Ossian said clearly, then hurriedly added as Lord Dorn gave him a sharp look, 'so they say.'

'You will still not commit your forces to actions outside the walls?' said Pentasian.

'We must stand firm,' said Dorn.

'Your firmness is commendable, but will ensure no Terra is left!' said Ossian.

'There will be no Terra if there is no Emperor,' said Dorn.

The Khan gave Dorn a sidelong glance. They disagreed on this matter.

'Guilliman will come. If he is delayed, then we must guarantee the Palace and the Emperor until he does,' said Dorn. 'The Legions cannot leave the Palace without jeopardising the Emperor. If the Emperor dies, we have lost, and so the Legions do not leave.'

'My lords,' said Adreen, 'let us not bicker. The primarchs favour us to give us this news. They do not have to. We have no authority over them, and the Praetorian is right. We cannot weaken the Palace defences, even if it costs billions of lives.'

'It *will* cost billions of lives,' said Pentasian.

'Then what are we to do?' said Ossian.

'We fight! The Imperial Army fights on,' said Adreen. 'We have plentiful support from Lord Kane's armies. The enemy's strength is concentrated here, at the Palace. While that remains the case, my armies shall do what they can elsewhere. It is appalling, I agree, but the legionaries and Custodians are needed here. We must resist as best we can.'

'That is all any of us can do,' said Dorn. 'Resist. We tell you these things that you might prepare, and save as many of our people as you can. That is your role in this, while we wage war on behalf of the Emperor. See to the civilians. Free us from this task, and I swear on my honour, it shall be enough. We will not allow the Imperium to fall.'

'What were you thinking?' said Dorn to his brothers, though primarily he addressed the Khan.

The Khan kept his silence. The three primarchs were in an unfinished side chamber off the Senatorum Imperialis. The building had been under construction for centuries, and still the outer chambers were yet to be completed. The one they occupied had bare rockcrete walls and was lit dimly by a single lumenglobe. It was freezing and damp; nevertheless there were bedrolls and other signs of civilian occupation all around the walls. 'Why were you on the same section of the wall?' Dorn demanded.

Again, the Khan said nothing, but stared at his brother with calm eyes.

'Providence,' said Sanguinius.

'You could both have been killed,' said Dorn.

The Khan chose to speak then. 'We all die eventually, brother. There is nothing more true than that. Even for us.'

Dorn clenched his fists. 'Why will you not obey my orders? Why will you not put the safety of our father above your own impulses?'

'We are different, you and I,' said the Khan. 'In the eyes of the actor, the action is justifiable. We know what the Dark Mechanicum are building. We would not if I remained here. Intelligence in war is the mightiest weapon.'

'I had already accurately deduced what was there,' said Dorn irritably.

'Then I have removed uncertainty from your calculations.' The Khan gave his brother a wide smile. 'I thought you would appreciate that.'

Dorn placed his fists upon a workbench. The bench was a crude thing, plasteel sheets bolted to scaffold-pole legs. The surface was neatly arrayed with tools. He stared at them in silence. They were covered with the dust of neglect, and left perfect outlines where curious refugees had moved them.

'No more risks,' he said. 'Either of you. Can you imagine the blow to morale alone if one of you died?'

'I am sorry, my brother, but I am going to disappoint you again,' said the Khan.

Dorn turned round so quickly the tools rocked.

'Do not take your Legion away,' said Dorn. 'I forbid it.'

The Khan held his eye. 'You heard the High Lords. The people of Terra are dying. You are sacrificing the population of this world,' he said. 'It is pragmatism, I know. You present a cold face to the world, brother, but your heart does not match it. You know this is not right. If we cannot protect the men and women of mankind's cradle, how can we claim the best interests of humanity are at the centre of what we do?'

'You have known of my strategy since you returned to the Throneworld, brother,' said Dorn. The shocking white of his hair accentuated the paleness of his face. In the dimly lit room, it seemed age had finally got its talons into him. 'Your objections are noted, but at this late stage, meaningless.'

'You shackle me to the Palace with too short a chain,' said the Khan. 'We fought the Great Crusade to free humanity, not to sacrifice it.'

Dorn nodded once, though not in agreement. He rested his hand on his sword hilt.

'Jaghatai, I understand. I feel your anguish that mortal men and women suffer to ensure our father survives. But war is a calculation, this one more than all the others. Life cannot be measured in absolute terms any longer. Every death must be set against one consequence alone – how much time it can buy us. Time is the currency of this battle. We must hoard seconds like misers. Lives we have in abundance. They can and must be spent freely, regrettable as that is.'

Neither of the others spoke.

'Do not be hasty, brother,' said Dorn, more gently. 'Horus continues his bombardment of the surface. He is still testing us, still probing the defences of the world. He is saving his best troops. He knows we cannot spare our own legionaries anywhere but here. The creatures assailing the hives of Terra are scum, dregs, opportunists and fanatics. While here our outwork forces arrayed against them are more than enough to keep them back. These attacks of the Death Guard are intended to draw us out. Their presence shows our strategy is working. Leave, and you shall be playing into Horus' hands.'

'The situation is fluid,' said the Khan. He spoke without rancour, but his objections were clear. 'Horus will land all his Legions soon. I prefer to act now, while I am still free to do so.'

'If you do, you will provoke his attack!' said Dorn.

'Making the enemy change his plans is strength. Force your enemy to react to you. A general who waits for the enemy to act is already defeated, I learned this as a child.'

'Your wars were different to mine,' said Dorn.

'Then perhaps you should listen to me,' said the Khan. 'The ordu are better served in swift battle. On the walls they are worth ten men – if we ride, twenty or more. I will not stand by while billions die.'

'Jaghatai!' said Dorn in exasperation.

'Brothers,' said Sanguinius. 'Arguing over eventualities that have not yet come to pass serves nothing.'

'Every strategic sense I possess tells me that Horus will direct his forces to reave the planet to exploit our concern for humanity,' said Dorn. 'He does this *expressly* to divide our efforts. When we are split, and our warriors spread, that is when the Warmaster will fall on us and seize victory. We must stand united.'

'Then you do not disagree with me,' said the Khan. 'The population is at risk.'

'I anticipated slaughter long ago,' said Dorn, 'and I regret that this chain of events came to pass, but we cannot respond to whatever provocation Horus presents to us. We cannot let ourselves be lured out. We cannot follow his plan. We will make ourselves weak, then all is lost.'

'Since when was saving mankind from the darkness a sign of weakness?' said the Khan. 'Sanguinius, my brother and comrade, what do you see? Lend me your foresight.'

Sanguinius shut his eyes. Like that, he appeared drawn and tired, a funerary monument to himself. Dorn suppressed a shudder.

'My sight is not so clear as father's,' said Sanguinius. 'The future is ever in flux. Only some events…' He paused, finding the words hard to say. 'Only some events are certain.'

'Do you see me? What will be the consequences of inaction?'

'I see fire, and blood, and a world laid waste if you do not act.'

'If I act?' said the Khan.

Sanguinius opened his eyes to look at him.

'There is grave risk to you. A confrontation unlooked for, and if you survive, a flight from one danger into greater peril.'

'Who will I face?'

'I cannot divine.'

'Will I save lives?'

Sanguinius nodded. 'Many.'

'That is what I was made for,' said the Khan. 'I will ride out.'

'We will save lives by holding the Palace,' said Dorn. 'So long as the Emperor lives, Horus cannot be victorious.'

'You hold the Palace,' said the Khan, turning his hard brown eyes back on Dorn. 'I will not leave the ordinary citizenry of Terra defenceless.'

'Jaghatai, I insist…'

'Half my Legion remains here, at all times.' The Khan spoke across him. 'This is my word, but I ride with the rest of the ordu. I will say no more other than to swear that I will return when I am needed. I will be here when the time comes. Do not try to stop me. I will not be dictated to, not even by you. If the Emperor Himself were to tell me I should not go, I would not listen.'

The Khan left the room.

Dorn let him go. Sanguinius rested a hand on his brother's shoulder.

'Trust to fate, brother. There are kinder powers at work who favour us.'

'I do not believe in such things,' said Dorn with a troubled sigh. 'But I shall ask them to watch over the Khan anyway.'

TWENTY-FOUR

The Lord of Iron
Iron circle
Superior intelligence

The Vengeful Spirit, *Terran high anchor, 9th of Quartus*

Perturabo arrived aboard the *Vengeful Spirit* in a foul temper.

His Stormbird put in to a small hangar high on the command spines of the vessel, where Sons of Horus in gleaming armour waited for him with all the pageantry of inter-Legion diplomacy. Were it not for the polished skulls hanging from armour upon cords and the bright red banners bearing Horus' baleful eye, the greeting could have taken place during the Great Crusade.

Those days were done. Perturabo saw through the display. There was nothing of the old glory nor anything of honour. He was insulted his brother did not greet him personally and saw only threat in the welcoming party, a feeling that intensified when Horus Aximand stepped forwards to greet him.

'My Lord Perturabo,' said Aximand. 'Welcome to the *Vengeful Spirit*. It has been far too long since you graced us with your presence.'

Perturabo had never warmed to Little Horus. He was a preening man, full of borrowed confidence. His resemblance to the Warmaster made him think himself better than others, when all he had been was an image of Horus reflected on dirty water. Now his face was ruined, he was not even that.

'Get on with it and take me to Horus,' grumbled Perturabo. 'There is no time for this pantomime. I must speak with my brother immediately.'

The side hatches of the Stormbird slammed down. The booming tread of iron feet on metal echoed from the belly of the ship. The Iron Circle, Perturabo's bodyguard of six towering battle robots, marched out, formed a crescent around their master and slammed their hazard-striped shields together to make a wall behind him.

'I see you have company,' said Aximand. His attempt to raise an eyebrow succeeded only in pulling at the scarred wreck of his face and making him even uglier.

'The Iron Circle goes where I go,' he said.

'You have more forces with you? Why don't you call them out?'

'There are always more,' said Perturabo.

Ten Iron Warriors in modified Cataphractii plate stepped onto the deck and took up position beside the battle automata. They aimed their weapons pointedly at their hosts.

'Is that Captain Forrix I see there?' said Aximand mildly, ignoring their show of strength.

'Him?' Perturabo said with complete disinterest. 'Yes. It is Forrix.'

'I shall see to it that they are refreshed,' said Aximand.

'They will remain here. They are staying to guard my ship,' said Perturabo. 'Refreshments are not required.'

Aximand looked over the Terminator-armoured Space Marines and the automata, and gave a little sigh. 'Your caution is a credit to your genius, but you should trust your brother, my lord,' said Little Horus. 'You are held in high esteem here. You have nothing to fear.'

Perturabo glowered. 'I fear nothing, but I trust no one,' he said. His cape of blades clanked behind him as he strode past Little Horus. 'Not even my brother.'

The Iron Circle came noisily alive, and stamped after their master.

Aximand looked at Forrix. The Iron Warrior acknowledged him with a tiny dip of his helmet, no more than that. Aximand smiled a crooked smile and followed Perturabo from the hangar, leaving the sons of two primarchs staring at each other over their guns.

Perturabo walked swiftly through the *Vengeful Spirit*, his Iron Circle clanking behind tirelessly. The ship shuddered in time to the firing of its guns. Having skulked behind Luna for several weeks, it had come out and joined the bombardment of the Throneworld. Horus was putting on a show of leadership from the front. A screen of destroyers and frigates protected the flagship from defence batteries that Perturabo would have destroyed many times over had his brother not kept him at the edge of the system. The story was the same as it ever was; Perturabo was exiled, ignored, called upon only as a weapon of last resort.

He would not let that stand. Already a master of the material sciences, he coveted the power of the warp. He saw possibilities beyond anything his genius could accomplish were it to remain shackled to the materium. But he was wary. His investigations were thorough. He would not follow his brothers into damnation and throw himself blindly upon the mercies of the gods, but circumvent them altogether and become a god himself.

As he proceeded through the vessel, his armour's auto-senses recorded everything for later examination.

The *Vengeful Spirit* was a living textbook on how not to grasp the warp's might. In every way, it had changed for the worse. The taint of mutation lay on all things. Perturabo deeply disapproved. The warp was chaos. If approached carelessly, it was uncontrollable. He prized order. He would impose order upon chaos where his brothers had not. In securing his own apotheosis Fulgrim had tricked Perturabo but ultimately, like Angron, he had become a puppet of his passions. Magnus had chosen the esoteric path and fallen from it. Mortarion had been humbled. Lorgar was abandoned by the creatures he had unleashed.

These things would not happen to him, for he was Perturabo. He was logical when the others were impulsive. Methodical when they were rash. Passionless when they were indulgent. He was the Lord of Iron, and he was better than them all.

If the *Vengeful Spirit* were his ship, he would have burned the rot out. Horus didn't even bother to hide it. Corruption was in plentiful evidence. The smell of spoiled meat blasted from atmospheric cyclers. Crew and legionaries bore the marks of flesh change. When he ascended a huge staircase leading up towards the command deck he encountered an entire wall subsumed by a mat of throbbing flesh, a tapestry of skin that presented a madness of rolling eyes and dribbling orifices. As the automata passed it, each chimed out a warning and powered its weapons. It was a supreme effort to order them to stand down, and not send them to cut away the canker.

Perturabo saw things other men did not. His psychic abilities were nothing compared to some, but he was nevertheless a primarch, and had an affinity for the warp. He had always been able to see the weeping sore in reality he had dubbed the Ocularis Terribus. Being on the *Vengeful Spirit* was like looking into the depths of the Ocularis and being unable to look away. There was a shifting of reality there. Nothing was real. Falsehood had stolen in behind every atom.

He wanted to be off the *Vengeful Spirit*. It reeked of slavery, and Perturabo was no one's slave.

He made good distance from the hangar without the irritation of Aximand, but the dog caught up with him to nip at his heels.

'My lord,' said Aximand, jogging to keep up with Perturabo.

'What do you want, Aximand?' said Perturabo.

'Where are you going?'

'Lupercal's court. I know the way, you need not follow me like a lost child. Begone, I am here to speak with the Warmaster, not a spoiled facsimile.'

'Horus is not in Lupercal's court,' said Aximand.

Perturabo stopped. The instant he did, so did the Iron Circle.

'Where is he?'

'In his temple. It is a new location on the ship. I must take you there.'

'Must you,' said Perturabo.

Aximand turned them about and led the party back down the stair and off towards a large lifter platform. Perturabo stared at it suspiciously before he and his robotic guardians clambered aboard.

'I prefer stairs,' he said. 'Less opportunity for assassination through mechanical interference.'

Aximand said nothing, but worked the controls, sending them down towards the base of the command spire.

At the bottom, he led Perturabo down a long corridor whose

portside windows showed a fine view of the fleet and whose
starboard side gibbered nonsense from thousands of chattering mouths. Presently they came to an ornate doorway carved
of black, faintly luminous stone with a bestiary's worth of leering faces. Perturabo had seen such stone before, in the Cursus
on Tallarn. Recognising the door as an artefact of the warp, he
greedily set the devices of his armour to analyse it. As always,
the stone showed only as a blank space to his equipment.

'The Iron Circle must remain outside,' said Aximand, inter-
rupting his evaluation.

'My machines pose no threat to Horus,' he said, still playing his instruments over the black stone.

'So you say,' said Little Horus. 'How can I be sure?'

Perturabo's furious grey eyes stared at him, but he held
up his fist and clenched it, and the Iron Circle took a simul-
taneous step backwards. Their hammers thudded onto the
floor, their shields they brought across their bodies, and
they deactivated as one, sinking into themselves with a hiss
of released pressure.

'Satisfied?' said the Lord of Iron.

Little Horus bowed his head; again there was an air of
mockery to his show of respect.

'You may enter, my lord,' he said.

The doors opened.

Perturabo stared at Little Horus long enough for his disgust to be known before passing through the portal.

The doors closed behind him, sealing him in a chamber
that should not have been there.

Perturabo took in the silent Unspeaking standing guard in
alcoves; the raised walkway; the black oil, strangely alive-
looking, in the channels cut into the floor; the windows
that looked upon an alien cosmos.

Horus sat upon a throne at the far end of the walkway, which was fashioned of the same black, lustrous stone as the doors. He sprawled carelessly, armoured legs thrust out in front of him, his hands on the screaming daemon heads worked into the armrests. A penetrating sense of unease had Perturabo in its grip; the warp was close here, its otherworldly tides practically lapping at his feet. The lights were dim, but they shone with painful wavelengths not found in the material realm, and Perturabo squinted against them to see his brother.

Horus was armoured, his hands encased in the huge machinery of his power claws, his great maul leaning against the throne. He stirred and sat upright. The machineries of his battleplate were loud in the sepulchral quiet.

'Brother,' said the Warmaster. 'It is good to see you.'

Perturabo hesitated. He should go to his brother. Caution held him back.

So much of the scene was wrong. The many Word Bearers vastly outnumbered the two Justaerin standing sentry at the entrance, whose presence was the only acknowledgement that this was a Sons of Horus ship.

'Brother,' said Horus again. 'It is unlike you to dither. Come to me and greet me. You have performed well. I wish to thank you. We have a great deal to discuss.'

The Lord of Iron advanced steadily to mask his worries. Perturabo felt no fear, but he was paranoid to the core, and the voice that whispered treachery and death into the hidden folds of his mind was screaming at him to get out.

'My brother,' he said. He believed he hid his internal conflict, but Horus watched him sharply, so that he feared he had betrayed himself.

With difficulty, for his famed battleplate, the Logos, was a massive construction, Perturabo knelt at his brother's feet.

'My Warmaster,' he said.

'Rise, Lord of Iron,' Horus said.

Perturabo had no choice. He had to obey. Horus' gift was his ability to command men. Long ago he had done so artfully, through argument and persuasion as much as force of will. His charisma had been such he convinced others to follow him gladly. Now his presence demanded obedience. There was such power in him, yet he was also lesser than he had been, to the extent that Perturabo barely recognised his brother. Imperiousness replaced nobility. The easy smile had become a knowing leer. His thoughtful countenance had become slightly wild, suggesting wisdom too terrible to hold. Yet there was a glimpse of the old Horus when he stood from his throne and looked upon Perturabo fondly, causing the Lord of Iron to doubt himself.

'We shall talk awhile, you and I,' said Horus.

A febrile heat rose off the Warmaster. The sourceless light shining up from his gorget stained his skin a lurid magenta. So much power was invested in Horus. Perturabo recognised authority when he saw it, and though he shied away from others who would dominate him, to Horus he grudgingly submitted.

'You have waited too long to summon me,' Perturabo said sourly. 'Why did you not allow me down with the Mechanicum landing parties? I have examined their work. It is pedestrian at best. Their contravallation is full of weaknesses. Had Dorn half the wits he ascribes himself, he would have overrun the siege camps a dozen times already. Lucky it is for us that he is arrogant, and afraid, choosing to skulk behind his fortifications. Let me at the Mechanicum to show how feeble Dorn's efforts are. Let me down to Terra, my lord, and I shall win this war for you. You promise me honour and respect, then leave me to languish in the outer system digging ditches. We delay when we should strike, we–'

'Perturabo,' said Horus, silencing him.

Perturabo's stolid face showed surprise as his words jammed in his throat and would not come out.

'Do not complain. Not until you have heard me out.' Horus stepped down from the throne dais to come to his brother's side.

'My lord,' Perturabo gasped, able to speak again.

'Dear brother,' Horus said. He rested his massive claw on Perturabo's shoulder. Perturabo's teeth and bones ached at the otherworldly power emanating from the Warmaster. 'Always looking for the poison in the meat and never at the feast. I did not summon you until now for good reason, and I assure you it is the exact opposite of the suspicions churning around in that mind of yours. You see deviousness when truthfully I set you to work as I do because you are the only one of our brothers I trust. Be aware of this. You are blind to the affection I have for you. It offends me.'

'My lord…' said Perturabo haltingly.

'Fulgrim is flighty,' said Horus. 'Angron is consumed with rage. Mortarion has fallen on the sword of his pride. Magnus cannot be trusted, for he serves only himself. But you are here, Perturabo, you are still strong. You have not cravenly begged for the mercies of the Four. You see in me what the true power of the warp can grant.' He held up his other hand. 'I am the master of the Pantheon, not their servant. The others are diminished creatures, slaves to darkness. The lost, and the damned.' Horus smiled regretfully. 'They were not strong enough. They give themselves to one small aspect of the warp. But you, Perturabo, you are too wise for that. Too clever. You preserve your individuality when the others have lost theirs without realising it has gone.'

'I broke with the Emperor to be free, not to enslave myself to worse masters,' Perturabo admitted.

Horus chuckled, a leonine growl somewhere at the back of it. 'The Four hear you. Your arrogance delights them. They respect you. The others...' He shook his head. 'They are tools. They are not respected. Not like you, Lord of Iron.'

Horus walked a few steps from the throne to look out at the vivid displays through the viewports.

'You are too important to waste. Your sons too – they are valuable! Why would I send you down to bleed with the dregs? I have greater things in mind for you.'

'Mortarion's sons are on-world,' Perturabo said peevishly. 'We are as indomitable, more indomitable, than the Death Guard. They are ill-suited to this battle. I should be there, fighting now.'

Horus dismissed his concerns with a gesture. 'They have a different role to play to the one I have for you. Mortarion's sons will die in their multitudes performing their task. I am saving you and your sons, my brother, for the real work.'

Perturabo's frown broke into a hundred different wrinkles around the input cables embedded in his scalp. 'When have you ever had a care for the lives of my sons, or for my talents?'

Horus looked at him pityingly. 'When have I not? You are the best of them, brother! This is a siege. It is *the* siege, Perturabo. There will never be another battle like this. You are the finest engineer in the galaxy. I protect my best assets. I preserve them for the right moment. You do not toss your advantage away.'

'Then... then you finally acknowledge my worth?' said Perturabo stiffly.

'Finally? I have always acknowledged your worth!' said Horus. 'That is why I speak with you alone. The rest of our siblings must be dealt with together, like children, but not you, bold, brave Perturabo. We can talk as men. You and I, we are more alike than the rest. Equals, almost, in the scale of our intellects and the scope of our ambitions.'

Perturabo bristled. He regarded his intelligence as superior to all others', even Horus'.

'Of course your Legion will perform better than the Ordo Reductor and Sota-Nul's lackeys,' Horus continued, smiling indulgently at Perturabo's pride. 'Of course you would already be forcing the walls. Was it not you who uncovered the vulnerabilities of the aegis? Was it not you who proposed the nature of the aerial assault? I rely on you, brother. This is a dangerous time. My attention is... elsewhere. We must be circumspect, not rush in where angels fear to tread.' His grin became impossibly wide at his use of the ancient aphorism. 'An egg is a strong vessel for the life it hides...' He held up his clawed hand. 'Pressure, pressure, pressure, the egg remains whole, until the pressure is too great, and the egg cracks.' His claws scissored together with a noise like striking swords. 'A small breach, a lone assault, these little violations can be overcome by the defender. The Palace must be forced wide on every front at once. So hard and so widespread our attack must be that it cannot possibly be countered.'

Horus' smile had no humanity to it. It was the sneer of a gargoyle on a pagan fane.

'You will go to the surface. You will direct your Legion to encircle the walls of the Palace with unbreakable siege lines. Yes, improve the contravallation. Yes, have your Stor Bezahsk show the others how to conduct a barrage. But this is not all I wish you to accomplish. Very soon the Emperor's grip on the warp around Terra will be prised loose. Mortarion, Angron and Fulgrim will then descend, and the Neverborn allies our patrons promise will be able to manifest soon afterwards. You will–' Horus broke off suddenly and looked up, hearkening to a call Perturabo couldn't hear. The Warmaster's gaze slid along the lines of motionless Word Bearers. He stared into nothingness for a while, then regarded his brother again.

'So there is nothing for me to do other than dig more ditches while false gods steal my victory?' said Perturabo.

'No, my dear brother. All the daemons spawned since time began will not win us victory. Nor will the Legiones Astartes. We require a greater power.'

'Titans,' said Perturabo decisively. 'Landing our Titans without their destruction is the key. Too far from the Palace, they are at risk of counter-attack. Too near, and their landing craft will be targeted and brought down.'

Horus nodded. A pointed tongue slid along teeth that appeared momentarily sharp.

'You will have your victory, and all the triumphs due you. When you accomplish the task I set you, every creature in the galaxy will know your name, all shall fear you. None shall doubt your brilliance.'

Perturabo listened, rapt.

'Only you can do this.' Horus gripped Perturabo's pauldrons in both hands and stared into his eyes. Heat from the Warmaster's body warmed his armour. 'You will find me a way to get Titans past the wall, Perturabo,' said Horus, 'and directly into the Imperial Palace.'

TWENTY-FIVE

Seven plagues
Nightmares return
The enemy speaks

Palace outworks, Daylight Wall section 16, 15th of Quartus

Katsuhiro was still alive. He did not know how. Sometimes, he thought he had died and been tossed into some punishing afterlife. He was so ill and tired. When the third line was abandoned, Katsuhiro was ashamed to retreat from it, but it had lost all use as a defensive position. Where clean lines of plascrete ramparts had crossed the land, now there were only heaps of splintered rock sculpted into hillocks and dells by endless bombs, all reeking with the corpses trapped in the ruin. Bastion 16 still stood, but now it was in front of Katsuhiro's position. He felt safer when it was behind him, as if it had his back. Now it was in front he watched it deteriorate, its guns fall silent, its surface pit and crack. Like the slow death of a valued friend, it filled him with despair.

But still Bastion 16 held. Others did not. Their remains lined the battlefield, ugly, rotting teeth in gums brown with decay.

A month limped by. If time could get sick, then it did, leaking putrid fluid from every day. One after another, seven plagues swept over the outworks, ravaging the defenders stationed there. First came the running boils, the trench pox and fungal rot: novel diseases that baffled the medicae sent to treat the troops. Red blindness, foaming madness, a plague of insectoid parasites that ate men from the inside, and finally, the humiliating, agonising death of the Bloody Flux. Jainan died. So many people died. The few people Katsuhiro knew were gone, save Doromek, who never sickened, and the woman Myz. He stopped talking to other people, saving his words for tearful monologues to himself that he mumbled into holes in the ground.

The enemy kept coming. Often the attackers were the undisciplined rabble they had faced before, but increasingly the merciless, nigh-on unkillable legionaries of the Death Guard came against them. The sole time the loyal Space Marines had come out faded from memory. When the Death Guard were driven back it was by dint of the wall guns, meaningless, short-lived triumphs that came at a terrible cost to the human defenders of the outworks.

The aegis continued to weaken, allowing more of the enemy's ordnance to fall through. Artillery emplacements in the fortifications encircling the Palace pounded them incessantly. Poisons and disease fell as often as fire. Toxic environment gear became the defenders' skin, gas masks took the place of faces.

Katsuhiro's company was merged three times with others, until they were a mongrel formation, stripped of the thin pretence they had of being members of the Kushtun Naganda. They were as motley and filthy as the wretches that attacked them. Only the direction they were facing told who was on which side, and that was not enough. Men from both forces broke in the middle of battles, going berserk and attacking anyone around them. Mistakes were common.

The nightmares that assaulted Terra in the months before the invasion, gone from Katsuhiro when he reached the Palace, crept back into his few hours of sleep. Horrible things, full of mutilations and blood, they were far more real and disturbing than even the traumas of war.

One rest period – it might have been the night or the day, the clouds of ash and fire long having removed differentiation from the two – Katsuhiro dreamed such a dream, of endless tunnels of black glass curved like a beast's intestines that he ran through in a panic, something clawed and silent gaining on him. He fell from the tunnel without warning into a sea of violent colours, where toothed hallucinations took on solidity for the sole purpose of tearing him apart, then tumbled through a door made of eyes onto the ruin of the Katabatic Plains. A bloody rain poured, and then, from the sky, a giant fell, huge and monstrous. Roaring in pain and rage, it came for him, a clawed hand reaching down to snuff out his life.

Katsuhiro woke screaming. No one came to his aid. Everyone had their own daemons to wrestle with. When he calmed himself from shrieks to moans and then to sobs, he feared for a moment he might be deaf. He heard nothing but his own, sickly breath rattling in the hood of his gas mask.

He stood on feeble legs. Hundreds of other soldiers were doing the same, looking across the grey wasteland of the Katabatic Plains in fear.

The bombardment had stopped. The heat of the constant explosions, which rose on occasion to heights painful to bear, was carried off by the spring winds and the temperature dropped rapidly. Poison gas and clouds of viral spores blew away. Katsuhiro felt the breeze's caress through the rubber of his tox-suit. The wind called to him.

For the first time in what seemed forever, he tore off the hood of his gas mask, not caring if he died, and stood gasping like a landed fish. He closed his eyes to enjoy the simple bliss of sweat drying on his skin.

Thunder boomed, then roared again – no bomb this time but a shout, a voice, a presence so large it filled the heavens from horizon to horizon.

The sky flashed, and all on the defences looked upwards, and there beheld a terrifying vision.

TWENTY-SIX

The Crimson Apostle
An offer of surrender
Blood rain

Daylight Wall, Helios Gate, 15th of Quartus

There were six hundred merlons on the parapets of each tower of the Helios Gate, huge tombstone blocks four metres deep, three wide and three high. Each one had its own firing step. Each firing step hosted a figure in blood-red armour. They faced out in every direction, silent sentinels, waiting for the petty battles of air and outworks to be done and the first true hammer blow to fall. They were men of the First Chapter of the Blood Angels, its men and their captains under Raldoron's command.

Another commander might have remained inside the tower command centre, but Raldoron still preferred to walk the walls. He paced around the circumference of the tower. The space between the central gun turret and the battlement was wide, but then everything about the gate was scaled for gods and not for men. The macro cannon fired every ten seconds, hurling its destructive payloads no longer upwards at the fleet, but across the plain towards the contravallation. The barrel was at its lowest elevation, close enough for Raldoron to reach up and touch as he passed underneath it. When it fired, the gate convulsed upon its foundations. Even to him, a veteran of a hundred wars, the effect was alarming, but he put his faith in the primarchs, and trusted that Lord Dorn had allowed for these violent forces when he designed the defences.

Raldoron's auto-senses failed to shut out the gun's roar. Dampened, the discharge still made his ears ring. He relished the sensation. While his orders prevented him from attacking, the gun was proof that the Imperium was fighting back.

Raldoron's vox pulsed. Thane's notifier rune blinked in the upper right of his helm-plate.

'On the walls again, First Captain?'

Raldoron paused in his patrol. He looked out between the mighty teeth of the crenellations over the blasted plain. War remade worlds so quickly.

'I could hide inside,' said Raldoron. 'It is safer. A few of my officers have intimated as much to me, but I will not listen to them. I am a Blood Angel. I am no logistician. My place is in battle, with sword in hand and bolter kicking in my fist.'

'I prefer battle myself,' voxed Thane, as he approached around the turret's giant turntable. 'If you would have me, I would accompany you.'

'You are welcome,' said Raldoron. He looked out over the tangle of wrecks. 'I feel that something is about to happen.' They spoke over the vox, insulated to an extent from the roaring of the wall guns, though no conversation could survive the macro cannon's report.

'Your lord is well known for his second sight,' said Thane. 'Do you share it?'

'In truth, I am not sure,' said Raldoron. 'I anticipate things, but I have always attributed that to my augmentations and training. I would not wish for Sanguinius' foresight. It is a curse as much as a gift.'

'It appears you perhaps do have a little of his power,' said Thane pointing. 'The bombardment has ceased!'

They looked upwards. A last shower of shells screamed down. Lightning flickered through the churning clouds, purple, yellow and green. The heavens writhed with dying winds.

'Fresh devilry,' said Thane.

'It is beginning,' said Raldoron tersely. 'Maintain bombardment of enemy positions,' he voxed to the gunnery command centres. 'All companies stand ready for assault.'

Thane looked at him. 'How will they come against us?'

'That, I do not know,' said Raldoron. 'But it is time. That I know in the pit of my being.'

The skies rippled like water, and in the clouds a face appeared, flat as a pict from a plastek flimsy projected onto an inadequate screen. It wavered with the movement of the clouds, unfocused at first, then became sharp as a knife to the skin.

At first, they took it for a sort of daemon. The face was horned. Its short muzzle ended in a maw surrounded by lamprey teeth. Six eyes glowed above it. But then, like the effect of a trick picture, the face changed in Raldoron's perception, and he saw he was looking at the distorted war-mask of one of the Legions.

'Word Bearers,' Raldoron said.

'Sorcery,' said Thane. 'They have fallen far.'

'Hearken to me, oh people of Terra!' the being said, its harsh voice penetrating the racket of the guns.

'Perhaps they have come to offer their surrender,' said Thane drily.

The Palace guns continued to fire.

'There's my father's answer to that,' he added.

'Predictable,' the Word Bearer said. 'But it is not primarch or Space Marine I address, but you, the common people, the subjects of Lord Horus who languish under the tyranny of the False Emperor.' The guns boomed on, but every word was clear, bypassing ears and auditory systems to ring in the minds of everyone on the planet.

The head turned, sweeping across the world. With that glance the legionary took in continents, and he laughed at what he saw with a low, monster's growl.

'Heed my offer!' the Space Marine said. 'I am Zardu Layak, the Crimson Apostle. I am the herald of the Warmaster Horus, rightful lord of mankind. I call on you all, people of the nations of Terra, to hearken to me and hearken well. There comes a choice now, twixt life and death.'

The voice boomed away across the valleys of the truncated mountains and tore around the globe. The Apostle waited for his words to be digested before he continued. Some of the warriors on the defences shouted up at the vision in defiance. Others screamed.

'I come with an offer to you all. Lay down your arms. Renounce your False Emperor. Raise your voices to the Warmaster and plead for your lives, and you will be spared.' Another pause. Where the maw of the Space Marine's mask projected onto the clouds, a vortex spun, and down it floated an island. That was how Raldoron instinctively named it. It was not a craft. It was not a platform or an orbital plate, but an *island* made of bone. Even from so far away, the ivory glint of it and the rough, compacted surface of the thing made it clear that it was formed of thousands of skeletons, crushed together.

The island ceased descending when it was level with the

walls. It came down close by the Helios Gate, and began a circuit of the defences, passing in front of Raldoron and Thane's position. Guns tracked the island, las-beams, plasma and shells hammering at it, but they did no harm. The island rippled, the shots passing through.

'A vision. An illusion,' said Thane.

'Maybe, but this Layak is there,' said Raldoron. 'Look. He shows himself to us.'

He pointed. Upon the top of the island was a pulpit formed of a monster's skull. From the empty brainpan, Layak delivered his sermon. Around the pulpit eight thousand mortal priests in purple robes swayed from side to side in worshipful silence.

'The Emperor is a liar,' said Layak. 'You have all been deceived. He has lived among you for thousands of years, biding His time, using your ancestors as He uses you now. The Emperor speaks of Unity. The Emperor speaks of the protection of the species. The Emperor speaks of the furtherance of mankind. The Emperor speaks of many things, and all He says is lies. Know this, people of Terra, He is false! The Warmaster, great Horus, has seen through His deceit, and commands me to relay to you the truth of the Emperor's ambition.'

The island rotated as it floated by. The wall guns continued to shoot at it, but it was a mirage called with magic, and it passed by unharmed. Seemingly serene, it nevertheless moved at pace, and was soon shrinking out of sight down the sweep of the Daylight Wall. Raldoron ordered surveillance automata to track it, giving him a doubled view. Via his auto-senses he looked down on the traitor. From the wall he looked up to the sorcerously projected image.

'The Emperor is a parasite! He uses your sacrifices to raise Himself up in the warp. Your blood and your souls are

His meat and drink. He wages a campaign to challenge the Pantheon of true deities. Listen to me, misguided, abused children of Terra. Let it be known to you that the Emperor desires only apotheosis. He would become a god and supplant the Gods of War, Life, Pleasure and Knowledge. He would transcend this plane of existence, and abandon you all to the monsters He pledged to rid you from. It is He who is the traitor to the species, not Horus! Horus will save you. Look to the sky and see his fleets. Witness how many others have seen reality for what it is, unclouded by lies and wishful thinking. Know that the coming of Horus is the coming of truth! He is the chosen of the gods, the powers in the warp who have watched over humanity for time immemorial until, to their dismay, the Emperor barred them from their worshippers. He has seen the gods' glory and serves them willingly. He does not wish to supplant them. He does not spoon-feed you pleasant fantasies. He is not a lying tyrant – he, Horus Lupercal, is the saviour of mankind!'

Layak pointed skywards, to the churning air and the fleet that waited beyond for Terra's answer. Raldoron's wall captains reported in, sending target locks for verification. He blink-clicked and thought-approved them all. They were as good targets as they could be, straight shots, but every beam of energy and solid round passed through the island.

'I am a prophet of the gods. I am Horus' servant,' said Zardu Layak, 'and I say to you, rejoice! The gods are coming here, to this world. They will bestow their power and their wisdom to any person strong and faithful enough to take it. Look upon me, and witness one of their champions. I swear to you that they will treat mercifully those who turn their backs upon the False Emperor. They will be kind to those who kneel to the righteous powers of this universe! This is my pledge! You will survive, you will prosper. You will know mastery of this realm, and glory in the next. This is their compact with me, and through me, with you.'

Again the figure paused. Again thunder rolled its drums.

'As I come to you with these joyous tidings, I must also convey a warning. If you do not embrace the true faith, if you do not acknowledge the true gods, if you do not pay obeisance to Khorne, God of War...' The sky shook at the speaking of the name. Men cried out. 'To Nurgle, God of Endless Life...' The sky shook again, and again as he spoke the names of the other powers. 'To Tzeentch, God of Knowledge, and to Slaanesh, God of Pleasure... then you will be slain by them and their servants, and your souls will be cast into the warp, there to be devoured. Only then, in the life that comes after this as surely as night follows day, will you know the magnitude of your mistake. There you will see through the Emperor's tissue of lies in despair. In the warp you will beg without hope for the chance to change your actions. There is but one choice!' Zardu Layak boomed. The island of bone had passed hundreds of kilometres to the south by now.

Through the automata's eyes, Raldoron witnessed the thrall-priests of Layak cast back their hoods, rip open their robes and expose their torsos. They were eyeless, every one, bloody sockets in their faces, and their bodies cruelly cut with ritual scars and burned with brands. In their right hands they held daggers of dull metal.

'This is the end!' Layak roared.

The priests lifted their daggers to the sky and howled praise with tongueless mouths.

'Grovel before the gods and beg for their mercy!' Layak demanded.

The knives plunged into the breasts of the priests. They fell as one, their blood rushing from their opened hearts and pouring through the gaps in the bone to sluice the land below.

'Now is the time, now is the moment! The way is clear! The doors open! Turn on the slaves of the False Emperor, repent before it is too late and liberate yourselves from His tyranny!'

The island rose up, rapidly vanishing into the crowds, chased all the way by a tempest of ineffectual gunfire.

Drops of rain plinked off Raldoron's battleplate, the few turning rapidly to many. It ran over his eye-lenses, smearing the view.

'What is happening?' asked Thane. He held up a cupped palm.

Only then did Raldoron see that the drops of rain ran bright and crimson on Thane's yellow armour.

'A rain of blood,' Raldoron said.

A great howling split the sky, then another, then a third. Three streaks of lurid energy shot down from above, each displaying brief glimpses of howling faces. One by one they slammed down. More thunder rumbled.

On the horizon, screeching horns blew.

Physical movement pushed through the line of shimmering energy fields guarding the contravallation. Constructs so large they were visible from the wall top across scores of kilometres of broken land emerged from the battlesmoke. Three huge siege towers pushed their way through the landing craft wrecks, taller even than the broken ships, and big enough to grind the smaller of them flat.

Sirens rose up from the city. Still the enemy fleet did not re-engage with their cannons, but across the land between siege line and wall sped the fire of more conventional weaponry as enemy artillery opened fire again. These hit the weakened shields, with many passing through to strike the wall itself.

'This is it,' said Thane. 'The circling is over. The duel begins in earnest.'

'There will be a landing soon,' said Raldoron, looking up into the bloody rain.

'Let us strike blood together, brother,' said Thane. He held up his yellow gauntlet. Raldoron crashed his forearm against the Imperial Fist's.

Explosions rippled over the aegis.

'I will not let that sermon rest without reply,' Raldoron said. He clambered up onto the firing step, and faced the mighty cannon. Framed by the fires of the enemy's impotence boiling off the shields, he raised his bolter and demanded the attention of friend and foe alike.

'Now! Now!' Raldoron shouted. He opened his communications to all the men under his command: his company, his Chapter, the warriors of other Legions pledged to the Helios section of the Daylight Wall, Martian cyborgs, mortal humans, grizzled soldiers and terrified conscripts.

'The oath! Take the oath!' he commanded.

His men turned about, took to one knee and bowed their heads.

'We are the sons of the blood of Sanguinius!' Raldoron shouted over the howl of weaponry.

'We are the sons of Dorn!' Thane echoed.

'In this moment we take our oath, solemnly to be upheld, that we defy these prophets. We deny their superstitions, their bloodthirsty idols, mumbled cantrip and fearful fetish. We deny these so-called gods. We deny their right to be. On this day, not one traitor shall pass this wall. Not one being who spits on the Emperor's name. Not one with treachery in his heart. Not one in thrall to these false gods. We fight to the last of our blood, for the Emperor, for the Imperium, for Unity, for Terra!'

'For the Emperor, for the Imperium, for Unity, for Terra!' half a million voices, human and transhuman, roared back, loudly enough to be heard over the guns.

'Let our defiance be our first blow!' Raldoron shouted. 'Let that be our oath!'

There were no parchments to be affixed by wax, or time to observe the proper rites, but in the gathering of warriors there was more solemnity than any official practice could contain. There was no distinction between man and superhuman, only brotherhood, and the shared will to prevail.

Raldoron rejoined Thane.

'Well said, Blood Angel.'

'Now I am ready to fight,' said Raldoron.

Dorn himself spoke then, a message that went to every helm, vox-bead and address system in the Palace.

'The time for speeches is done,' said Dorn. *'The first great test is here. My order to you all is simple, yet heed it well, and exert yourselves to see it done.*

'They are coming. Kill them all.'

TWENTY-SEVEN

Angels of Death
Angron freed
First on the wall

The Nightfall, *Terran orbit, 15th of Quartus*

A single note sang through Horus' fleet, calling all to action. Upon the *Nightfall* it was greeted gladly.

'That's it. That's the signal. All engines full ahead!' bellowed Terror Master Thandamell, wild with excitement.

All mutual respect between the Legion and its servants was gone aboard the *Nightfall*. The bond had been failing for a long time, a process of erosion quickened since Skraivok had installed himself, and come thence to collapse. It was not so on every ship, but under the Painted Count's overlordship, the crew were reduced to chattels. The slave masters moved among the thralls, laying their scourges across the backs of those deemed to be performing their duties too slowly. No Night Lord would lower himself to the tedious administration of day-to-day discipline. Every overseer was drawn from the thrall-stock of the ship. All were desperate men, and

sadists. Their eagerness to perform their duties exhilarated
Skraivok. He had never been a gentle man, but his character
was changing under the influence of the sword, becoming
more wanton in its cruelty – quickly enough that he could
see it himself, invigorating enough that he did not care.

'Thandamell!' Skraivok crowed from the shipmaster's dais.
'What glories await us! What fine adventures we set ourselves
upon. When the bards compose their sonnets of this war,
come victory or defeat, the name of Gendor Skraivok will be
remembered, and that is very fine. When the chroniclers of
the future ask where Konrad Curze was at the moment the
first assault crashed against the walls and find no answer,
they will know that I, the Painted Count, was there in his
stead! As Curze blunders his way across the cosmos whining
for his father, it is I who bring the sons of the sunless world
to glory, for power, for plunder and for pain! Onwards, sons
of the night! Onwards to victory.'

Thandamell grinned savagely. 'What a lovely speech,' he
said. 'Are you all done now?'

'Of course, Thandamell.' Skraivok gripped the hilt of his
sheathed sword and gestured to a slave to bring him his
helm. 'If you would be so good as to release the primarch, I
have a ship to board. Order the Raptors to depart immediately. Take the enemy by surprise, clear a safe zone. I wouldn't
want my crowning achievement to be spoiled by my death.'

'How do we get him out?' said Thandamell.

Skraivok, on his way to the nearest lifter, stopped.

'Who, terror master?'

'Angron. How do we get him off the ship?'

Skraivok waved a hand around dismissively.

'I shall let you decide on that. I've other prey to hunt.'

The *Nightfall* shuddered from stem to stern with the push
of its engines. Terra's tortured orb swelled. Klaxons alerted

all aboard to imminent planetfall. On decks below, warriors readied themselves for the drop.

'You, serf!' Thandamell barked. 'Prepare to cut power to the labyrinth.'

Angron blundered from a smoking chamber. Delicate crystalline pain engines lay broken on the ground. The daemon primarch panted with effort, his red skin crossed with a thousand welts. The pain engines could keep a normal man occupied with an eternity of torments – yet another trap in Perturabo's maze. Under Angron's fury, they had lasted four minutes. Behind him stretched a trail of destruction through the intricate workings, a road of smashed priceless technologies, caved-in walls, ruptured conduits and broken machinery.

The next room came alive. A labyrinth of screaming faces trapped in mirrors, all pleading to be saved, all in peril, shouting endlessly.

There was perhaps a way through. Once, Angron had possessed a mind sharp enough to best the challenge by intellect alone. Now, he did not need to think. Brute force served him better. His wings were tattered, one eye blinded. Las-burns, rad-burns, cuts and bullet holes covered him. The labyrinth had tested him, but it could never, ever stop him.

Angron heaved in a wheezing breath and spat it out as a blood-curdling roar. He was not done with the maze.

He ignored the faces pleading for mercy. He passed by the slaughter of innocents without care.

'Blood!' howled Angron. *'Blood and skulls!'*

The black sword sliced. A mirror burst. The face within screamed. Blood spattered the primarch, followed by a burst of tinkling clockwork. Perturabo had put all his artistry into the creation of the maze. It was lost on Angron.

'Blood!' he roared. *'Skulls!'* Furious at his captivity, he was reduced to a vocabulary of two words. A fist, the skinned knuckles shockingly white against his red skin, caved in another mirror artwork, crushing the weeping mortal trapped inside.

'Skulls!' he howled. The black sword fell, umbral flames roaring along the killing edges. It melted as much as cut through the next mirror. Arcane energy fields exploded with a crisp bang. Powdered glass burst everywhere.

Angron was in the thick of slaughter, and there alone could he find a scintilla of peace. As he smashed apart the machines and the beings within, his fury blotted out all thought, removing the troublesome weight of sentience. He did not stop to contemplate whether the people were real, and if so, how they had come to be trapped. He was as unaware as an earthquake, and as destructive. He battered his way through every mirror, silencing the screams, then smashed in the door at the end of the chamber with three blows that dented it and sent it clattering over the floor of the next room.

Flashing lights lit figures juddering into life. Dragging footsteps approached Angron. Bladed fists whirred. Mindless voices moaned. Each one was a Salamander of Vulkan's Legion, their bodies violated by cruel cybernetics. Insanity blazed from their red Nocturnean eyes. Hints of sentience lurked there. More torments for their father, but Angron did not notice nor would he have cared. He saw skulls and blood for the harvest, and charged without thought.

They cut him. Black blood ran from his wounds and fizzed on the deck as it dissipated, taking his essence back to the warp. Buzz saws and power shears gouged at him. The enslaved Space Marines could harm him. They could kill him. He would not stop fighting until he was hacked apart.

A cut nearly chopped his wing from his back. With his sword gripped in both hands, he spun around in a deadly circle, wrecking every slave-cyborg within reach. Yet still there were more.

They stopped moving. The lights went out, and he didn't notice, hacking at the Salamanders until most were rent into slivers of metal. He was still battering away at the floor, shouting, *'Blood! Blood! Blood!'*

The last was slashed to bits, its flesh mashed to red pulp and its mechanisms broken.

Angron snuffled in confusion into the dark.

Something had changed. A door opened. He turned. No more tricks or foes. An empty corridor.

His rage ebbed. His mind cleared. He had wandered the maze for hours, fighting and destroying, only to be brought back every time to the central chamber, no matter which route he took.

Far off a klaxon blared, and the maze shook with the movement of heavy machinery. A breeze tugged at Angron's legs.

'Freedom,' he grunted. *'Blood.'*

The breeze grew into a raging torrent of air, sucking at him. Door after door opened, drawing him through inactive rooms outwards, until the air howled, and he came to the end of the labyrinth, and passed out through vast, patched adamantine doors into a cavernous hold.

The maze filled most of the space, the iron mask of Perturabo stamped regularly along the exterior. Angron barely comprehended it, but followed the gale, turned a corner and was presented with the sight of giant loading doors open to the void. He ran to them, and stood upon the lip of the hold, buffeted by the gale. Terra was before him, its tortured atmosphere flashing and roiling, its orbits shoaling with a hundred thousand ships. From them fell drops of fire. Angron's last remaining shreds of humanity dimly recognised a drop assault of a magnitude that dwarfed any unleashed during the Great Crusade.

The wind died to nothing. Angron stood unharmed in open space.

A little of his mind returned. He saw the white-and-blue ships of his own Legion shoot out their landing craft.

Sol rose around the globe, spreading its wide beam of golden light over Horus' fleet, and silhouetting the *Vengeful Spirit*.

'Horus! Horus!' he shouted. Against the laws of nature, his voice was heard in the vacuum. *'Give me my due!'*

With that, he spread his wings, and leapt into the void.

Himalazian airspace, 15th of Quartus

Dropping at several hundred kilometres an hour into the most dangerous warzone in history, Lucoryphus of the Night Lords was preoccupied with one thing, and that was that his feet hurt.

He lifted up his right boot for the fifth time and stared at it.

The vox clicked.

'What are you doing?' asked Tashain.

Lucoryphus put his foot down.

'My foot hurts,' he said.

'See an Apothecary then,' Tashain said disdainfully.

He could have added that Lucoryphus shouldn't need to see one. That his foot shouldn't hurt. He was a legionary, and beyond the petty aches that plagued unmodified humanity. Lucoryphus could equally have responded that he had already consulted with their company medicae staff, but then he would have to tell Tashain that his foot was not as it should be.

He had been to Estus, because he could trust him. When so many Apothecaries abandoned their role or turned from healing to torture, Estus still did his job properly. Many standards had slipped in the Night Lords, but Estus could still be relied on. In his notes were annotated scans of Lucoryphus' feet, arrows picking out metatarsals in the process of fusion, the calcaneus atrophying, phalanges lengthening, and smaller bones dissolving altogether.

'A malfunction of the ossmodula,' Estus had said, somewhat uncertainly, marking his comments down in a book of meticulous records. 'There is not much I can do. I am busy with the wounded. I do not have time for your problem.'

He had given Lucoryphus a stabilising compound to add to his suit pharmocopia. It had not helped.

That was weeks ago. Lucoryphus' foot had changed further since then. He was too canny to go back. The Night Lords were degenerating, but they still had only contempt for mutants.

The Thunderhawk bounced through a storm of turbulence. There was not a still pocket of air in all of Terra's atmosphere. Crosswinds and pressure changes were violent enough to tear gunships from the sky and dash them on the ground without any help from the loyalist guns. But though the Night Lords had a reputation for cowardice it was undeserved. They were Space Marines; they knew no fear. Lucoryphus didn't want to die, not one bit, but he did not fear death. The very idea of being afraid was slightly absurd. His disregard for danger was not down to conditioning, or bravery, but because of one simple fact.

Lucoryphus knew he was going to live forever. He felt it to his core.

So as the ship bounced and screamed through the dried-up valleys of Himalazia, out of sight of the Palace wall guns but on a collision course with them, Lucoryphus stared at his feet. The lengthened toes of the right curled uncomfortably against his boot. He had no heel to speak of on that foot any more. A backwards-facing digit tipped with a claw was growing in its place.

He could no longer deny it. His right foot had become the image of a bird's talon.

The left foot was not far behind. Their confinement in boots made for human feet was the source of his discomfort. He had wondered if he could find an armourer willing to make him new boots more fitting to his condition, until he wondered again if he was going to need to. A mark had appeared on his right boot recently. An indentation in the ceramite that would not polish out, and no matter how many times he filled and sanded it, grew deeper. The boots were hot with some machine fever, as though they were changing to fit his new form.

He looked around the shaking crew compartment. He was not alone in his change. The Raptors seemed like Night Lords, until one looked closer. The helms of some had been refashioned with a distinctly birdlike aspect. Through personal choice, the armour was diverging already from that of the rest of the Legion, but the alterations that armour hid were telling. When on the ground some of them moved awkwardly, their steps exaggerated into avian hops. Several had strange birdlike twitches and hunched postures, as if the jump packs they wore were folded wings, not jets.

Lucoryphus lived for flight. All of them did. Being a Raptor was becoming more important to him than being a Night Lord.

He looked at his feet again. How would his comrades

judge them? He thought how much more useful talons would be to him as a flying being than human feet, how they would allow him to grasp and hold himself fast after a jump.

The engines screamed. The Thunderhawk nosed upwards into a rapid ascent. Suddenly the sky around them was full of the bang of explosions and clatter of shrapnel as the ship came under fire. A heavy lascannon beam cut through the front hatch, skewering three of Lucoryphus' brethren on a shaft of light, leaving them dangling in their restraints when it snapped off.

Another hit moments later, smashing the left engine. The ship dipped, its wounded jet coughing, and lost height.

The ready lights switched from red to green, bringing a little more illumination to the dingy interior through the smoke rising from the dead. The damaged front ramp flapped open, the extra drag pulling the gunship faster towards destruction. The rear ramp followed with more mechanical discipline. The side doors ratcheted wide. Fire flashed on every side as the Emperor's slaves tried to bring them down.

Lucoryphus stood first. He drew his weapons as he walked down the aisle to the prow, trying to suppress his growing limp. His armour whined at his awkward movements. Sometimes he thought it would be more comfortable to run on all fours.

'Brothers!' he voxed his command. 'We fly! First to the wall! First to the blood! *Ave Dominus Noctem!*'

The others were rising as Lucoryphus ignited his jets, ran from the prow and leapt into the maelstrom of fire. Thirty Raptors followed him, bright comets of exhaust joining the flare and flash of war. Its task completed, the gunship rolled in the sky and fell, fatally wounded. Smoke chased it to the ground, where it died in orange flames.

Lucoryphus' hearts pounded with the thrill of flight. Bloody rain splashed from his war-plate. A billion people were trying to kill him during that glorious fall. The wall rushed at him, a giant's hand to swat a fly. He fired his jets to slow himself, passing through the failing aegis with a searing crackle of energy that shorted out half his suit's systems and left the smell of burnt circuitry in his nostrils. The wall grew from a black slab to a layered stack of defences manned by tiny figures in yellow and red. Behind them rose the Palace spires, daunting in their height, and the inconceivably huge whale-ridge of the Eternity Wall space port. The figures saw him, and fired. Smaller humans among the legionaries turned their attention to him. Pintle stubbers streaked tracer fire in his direction. Lasgun beams flickered out their short-lived displays. It seemed he was the one stationary in all that fury, and the bullets, and the wall and the world rushed at him, as if he were the offended party and they attacked without provocation.

He was so intoxicated by his flight that he remembered to fire his own gun only moments before impact. Three rounds he allowed himself. Two went wild. The third blew apart a mortal man in a gaudy uniform whose body flowered with stamen ribs and chest wall petals.

The wall punched up to meet him. Lucoryphus altered his course to slam into an Imperial Fists legionary with force enough to kill. The Emperor's slave flew back so hard he cracked a chunk from a merlon before pitching over into the fire-dazzled twilight and falling from the wall. Lucoryphus was sent spinning off by the impact, slamming into the rockcrete with his jets still burning. The surface was slick with vitae pouring from the heavens, and for a moment he teetered on the brink of the inner crenellations. The chasm of the canyon road dividing city from defences yawned at him. A burst of jets and a painful push from his twisted feet sent him back onto the parapet, where men ran at him. Staggered, he brought up his inactive chainsword to deflect the desperate bayonet jabs of three Imperial Army soldiers. They fired their guns as they stabbed, scoring his livery. He punched at them clumsily, breaking their skulls with his fists. Time slowed. His head rang. Imperial Fists were running at him, bolters barking. A macro shell hit the wall fifty metres away, sending out a cloud of fire, flailing bodies and a storm of deadly rubble.

Time ran true again. He launched himself up, finger gunning the chainsword trigger. He met the first attacker with a sweep at the torso. The sword's teeth did not bite, skidding off the ceramite with a spray of sparks, but it threw off the legionary's aim and his bolt burned past Lucoryphus' head, wounding his vision with rocket motor flare. The Night Lord was fast, working on instinct, and finished him with a round through the eye slit that obliterated his helmet and painted Lucoryphus with blood.

A second warrior came for him, only to be hit by a howling Raptor whose falling kick was strong enough to shatter ceramite.

Night Lords thumped down around him, guns firing, chain weapons growling. A flurry of violence, a popping chorus of bolt explosions, and there were no more of the Emperor's slaves there to oppose them.

Lucoryphus was on the walls. After all this time, he was *on the Palace walls*. Their attack had taken the defenders by surprise. There were no other of the Warmaster's forces on the battlement; only the blue and red of Night Lords battle-plate was visible, both colours close to black in the fire and murk. He looked up at the spires of the Imperial Palace, bathed in light and glorious despite their embattled state.

Lucoryphus' hearts pounded with the scale of his achievement.

He raised his arms and shouted at the sky. *'Mino premiesh a minos murantiath!'* he cried in Nostraman, the words as liquid as the rain. 'We are first on the wall!'

He gathered in his warriors, and ordered them to secure the landing zone.

Skraivok was coming.

TWENTY-EIGHT

Second line
Ordo Reductor
Myzmadra plays her part

Palace outworks, Daylight Wall section 16, 15th of Quartus

There was only noise.

Guns were firing from both sides in such great numbers their reports had no individual existence, but became a single block of sound as tangible as stone. The racket stole every other sound and made it into part of an unyielding, physical whole. Moving against this force required effort. It permeated the earth. It shook every cell in the human body.

In this realm of war, noise was the king, oppressing every sensation ruthlessly. Occasional louder eruptions would surface from the racket: a jet's roar, a direct macro cannon hit on the line's revetment, the warbling shrieks of dying void shields, the explosion of a nearby bomb. They would exceed the volume of the noise, then be swallowed up by the greater whole.

There was no question of Katsuhiro hearing orders. Even touch was blurred out by the noise's relentless vibrations, and the slaps sergeants gave to attract attention were hardly felt.

Men died to the left and to the right of Katsuhiro, felled by buzzing swarms of shrapnel or shots from the seething mass of the foe coming at them. They fell unnoticed, their screams unheard. He would reach for a fresh power pack, and then see the fellow beside him had been blasted into scraps, or realise that a bunker which moments before had been slaughtering the enemy had become a burning ruin.

In the pouring rain of blood, the conscripts fired down from the second line rampart. Once more, the lost and the damned of Horus' grand army surged at them with no care for their own lives. Abhumans and mutants had been replaced by worse abominations. Every squint through Katsuhiro's iron sights brought a new horror to his attention. Months ago any one of them would have had him gibbering in terror, but now he shot them and moved on to the next target.

The last bastions fired their guns until the barrels glowed hot. They killed and killed, but the enemy would not stop coming, nor would they break and run. Behind the foe the three siege towers rumbled forwards, crushing everything in their path. Smoke obscured them from Katsuhiro, and he saw them only as looming shapes lit up by the aching glow of shield discharge. Another threat ready to destroy him should he survive the horde.

The Palace aegis shook to the drum beat of plasma, las and shell. The shrieks of the voids were the worst of the noises deafening Katsuhiro: otherworldly, moaning howls as each lenticular field collapsed which gave the impression that the shield was a tormented being. Collapses happened with increasing frequency. Each time the voids reignited they came back weaker. Permanent gaps were forced and targeted by the foe, and thereby widened, exposing the wall to the attentions of artillery. Behind the wall the shields held, but over the outworks the aegis flickered with dying light.

Gunfire battered at the Palace walls. Among the outworks the bombardment wreaked havoc, tearing up the ground, breaking the ramparts into islands of resistance amid a sea of hatred. More bombs were getting through. More streams of incinerating plasma slashing into the defenders and boiling them to steam. More las-beams obliterating bunkers and breaking the bastions.

Katsuhiro fired and fired as his comrades were slain. At the beginning of the siege, the conscripts had stood in such numbers they packed the ramparts and tangled their weapons. Now there were too few of them to cover all the defence line. They relied more than ever on the Palace guns and the closer-ranged weaponry of the bastions. They had all become snipers, thought Katsuhiro, which made him think about Doromek. He was certain the veteran had killed Runnecan. Were it not for the million traitors to his front, that might have worried him.

Enfilading fire cut the enemy down some way out from the ramparts, but the dead were so numerous and heaped so high they created cover for those coming behind. Phosphex grenades launched from the tops of the bastions set fires among the slain that reduced them to ash, but the enemy used the black smoke pouring from these ragged pyres to press even further forwards.

Overhead the gunships of the Legiones Astartes roared in to attack the walls. Aircraft duelled around them. Such violence was inflicted on every level of the battlescape, but Katsuhiro was unaware of the larger fight. All he saw were bestial faces twisted in rage, fusillades of las-beams stabbing towards him, and clawed hands reaching impotently from the ground towards the rampart top.

The fumes and poison gases blown away earlier in the day returned. Blood fell in sheets from the racing clouds. Such fury and tumult had the world, Katsuhiro could not hope to survive; but whether he lived another minute or another hundred years, one thing was certain.

The second line was failing.

Siege Camp Penta, 15th of Quartus

Clain Pent watched the battle raging against the wall's feet. His precious constructs rumbled across the littered plain, each engine fuelled by burning souls and directed by the essences of captive daemons. They were but the first Neverborn on Terra, the machina diabolus. They were protected from the Emperor's psychic might by their half-material forms. Untold legions of daemons waited beyond the veil, but more blood must flow. Pent's efforts were key to that.

Pent was nervous. His siege towers were among his finest creations, yet they moved against the greatest fortification in the galaxy.

<Are the shield-banes ready?> he demanded via datapulse of Penta-4. <When will the Ordo Reductor open fire?>

Around the *Pent-Ark*, teams of Dark Mechanicum thralls laboured under electro-scourges to load and prime the great cannons. The barrels alone were dozens of metres long, larger than any weapon carried by a Titan, as large as the capital-ship killers mounted on void fortresses. Scores of tracked trucks supported their frames. Platforms along their sides allowed access to unfathomable workings. Grim techpriests by the hundred oversaw the efforts of their creatures.

<Now, oh knowledgable sage,> said Penta-4.

Clain Pent's grotesque body nodded stiffly.

The great guns started to draw power. Giant cables snaked

off to trailers behind the cannons, where plasma reactors were lit and coaxed to full power output. Stray arcs of electricity leapt over the surfaces of the weapons. Giant finned energy sinks were filled with coolant in readiness for the cannons' firing.

The lords of the Ordo Reductor held their machines, waiting for the command to come down from the fleet. In the eight siege camps, Sota-Nul's disciples, reliant on the ordo's protection for their infernal devices, watched impatiently.

The order came. Horus Lupercal himself issued the command, a single, rasping sentence broadcast to each of the cyborg siege masters.

'Unleash your weapons,' the Warmaster said.

The guns spoke.

Palace outworks, Daylight Wall section 16, 15th of Quartus

Something imperceptible changed the moment before the cannons fired, causing Katsuhiro to cease shooting, and look to the wall to the south of the Helios Gate.

Out over the wastes before the wall, there was movement. From the siege camp came first a flash, and then a spear of black light that crawled across Katsuhiro's vision. It was energy of some sort, but it moved with a malevolent slowness a man's eyes could track.

A shock wave preceded it. Although the beam itself did not touch the ground, a line of force surrounding it ripped a furrow through debris, the defence lines, the defenders and the attacking armies. Like an attacking serpent, it slithered quicker, then struck, planting itself against the shields, which wavered and sang with tortured harmonics.

Upon contact with the void barrier, the beam thickened, its strange energies dammed by the aegis. A living tar spread over the voids, some arcane reaction making the lenses of the Dark Age energy field constantly visible on normal wavelengths. Like an overlapping wall of shields, the lenses stood against the strike, but as Katsuhiro watched, their vitality was bled away. Where the play of black energy caressed them, the lenses dimmed from healthy blues and greens to angry reds, then through lower frequencies to sulphurous, glowering oranges.

A horrible, discordant squealing came from the contact point, building in volume and intensity, until it overcame the thundering guns completely. The detonation was immense, sending warriors on both sides reeling from their fight in pain. Something gave in Katsuhiro's right ear. Hot wetness trickled down the angle of his jaw. His left ear screamed with discordancy.

The shields bled light.

He fell to his knees, jaw clenched tight enough to break his teeth. The pain went beyond any suffering he had so far endured. His eyes shook, blurring his vision. He wished then to die, but could not stop watching.

Like dying embers, the lenses under fire burned out, and their failing set up a chain reaction in the cellular construction of the aegis. With painful flares and whooping screams, a great swathe of the landward shield collapsed, robbing fifty kilometres either side of the Helios Gate of shelter, opening the way for the Warmaster's forces to assail the walls directly. Uncountable thousands of land-based artillery pieces hammered the great walls, or shot over the defences to target the giant buildings they guarded.

The moment had come. Huge chimneys on the motive units of the siege towers belched green smoke. Wheels ten times the height of men churned up the ground, and the massive constructions lurched forwards, their fronts alive with shield flare as Dorn's defences tried to bring them down.

Dauntlessly, the Death Guard's towers made all haste for the breach in the aegis and the walls behind.

The ruination of worlds poured down upon the outworks. Quake cannons ripped up the ground. Macro shells gouged craters from the stone. Plasma reduced rockcrete to boiling geysers of atoms. Weapons exotic and mundane hammered into the second and first lines. Now completely unprotected by the shields, they were ripped apart. The bombardment was intense and indiscriminate. Hundreds of thousands of Horus' followers were obliterated to kill a few thousand defenders. The ground bucked and heaved, swallowing the living and the dead. Bastions up and down the line were smashed like skulls under hammers.

The defenders broke and ran. The veterans who had watched over them fled as readily as the depleted regiments of conscripts. There was no other choice.

Katsuhiro ran when the others did, abandoning his post in a state of detachment. Weeks of horror had numbed his soul. The deafness in his left ear isolated him a little from the battle's fury. Tiredness cocooned him. He felt as if he floated over himself. The pathways of his body raged with adrenaline that muzzled his consciousness and pushed him only to survive, so that numinous piece of Katsuhiro which existed apart from the slosh of blood and muscle watched disinterested from on high.

He leapt from explosions, he sprinted past glowing lakes of cooling rock. Everything was on fire. Where it was not molten, the ground was a steaming mix of mud and blood. His feet splashed in scalding red puddles. His face burned.

His hair crackled back on his scalp. Blood was in his eyes and in his nostrils and mouth. Tears streamed down his face. The few survivors of the lines were black figures, fragile in the roil of flame. They ran without in panic, all of them heading towards the soaring citadel of the Helios Gate. The gates were shut tight against the world, and the towers under ferocious attack that would see all the soldiers dead before they came anywhere near shelter, but there was nowhere else to go, so they ran away from one source of certain destruction towards another.

Behind Katsuhiro a wall of fire reached for the heavens, its glare and heat obliterating every other sight. Silhouetted in black before the inferno, Bastion 16 fired wildly when so many others of the outwork forts were gone. The call of wheezing trumpets sounded out in the wastes that even now crept closer to the feet of the defences proper, and from the blasted lands of the plain the giant shape of a siege tower burst through the flames like an axe breaking a shield.

The tower was as tall as the walls that it set itself against. Its forwards arc flashed as incoming fire was annihilated by its void shields, sending oily swirls all around its height. The front was armoured with giant bronze faces stacked atop one another, seven in number, as grotesque as any feral-worlders' totem pole. Their screaming mouths vomited words of coherent light from cannons in place of tongues, scoring molten streaks across the walls.

The scale of the thing defied sense. It was hundreds of metres tall, its wheels immense. It should not have stayed in one piece, let alone move, but it did, flattening the land with a great dozer blade, smoke pouring from whatever engine propelled it forwards.

The incongruity of the tower struck him as wildly funny, and he laughed as he ran. To see a sight like that… In a time of reason, unreason was let loose. Impossible towers in an era of high science and rediscovery. The world had gone mad.

He cried tears of fear and tears of laughter. His throat hurt from smoke inhalation and from screaming. A shell sent up a fountain of earth in front of him, and he skidded to a stop. The tower ground forwards faster than he could run, crushing everything, its protection of energy and of metal impervious to all weaponry.

Katsuhiro sank to his knees.

'It's hopeless, hopeless,' he said. 'There is no escape.'

War trumpets blared from the construction once again, weakening his grip on sanity. His mind might have collapsed entirely, right then, and left him gibbering to perish in any one of a thousand ways, had the glare of a plasma strike not illuminated the area with more certain light, and shown Katsuhiro a familiar sight. The trenches had been pounded so hard they were hardly recognisable, and the small bunker was half buried in rock and shattered plascrete, but it still stood, and the door was ajar. A rivulet of blood rain poured inside from the wounded earth.

Nexus Zero-One-Five.

Without realising, Katsuhiro had run close to the tunnels' entrance.

There was a way out after all.

The door was jammed open by a fan of rubble. There would be no closing it, though he dearly wished he could shut out the awful battlefield. Nevertheless, as Katsuhiro descended into the network the tumult receded a little. The inferno became a glow, the noise almost bearable, and when he got to the bottom and set out into the network, it dwindled further until, when he turned a corner into cool blackness, it faded away to a quiet, faraway roar.

He became acutely conscious of his lost hearing. Everything on the left felt muffled. His right ear functioned, but rang with tinnitus.

When he set a foot forwards and heard the soft crunch of fallen debris under his boot he was a little relieved, and he set out deeper into the network, intending to turn north and make his way nearer to the wall in safety. Darkness pressed in. The lumens were all out. The ground shook with the bombardment, sometimes violently. Debris pattered off his head. Without the immediate danger of the explosions and the enemy to keep him occupied, his fear built, and he went cautiously.

He did not find the way towards the wall. Somewhere, perhaps several somewheres, he took the wrong turn, and ended up in the corridor leading to the base of Bastion 16. Once more he smelled blood. His foot rolled on a corpse, and he nearly fell. Stumbling probably saved his life, for it prevented him from blundering into the dead man's murderers.

Around the corner, dim red light shone, and he heard voices.

He crept forwards, not daring to breathe.

Away down the tunnel, by the base of Bastion 16, Myz and Doromek stood by a crate of explosives. Two more dead soldiers lay close to them. They were talking in urgent whispers. Despite Katsuhiro's impaired hearing, it was quiet enough in the tunnel that he could hear what they were saying. With growing alarm he eavesdropped on their conversation.

'It's time,' Myzmadra said.

Ashul's face set.

'Maybe we should stop a moment. Take a pause to think.'

The detonator nestled in Myzmadra's palm. Her finger was close by the button, the nail still beautifully shaped under its covering of dirt.

'There is nothing to think about.'

Doromek looked away. He found it hard to formulate his words when Myzmadra stared at him like that.

'Do you ever question why we're doing this?' he said eventually. 'If we're on the right side even?'

She stared at him hard. 'No. You do though, apparently.' Her free hand moved smoothly to her holstered laspistol. 'Should I worry?'

'No,' he said. 'I won't stop you. But...' He looked at his feet. 'After Pluto,' he began again. 'It got harder. I don't know what I think any more. I forgot what I believed once. It's changed so many times.'

Myzmadra could have shot him right then, and he half expected she would. But she didn't. Her face retained the same fixed, slightly fierce expression it usually wore. They'd escaped the sicknesses that killed so many, but they were underfed. She was frighteningly thin. The war was using them up.

'You used to trust me.'

He shrugged. 'I still do.'

'Then listen to me,' she said. 'I have always said this was for the Emperor.'

'You did.'

'That this is the only course of action.'

He nodded.

'I never told you why.'

He shrugged. 'I did not need to know why. I believed you. I never believed *Him*.'

'I was not lying. I do not think the Legion were, when they came to me, and told me that this was the only way. It all makes sense now, seeing the things we have.'

'Myzmadra,' said Ashul. 'Come with me. We can get into the city. Ride this out, see which way it goes. We have no orders. No contact. We're making this up as we go along. Destroying this bastion is an insignificant action. You're throwing your life away for the sake of it.'

'Every death is a triumph for us,' she said defiantly. 'Every act of destruction serves. This bastion is the last obstacle between the traitors and the Helios Gate. If I bring it down, they may get inside today.'

'You can't believe that,' he said.

'Does it matter if I do or if I don't?' She looked him in the eye. She was so proud. He admired her more than any other person he had ever met.

'You can go now,' she said, distantly, as if he were a servant to be dismissed. 'There's no need for both of us to die.'

'There's no need for either of us to die,' he said. 'What's the point of this? This is one bastion from hundreds. We've done our part, why keep fighting?'

'There is no wasted action in this war. We are here because we are meant to be. This action will mean something.'

'How do you know?' he said.

'I just do,' she said, with conviction.

'That doesn't sound like you.'

'How do you know what I sound like?' she said. 'We don't know each other at all.'

He stared at her. He could have said she could go, that he would stay. He could have told her the truth, that he'd had enough, and was sick of the war and his role in it. But he didn't. Life finds a way to make itself persist, even if it means turning a man into a coward. He had already made his choice. He wouldn't give his life up for anyone. Not even Myzmadra.

'All right,' he said. 'All right.'

She looked relieved. 'There's more for you to do before this is all over. But my story ends here.'

Ashul held out his hand. She clasped it.

'Alpha to Omega,' she said. Her smile was small but brave, and bright as polished steel in her dirty face.

'Alpha to Omega,' he replied.

They held hands for what seemed to be an age. Ashul had never touched her like that before. It was a simple, warm, human gesture, and he wished he had done it a long time ago. A different version of his life with her by his side flashed through his mind, the two of them against the universe. Once upon a time, he had wanted a life like that.

As if guessing what he thought, she frowned and she shook his hand free. A woman like her would never be with a man like him. She had her cause, and so did he.

'Get out of here,' she said coldly. 'I'll give you one minute, no more.'

Katsuhiro waited for the next earth-shaking detonation, and slipped away before Ashul caught him.

TWENTY-NINE

Daemonfall
Lord of the night
Red Angel

Daylight Wall, Helios section, 15th of Quartus

Midnight-blue gunships set down on the parapet under heavy fire. Gun positions in the city spires raked the wall tops where the enemy landed, but Skraivok chose his drop-craft carefully. All were of the increasingly rare Stormbird Sokar pattern, and void-shielded. They landed in a tight group, ramps slamming down simultaneously. Support squads poured out first into the rain, arraying themselves near the Stormbirds and targeting the nearer weapon installations with missiles and lascannon fire. The gunships angled their ball turrets up and added to the infantry's efforts. Breacher squads came next, heading off away from the Helios Gate to block Imperial reinforcements coming up from the south. Rapier weapons platforms were dragged out from the holds. Further down the wall a heavy transport deposited a pair of Predator tanks to bolster the line. Lesser vessels flew as air support, strafing the buildings with their cannons, their

missiles demolishing fortified balconies and bolted-on gunnery blisters before roaring past and coming about to make
further passes.

Relieved of their cordon duty, the Raptor packs ignited
their jets and bounded down the wall out from the landing zone.

The Night Lords worked quickly to secure the area. A final
ship thundered down through the sky, breaching the weakened aegis in a flare of orange and sickly green. The torrent
of blood raining from the sky ran off it in black falls, but
it could not hide the ornate nature of the ship. Decorated
with precious metals, lavishly painted, the Stormbird carried
the personal heraldry of Gendor Skraivok, self-proclaimed
leader of the Night Lords Legion.

The ramp opened as the ship was landing. Space Marines
leapt from the exits before it had touched down. When
landing claws kissed rockcrete and the ramp opened, a
unit of Atramentar strode purposefully forth, slower than
their power-armoured brethren but massively better protected. Lesser Night Lords took hits from the buildings of
the Palace and died, but these giant warriors stood firm
as las-fire flashed off their power fields without effect, and
bolts and solid slugs were deflected away by their angled
armour plates.

Gendor Skraivok marched out with a confident swagger,
his hand gripping the hilt of his sheathed warp blade. He
surveyed his troops from the top of the ramp before joining his Terminator guard. His chronometer told him it was
day, but the world was deep into a war gloom as black as
any Nostraman noon.

Night suited him perfectly.

'An exemplary deployment, Captain Ashmalesh,' Skraivok
voxed. He drew his sword. The comforting power of the

Neverborn flowed into his body from the naked blade, and he smiled within his helm. Why had he resisted its gifts? He saw how foolish he had been now, and it made him smile.

'Get a shield line of breacher squads at the fore of our advance,' he commanded. 'We move on the Helios Gate.'

Daylight Wall, Helios Gate, 15th of Quartus

The smell of the blood pouring from the sky permeated everything. It filled Raldoron's helmet long after he activated the void sealing on his armour. Though it was sickening by any human measure, he found it alluring, appetising even. The odour fogged his mind, encouraging him to throw off restraint and slaughter the enemy.

The world had lost all colour barring red, black and orange. Fire lit everything. The sky was so dark it was hard to believe Terra had ever enjoyed sunlight. The aegis' displacement glows were guttering pinks and purples.

'Captain.' Thane's voice penetrated the fog in Raldoron's mind. 'Captain!'

Raldoron shook himself out of the fugue. They were under attack from all quarters.

'The Night Lords to the south of the gate have reinforced and are moving on our position. The siege towers are closing, two to the north of the gate, one to the south. The aegis has collapsed across the entire front of our section.'

'Elsewhere?'

'Hardline vox reports say the wall is under assault in the seven other places facing the siege camps,' said Thane. 'The shield-banes burn away our protection. The upper aegis holds for now, but we have lost many generators, and the system is under great strain, so the adepts say.'

Raldoron surveyed the wall top. It had taken the enemy

minutes to sweep the rampart free of defenders, secure their landing zone, then bring in more troops. Now the Night Lords were advancing in force, before he and Thane had rallied a counter-attack. The great black snake of the shield-bane cut a darker channel across the murk. Meanwhile, the siege engines had gathered speed, and were dark shapes in the downpour, revealed by flashes of gunfire like shock images in vid-plays made to frighten.

'We do not have enough warriors to hold the wall against this attack,' said Raldoron.

The macro cannon on the gate tower roared, shaking him to his core.

'Take one in every two men from sections twelve, thirteen, fourteen, seventeen and eighteen. I shall provide you with my authorisation coding.' He blink-clicked an icon to send the data key over to Thane's warsuit. 'We will have to trust that the enemy will not attempt an escalade there. Inform Bhab command that those sections will be vulnerable. Request reinforcements, whatever they have. The siege towers here must not be allowed to make contact with the wall. Concentrate all fire on them. If one gets through, then our situation here will be greatly compromised. And watch the skies. If one Legion is willing to attempt a landing on the rampart, others will.' He looked upwards through the dying aegis, half expecting to see the trails of falling drop-craft. 'They will attack us here at section sixteen, where the aegis is weak. We can trust the sections we draw our reinforcements from will be safe, for now.'

'As you say, Lord Raldoron. If I had command, I would do the same.' Thane said. 'And I tell you, I am glad I do not have command.'

'You hold here. The Blood Angels must deal with the threat to the south. The Night Lords must be swept from the wall before the siege towers come into contact with the ramparts. Give me covering fire.'

'We shall bring up heavy weapons to cover the wall top, both sides.'

'Make it so. Target their heavy armour and their Terminators. Your Legion is the holder of gates,' said Raldoron. He looked south again. The Night Lords were close enough for him to pick out their heraldry under the coursing blood. 'Night Lords are an insignificant threat to the Blood Angels. I shall give our guests below a warm welcome they will not quickly forget.'

Calling up his veteran squads, Raldoron gathered his warriors within the guard chambers of the Helios Gate, then led them out from the doors onto the ramparts. They came under immediate fire from the Night Lords advancing on the gatehouse. Breacher squads went to the fore of both lines, shielding the warriors behind them. Shield walls drew closer to each other, the thick breachers dancing with bolt impacts. Heavier weapons from both sides gunned for their opponents, the exchange becoming more violent the closer they came. Impacts from the wasteland and increasingly from the void blasted chunks from the fortifications, but the Night Lords and the Blood Angels were intent on each other. Warriors fell, opening gaps in the walls of shields that were quickly filled. Though the Night Lords suffered heavier casualties from Thane's attentions and the gunfire coming in from the Palace hives, they were greater in number.

So it was that two forces came within striking distance of one another upon the walls.

This was a contest that would be decided by blades.

The space between the two groups was a storm of explosions and microshrapnel. They were one hundred, then seventy, then fifty metres apart.

When the foe were forty metres away, Raldoron held aloft and ignited his power sword. It glittered in the bloody rain as droplets burst to atoms in the disruption field. Timing was all. They must charge first.

'Drop shields!' he shouted. 'Charge!'

A hundred veteran Blood Angels roared out their battle cry.

'For Sanguinius! For the Emperor!'

The ramparts shook to the thunder of ceramite.

A replying call of '*Kelish!*' sounded from the Night Lords' line. 'Brace!' it meant. They stopped, shields angled and planted against the parapet, pauldrons butting them. Each shield bearer was supported by the hands of the legionary behind.

Raldoron ran ahead of his warriors. Guns barked on both sides, but the Blood Angels, their shields abandoned to grant them speed, took the brunt of the damage. Several fell dead.

The lines met with a deafening crash.

Raldoron leapt, sword buzzing down. It caught the edge of a shield. Searing light dazzled him as ceramite was annihilated by the disruption field. The sword boomed and crackled, slicing across, taking the shield bearer's arm off.

The line bowed under the impact of the Blood Angels, but held. Guns fired from behind the shields, dropping more of the sons of Sanguinius. The Blood Angels wrenched at the Night Lords' protection, dragging shields down and firing their bolters at the men behind, but they held. The line rearranged itself, and set firm.

'*Ilashovarath!*' The Night Lords officers shouted through their voxmitters. 'Advance!'

The Night Lords gave a wordless shout, and set themselves hard behind the shields. Arranged as a giant, pressing scrum, they pushed forwards. Blood Angels battered at them, killed them, but the pressure was immense. Red boots rasping on bloody rockcrete, the Night Lords pushed forwards three steps, and set their shields down again, rearranging themselves for another push.

'*Ilashovarath!*' The Night Lords commanded a second time.

They shoved hard, pushing Raldoron and his men back another few steps towards the tower. The ground gained, they slammed down their shields and braced once more.

Raldoron smote at his foe, but with the shields angled as they were, it was hard to land a telling blow, and though the shield in front of him bore several smoking gouges, it held. Raldoron reversed his grip, and pushed the point at the shield. Point and energy field worked together to cut into the surface. The breacher shield was thick, and though he strained with the effort, it nibbled only slowly through the metal towards its bearer.

'*Ilashovarath!*'

Night Lords' shields squealed against the Blood Angels' armour, forcing them back. Raldoron counted the distance to the southern tower of the Helios Gate. Two hundred metres. Each push brought the Night Lords a few metres closer to their gatehouse. They were dying from Thane's shots angling in from above, but not quickly enough.

'*Ilashovarath!*
'*Ilashovarath!*
'*Ilashovarath!*'

The shield wall pushed on. The racket of weapons hitting shields was a hundred drums played to different rhythms. Raldoron had no need to push his blade. His sword sank into the shield before him as the legionary behind it was forced forwards. Bolts shot from the firing loops of the shields burst on his armour.

Raldoron waited as long as he could.

'*Ilashovarath!*'

Until their backs were almost against the wall.

'*Ilashovarath!*'

The tower was behind them, massive, indomitable, its reinforced portals standing between the Night Lords and the taking of the gate.

'*Ilashovarath!*'

At the other points of the wall, similar things were happening. He wondered if any gates had fallen, if the enemy were on the wall elsewhere, or had come over it and got into the Palace.

'*Ilashovarath!*'

He had little vox contact with Bhab command. No guidance.

'*Ilashovarath!*'

Thane's guns rained down their slaughter on the Night Lords. The Night Lords responded in kind, firing plasma guns up at the ramparts. Yellow-armoured figures fell back ablaze.

'*Ilashovarath!*'

The gate was ten metres behind him.

The moment had come.

'Now!' Raldoron voxed.

The portal ground open, rolling aside like the stone of an ancient tomb. Lens lights blinked at twice the height of a man. Servos purred in the darkness of the chamber.

'Split!' roared Raldoron.

He yanked his sword free. His men stepped back. The shield wall, relieved of pressure, surged forwards in disarray.

Giant footsteps thumped in the tower chamber towards the wall walk.

Before the Dreadnoughts emerged onto the rampart, they were already firing.

* * *

The first shots of the rotary cannons mowed down the leading ranks of Skraivok's men. Shields shattered under thousand-round-a-minute blows. The shield wall broke. Three Contemptor-pattern Dreadnoughts in pristine red thundered out from the tower, the blood rain slicking them a bright gloss, and smashed into the Night Lords' advance. Blue-armoured warriors were bowled over. A power fist smashed a Space Marine into the air, sending him shouting madly over the battlement to plummet down on the far side.

The Blood Angels followed their walking dead, hacking and shooting. They roared like beasts, their famed refinement gone.

The Dreadnoughts ploughed deep into the Night Lords' line before the mass of troops slowed them to a halt. They stood embattled by dozens of Space Marines, and the real work began.

The first Dreadnought fell a moment later, its leg blasted off by implosion charges.

'My lord,' growled Skraivok's Atramentar sergeant. 'We must take you to a place of safety.'

'What, now, at the moment of my triumph?' Skraivok scoffed. 'When word of my deed reaches the Warmaster, I will be rewarded with power and with riches. If I depart now, I will be known as nothing but a coward.'

'The leader!' Another of his escort raised his combi-bolter, sighting it on a veteran captain whose armour was encrusted with high honours.

Skraivok put his hand on the top of the Terminator's gun and pushed it down.

'He's mine,' he said. 'I want him. I want it to be known that I killed the captain of this gate myself.'

Skraivok pushed forwards into the fray. His Atramentar followed behind.

The first Blood Angel he encountered died so easily Skraivok barely felt the ceramite part. The sword shifted in his hands as he swung, perfecting the strike. The edge cleaved through the warrior's helm, cutting it in half, and passing deep into his torso. A lesser blade would have stuck, but not his sword. He pulled it out with a light tug, easy as plucking a blade of grass. Skraivok smiled to himself. Power flooded him. His body tingled with it.

'Blood Angel!' he shouted. His Terminators pushed aside the combatants, clearing him a path. 'Blood Angel!'

The ramparts were broad, but crammed with fighters. The fighting was close and dirty work. There was little room for finesse.

Another Blood Angel died to Skraivok's blows. The Atramentar laid about themselves, the booming of their power fists and the roar of their heavier weapons drawing the attention of one of the Blood Angels Ancients. It crushed the Space Marine it was fighting and threw down the leaking body. Bullets sprayed from its rotary cannon. One of the Atramentar was hit hundreds of times. The cannon overloaded his field generator, chewed through his layered ceramite and plasteel, and tore into the adamantium frame beneath. The man died inside his giant suit, and fell over heavily.

'Deal with that for me would you, sergeant?' said Skraivok. 'I do not wish to be distracted. I will have that captain's skin for my cloak.'

'Our role is to protect the leader of–'

'Do it!' shrieked Skraivok. 'Bring it down.'

His sergeant said no more but moved with his men to engage the Dreadnought. Skraivok pushed on. The lines of the two warring Legions were by now thoroughly blended. Bodies clogged the rampart. Footing was treacherous, but the enemy captain was near.

'Blood Angel!' Skraivok yelled joyfully. 'Face me!'

The Blood Angel finished his opponent and turned to face the Night Lord. Upon his left pauldron, his name was emblazoned across a scroll plate, just legible under rivulets of blood.

'Raldoron?' said Skraivok. '*The* Raldoron?' He made a few passes with his sword, revelling in its lightness, in its killing edge. 'This will be a day to celebrate, the day I slew the hero of the Blood Angels!' He saluted, and declaimed pompously, 'I am Gendor Skraivok, the Painted Count, Lord Commander of the Night Lords Legion, and I am your end.'

The Blood Angel was unimpressed. 'Never heard of you,' he said, and came in to attack, his power sword buzzing.

Skraivok laughed and parried. The daemon sword moved with a mind of its own to block the blow so fast Raldoron was almost taken down by Skraivok's riposte, only a wild slicing deflection turning it aside. A second strike was thus deflected by Raldoron, and a third. The First Captain of the Blood Angels was as good as his reputation suggested, but Skraivok was filled with sorcerous foreknowledge and supernatural speed. He saw an opening, and moved in for the kill.

He missed. He was too slow. Raldoron sidestepped the blow and twisted it aside with a slight flick of his blade.

Skraivok stepped back. The delicious feeling of power was gone. The world lost its sheen. He was in the rain, on the wall, surrounded by the dead, and he could not beat this man.

Panic gripped Skraivok's gut. The blade was heavy. It would not respond as it had. Where before it accentuated his skills, lending him greater speed and strength, now it did nothing. Raldoron pressed his attack, battering at Skraivok with a flurry of blows that he could barely deflect.

The daemon had deserted him.

'No,' said Skraivok. 'It cannot be!'

Raldoron's power sword banged against the edge of Skraivok's blade, sending him stumbling backwards.

'That always was the problem with your Legion, Night Lord,' said Raldoron. 'You are quick with your torturer's knives, but so few of you are worthy warriors.'

Raldoron swung his sword overarm, building momentum into a blow that would cut a power-armoured warrior in two. Skraivok parried it only just in time, stepping back and nearly tripping on the corpse of a Night Lord. Raldoron followed with another blow, and another. Skraivok struggled to stop him. He was so fast. Skraivok was a Space Marine captain, and more than a passable swordsman, but Raldoron was a hero of the Imperium whose name was known across the galaxy.

Raldoron attacked with greater ferocity. Skraivok's arm was numb from deflecting the blows. He forayed a few attacks, but they put him in more danger, as Raldoron caught and countered every one. His latest riposte was turned away, and Raldoron's power blade scraped sparks up the side of his breast-plate.

'Atramentar!' Skraivok called, his panic rising. 'To me!'

If they heard, they could do nothing; they fought the Blood Angels Dreadnought still, their number reduced to three.

'Night Lords! Help me!' His power pack scraped on rockcrete. He had his back to the outer crenellations, and could retreat no further.

Raldoron faced him. His sword energy field buzzed in the downpour.

'Listen to you,' Raldoron said. 'The masters of fear. You are cowards, like all cruel men.'

Raldoron's power sword slashed across Skraivok's chest,

breaking open the ceramite and severing his power cabling. The Painted Count staggered, unbalanced by the sudden loss of energy to his war-plate's systems. Raldoron lunged forwards, stunning Skraivok further with a blow to the face from the punch guard of his sword. Cracks crazed over Skraivok's eye-lenses. His faceplate systems fizzed and broke down into a display of meaningless blocks. He feebly attempted to parry, but Raldoron smashed it aside and turned the blade downwards, his own sword cutting deep into Skraivok's greave, cleaving through ceramite, undersuit and flesh, and sliding into the bone.

Skraivok staggered to the side, slipped and fell backwards into the chute of a crenel. A wedge-shaped gap between merlons, the crenel sloped down and narrowed towards the edge. Skraivok scrabbled at the smooth, polished plascrete of the surface, and succeeded only in making himself slide towards the killing drop.

A red boot on his wounded leg pinned him in place.

Skraivok cried out in pain.

Raldoron leaned forwards to address him.

'You are and always were an evil Legion. You took the Emperor's mission and twisted it. Selfish. Monstrous. Tormentors of the weak,' snarled Raldoron. 'If Horus had not turned, I would have gladly led the hunt for your kind myself. I thank you from my heart that you came to my sword and saved me the trouble of looking.' He shifted the weight of his foot, bringing another cry from Skraivok.

'Wait!' the Painted Count said. 'I give you my surrender. You beat me. I am your prisoner!'

'There can be no prisoners in this war,' said Raldoron. 'How much mercy have you shown to all those that you harmed? I have as much mercy for you as you had for them. Now get off my wall.'

He shoved hard with his foot, sending Skraivok skidding towards the drop. The Night Lord dropped the daemon sword to grip at the polished rockcrete with both of his hands, but there was no purchase on the blood-slick surface. He managed to brace himself on the merlon's rounded corners with his elbows, and for a moment he thought he might save himself. He looked up to see the Blood Angel still staring at him.

'You are a pompous man,' Skraivok said.

Raldoron raised his bolt pistol.

Screaming in defiance, Skraivok shoved himself over the edge, whence he plummeted, reaching terminal velocity long before he hit the ground and the stone broke him.

The Night Lords were retreating. More than half their number had fallen. Three Terminators fought Ancient Axiel, but they would not last long. All those near Raldoron were dead. Thane's men continued to shoot down onto the enemy, while his own warriors were reforming their squads to better discipline their firing at the retreating foe. A report from Captain Galliard of Raldoron's Chapter crackled in his ear, informing him the Night Lords rearguard was falling back. Their gunships were powering up. True to their nature, some were taking off without their passengers, the pilots seizing the opportunity to save their own skins.

But the battle was far from over.

Siege towers lumbered on towards the wall, the nearest now approaching the cratered zone where the third outwork line had been. Enemy artillery pounded at the wall directly. Overhead the failing aegis held out the bombardment, but would not for much longer, while in the sky lines of fire marked the approach of hundreds of drop pods.

'Thane,' voxed Raldoron. 'Imminent drop strike. What is the status of our reinforcements?'

'*Incoming,*' said Thane. '*Requested Ninth and Seventh Legion reinforcements estimated arrival within fifteen minutes. Bhab has commanded four Imperial Army regiments to be redeployed from the inner districts as reserves to our section of the wall.*'

'I would prefer more legionaries.'

More drop pods were hurtling through the clouds.

'You have re-established contact with the Bhab Bastion?'

'*Hardline only.*'

'What occurs elsewhere?'

'*The same as here. Direct assault on the walls. No breaches reported.*'

Raldoron looked down the wall after his men. Close at hand, the final Atramentar went down to a piledriver blow from the Dreadnought. The fighting had drawn away from his position. The Night Lords were boxed in on both sides. The last ship was lifting off under fire it could not survive.

'The threat here is contained,' Raldoron said. 'Concentrate all fire on the siege towers. If we can weather their assault, and that of the drop pods, then we may yet–'

A squeal of feedback cut off the line between Thane and Raldoron.

'Thane?' he said. 'Thane?'

He scrolled through other channels. The vox was silent, then half deafened him with a cacophony of screams, like a million people dying at once. He shut it off.

Flame burned in the sky. Lightning spread out in a ring around the fire. Thunder rolled.

A fireball fell from the churning heavens towards the land before the Helios Gate; too big to be a drop pod, too controlled to be debris from the fleet, too slow to be a shell or mass round.

Raldoron followed the fireball down, the blood running over his helm blurring its outline.

It hit the ground, sending out a billow of flame that raced over traitor and loyalist alike.

The vox burst back into life.

'What was that?' said Thane.

Raldoron increased the magnification of his helm lenses, revealing a smoking figure crouched in the glowing, eight-pointed emblem of the enemy stamped into the ground by its arrival. Bat wings wrapped around the figure protectively. Its head was bowed, a giant, black sword placed point down into the earth, both hands resting on the hilt. Fissures raced away from the sword point, and fires glowed within. The fissures widened, becoming chasms, and from them leapt sheets of flame.

The figure at the centre of the octed rose, spread its wings, and lifted its sword to show the world it had arrived. Raldoron didn't recognise it at first. The being was vast, a daemon-beast of a size that exceeded those he had battled on Signus. But something in the way it moved made him suddenly sure of its identity.

'Angron. It is Angron,' said Raldoron quietly. 'By the Emperor, what has happened to him?'

Even from so far away, the primarch's fury touched Raldoron, stirring something hot and vile in the Blood Angel's being.

Angron howled. Horus' mortal armies surged forwards over the carpet of dead fronting the outworks and the walls. The first drop pods hit the ground among them, hatches blowing wide, bringing more Space Marines into the attack. Dreadclaw pods angled down at the walls. The dying aegis destroyed some; others hit the fortifications and glanced off. More extended their claws at the right moment, catching the crenellations and holding fast. Two landed close together, between Raldoron and his men engaging the remnants of

the Night Lords. World Eaters leapt from inside into the
downpour of blood.

'Father!' roared the giant; his furious, brazen voice was
empowered by the violence, thundering louder than any
cannonade and audible over all the racket of battle. *'I have
come for you!'*

THIRTY

The breaking of the line
The gates open
The Great Mother

Palace outworks, Daylight Wall section 16, 15th of Quartus

Katsuhiro was running from the tunnel when Bastion 16 exploded. Flaming chunks of rockcrete rained down over that section of the battlefield, as deadly as any weapon. The outer lines were deserted, and with the bastion gone there was nothing to hold back the enemy. They poured over the shattered ground. Worse things were joining them, emerging from the smoke and fire to kill. Surrounded by flames, Katsuhiro did not see Angron fall from the sky, but he heard his call, and he saw the things the fallen primarch summoned.

'Father! I have come for you!'

The words shook the world. Terror and fury swamped Katsuhiro's mind, leaving him fighting with himself. When the World Eaters came loping from the fire with their chainswords and set about their grisly work, cutting down men and hacking skulls from the dead and living alike, he

ran harder. One saw him, and came springing after him, the
mass of the legionary's armour making the ground tremble even through the bombardment. Skulls bounced on
chains from battleplate whose white-and-blue livery was all
but obscured by a thick coating of gore. In his warsuit, the
Space Marine was far faster than Katsuhiro could ever hope
to be, and ran at him, joints grinding, his chainaxe gunning.

'Blood!' the legionary shouted, so thickly he hardly spoke
words. 'Skulls!'

Katsuhiro tripped, sprawling on the ground. He rolled
over to see the monster leap at him, weapon lifted to sever
his head from his spine.

He threw up his hand. A loud bang and a blast wave of
superheated air thumped the wind from him.

No axe fell. He looked up to see he was alone. Only
when he scrambled to his feet did he find the Space Marine
scattered in bubbling pieces across the ground.

No time to think. No time to see. More World Eaters were
bounding through the fires and the explosions. Brazen horns
blew. Drop pods slammed into the ground and released
squads of legionaries. The siege towers ground on, and
behind were the mortal hordes. All would kill him just as
well, no matter their method. From the walls death was
flung indiscriminately. Away to the south one of the great
siege towers' shields failed. It caught fire and detonated,
going up like a resin torch thrust into a fire. Seconds later,
metal from its destruction rang down around him, missing him, but there were more towers, and there were more
deaths for him.

The red giant ran through the flames between the towers,
his sword sweeping before him, slaughtering all he encountered. Guns rained every form of technological destruction
down on him, but he was unharmed in the main, and what

damage was inflicted was smoothed away, as if the wounds were washed off by the bloody rain.

'Blood and skulls!' the giant howled. *'Blood for the Blood God!'*

He ran with lowered head towards a trio of tanks that had somehow survived the destruction. His horns connected with one, rocking it on its tracks. The giant pushed a hand beneath its treads and heaved it over. A point-blank shot from the main armament of its squadron mate made the giant reel and roar, but he seemed only enraged by the blow. The sword sang through the air. Katsuhiro gaped as it sliced cleanly through the hull, setting the metal alight with black fire.

When the giant turned on the third tank, striding through a storm of bolts to ram his blade into its engine block, Katsuhiro ran again.

Somehow, he avoided the myriad forms of extinction that sliced, blasted and bludgeoned over the ruined outworks. Finally he crested the ridge of broken ground the first line had become, the roaring of the winged giant echoing behind him. Through the tempests of fire he beheld the grand portal of the Helios Gate. Little trace remained of the outwork fortifications there.

The gate was only a few hundred metres away, but firmly closed. He stumbled towards it, all strength spent, not sure what he would do. If he approached, he would die under the enemy bombardment, and there was no way through in any case. Not far from the gate one of the great siege towers was making its final approach to the wall. Between them there was no hope.

One more minute to breathe, he thought. One more moment to hear the pounding of his heart, that was all he could ask for.

There were other soldiers converging on the Helios Gate

from all quarters, scattered survivors, a small proportion of the conscripts sent out to fight, but numerous in terms of absolute numbers.

Then a miracle occurred. Multi-throated horns sang orchestral warning cries. The great locking plates along the hinges of the gates clunked open, withdrew and lifted back. Grinding debris to powder, the gates swung open – slowly at first, but then, as their enormous mass was bullied into moving, with surprising speed.

Light flooded out from the open gate. Enemy weapons fire that had slammed into the portal was caught by a void shield spread over the arch. Figures, small as ants, formed up behind the sparkling aegis into firing lines. All were transhumans, their yellow armour golden in the city's light. Tanks and Dreadnoughts supported them against the foe making for the gate.

'Loyal men and women of the Imperium,' a greatly amplified voice boomed from the gates. 'Look now to your salvation. Make your way into the Emperor's protection.

'You have three minutes.'

A cry of anguish went up from the fleeing soldiers. Exhausted as they were, they redoubled their efforts, and fled through the field of death in hope of life.

Daylight Wall, Helios section, 15th of Quartus

Chain teeth growled past Raldoron's face with a hair's breadth to spare. He leaned back, and slashed down with his power sword, cutting the axe head from the World Eater's weapon. It flew off, teeth still spinning. The Traitor legionary slammed a fist into Raldoron's face, knocking his helmet into his cheek, and then grappled with him. Raldoron jammed his bolt pistol into the neck joint of his foe's armour and pulled the trigger, emptying the ammunition clip and blasting the World Eater's head from his body.

He heaved the warrior's limp corpse away and moved on.

Several dozen World Eaters were on the wall. More drop pods were screaming down from the sky. The last of the siege towers was approaching, now only dozens of metres off the rampart. The uppermost storey was higher than the crenellations, its drawbridge held up on rusty chains the thickness of a Titan's leg, and ready to drop. The size of it was ridiculous; it was so huge it should not be, and yet it was. From a castellated firing deck atop, Death Guard fired down onto the wall.

There was space within the tower for hundreds of legionaries. The difficulties the Blood Angels were experiencing would pale into insignificance if the siege tower made it all the way in.

Three had come out of the enemy camp. Two were now ablaze out from the wall, brought down by the Palace guns, but nothing, it seemed, could stop the third.

World Eaters reinforced the few Night Lords left on the rampart. They fought with astounding savagery, with no thought for tactics or self-preservation, but went berserk as soon as their Dreadclaws snagged themselves on the crenellations. The aegis had weakened to such an extent that drop pods were falling into the city now, slamming into hive spires and putting down in plazas. Not enough warriors made it through the air defences to take the Palace on their own, but they cut bloody slaughter through soldier and civilian alike before they were taken down, diverting the reserves coming up to hold the wall top against the main assault.

Mortis runes peeped for Raldoron's attention as warriors of the First and Fourth Companies died around him. Thane's weapons fire was diverted by the tower as his men engaged in a gun duel with the Death Guard riding it in.

The World Eaters expended their lives in savage explosions of violence, taking three of Raldoron's men with them for every one slain.

'Finish them!' Raldoron voxed. 'Get them off the wall!'

Behind him, another Dreadclaw hit the wall at a poor angle, ripping out several of the giant merlons and ricocheting off. It hit the tower on the way down, losing half its mass to the shields cocooning the construction, and cartwheeled uncontrollably end over end towards the ground.

The enemy surged around the tower base, certain it would reach its target: mutants, traitors, abominations, readying to flood up its steps and into the Palace after the Death Guard, their baying filtering up to Raldoron from all the way below. The ground was black with them, studded with fires from torches and burning effigies. Enfilading shots from the Helios Gate tore into them, slaughtering them by the dozen, but there were no big guns that could hit the tower itself, not at that range.

'Get them off the wall!' Raldoron repeated.

A World Eater came at him, his armour overpainted with gore. Chains bearing jawbones whipped around him. He was bareheaded, nothing but pure rage and hatred on his face, the tendrils of the Butcher's Nails buried deep into the back of his scalp.

Raldoron shot him down, turning his skull into mist. The warrior dropped, blood pumping from his neck, fists beating at the rampart when his body hit the ground.

To the south, loyalist reinforcements finally arrived, bolstering the thinning ranks of the Blood Angels coming from the direction of the broken Dawn Tower. Howls and battle cries filled his vox. Making any strategic sense of the situation was impossible.

A lance strike punched through the aegis several kilometres

away, cutting down into a small spire behind the fortifications. The weapon burned through, slicing the building diagonally. It collapsed with the screech of tortured metal, the top part falling on the wall, crumpling as it hit and blocking the wall walk.

Another World Eater came at him. Raldoron met his blow. Disruption lightning wreathed them both as his blade chopped off the legionary's arm. The traitor barely seemed to notice the amputation, but launched himself head first at the captain. Raldoron stepped to the side, letting the warrior throw himself onto the paving of the rampart, and stabbed him through the back. The blow obliterated the World Eater's power pack and the back-plate beneath, leaving his spine exposed to the air.

The first siege tower was mere metres away, and the rain was pouring down.

Between the north and south forces of the Blood Angels, only three World Eaters remained, then none, gunned down rapidly by the two lines of loyal legionaries meeting. Another drop pod speared towards the wall, retro thrusters burning to line it up for a perfect landing on the rampart, but as it was poised to cut out its jets and drop, guns within the Palace blasted it to scrap, dropping its wreckage on the wall.

'Form up!' bellowed Raldoron. He looked to the siege tower. Another few seconds and it would lower its bridge. Armoured loophole covers rattled up, and banks of melta-cutters extended, angled down.

'Stand clear!' he said. 'Two lines! Two facing lines!'

Sergeants ordered squads over the gap between the groups of Blood Angels, bolstering Raldoron's depleted units. They jogged over an uneven ground of power-armoured corpses, Night Lords, World Eaters and Blood Angels intermingled, their rounded armour slippery with blood and treacherous underfoot.

'Stand ready!' Raldoron called. 'Stand ready!'

The siege tower moved forwards slower than he expected. It shuddered under fire and adjusted its course. A blaze of bolt-rounds hammered from its roof, forcing the Blood Angels to duck down behind the crenellations, their return fire ineffectual owing to the angle.

Raldoron took stock of his men. Three hundred left from two companies waited for the riders of the tower. A terrible stink came off the siege engine, of sickness and putrid wounds, that he smelled even though his armour was void-sealed.

More reinforcements were coming. Thane's men were running down from the gatehouse, more arriving from the north, and a sixth company of Blood Angels speeding along the road behind the defences. This was the risk. This siege tower. If they threw back this assault, the Helios section of the Daylight Wall would hold.

We will triumph, he told himself. We are worthy.

The trumpet chorus of the gate's war-horns snatched his attention from the siege tower. For the first time in centuries he experienced dread. Not even the daemonic horrors of Signus Prime had unnerved him; what he saw at the Helios Gate did.

The gates were opening.

They swung wide, pouring the pure lumen light of the city onto the field of battle. His hearts pounded. If the gates were open, they were lost.

'Thane! Thane!' he voxed. 'The gates are opening! Angron is outside! Thane! On whose authority do the gates open? Are we betrayed?'

There was a rush of air behind him, and the thump of boots upon the stone. He turned to see Sanguinius alight on the wall, sword drawn in his left hand, the *Spear of Telesto* in his right, his golden armour running with the bloody downpour.

'The gates open by my authority, captain.'

Sanguinius strode to Raldoron's side.

'My lord, why?' For one terrible moment, Raldoron doubted his genefather's loyalty, and feared he had turned against the Imperium at the last. If that were so, the Death Guard were in ignorance, for they turned all their attention on the Great Angel. His armour sparked with bolt impacts, but he stood in contempt of their efforts, even his bare wings untouched, and spoke.

'My brother, the Khan, reminded me that we must not forget our ultimate duty. The Emperor works for mankind, but while I live I will not forget the individual men and women who make up that whole.' He swept his spear out over the ramparts. Tiny figures pursued by all the horrors of Horus' mutant legions were running for the gate, while Angron rampaged through friend and foe alike. 'I will not abandon the human troopers to this vile death while some might be saved. In them, I see bravery, I see loyalty, but above all, I see faith in my father's vision. I shall not let them die while there is blood in my body and strength in my limbs. Fear not, my son, the Imperial Fists hold the arch, and even now allies come to their aid. Now, prepare. The enemy comes against us, and we must look to our own task.'

The fire from the roof of the siege tower cut into the ranks of the Blood Angels. The melta arrays upon the front discharged, their beams agitating atoms to the point of destruction. A swathe of the downpour evaporated into meaty steam. The crenellations glowed red, then orange, then white, and collapsed into slag. Where the beams cut across the bodies of the fallen, flesh exploded. Ceramite resisted the arrays for mere seconds before collapsing into powder.

The Blood Angels waited either side of the beams' tracks, now separated by a trench of molten rockcrete.

Sanguinius stood unafraid in the storm of bolt impacts, unharmed while his sons were felled.

'We shall repel them!' he said.

'My lord, I suppose my telling you to get off the wall will do no good,' said Raldoron. 'But I am honour bound to say you should. We cannot lose you.'

Sanguinius laughed, a musical, pure sound in the blood rain and the slaughter. 'You are right, my son. I would not leave you if I were sure it would be my end,' he said. Then he spoke the awful words Raldoron had heard so much of late. 'But I know I do not die today.'

The gargantuan chains rattled. The siege tower's drawbridge fell forwards, rusty teeth in the underside biting into the softened fabric of the wall. The boltgun fire from the top roared on.

From within, a throng of Death Guard ran out, rasping their praise of Mortarion and their new-found god, and poured onto the battlement.

'For the Emperor!' called Sanguinius, and led his sons into the fray.

The Imperial Fists shot with incredible discipline, killing traitor humans and monsters alike, yet avoiding the majority of the fleeing soldiery.

The conscripts ran between their saviours, staggering into the safety of the city. Those that collapsed were lifted up and carried away. Katsuhiro fled towards the yellow line, not daring to look back. He heard the shouting of the enemy behind him, and the bellowing of the red, winged giant. To his utter disbelief, he made it through the whistling bolts to the line of Imperial Fists, was grabbed and dragged through.

Guns all around the arch fired down. The Imperial Fists swept the field clear. He dared not think himself safe, and looked back, immediately regretting it.

Through the legs of the legionaries, he saw that the giant was nearly upon them. He had abandoned his rampage and was making right for the open city gate. Tens of thousands, hundreds of thousands perhaps, of bolts impacted on him, blasting divots from his flesh, obscuring the greater part of him with the gathered flashes of small explosions. Las-beams punched smoking holes deep into his body. Plasma streams scorched muscle from bone. He would not fall, but he was slowing, encountering some obstacle invisible to Katsuhiro, leaning into it like a man battling against a hurricane. The giant roared in frustration. Flesh boiled off him from an attack that had little to do with legionary weapons. Fire ran over his body. Katsuhiro's teeth ached. He tasted metal.

'Father!' roared the giant. *'I will destroy you!'*

But the giant went no further. Something was holding him back.

A frantic stalemate was reached. The enemy died in droves at the threshold. Their daemonic leader could make no more headway.

More giants were required to tip the scales.

The ground shook to steady beats, and Katsuhiro turned to look into the Palace. To his amazement a group of Titans were advancing down the main road to the Helios Gate, green and red and white. They blew their war-horns in outraged cries, lined up in the gate, steadied themselves on splayed feet, and powered their weapons. Katsuhiro was hustled beneath them, enduring the soul-wrenching shock of passing through their void aegis. They sang their war songs once again, and the largest spoke.

'The Emperor Protects.'

It opened fire.

Twinned cannons blasted volcano heat. Las weaponry of a scale that dumbfounded Katsuhiro cast double spears of hard light at the enemy horde. They both hit the raging giant, who was caught upon the cusp of entering the city, throwing him back, and vaporised the greater part of his charging Legion. The other Titans opened up, war-horns still howling, blazing fury across the sky. The enemy streaming for the open gate were annihilated, the survivors retreating in disarray.

War-horns blared again. Legs straightened, and the last of the Legio Solaria strode out of the Imperial Palace, weapons still firing.

Sanguinius slew the Death Guard with such speed and power. All that came against him died. With blasts from his spear and the sweep of his great sword he ended their treachery once and for all. He leapt from wall to drawbridge, knocking as many foes from the edge as he slaughtered directly; then having cleared a space he leapt from the bridge, beat his wings and flew up and round, landing upon the siege tower roof, and there lay about himself with his blade, bringing to an end the hail of fire that so troubled his sons. At the lip of the wall the Blood Angels fought in a line against their fallen cousins, no quarter asked and none given. An equilibrium held there, the Blood Angels' fury matched by the Death Guard's tenacity. The XIV Legion were far more durable than Sanguinius' sons, taking blows and bolts that would have incapacitated other legionaries, but they were slow, bloated by sickness, disabled by infirmities. The Blood Angels moved with a grace that their counterparts could not match and found hard to counter. Just as much stinking blood was spilled as pure, legionary vitae, and the line held.

Pushed at by the mass of warriors at their backs, Mortarion's diseased progeny fell from the sides of their ramp, but the thin barrier of red would not give.

Sanguinius was captivated by the sight of his brave sons holding back the tide of the traitors. Such pride stirred in him at their sacrifice, such sorrow that he would behold their valour only a few more times before the final act of his life played out.

Until that moment, he was safe. He could not die. He would not. That was his advantage.

Time was running against them. The hordes of the enemy were converging on the tower. They would keep coming, brave in their madness, and no matter how many Raldoron and his warriors slew, eventually they would overcome the defenders. The tower had to fall.

Aid was at hand. Five towering walkers were making their way out from the gate. Sanguinius looked upon them from the siege tower. Many times the height of the war engines, the tower's very existence made a mockery of the laws of physics. No mortal engineer could build such a thing and expect it to hold up against gravity, but, he reminded himself, they fought the wars of gods now.

And yet the mortal realm still had might of its own.

'Great Mother, I am pleased you heeded my call,' he voxed. 'I salute you for overlooking factional division in the name of the greater cause. We will stand together in victory.'

'This war construct at the walls, you wish it gone?' Esha Ani of the Legio Solaria responded.

'Indeed,' said Sanguinius. 'The hour hangs on you.'

'Then stand clear,' she said.

In the command czella of *Luxor Invictoria*, Esha Ani Mohana Vi drew a bead upon her target. Her new augmetics troubled her, but they had certain advantages, bringing her closer to the roaring soul of the Warlord through the holy unity of steel with flesh.

Through his eyes she saw the rear of the daemon tower, where was mounted a gargantuan steam engine, meshed in fleshy sinew, and powered by a furnace of damned souls. From the engine great pistons led to the drive wheels of the tower. It idled, having done its purpose of bringing the tower to the wall, but she had another use for it.

'Increase reactor to maximum output,' she commanded. 'Disengage fail-safes. Remove limiting protocols. Stand by for core venting.'

In ordinary wars, her orders would have been rigorously questioned by the Titan's engineers. Overpowering the plasma core of her god-engine carried a high chance of its destruction, but this was not an ordinary war.

'Legio Solaria,' she said, voxing the other Titans in her mongrel maniple. 'We stand on the brink of annihilation once again. Let this not be the last action we undertake. Keep the enemy from me while I serve the Lord Sanguinius, and prepare for immediate retreat.'

Her mind meshed with that of her Titan. They had yet to know one another perfectly, she and *Luxor Invictoria*, but they held a common bond in their grief for Esha Ani's lost mother, and that made them strong together. His systems gave her insight into the abominable engine they faced, and his bold spirit picked out two sites for her, one for each of the Titan's volcano cannons, that would bring the damned thing low.

Tocsins rang, klaxons grated at her hearing. The soft alarms of the Warlord's servitor clades whispered in her mind, their voices still human, though they had but one thing to say.

'*Danger, danger, danger.*'

Solaria were spotted. Punishing fire from the enemy con-travallation zeroed in on them. Void indicators flickered with troubling portents of failure. She did not have much time. At *Luxor Invictoria*'s knees, Warhounds and Reavers burned back enemy infantry and armour with plasma, flame and bullet. The enemy were so many.

She could not fail.

The whine of the reactor climbed. The great god-engine trembled with barely contained power. More alarms pushed into her being, prodding at her soul through the manifold.

Gauges slid into the red. Target locks screamed at her. The machine-spirits of the volcano cannons begged for release. Still she did not fire. She waited for maximum power, the very acme of destruction.

Alarms shrilled. The moment came.

'Legio Solaria, switch fire – all weapons to the siege tower, now.'

Immediately the god-machines obeyed, swinging their great limbs to bear, and opened fire. The shields of the tower, weakened during its advance on the walls, finally collapsed under the pounding of the Titans' guns.

'Loose,' she said.

Luxor Invictoria sighed with machine pleasure as its can-nons were unleashed. Alarms screamed. An overbearing wailing resounded through the entire machine, promis-ing imminent destruction, but she did not shut the energy stream off until the last.

The giant las-beams slammed into the tower engine, itself bigger than the Warlord. They burned through warp-infused bronze, put out the hellish furnace.

The Titan's reactor howled.

'Dump all coolant. All Titans retreat to the Helios Gate.'

Clouds of superheated gas burst from the cannons' thermal

vents, shrouding the maniple in pure white steam. Alarms still shrieking, still under heavy fire, *Luxor Invictoria* turned about as the daemon tower's engine exploded.

Scalding fluid blasted out in every direction. The tower shook, spilling the tiny figures of battling Space Marines from its broad ramp. Chained explosions raced up its many floors, blasting flames from its firing slits and windows. Magazines caught. Energy sources detonated.

Esha Ani did not see the tower's final demise; she wrestled with her Titan's desire to fight while her tech clade brought down its internal temperatures, until it arrived, still spraying scalding gas, back at the Helios Gate, and returned through the wall.

The cannons hit the tower, shaking it from top to bottom. Sanguinius staggered. The Death Guard coming up the main stairs to confront him fell back. Sanguinius used the distraction to jump at them, incinerating them with his spear's energy cast, and took again to the air.

'Retreat from the bridge, my sons!' Sanguinius shouted. He blasted down with the *Spear of Telesto* directly into the melee, its strange energies leaving his own warriors unharmed, but turning the Death Guard into shattered husks of broken armour.

'Fall back!' Raldoron said, passing on Sanguinius' order. 'Fall back!'

The Blood Angels gave way, and the Death Guard spilled from the drawbridge onto the ramparts. For a moment the sons of Mortarion were triumphant. They fired as they advanced, killing many of the retreating Blood Angels, before the illusion shattered along with the tower.

The first explosion was so distant it was lost in the general roar of the battle, but as those that came after sped upwards, the noise grew to deafening thunder, shaking the whole structure so that warriors fell screaming to their deaths, until the top half was obliterated in a fountain of green fire, and a tempest of shrapnel burst over the rampart, slaying warriors on both sides. A pressure built in Raldoron's head, and released again when a malevolent presence roared from the broken interior of the tower in a column of black flies. Glowing eyes stared down from the swarm's midst, then the flies dissipated across the night sky, and the eyes faded away with a howl that made men vomit.

Raldoron grabbed the standard from a dead banner bearer and waved it over his head. The tattered flag snapped beneath the winged blood-drop finial.

'To me, sons of Sanguinius! To me!'

The Death Guard had taken the brunt of the explosion, but they were hardier than they had ever been, and some dozens of them were on the rampart. The Blood Angels rallied themselves for a hard fight, warriors again attacking from both sides and running up against a wall of rotting ceramite and iron will.

'The battle is almost won! Do not falter!' Raldoron shouted. 'Cast them from the rampart! For the Emperor! For Sanguinius!'

Called down from on high by his name, Sanguinius, most perfect of all the primarchs, hurtled into the middle of the Death Guard. His landing killed three even before he set his spear and sword whirling through them, cutting them down with contemptuous ease.

'To the primarch! To the primarch!'

Bolters and voices roaring, the two lines of Blood Angels crashed back onto the ruined section of the wall walk, slaughtering the traitors utterly, so that not one was left alive.

Sanguinius swept his gaze over the battered remnants of the Blood Angels.

He held aloft his spear.

'It is done!' shouted Sanguinius, and his sons cheered him.

'My lord! Look out!' Raldoron pulled at his genefather's arm, but no Space Marine could move a primarch.

Angron was flying straight at them, wings beating, howling madly, black sword drawn back to strike. The Blood Angels opened fire. Bolts ricocheted from Angron's armour and his flesh without effect.

But Sanguinius stood there, and lowered his weapons.

'My lord!' screamed Raldoron in anguish.

'Do not fear. He cannot pass. The Emperor's ward is weakening, and soon the Neverborn will walk upon Terra, but for now, even Angron is forbidden entry to the Palace.'

There was truth in Sanguinius' words. Angron spread his wings and came to a halt some way out from the wall. He swooped back and forth, his yellow eyes fixed upon his brother.

'*Sanguinius,*' growled Angron. '*Face me. Let us fight, you and I.*'

'You shall not pass over these walls, nor under or through them until our father decrees it,' said Sanguinius. 'You know this to be true.'

Angron snarled. '*Then come out and fight me, red angel to red angel, upon this field of battle where father can no longer interfere.*'

Sanguinius saluted his brother as if Angron remained the troubled warrior of before.

'We will fight, my brother, but not today.'

Angron roared and wheeled around, but he must have seen the truth of the Great Angel's words, for he did not attempt to pass over the wall, and flew back to the burning plains below where the last unfortunate few of the outworks' defenders were being hunted down.

Sanguinius stood at the edge of the ruined wall section.

The crenellations had been entirely stripped away by the melta arrays, and the rampart cratered deeply. The wrecked stump of the siege tower burned some distance down. He looked out over Horus' hordes, mutants and Traitor Space Marines, held up his sword and shouted.

'None of you shall pass within!' he told them. 'You shall all perish! This is the judgment of the Emperor. Remember these words, for they shall haunt you when the moment of your death comes and you learn to regret your treachery.'

He turned away from it all.

'Remove the corpses, Raldoron. Burn the Death Guard and throw the ashes over the wall. Have the Librarius check for warp taint. Mortarion's sons have strange new gifts.'

'My lord,' said Raldoron.

'And rest while you can.' Sanguinius looked to the heavens. 'They will try again and again. The veil between worlds weakens. The Neverborn are coming.'

Raldoron's genesire had no further words for him, but leapt skywards and passed as a flashing mote of gold and white feathers towards the Palace centre.

Raldoron looked out over the zone of battle atop the wall. The Apothecaries and engineers had much work to do. Dozens of Blood Angels were dead or dying. The wall was badly damaged. The place where the outworks had sheltered the wall's feet was covered over by the servants of the enemy. As his men worked through long hours to set things right, reports finally came in from Bhab command. At every point the enemy's escalade had failed.

The walls held.

The attack was over.

Titans swayed through the Helios Gate, their ponderous footfalls shaking the ground. Again the voids slipped over

Katsuhiro, making him sick to his soul. The Legio Solaria
hooted a mournful salute to the fallen as the last came in.

Still firing into the enemy, who would not give up their
suicidal attempt on the gate, the sons of Dorn fell back, covered by their tanks and the guns of the walls.

'Close the gates!' the cry went up, taken up by others.

Three minutes. That was what they had been offered. That
was all that was given. Katsuhiro saw desperate men sprinting
for the gateway. Three minutes was a lifetime quickly spent.

Once more the gate's array of war-horns blared out their
tune, the Palace itself giving a valediction for the dead. The
ground thrummed with powerful motors, and the gates swung
inwards. A last few conscripts sprinted through as they swung
closed. Katsuhiro tried to go to them, but he was pulled away
from the gate by shouting people he could barely hear.

Hands pulled him onto a low cot at the edge of the great
canyon way behind the wall. There medicae personnel performed triage on a group of filthy, shell-shocked soldiers.
Many thousands had manned the outworks in their section.
Katsuhiro reckoned there to be less than one thousand left.

The Imperial Fists in the gateway altered their formation
to intensify their firing through the gap of the closing portal. It shrank with increasing rapidity.

Guns fired nearby. A group of legionaries festooned with
skulls ran at the rear of the gates from within the city and
were cut down by bolter fire from loyal Space Marines, who
turned around on the spot and smoothly switched targets.
The Titans sang again as they moved off into the Palace.
He watched them go. They moved so quickly despite their
plodding pace. Then the gates swung closed with a boom,
shutting out the battle and the horrors beyond the wall,
drawing his attention back.

Katsuhiro stared at the rear of the closed gates. Transhumans moved all around the square behind the gatehouse. Now combat was done, they went about rearmament and repair without the post-combat shock lesser humans experienced.

A captain of their kind walked by, shouting orders from his voxmitter.

'Please, my lord,' Katsuhiro said, reaching up his hands.

He expected to be ignored, but the captain stopped at his cot and looked down on him.

'Why did you save us?' Katsuhiro asked.

As the Space Marine wore his helmet. Katsuhiro could not gauge his expression. Green eye-lenses stared at him hard, so soullessly he regretted speaking.

'We were ordered to,' said the Space Marine.

'Then you think it a waste of resources,' Katsuhiro said. 'I do not blame you. I am a coward. Every time I think I have overcome my fear, then some fresh horror is revealed, and I am a coward all over again. The city was put in danger for our sake. I am sorry.'

The Space Marine lord stared down at him. He was so tall, so distant, the last bits of his humanity hidden behind the angled mask of his war-plate, and when he spoke his voice was near robotic thanks to the voxmitter; and yet Katsuhiro heard his compassion, even through all of that.

'Hear me, son of Terra. Not one of you who fought upon those lines is a coward. You did what was asked of you. You performed your duty. I am proud to call you my comrade in arms, whatever the cost in blood and the risk of bringing you within these walls. This I, Maximus Thane, swear to you. Now rest. You will be needed again.'

The Space Marine walked away. A medicae orderly came to Katsuhiro and pushed him gently onto the cot. But Katsuhiro saw something behind Thane's huge, yellow bulk that made him sit up.

'That man! That man! Stop him!'

'That's the commander of the gate.' The medicae muttered to his attendants. 'Delirious. Battle shock. Administer somna vapour.'

A soft plastek mask was pulled over Katsuhiro's face. He struggled against the hands pushing him down. Gas hissed down tubes beaded with condensation.

Thane moved on, calling to his men, revealing Ashul at the edge of a crowd, the man Katsuhiro had known as Doromek. The traitor.

'Stop him, stop him,' Katsuhiro muttered, already losing consciousness.

Ashul saluted ironically. Katsuhiro's eyes slid shut. He forced them open one more time, but Ashul was gone.

Hissing filled the world, and Katsuhiro fell into welcome, dreamless sleep.

THIRTY-ONE

Ascension
Absent father
A new champion

Daylight Wall, Helios section, 15th of Quartus

A broken man in broken armour stirred at the foot of the wall. A single casualty among thousands, he was not noticed in the battle's aftermath by either side.

Gendor Skraivok was dying. The fall had brought him down across a lump of rockcrete and his back had shattered on it. He could move his arms. Everything below his shoulders might as well have been sculpted from clay.

The hum of his warsuit's reactor had stopped. No power ran through the armour's systems, and much of its ceramite shell was broken open. Skraivok could see very little past his collar and his pauldrons. The walls soared above him, as if placed there with the sole purpose of framing the sky, where the living art of orbital bombardment danced in ever-changing patterns on the aegis. From a lump of stone his helmet looked at him accusingly, having been torn off as he slammed into the wall. It had contrived to land upright, solely, it seemed, to silently condemn him with cracked glass eyes.

Blood was leaking into Skraivok's mouth. He spat weakly to the side, an action that stabbed his organs with a hundred knives of agony. The blood flowed faster than he could spit.

He groaned. If his other injuries did not kill him first, he was going to drown in his own vitae.

Gendor Skraivok did not wish to die.

'Daemon,' he whispered. 'Daemon!'

He patted the ground to his left and his right. Amazingly, his hand touched the familiar hilt of his warp blade. Gripping it cost him greatly in pain, but he managed to bring the weapon onto his chest, where it clanked against his armour.

'Daemon, can you hear me?' He spat again. Blood was running down his throat.

The sword trembled.

'You are here with me!' he croaked in relief.

Skraivok's smile became an expression of dismay as the metal's trembling turned to shaking so pronounced it clattered on his armour. The blade began to fizz, boiling off into black smoke that fled upwards towards the flaring sky.

'No!' he said. 'No! Daemon, wait! Do not desert me!'

The rattling died away as the weapon evaporated into nothing. Skraivok stared at his empty hand.

'I don't want to die!' he said, weakly. He felt intensely sorry for himself. 'I'm not ready! Daemon! Daemon...'

'I have not deserted you, Gendor Skraivok. Not yet.'

Dragging footsteps approached. Skraivok turned his head. Relief turned to horror at what he saw.

The daemon came fully formed, solid as a man of flesh and blood. It was a scrawny thing with skin covered in tumorous lumps. Its head had something of the equine to it, being long, with eyes set far back and to the side of its face.

The teeth were predatory, however: sharp along the front, large incisors lying neatly together, like the scissor-blade tusks of Terran boars. The head carried four short growths that were more nobbles than horns. Its ears, Skraivok noted, were very small and delicate.

It came closer.

'Get away from me!' Skraivok gasped, suddenly afraid.

A famine-swollen belly dangled from an emaciated ribcage. Its legs were knock-kneed. It limped. Its arms were overly long, held awkwardly across its body, with grasping, twitching fingers covered in warts. Dragging misshapen feet, it approached Skraivok slowly, as if bashful, unsure of how to greet a potential mate, but Skraivok could see even from his limited view how triumphant it felt.

'*Do not be afraid. I am your sword. I am your daemon. We spoke before, on Sotha, you and I. We are important to one another.*'

'I do not know you!'

'*I have many forms, and many names. You know me well, and always have, as you shall soon see. The walls between our spheres are breached. I can be here now, thanks to my connection with you. Others of my kind will come soon enough, but not for you. I am the first, and you are mine.*' It came to a halt at Skraivok's side and looked up at the continuing battle. '*Soon the Anathema will fall, and this sphere of being will be like ours.*'

It stared down at Skraivok with huge brown eyes that might have been beautiful in another creature, but in its lumpen face were abhorrent. Thick, clear fluid wept from them, dribbling down its long snout and coating its teeth.

'*Now what do we do with you, I wonder?*'

The Neverborn knelt over him, and rested a knotted hand upon Skraivok's broken armour. Its fingers dabbled in his blood.

'Why did you leave me on the wall?' said Skraivok.

'*Because I could,*' it said. Its voice was wet and laboured. '*Because you needed a lesson. I made you strong, Skraivok, and you assumed that strength was your own. You are a traitor and a murderer. Ruthlessness and a little cunning are your only gifts, but you mistook my talents for yours.*' It snickered. '*Can you imagine, the Painted Count thought himself the equal of the First Captain of the Blood Angels? A priceless error.*'

'I slew Lord Shang,' croaked Skraivok.

'*I slew Lord Shang,*' countered the daemon, '*not you. Truly you are gloriously arrogant,*' it said with satisfaction. '*A fitting bondsoul for me. We shall have such times, you and I.*'

'I am a captain of the Night Lords.'

'*You are, you are,*' the daemon said, patting him. '*But you cheated your way to your command. You never had the patience or the discipline to properly master the gifts the Anathema bestowed upon your mortal body. You are no warrior, Skraivok. You never were. You are a parasite. You are a gutter politician. You are devious, and false. Nothing more.*'

'What do you want of me?' Skraivok said. His life was ebbing away. Not long now. He almost welcomed it.

'*You have a choice to make,*' it said with relish. '*You can die here, now, and your soul will flee into the warp where it will be torn to pieces by my kin who dwell there.*'

'The alternative?' His eyes were heavy. Blood dribbled into his lungs.

The Neverborn leaned closer, and whispered with rank breath into his ear.

'*You can offer yourself to me, wholeheartedly, with no reservation or doubt, and I will take you into myself. You will become a part of me and I will become a part of you. Together, we shall live forever, and freely tread the materium*' *and immaterium both. We shall bring such pain upon this sphere of being that it will wound the very light of the stars.'*

'I will die otherwise?' he said.

'You will do more than die. You will cease to be.'

'Then yes,' said Skraivok. 'Yes! Anything but death.'

'Anything?' crooned the daemon.

'Yes!' said Skraivok. Fear sent a last jolt of energy into him. He lifted his head. 'Anything.'

'Then say the words,' growled the Neverborn. Its thin lips were close enough to kiss. The fluid from its eyes dripped onto Skraivok's face.

'I pledge myself to you! I shall become yours! You will be me and I will be you! Is that right? Is that right? Please, do not let me die!'

The daemon chuckled. *'I chose you so well. Yes, those words will suffice. This is your first lesson – the form of the words do not matter, only their sincerity, and I see that for the first time in your life, Gendor Skraivok, you are sincere.'*

'I am! I am!'

A long, reeking tongue slipped between the daemon's lips, furred green and ulcerous, and pushed roughly into Skraivok's mouth. It slithered into his throat, growing longer and thicker, plunging down, down inside him, blocking off his air, choking him. The daemon's mouth parted wider, and wider. The tongue grew thicker while the rest of the being deflated, pouring itself through the serpent of its tongue into the Night Lord. Skraivok goggled and choked, his eyes wide with terror.

Did I mention, said the daemon into his mind, for the mind was its now too, *that for you to deliver pain correctly, you must learn what pain is. I will take you now, into the warp, where for six times six hundred and sixty-six years you will learn the depths of agony. This is a great gift. No living being could survive the torments that await you, my friend, my soul bond, my Painted Count, but you will... You will become expert in pain.*

Skraivok's eyes bulged. The daemon slithered inside him, pulling its empty skin after it. Skraivok's flesh glowed lurid purple, too bright to look at.

When the light went out, his armour was empty, but the daemon was good to its word.

The Painted Count was not dead.

In the depths of the warp, Gendor Skraivok began to scream.

The warp

Horus coalesced from shreds of smoke and blood fume, striding from one existence to the next as if he walked from one room to another.

He stopped to take in his surroundings.

There was a place his father had taken him soon after his arrival on Terra. A rotunda tower in the young Palace, whose colonnaded sides were protected from the freezing winds of Himalazia by shimmering atmospheric shields. The room at the top was of simple luxury. Nothing ostentatious, but everything fashioned to the highest standard, and of the finest materials. The floor was chequered with black and white marble fitted to the room's circular shape, the flagstones rhomboids with curved edges that grew more slender until they reached the middle of the room, where they became tesserae locked into a geometric prison. At the very centre was an ancient symbol, a circle divided into two tailed shapes of black and white by a curved line, a small dot of black within the white and vice versa. The Emperor had told him that this symbol represented equilibrium.

Where he was now was an echo of that chamber. He saw it as it had been, and he saw it as it would become, its energy shields out, curtains shredded, floor cracked. The rotunda offered a view of the whole Palace, and it showed now a vista of fire. Hot breezes laden with embers wafted between the pillars. Horus looked on approvingly.

'Why did you bring me here, father?' he said. The Emperor did not show Himself. Horus felt His presence all around him, but no contact came. He remained hidden.

The Warmaster raised his eyebrows at this display. He felt the consternation of the Four, but he was not unduly concerned. His father had never liked to give a straight answer. His gaze wandered over the chamber, touching on a pile of cushions where he and the Emperor had talked long into that first night, then over the table where they dined together when time allowed. The Emperor was always occupied with His great work – *His great lie*, Horus thought – but at the beginning of it all He had had more time for Horus than He had for any of the others that followed.

That had been important to him, once. In truth it was so meaningless. Days full of lies to feed a tyrant's vanity. It saddened him. Such a waste.

At one side of the room was a regicide table of ancient origin. Upon a single curled leg a round board sat, its surface inset with wooden squares to make the playing surface. The wood was so old the whites had darkened and the blacks mellowed, until they were nearly the same shades of brown. A game halfway through was set on the board. Ivory pieces aged to a mellow cream were on the defensive, half their pieces off the playing surface already. A nearly full set of ebony was arrayed against them. Over the heads of their servants the black king and the white king looked directly at one another. Horus ducked down to get a better view.

The attack was deeply flawed. The defence had many holes. Grains of dust and debris littered the board. Ash drifted onto it from the fires outside. It was when one of these grey smuts settled next to the black king that he saw that the piece rested in a puddle of blood.

He shook his head at the symbolism. Unsubtle.

He stood up, picked up a thrall piece on a whim and moved it to block a white keep.

The base clicked onto the ancient wood with a soft finality.

'I have tested your walls, father. My armies stand ready to begin their attack. Why do you still resist? You can see the end, I know you can. Your resistance is pointless. You damn humanity. Release them. Let me save them.'

There came no reply.

Horus stood back from the game.

'Your move, father,' he said quietly.

The Vengeful Spirit, *Terran near orbit, 15th of Quartus*

The air was foul in Horus' nameless sanctum where Abaddon watched over his father.

As always, Layak and his tongueless servants had followed him there, giving him no moment of peace.

'He spends too much time in his meditations,' said the First Captain.

Horus' eyes were wide open, staring at nothing. His mouth gaped. He looked an imbecile, or dead. Abaddon was glad few others saw the Warmaster like this. He wished he did not see it himself, but he could not stop looking.

'How do you think that Angron walks on Terra?' said Layak mildly. 'He will not be the first child of the warp to do so. The Emperor's might dwindles because Horus confronts Him in the warp. Without these attacks your father makes upon the Terran despot, our allies would never break through.'

'Erebus would have claimed those triumphs for himself,' said Abaddon.

'I am not Erebus,' said Layak. 'The First Apostle served himself first and the gods second. That is why the Warmaster banished him. He and Lorgar were faithless in the end.'

'What about you, Layak? Do you keep faith?' he said dismissively.

A burst of angry heat radiated from the Apostle. 'I serve only the gods,' said Layak, 'for what use is mortal power in the face of eternity?'

Abaddon stared at the Warmaster.

'The price of this is too high. We can bring the Emperor down without the Neverborn. I do not like what these sorcerous journeys are doing to my father, and I hold you responsible.'

'Kill me, and it will make no difference. It is too late to change the Warmaster's path,' said Layak. 'The deal has been struck. The daemonic legions wait to add their might to yours. There is no going back on that.'

'We could have obliterated this world.'

'Then you would have lost. The Emperor is no ordinary foe,' said Layak. 'Slay His body, and He will persist. He must be destroyed, face to face, in body and in spirit.'

'Then we should have tried it on our own,' Abaddon said. 'If Horus continues with this harassment of the False Emperor, he risks himself. Do not underestimate the power of the Emperor, Layak. I do not. Do your masters?'

Layak did not answer Abaddon's question. 'There are pressures upon our labours,' he said instead. 'They must be completed quickly, or the war will be lost.'

Abaddon looked at the masked priest. 'Such as? Guilliman

is nothing. I will break him. I will break them all, these loyal sons. These primarchs. They are weak.'

Layak's six eyes flared. 'Do you believe that Guilliman's advance is the only limit on our time?'

'Layak, I have no liking for you. You are useful, and Horus has decreed that you are not to be harmed, but I would require little excuse to overlook both these protections you enjoy.'

'I will say what needs to be said, threats or not. I serve the gods. My life means nothing.'

Abaddon's fists flexed. 'Then if you are so faithful, I dare you to speak, and we will see what affection the gods hold you in.'

'You have seen it,' Layak said steadily. 'You can sense it. Horus is failing. He is too strong to defeat, but it may be that he is too weak to claim victory. The Pantheon gift him with great ability, but the favour of the gods carries a steep price.'

'Speak clearly,' Abaddon said.

'Horus' soul is bright with divine might, but it burns. Mighty as his being is, it is finite. He is not invincible in this world or the other. If we delay too long, he will be devoured by the power he commands.'

Abaddon did not want to recognise it. He could not, but he knew, looking at his father's blank face, that what Layak said was true.

'How long does he have?'

'Long enough, perhaps,' said Layak. 'His will is strong.'

'But if it is not strong enough? If he fails now, if his soul burns out before the task is done, what will happen?'

'Then, my lord, what happens will be what has always happened before.' Layak looked at Abaddon. 'There shall come another champion of Chaos.'

ABOUT THE AUTHOR

Guy Haley is the author of the Siege of Terra novel *The Lost and the Damned*, as well as the Horus Heresy novels *Titandeath*, *Wolfsbane* and *Pharos*, and the Primarchs novels *Konrad Curze: The Night Haunter*, *Corax: Lord of Shadows* and *Perturabo: The Hammer of Olympia*. He has also written many Warhammer 40,000 novels, including the Dawn of Fire books *Avenging Son* and *Throne of Light*, as well as *Belisarius Cawl: The Great Work*, the Dark Imperium trilogy, *The Devastation of Baal*, *Dante*, *Darkness in the Blood* and *Astorath: Angel of Mercy*. He has also written stories set in the Age of Sigmar, included in *War Storm*, *Ghal Maraz* and *Call of Archaon*. He lives in Yorkshire with his wife and son.

An extract from
The First Wall
by Gav Thorpe

Patches of static in the holo-display vexed Perturabo, causing him pain in a way that a wound to his flesh could not.
Every blur marring the projected image was a failure of sur-
veyors, each a gap in his knowledge.

His only companions were the six automatons of his Iron
Circle, stationed at regular intervals around the periphery
of the octagonal chamber. They stood with their shields
raised, mauls dormant, the only movement that of their
ocular lenses, which whirred and clicked as they followed
the pacing of their creator.

'I could extrapolate the defences hidden from me,' Perturabo thought aloud to his bodyguard. Their unquestioning
silence was a welcome break from the ceaseless doubts and
queries that spilled from his subordinates of late. 'I have
perfect recollection of other works raised by Dorn, and by
patterning those memories with what is shown here I can
fill the gaps to a high degree of accuracy.'

He stared at a glimmering hololith that filled most of his planning chamber aboard the *Iron Blood*, as though force of will could make it offer up its secrets.

'Extrapolation is not fact,' he growled. 'There is too much at stake for assumption, no matter how well informed.'

His mind, his military genius, was the key Horus needed to unlock the palace of his father, but it needed data like an army needed supplies.

He stepped into the display, his massive suit of armour hissing and wheezing. Its shadow obliterated whole sectors of the Sanctum Imperialis as he strode to examine one area in particular. He crouched, coming eye to eye with a fictional defender standing on the Ultimate Wall.

The yellow of Dorn's Legion was spread everywhere, though it was concentrated around the north-east and south-west. The red of the Blood Angels was strongest to the south-east, where Mortarion's Death Guard had launched a damaging but ultimately unsuccessful assault near the Helios Gate.

The Khan's White Scars were harder to place. They had sallied forth against Mortarion in support of Sanguinius, but had since been seen in several other battles to the north and west of that attack. The precise whereabouts of the primarchs themselves was a factor to be considered, but impossible to ascertain with any degree of timeliness or certainty.

Raising the fingers of his left hand, he gestured and the display rotated around him, placing him behind the wall so that he was looking out across the Katabatic Plains surrounding the Palace.

The Warmaster's forces were rendered in a more abstract sense; series of runes, numbers and sigils denoting troop type, strength, current morale estimates, longevity of engagement, and half a dozen other factors.

And there were more features, sketched with a nomenclature

he was still creating. These were the forces of the warp, whose powers he had only just started to investigate. Daemons. Possessed legionaries. Word Bearers and Thousand Sons sorcerers.

And his brothers. Swirls of arcane conjunctions between the real and the imaginary, with a foot in the world of the mortal and immortal alike. Angron, so determined to prove himself, unable to hold his wrath, was still trying the defences at Helios. Mortarion had not personally attempted to breach the Emperor's shield yet, and at the command of Horus was redirecting efforts to the south-west, attacking a twenty-kilometre stretch of wall near to the bastion of the Saturnine Gate. The Emperor's Children and Fulgrim, who Perturabo considered the least trustworthy of Horus' other lieutenants, had been engaging the defenders to the west and north, without any breakthrough.

Of Magnus there was no sign, but his Legion commanders had been content to take assignment from Perturabo and invested the south-west of the continent-city, supporting the efforts of the Death Guard.

All of his brothers were baulked at the walls still, held back by the last and most powerfully enigmatic variable in the whole war.

The Emperor.

So many questions Perturabo could scarcely think of them, much less attempt to provide answers. Queries that stretched back decades, strategies and decisions he had been picking apart since first he'd come into the presence of his creator.

But it was equally simple to dismiss most of the unease. Questions of why his father had acted in certain ways, why He had treated His sons the way He had, were now irrelevant. All that was left was the how of the matter. It was connected to the powers of the warp. If Perturabo could unpick that relationship, he could break apart the psychic wards that held back his brothers.

'Titans,' he reminded himself. 'The Warmaster needs our Titans to break the siege. He is right – the war engines of our foes' Legios are a force we cannot yet counter.'

The reinforced plates of his armour rippled with projected light as he stepped back, fingers clenching and unclenching as he surveyed the Palace again.

'There is only the one place,' he said, gesturing to zoom the display to the middle of the Palace, where the two great loops of the Eternity Wall and Ultimate Wall met. It was both the weakest and the strongest point of the entire complex. If it were to fall, the entire fortress-city would be vulnerable; protected from both sides by immense fortifications, it would be death to any enemy that dared entry.

'But you left a key in the lock, Rogal,' said Perturabo. The display cycled closer, flickering with more static as the required data for the level of detail was unavailable. Even so, the edifice that drew his eye was plain to see, so tall that it made the surrounding walls and Palace seem like models though they were each ten kilometres tall and more. The lord of the Iron Warriors grimaced at the lack of recent reconnaissance. 'The Lion's Gate space port. All but part of the wall itself, like a growth on an artery. One cut here and Horus can move whatever he desires into the Palace.'

Yet failure would be costly, and victory only a little less so. The Lion's Gate space port was an immense fortress in its own right, an orbit-piercing city protected by shields, cannons and hundreds of thousands of soldiers.

'Perhaps an attack against the wall, after all,' he said, panning the view to the north, drawing back to see more of the Imperial Palace.